Wings on the Mountain

To the wonderful Patty Ellison,

Thank you again for helping me with this book! Your advice & editing talents were extremely helpful & very much appreciated!

God bless you!

Love, Lynn Congiano

12/15/2020

ISBN-13: 9781517179403
ISBN-10: 1517179408
Library of Congress Control Number: 2015914655
CreateSpace Independent Publishing Platform
North Charleston, South Carolina

Cover Art and Design by Linda Hamil

Bible References from The Holy Bible:
King James Version
New King James Version
New Living Bible
New International Version
International Standard Version
(ISV used for Ma Riley's Bible Code)

Wings on the Mountain

Colorado Trilogy - Book Two

L. Faulkner- Corzine

"In the shadow of your wings I will make my refuge,
until these calamities have passed by." Psalm 57:1

Heavenly Father, please bless this book.
May it be entertaining so readers will turn to the next page.
May it be inspiring so they will turn to You!

DEDICATION

To all those who have suffered from abuse of every kind.
My prayer is that God will use the characters in this book,
and the challenges that they endure and overcome,
to give hope and encouragement!
That those who feel broken will discover that
God is still in the business of binding up wounds
and healing broken hearts!
That when we place ourselves in the Master's care…
All things are possible!
All things can become new!

SPECIAL THANKS

To my husband Gary, who has been my staunch supporter,
wise and constructive critic, greatest advocate
and my best friend!

Another heartfelt thank you to my family and friends:
Jan and Kay Knigge, Sandy Mathis,
Mike Corzine, Nancy McMahan, Rachel McKeever
Donna Armstrong and Patty Ellison.

You all have been so wonderfully supportive
and encouraging as I struggle along,
attempting to do the work,
I believe God is leading me to do.

Dear Reader,

I hope you will enjoy reading Wings on the Mountain. When you've finished please continue turning the pages or swiping the screen. There are Discussion Points in the back and a Prologue Preview for Book One of the Colorado Trilogy, Giant in the Valley. Please note that the characters in these two books are experiencing their adventures in a parallel time period (1864-1867). You will see that a few of the characters and places from Book One will make cameo appearances in Book Two. Their worlds may touch briefly, but only now and again. Book Three in the Colorado Trilogy, will take place a number of years later, allowing time for the characters to expand and mature. In some cases, the characters from books one and two will not only touch, but…**collide!**

Thank you and God bless you.
Lynn

Please visit my website at http://lfaulknercorzine.com

TABLE OF CONTENTS

PROLOGUE

TEXAS -1860

The fog shifted and swirled about Dirk Culley as he walked through the moonlit forest. He waited in the shadows, watching the old gypsy woman, as she sat on a stool and warmed herself beside a crackling fire. She couldn't have known he was there, but suddenly she looked through the fog and with her gnarled hand, beckoned for him to come closer. Her face was ancient, but her eyes were fiercely perceptive, dark and keen. They seemed to look right into his soul as she stared up at him.

"Sit down young man," she crooned. "I have been expecting you." Her voice was deep and her words heavily accented. "I have had dreams about you. There are things I must tell you…and warnings I must give!"

He paid little attention at first, just an old woman's words for a young man's ears. Easily spoken and more easily forgotten. Then, as the fog and the smoke curled about the old woman's head, her words captured him.

"My first warning is one you must heed. If you trifle with a married woman, it will bring disaster upon you! I say this most forcefully, for I have dreamt of two women who will cross your path." Staring off into the forest, her dark eyes reflected the firelight. It seemed as if she could see before her, the days and years to come. "One woman will have hair the color of sunset and eyes as green as clover. She will lead you to something important. Something—I think of great value! The other woman stands in the light, and in my dreams, she stands so close to you that I cannot see her clearly. All I see is that she wears a band of gold on her left hand, and she is covering a wound. Red blood is bubbling up through her fingers. I do not know if this blood is her blood or yours—and yet I know this wound will cause *you* great pain! It will also lead to great danger and death, to some whom you know well."

Dirk scowled as he stared into the fire, not knowing what to think of the old woman and her strange words.

Gently touching his arm, she added, "There is one more thing I will tell you. Then you must go—for my people do not trust you. When these women come into your life, they will force you to face a great darkness—a darkness you have feared all your life. The outcome, however, will be of your choosing, for these women will lead you either to—ruination or salvation!"

"There before me were two women, with the wind in their wings." Zechariah 5:9

Chapter 1
Freedom

Colorado Territory – 1865

"Masters, give your bondservants what is fair, knowing that you also have a Master in heaven." Colossians 3:18

He knows I can't mend this…he just wants an excuse to use his belt tonight!

Copper Delaney glanced up from the ragged garment on her lap as fear knotted in her belly. She knew instinctively that there was more to her growing anxiety than dread over another beating. Her intuition had never failed her and tonight it was unmistakable. First, came a bleak foreboding that hovered over her like a dark phantom. Then the trembling began; a slow shudder rose from deep inside and refused to be stilled.

Warily, she studied the old man who sat across the campfire. She'd been the bondservant of Percy Barr for two years now, but never had she seen him in such a strange humor. Something was surely amiss and it began with him guzzling down his last bottle of whiskey. He was a poor man, and though he was in the habit of flavoring his evening coffee with a splash of hard liquor, he was always careful to make each bottle last. So, why was tonight different, she wondered? The sour old man seemed almost cheerful, as he sang bawdy tunes and drank as if he had an endless supply. Percy's wife had died two weeks earlier and he hadn't taken to the bottle then, but now, for no apparent reason he was behaving as if—he had something to celebrate!

Percy Barr was indeed making merry and it added to his pleasure to see the fearful look on Copper's face. However, if things went according to plan, there would be no more beatings, at least not from him, ever again. No, from now on he must be careful not to bruise the merchandise. The Manor College for Young Ladies, built on the outskirts of Denver, accepted only comely orphan girls of a certain age, and Copper had finally turned sixteen.

Tomorrow they'd be in the 'Mile-High City'. Yes, everything was working out just as he planned.

He took a long pull from his whiskey bottle and then a predatory expression spread across his face. The girl really did make a pretty picture as she sat by the fire. The amber flames matched the color of her hair as it fell over her shoulder in a straight cascade of shining silk. Percy knew she thought of herself as ugly and awkward. Of course, he had fostered that belief, and had encouraged her distain of her straight red hair and freckles. In fact, Percy went to great lengths to make sure that Copper remained unaware of her talent as well as her beauty. And yet, she was like the humble caterpillar that falls asleep in her cocoon, only to awaken as a butterfly, having no idea that she is now the most beguiling of all creatures. Fortunately for Percy Barr, Copper was too unassuming to think herself as anything but plain—and much too jaded by her past to hope for a better life.

Even as her intuition warned of changes ahead, Copper found it difficult to imagine how her life could get worse that it already was. After all, she was bound to this disgusting, shriveled up little man, until he acknowledged that her debt was paid in full. When they'd made camp that night, Percy had tossed his raggedy black suit at her and told her to mend it. The promise of a beating if she didn't do a good job was unnecessary, for that threat always hung in the air. Tonight Copper was sure to be punished, for although she was a fair hand with needle and thread, the fabric of the suit was too thin to bear the weight of a patch. As she realized the futility of her efforts, her mouth went dry.

Percy Barr was proud and arrogant, and one of his greatest joys it seemed was in finding fault with his bondservant. If she didn't work quickly enough, she'd feel the sting of his belt. If one of her drawings sold for more coin in a day than he had earned all week, he would cut a switch, saying that he had better take her down a peg or two. As his rheumatism grew worse, he didn't strike her quite as often or as hard, but on those days he made a point of taunting her. *'Copper Delaney'*, he would say, *'iffen we hadn't bought ya, ya'd be nothing but a worthless bindle stiff, yer not even worth as much as that mule ya love so well. All ya'll ever be good fer is to servin' yer betters.'*

Copper trembled at the thought of telling this pretentious little man that his very best suit was little more than a rag with buttons. It seemed as if she could already feel the sharp edge of Percy's belt slicing into her back.

Just then, however, she remembered Matilda Barr's final words to her, 'When it comes to handlin' Percy, just remember that if you want to keep a bee from stingin', then ya gotta blow smoke in his face.' Copper took in a deep breath, then as calmly as she could manage, she said, "Mister Barr, I think you deserve a new set of clothes—don't you? I'm sure your sister and her well-to-do husband would be favorably impressed if you met them dressed in a fine black frock coat and matching trousers. Once we arrive in Denver, we could make a few stops along the way and with a bit of luck I'm sure you could talk some folks into buying a few of my simple drawings. I'm sure it would make quite a difference if you met your family looking your very best."

The old man focused his red—watery eyes across the fire, pretending that he had just then remembered that Copper was even there. He took another gulp from his bottle. When a rivulet of brown liquid slid down his chin, he frowned and wiped his face with the back of his hand. Then not wanting to waste a single drop, he sucked loudly on his knuckles.

"Sssure." He slurred. "That's a right good idea, Copper." Percy lifted his nearly empty bottle in salute. "I reckon it is time I had me some new duds." But then his beady eyes turned hard and his voice became a growl, "But…I ain't needin' any of yer scribbles to get it done—neither. My pockets are gonna be plum full by mid-day tomorra. That's—why I'm ce—leb—ra—tin' tonight."

Copper couldn't presume to know what the old man could be talking about. Matilda and Percy Barr were tinkers by trade, and when they were younger, they could mend or repair most anything, from a lace tablecloth to an antique chiffonier. However, in their elder years they'd both become so crippled that they struggled to make even a meager living. What little money they made came from Percy's cheating at cards. In the past two years the couple had relied heavily upon whatever Copper could earn, especially—from her drawings. Beginning when she was a small child, Copper had been able to look at something or someone, and then sketch an exact likeness using charcoal and paper. When the Barr's saw one of her drawings, they knew immediately how to turn her talent into a profit. As they traveled from town to town and farm to farm, wherever they stopped Copper was told to sit where people could see her and then sketch something. When onlookers gathered near and saw the remarkable realism of her drawings, they would ask her to draw something that was dear to them—and of course, the Barr's would charge accordingly. Copper did many portraits of entire families; she even did one of a farmer's favorite bull. However, if no one wanted a drawing, then the Barr's would hire her out to wash windows or scrub floors. Nearly every time they stopped, the girl was able to earn a few coins or barter for supplies.

When Percy's wife Matilda had died a few weeks earlier, they had sold just about everything of value to give the woman a decent burial. And yet, Percy had boasted that his pockets were going to be full—and that the money would not be coming from her scribbles, as he called them. *How could that be?* She wondered. *He has nothing left to sell.* Suddenly a chill slid down Copper's spine—***or has he?***

Percy watched as a look of awareness and anguish spread across Copper's pale face. Usually he delighted in her despair but tonight, as she rose slowly from her stool to put the fire out, her despondency irritated him. Suddenly he wanted her out of his sight, "I'll do that, go to bed, gal," he ordered. "Now."

The hour was late, and after watching Copper quickly roll herself into her canvas hammock that hung beneath the wagon, it wasn't long before Percy grew tired of his own company and struggled to his feet. On legs of rubber, he tossed his empty bottle into the bushes and then he upended the coffee pot over the campfire. His mind wandered as the last of the gray and red embers hissed and died away. All evening the flames had reminded him of his copper-haired bondservant. However, by this time tomorrow night—the girl would be but a memory.

Finally, Barr managed to stagger his way towards the wagon. He braced his hand against the splintered side as he thrust his baldhead underneath, "Ya got ssssomething to look forward to, gal," he mumbled. "By this time tomorrow, you'll see the Rocky Mountains, just like ya've always wanted. Yep, and we're both sssstartin' a new life, me in Californey and you in Denver. Yes, sireee—tomorra night you'll be sleepin' in a fine bed, in a big fancy house."

A cold knot fisted in Copper's stomach, and yet she hoped that perhaps his words were just the ramblings of a drunk. Her large green eyes peered over the hammock, and though she had a dozen questions she knew it was best to hold her tongue. Her silence however, seemed to anger the old man and he grunted a drunken curse as he stumbled up into the wagon and fell onto his small bed.

The misery Copper had felt earlier in the evening suddenly surged through her body and she knew what was going to happen. "I've earned my freedom." She moaned, her voice no more than a whisper. "But you're going to sell me anyway—Percy Barr—I just know it."

The confirmation that her intuition had been right and that everything was about to change again was terrifying. Her fear was something of a paradox because she hated her life as it was now—hated it with every thread of her being. And yet, her present life, as bad as it was, seemed preferable to the unknown. Copper's life had never been pleasant. Her mother had died when she was a year old. Her father, a country schoolmaster had been cold hearted and distant. She had hoped that someday she would earn her father's love and respect and then their lives would be better. Instead, Jarvis Delaney had died in his sleep and left her to pay off his debts. Copper had thought her childhood dismal and lonely but the four years of being a bondservant had been far worse. Now, Percy Barr was celebrating because he was going to sell her. That was the only thing that made sense.

If I wasn't such a coward, I'd run away. That's what I should do...I know it, but...

A sudden chill overtook her and she ran her hands up and down her arms. Her fingers traced the slanted scars that ran from the backs of her hands to her elbows. They always reminded her just how dangerous and foolhardy it was, even to consider running from Percy Barr. She had learned that lesson just two weeks after the Barr's had bought her. Matilda was teaching her to bake biscuits outside over an open fire. Somehow, Copper had allowed them to burn and the next thing she knew Percy was shouting at her for wasting food and lashing at her with his whip. When he didn't stop after five or six lashes, she tried to run away through the forest. Her defiance seemed to unleash an uncontrollable fury inside him. "Don't you dare run from me you little redheaded whelp," he screamed as he chased after her. "Come back here—and take yer punishment."

The next thing she knew he caught her by her long hair and flung her to the ground. Then he stood over her and lashed at her again and again, his whip slicing through her clothing and skin. Unable to fight or run, she finally just rolled into a ball and covered her head with her arms, trying to shield herself until he stopped. But Percy wasn't going to stop. Instead, he kept bringing the whip down in a growing frenzy. Copper knew that he would have killed her, had it not been for Matilda. Even so, when his wife grabbed him by the arm, Percy was in such a rage that he spun around and struck her instead of Copper. As it happened, that was the only thing that could have stopped him. Seeing his sweet and gentle wife, lying at his feet, weeping as she struggled to pull the bloody young bondservant into her arms, seemed to shock the man back to his senses. He frowned down at them, then dropped his whip and staggered away.

Copper's misery, unfortunately, was far from being over. The tender flesh on her arms was split open in a number of places and Matilda wept right along with the young girl as she began the painful process of cleansing her wounds and applying needle and thread. The scars were constant reminders, lines and dots showing clearly, where each cut and stitch had been. Over the past two years, Matilda Barr had protected her many times against Percy's unreasonable and often vicious temper. Now that the old woman was dead, Copper was terrified to stay, but somehow she was equally or perhaps even more afraid...to run.

"Oh, do go to sleep, Copper." she demanded. Even though she wanted so badly to run away, she couldn't conjure up enough courage to even think of doing such a thing. Right now, her only escape was in the shadowed world of slumber. The old man's words troubled her, like nettles in the sheets, and she couldn't even enjoy the comfort of a few hours of sleep. With practiced stealth, she quietly slipped from her hammock. Wrapping a blanket around her shoulders, she walked towards the forest, gazing up at the canopy of dull gray clouds. They matched her mood, making her feel as if she sat beneath a dingy umbrella. There was a small break in the clouds and she spotted a single star in the night sky. Alone and friendless, she thought, just like me. Had she been a child she might have wished upon that forlorn little star. Copper smiled sadly and shook her head—it was almost laughable—when had she ever been a child? It didn't matter, she was a very old sixteen and far too grown up for wishes—or luck—or even prayer. Wishing was a waste of time. If there was such a thing as luck—hers had always been bad. And prayer? No, she'd given up on the idea of a loving God even before her father had died. The town leaders had required all schoolmasters to sign a statement of faith, declaring that they were God-fearing men. Jarvis Delaney had signed their statement, but secretly he believed only in himself, science, mathematics and geography. Copper, by necessity, had done well in those subjects, with a true fascination for geography. She was especially intrigued by the vast Rocky Mountains. Letting her imagination run wild, she had pictured the earth as an enormous living creature, all curled into a ball. The tall and jagged Rocky Mountains ranges were the creature's spine or perhaps its armor, rising up high and proud, like pictures she had seen of mythical dragons or even the great and terrible lizards of old.

Oh yes, seeing the Rockies for herself one day was Copper's fondest wish. Now that seeing them was linked with her life changing yet again, the prospect had suddenly lost its appeal.

What is Percy Barr up to anyway? 'Something for me to look forward to.' he had said. More likely, it's something for me to dread. Oh how I wish tomorrow would never come.

The long night offered no sleep for Copper and the following morning held no comfort. In fact, she couldn't help but feel betrayed when a glorious dawn broke over the horizon. Though she had neither wished nor prayed, she had allowed herself to hope. She'd spent the night searching the clouds, longing for a sudden blizzard or maybe a flash flood. Anything that might delay their arrival in Denver. Of course, since she had dared to hope for a white squall, she wasn't surprised in the least when she awoke to find the sun had risen in the east like a soft yellow buttercup, accompanied by a sweet and gentle breeze. And of course, the road ahead looked as smooth as a whisper across the plains. No, Copper was not surprised. It seemed even nature had become her enemy. For as long as she could remember, things never seemed to get any better and yet somehow—they could—always—manage to get worse. For the most part, she'd been able to take her hardships and trials in stride, and if she hadn't been so close to tears all morning, she might have found the irony of it...almost amusing. Just now, she didn't have the strength to feel anything but misery about the day ahead. In an attempt to delay the inevitable, Copper dawdled over her morning chores; she managed to twist the harness as she hitched the mule to the wagon, and then fumbled awkwardly as she straightened it out again. Even though she slowed their progress down as much as she dared, all too soon, they were on their way!

As each mile took them closer to Denver, the rocking of the wagon coupled with her nervous stomach made her seasick. Then, she heard the sound of rushing water just ahead. She had nearly drowned two years before and hated river crossings with a vengeance. The smell of the muddy water was in the breeze that cooled Copper's cheeks and pulled silky strands from her rust colored braid. Though she hated fast moving water, she had always loved the wind and she closed her eyes and leaned into the sharp-edged breeze. Its invisible strength always made her feel more alive somehow, as if she could take wing and leave all her troubles behind. Just now, the feel of it against her skin stiffened her resolve and filled her with courage. It whispered to her of what she longed for most of all—freedom.

Percy Barr sat beside her holding the reins in his crippled hands and calmly puffing away on his pipe, as if nothing out of the ordinary was going to happen that day. Copper felt herself trembling all over, but she knew that if she had any chance of changing Percy's mind, it was now or never. That morning as she prepared their breakfast he had told her that she would be going to school. Copper was young, not stupid. Schools don't pay to have students; it's the other way around. Percy never did anything without making a profit. So, what kind of *school* would pay someone for bringing them a young female student? Copper took in a long breath, swallowed down the bile that rose in her throat, then turned to the old man riding beside her.

"Please, Mister Barr," she said tremulously. "I think I know what you've got planned for me in Denver, but I beg you, don't do this. Sign my bond papers and release me."

Unaffected by her words, the churlish little man narrowed his eyes and belched loudly. Then he drew on his pipe, turned and blew a cloud of swirling smoke into Copper's face.

Coughing and waving the smoke away, her temper suddenly got the better of her. "Listen to me." she hissed. "You know you're just as afraid of this river as I am! You know Remy will fight you. She won't take one step if I don't sit on her back and talk her across."

Percy grabbed his whip and shook it, "Gal, ya best mind what ya say and how ya say it. Or do I need to teach ya respect—like I done when I first bought ya?"

Copper well remembered the first beating she had received at Percy's hands, as well as everyone there after…and she couldn't help but cringe. She hated being so afraid of this odious little man, but the memory of his cruelty ran deep. Just then, another breeze brushed against her and she found enough courage to try once again. More calmly, she said, "When my father died he owed Crookshank's Emporium fifty dollars. I worked off thirty dollars in two years. You gave Crookshank twenty dollars paying off the balance. I've been with you two years and two months—I've more than paid you in full."

The cloud of pale gray smoke curled about the old man's head as he pondered what he should say to the girl. He knew he shouldn't have threatened her—not today of all days. The truth was that he could no longer earn a living, either honestly or dishonestly. The only thing left for him to do was head to California with his sister and her wealthy husband. Still, Percival P. Barr could not abide his brother-in-law's pity, and he refused to travel west with his sister and her family as their poor relation. Instead, he would at least appear to be a man of means.

Copper recognized the old man's deceitful expression all too well. He was planning something and was already savoring the rewards. Never in Copper's life did she have a choice about anything and it seemed that this day was going to be no different. Still, she just couldn't give up.

"You're planning to sell my bond for a profit, aren't you?" she demanded. "You do not have the right to do that. I've fulfilled my service to you." Softening her voice, she added, "If you'll sign my papers I will still help you and your family get to California. I'll cook and clean and tend to the stock, like I've always done...but please...don't sell me!"

The old man set his thin lips in a hard line. The girl could cry and plead all she wanted—nothing would change what he had planned all along. Two years earlier when he had seen the pretty, little redhead working in Crookshank's Emporium, and then learned that she was an orphaned bond-servant, he knew just what he'd do. Though Percy would have paid more, Crookshank was nervous and seemed in a hurry to get rid of the girl. He had jumped at the old man's offer of twenty dollars. At the time, Copper Delaney was an awkward fourteen. However, Percy could easily imagine how she would look at sixteen. His plan was to keep the girl for a few years, allow her to make life easier for his sickly wife, and then—when she began to blossom like a rosebud kissed by the sun...he'd take the little beauty to Denver and sell her for a price.

Percy allowed himself a rare smile as he glanced at the girl sitting beside him—for she had indeed—blossomed. Copper was aptly named, for her hair shown like a newly minted penny, and her skin was as creamy as fine porcelain with a dusting of russet freckles across the bridge of her delicate nose.

The tiny imperfection seemed only to increase the girl's charm. It was her heavily lashed, large, sea green eyes, however, that captivated everyone that saw her. They were not only beguiling, but also intelligent and expressive. Percy was especially pleased that, daily her young body was transforming from that of a child to that of a woman. Her figure, even at sixteen was morphing from a thin willow branch into the shape of an hourglass.

As they rode closer and closer to the river, Copper tried to think of what she might say to sway Percy while silently the old man contemplated his own plans.

I'll have her wear the green dress Matilda made for her—brings out the beauty of her eyes. Have her put her hair up...no...I'll tell her to leave it down, have it flowing long and silky over her shoulders. Yep, should get a real good price for this one. The Manor College for Young Ladies, what a joke. I wonder if Lavinea Wrenford is still runnin' the place. Now, what was it she called herself? It wasn't Madame. Oh yeah... the housemother. Sure, I'll have to remember that. Like all the other girls, I'll tell Copper that this is a fine Ladies College. She won't find out the truth until I'm long gone and she's locked away in one of the upstairs rooms. It'll work—always has before.

Although Percy had sold two other orphaned girls to the so called—Ladies College, this time would be easier for it had always bothered Matilda. Eventually Percy would persuade his wife to go along with the pretense that The Manor really was a school and that this was best for the girls. In the end, Matilda found that denial was less painful—for her at least. Percy missed his wife but he was relieved not to have to argue with her over Copper's fate. Now he was free to do as he pleased, and the price he'd get for Copper would help him look respectable before his kinfolk.

As Percy shook the reins, he decided it was time he explained a few things to the girl. Turning to Copper, he grunted, "It ain't like you to make a fuss. Told ya before, yer a bondservant, and that's all ya'll ever be. Ya haven't paid off yer debt, so there'll be no signin' of papers. It ain't just what I paid out fer ya. Haven't I put clothes on your back and fed ya fer these two years? And didn't Mattie teach ya to sew and draw them purty pictures? I can't just let ya go after all of that investin'. I may be old and poor, but I'm still a good man o' business—gotta make a fittin' profit. Besides, the place I'm thinkin' of is real nice. If ya settle in and behave yerself, why—ya'll do fine. Ya won't have to work hard and they'll give ya purty clothes and a nice room all to yerself. But if ya try to run gal, I'll be quick to bring the law down on ya." Softening his tone, he added, "Now, once we get across the river, ya be a good girl and put on that frilly green dress Mattie made ya. If things go well, I'll even give ya her china doll—I know ya've always admired it."

Copper didn't give a hoot for that doll. And the conniving look on old Percy's face was turning her stomach. She'd grown to loathe the old man, and thought just about anybody would be preferable to him. Then again, she knew deep down that her situation could be worse. Nothing in Copper's experience, had given her reason to put her trust in men. Even her schoolmaster father had been liberal with the use of the ruler or a switch if she didn't achieve the highest marks in the class. After her father's death, Copper had been forced to live in the storage room at the Emporium. The owner, Mister Crookshank, had also been hard to please, applying his razor strap if she so much as spilled a bit of flour or failed to keep the tins straight on the shelves. Percy Barr, on the other hand, struck her with whatever was most handy: his belt, a buggy whip or even his booted foot to kick her whenever she displeased him. Still, she knew there were men who hurt women in even more brutal and personal ways, and her stomach churned at what might be in store for her once they arrived in Denver.

"Whoa mule." Percy called as he pulled back on the reins.

Finally, they had come to the very edge of the river and Copper's eyes grew wide as she stared at the dark undulating water. Her throat was dry and her heart was pounding like a drum. Matilda Barr had taught her how to float while bathing in a farm pond, but she didn't actually know how to swim. As Copper studied the river, she was certain that if she fell into that dark, swirling waterway—she would never remember how to float. It would simply be the end of Copper Delaney.

"Gal," the old man barked, "Will ya quit lookin' at that puny river like it was a rattlesnake. Just do what ya've always done before, and everythin' will be all right. Now shinny up on old Remy's back and sweet talk her across."

Copper's huge green eyes were wide with apprehension and, except for her freckles; her face lost all color as she looked at the muddy, fast moving river. Another sudden gust of wind blew hard against her and she turned and frowned at Percy Barr with defiance. "If I help you…then you have to at least let me have a say in who buys me? Missus Barr would have."

The old man grabbed his whip again and shook it in Copper's face. "What'd ya mean, *IF* ya do what I say?" His eyes narrowed and his lips trembled but he managed to hold back his temper, reminding himself once again that he would be selling this little vixen in a few hours. He didn't want to risk marring her soft skin and the truth was—he needed her to behave when he introduced her to Lavenia Wrenford. Slowly, he put the whip back and scratched his beard as if considering her request.

"Well?" He muttered, after a long pause. "It ain't that I owe ya nothin'. But in honor of Mattie, I'll allow ya one choice." he mumbled. "I'll give ya one chance to say no, but after that—I'll do what I have to and you'll behave yerself. Agreed?"

Copper pondered for a moment, then she gave a nod of her head, "Agreed." Percy smiled to himself: *Maybe this won't be so hard after all. I'll take her to the roughest* place in *Denver. When she refuses to even step inside, I'll head straight for The Manor. It'll be the easiest money I ever made."*

The arrogant look on Percy's face troubled Copper and it really wasn't much of a concession, she was agreeing for her bond to be sold to someone else. Who they were and what they would expect from her—she still didn't know. At any rate she guessed, it was better than nothing. She put her hand out and they shook on it. With that done, there was nothing else for her to do…but face the river.

"All right Remy, here I come." She called, as she climbed down from the wagon. Copper loved the big ugly beast, and had been the one to name the huge dapple-gray mule, Remy, for the creature looked like bits and pieces of many other animals—remnants all rolled into one. Trailing her hand gently along the animal's side, Copper continued to speak softly as she stepped onto the left harness pole then jumped onto Remy's back. The big mule turned her moose sized head and gently nibbled at the girl's bare toes, while Copper leaned forward and rubbed the mule's forehead.

"Ok, sweetie, here we go again."

When Remy turned back to the river and snorted her displeasure, Copper pressed her heals into the mule's sides and lowered her voice, "Hey now—" she cajoled, "you be a good girl—and we'll make quick work of this. Sooner begun—sooner done."

Cautiously, Remy dipped one griddle size hoof into the water followed by the next. Copper continued her words of praise all the while forcing her voice to sound calm and sure, even though she gripped Remy's mane so tightly her knuckles turned white.

Percy bit down on his pipe and nodded his approval, for everything was going smoothly. Copper's way with animals had come in handy many times. If he took her to California, he could get a better price for her. Still, he knew The Manor would pay well enough, and he needed the money now. He smiled at the thought, they were nearly half way across the river, and soon they'd be in Denver.

Just then, Percy noticed a huge log floating downstream; it was heading straight for the wagon. He shook the reins, and brought the whip down hard on Remy's back, even as he shouted for Copper to hurry. Startled, the mule lunged forward, pulling the wagon almost out of danger. Unfortunately, the massive log hit an underwater snag, and the strong current spun the log around and rammed it right into the back corner of the wagon. The jolt was so powerful that both harness poles snapped in two and the wagon began to tilt precariously. Remy brayed and pulled hard, breaking the rusty trace chains. Unexpectedly free of all restraints, the mule put her head down and bounded for the riverbank.

"Whoa Remy—whoa." Copper cried out as she grabbed the reins and pulled hard. Still, she wasn't strong enough to hold the mule back.

Meanwhile, Percy was already cursing and shouting his demands, "Copper Delaney." he screeched, "You better turn that stubborn mule around—we gotta save this wagon."

Copper struggled with the frightened mule, trying to do what he asked, even though she was just as terrified. With great effort, she finally had Remy facing the river, only to see that the wagon was pitching farther and farther to one side while Percy struggled to secure a hold on the wooden frame.

As the old man realized that he was in jeopardy of losing his life, and not just the wagon, he began to shriek, "Save me—gal—I can't swim. If ya get me out o' this—I—I promise not to sell ya. Not to anyone—ya hear me? I won't sell ya." Ironically, he made his vow even as he shook the whip he had often used to beat her. "Please," he wailed, "Gal, ya can't let me die like this."

Copper bit her lip. "Oh blazes!" she cried. Though she detested the little man, she wasn't about to watch him drown. Digging her heels hard into Remy's side, Copper urged the mule back into the swirling water. "Come on Remy, we've got to get him."

They had nearly reached the floundering wagon when a black river snake slithered across the water. Copper's attentions were focused entirely on reaching Percy. However, when Remy saw the snake gliding towards her, she reared and brayed and spun right out from beneath her rider. It all happened so fast. Copper was in mid-air one second and the river was closing in over her head the next. Screaming from fright and gasping from the cold, she sucked down a lung full of dirty water while the river wrapped itself around her and began tugging her downstream.

When she finally managed to get her head above water, she saw the wagon tip over and dump Percy Barr into the river. Even in her predicament, the irony of the moment wasn't lost on her, when she heard the silly little man still barking out his threats, ***"Copper, Copper."*** he called, ***"You better help me."***

"Hang on—to—the wagon." she called, but her words were a waste of breath, for just then the old man lost his tentative hold. The fast moving current had them both now and was swiftly carrying them downstream.

This is it...she told herself. *We're both going to drown.*

Chapter 2
I Do or Die

"The evil deeds of the wicked ensnare them; the cords of their sins hold them fast." Proverbs 5:22

Just then a buzzing sound zipped over her head, and something tightened painfully around Copper's shoulders. At first her body simply jerked to a sudden stop, but then she felt herself being yanked backwards through the water. It was a strange sensation, and then oddly enough the thought came to her; *this must be how a trout feels on the end of the fisherman's line.*

An instant later a young man roughly hauled her up onto the riverbank. He took the rope off her shoulders and then pounded on her back while she coughed and sputtered and shivered.

"That's it little darlin'…get that dirty water out of yer lungs and…I think ya'll be all right."

Clawing the wet hair from her eyes, Copper struggled to focus on the man that had apparently just saved her life. He turned his back while he untied his bedroll and then draped a warm blanket around her shoulders.

"We best get ya dry before ya catch yer death." He grunted as he knelt beside her and began rubbing her back and arms with the scratchy woolen blanket. Although it seemed to Copper that he was being awfully familiar…she was too busy trying to catch her breath to complain about it.

When she was finally able to speak, she looked around and asked through chattering teeth, "Wh-wh-where's—M-Mister Barr? Didn't you pull him out too?"

The man that looked down at her was a plain looking fellow, with wavy brown hair that curled around his hat. He wasn't that much older than she was, but his eyes were old and as hard and gray as gunmetal.

He shook his head and scoffed at her question, "Ya think I'd help that sorry little reprobate? He wasn't worth m' trouble."

As if allowing the old man to drown needed no further explanation he simply stood and coiled his lariat, then retied it to his saddle. As he gazed down the river, he rubbed a two-day growth of beard. "I'm bettin' he wore a money belt though, 'cause for a little guy he sure didn't bob up and down much." Once again his gray eyes fell on Copper, "Don't tell me ya care. I heard that scallywag promise not to *sell ya*, if ya saved his sorry hide."

When Copper looked embarrassed that he knew such a thing, the man added, "He was lyin' ya know. He would a sold ya to me before yer clothes were dry." He lifted his black Stetson from his head and gave Copper a slow appraising look. After running his hand through his thick brown hair he re-settled his hat adding, "And I would have bought ya." When Copper's green eyes sparked with both fear and anger, he gave a slight chuckle, "Don't worry Red, my name's Vernon Riley and ya caught me on a good day. I'm as de-cent as I ever get when I'm this close to Ma's house. And that's where we're headed now. Ma will take good care of ya."

Suddenly, another man came riding up on a solid black horse. He spurred his mount between them and Copper scrambled to her feet for fear of being trampled.

"Oh, no ya don't, Riley." The man sneered angrily, "Since when do we take the girls we find to yer Ma's? Besides, she's a redhead—she's my redhead." Then he turned towards Copper, "I'm Dirk Culley and you best get used to me, 'cause you're mine! A gypsy told me a long time ago about you. You are meant to be my woman—ya hear? It was foretold to me and I won't give ya up."

Copper pulled the blanket more closely about her, as she appraised this strange man. He sat tall on a horse that was as black as night, and from his boots to his hat, the man himself wore nothing but black. Though his fea-tures were handsome, his skin was like that of a ghost; his hair and face were as white as the clouds that floated overhead. His eyes were like glass—pale and colorless. He looked to be in his late twenties even though a braid of snow-white hair trailed down his back. Both men frightened her, but the cruel expression on this man's face made her take a step closer to Vernon Riley.

"Hey partner..." Vernon said, "Your horse threw a shoe back yonder and you weren't here to see her fall in the river. And you may be fast with yer gun, but you know as well as I do that you can't rope a slow moving fence post. I saw her and I'm the one that saved her. That gypsy told ya a redhead would lead ya to treasure, right? Trust me; this ain't *your redhead*." Then he turned to Copper, "You're a bondservant, ain't ya?"

Copper stiffened, "Not anymore."

Vernon laughed then looked up at the albino, "See, she's got spunk but she's as poor as Job's turkey. She doesn't even own the clothes on her back let alone a treasure."

When Vernon saw the alarm in the girl's large green eyes he quickly turned his back on the albino and adjusted the blanket more tightly around her shoulders as he whispered, "Unless you want to be his, you best do what I say."

When she gave a slight nod of agreement, Vernon scooped her into his arms and with no effort at all, he stepped up into his saddle carrying Copper with him. With the girl settled on his lap he turned back to the albino and said, "Now, there's no need for the two of us to butt heads over this. You know we always live by the book when we're within a hundred miles of Ma's house. The girl doesn't change the fact that we've been headed to Ma's all along—and we're only a skip and a holler from the farm right now. We'll figure this out later."

Just then another rider cantered up to them, he was a smooth faced sandy-haired boy and looked even younger than Copper. He reined his horse to a stop, saw the wet girl in Riley's arms and blushed crimson.

"Hey Boss." he said looking at Vernon. "It was just like ya said; he got all tangled up in the shallow waters downstream." Suddenly embarrassed, the boy gave Copper a sheepish look, and then he nodded to Vernon while he slyly patted his saddlebags.

Copper wasn't fooled; she knew Mr. Barr had indeed worn a money belt and that it was now in the boy's possession. The joke was on them however, for Percy's money belt held mostly fake bank notes and a pouch of gold dust, but was actually just lead and sand. The old scoundrel had used these things for show, whenever he wanted to sucker a man into a game of chance. Still, the boy's words had confirmed her suspicions that these men were outlaws and that Vernon was their leader. As usual, Copper's life was taking her right from the kettle—into the flame.

Feeling the young girl trembling in his arms, Vernon pulled her closer, and it was at that precise moment that he decided what he would do with the prize he had fished from the river—he would keep her. She was young and innocent, soft and pretty and she felt just right in his arms. Vernon smiled as the thought took shape. This would infuriate Dirk as much as it would please his mother—and most all—it would please him.

Although the albino was staring daggers at him, Vern only shrugged, "Listen Dirk, we'll work this out. Right now I don't want that man's corpse putrefying the waters around ma's house. So, I need ya to take the girl's mule and get that old codger and bury him off in the forest somewhere. Then see if you can scare up some game. Ma saved your life last year and it ain't fittin' that we show up empty handed with four mouths to feed."

The muscle in Dirk's jaw jerked and he scowled at Vernon. He had no intention of giving up on the redhead, she was meant to be his. The trouble was, he owed Ma Riley. That woman had treated him better than anyone else ever had. So for now at least, he would wait until after the visit was over.

The big mule was grazing a few yards away and Dirk rode over to her and reached down to grab the reins, but the ornery beast laid her ears back and tried to bite his hand.

Cursing, the albino spun his horse away from the mule and drew his gun.

"No. Don't shoot her." Copper screamed. "She just doesn't like strangers." Putting her fingers to her lips, she whistled and the big mule trotted over to where she shared a horse with Vernon. Copper reached down and grabbed Remy's reins then glanced back at Vernon, "She'll be good now, I promise."

"I'm not foolin' with that crazy mule, Vernon. You deal with it or I'll shoot that ugly thing."

Vernon only laughed, "Fine, just go do what I asked ya to."

Dirk spurred his horse and headed down the river, cursing as he went.

As soon as the albino was out of sight, Vernon turned to the younger man who was still staring at Copper. "Hey Smitty, ya've done good, but now I've got somethin' else fer ya to do."

Grinning, he shook his head as if he were surprised by his own decision. "Listen boy, ride into town—nobody there knows ya. Find the preacher and tell him a man's been drown out on the crossing and he's been taken to Ma Riley's for burying. Tell him that Ma asked that he come alone and as quick as he can."

Copper watched the young man hurry away. This outlaw, Vernon Riley, sending for a preacher just didn't make sense. Shaking her head, she asked, "You didn't think it worth the trouble to save Mister Barr from drowning so why would you bother to send for a preacher to speak over his grave? He wasn't a religious man and you don't strike me as one either."

Vernon leaned close to Copper's ear and said softly, "I know the men that ride with me. Dirk Culley does what I say—*most of the time.* But he's still the meanest man I know. If you're smart, you'll take my advice."

When he felt Copper tremble again, Vernon enjoyed the excuse to tighten his hold. "Hey now, no need to be scared, little darlin'." He assured her, as he nudged his horse forward, "Why don't ya tell me who ya are and what's yer story? How'd you get yerself in such a fix as this, anyway?"

Pushing a damp wisp of hair from her eyes, she shrugged. "My name is Copper Delaney, and I'm almost always—in a fix like this. My mother died when I was a year old and my father was a schoolmaster. He died four years ago. While I was working off his debt to the general store, I slept in the back room. Late one night the owner came in and...well he became very angry when he found out that I always slept with a knife under my pillow and I wasn't afraid to use it." Just then Copper slanted her eyes at the man holding her.

"Good girl." Riley said with a chuckle, knowing she was giving him a warning. "So what'd he do then?"

"Well, he was madder still when I told him he better leave me alone or I'd tell his wife! The next day when Mister and Missus Barr offered to buy me, he was eager to sell." Copper shook her head and sighed, "I hated Percy Barr, he was even meaner than Crookshank, but I could never wish anyone dead." Glancing back to make sure Remy was following, she added, "I liked his wife. For the most part, Missus Barr was good to me and she taught me things. I always thought she was intelligent, however—I must say—her discernment regarding the choice of a spouse was—extremely—unfortunate."

Vernon threw his head back and laughed, "Yer a funny little thing, and ya sure talk like the spawn of a schoolmaster. But darlin', I think maybe yer luck has changed. Ya sure picked the right day to drown. I'm a pretty bad hombre most any day of the week but I've always been good with a rope and when I'm headed to Ma's...I live by the book."

"The book?" Copper asked.

"Yep, my Ma lives by the good book—the Bible. I don't put much store by it, but my Ma's the best there is. So, I made her a promise that when I am within a hundred miles of our family farm—well—I don't do anything that would shame her. I at least try to act like the kind of man she wants me to be."

Copper didn't quite understand what he meant by that, but then her thoughts turned to the frightening man that had gone on to fetch Mister Barr's body and her curiosity suddenly got the better of her. "I don't like your partner and I don't like what he said about my belonging to him. He frightens me."

Vernon nodded in understanding, then he spoke softly even though Dirk wasn't anywhere near

"Listen Red, you best be careful around that man. Like yer the spawn of a schoolteacher, he's the devil's spawn if ever there was one! Like I said… he's the meanest man I know—and he aims to have you as his woman—but I don't think you'd like it much."

When Vernon saw the fear in Copper's eyes he continued, "I see you agree with me. So, little lady, I can think of only one thing I can do to keep ya safe. Dirk Culley has only one weakness; he's scared nigh to death of one thing. I laughed the first time I heard it, but I'll never laugh at him again. Like he said, a gypsy once told him that she saw terrible things in store for him if he ever trifled with a married woman. If he knows a woman is married…he always steers clear of her. The other thing she told him was that one day he would meet a redheaded woman and she would lead him to great treasure. Yer in big trouble Red. If you don't want to be his woman—then you—are—just gonna have to be mine. That's—why I sent for the preacher."

The Riley Farm was nestled at the end of a winding road through a grove of elm trees. The house was small and gray. The rough cut siding had probably never known a coat of paint. Nor had the old wooden barn that stood just beyond with a chicken coop attached to one side. Vernon stopped his horse at the hitching post, but before he could dismount a round little woman with salt and pepper hair wound into a tight bun opened the front door and hurried across the porch. The woman had the exact same shape and shade of gray eyes as her son, but there was no harshness in them. Instead, they danced with joy as she clasped her work worn hands together and came down the steps, laughing and crying. "Oh, welcome. Welcome home, son." she cried. "Get down from that beast so I can give you a proper hug."

Vernon grinned and began his explanation even as he stepped down from his horse carrying the still damp and disheveled girl with him. "Ma, I brung ya a present!" He said proudly, setting Copper at his mother's feet. "This pretty little thing is about to become that daughter-in-law you've been hankerin' for, this is—uh—" Vernon turned to Copper and frowned, "What did ya say yer name was?"

The man's off handed remarks astonished and then infuriated Copper. How dare he offer her as a gift to his mother. As if she were a figurine for the mantelpiece or worse yet a servant girl. Up until that moment, Copper had been confused, but now suddenly she felt the starch flooding back into her spine. She was finally free now—there was no way she was going to be indentured again, especially not to this arrogant outlaw or his mother. The man hadn't even bothered to remember her name. Pressing her lips together, Copper placed her hands on her hips and glared at the older women, believing that Vernon's mother would surely be as outraged as she was. But to Copper's dismay, the elderly woman's soft gray eyes became tender, her smile hopeful as she pulled Copper into a gentle embrace, "I'm Ma Riley, welcome home my dear." she said, treating Copper exactly as she had her own son, and the look in the woman's eyes was one of sincere joy.

Ma Riley's surprisingly kind reaction to her was more than the young bondservant could comprehend. Copper understood belittlement and cruelty all too well, but genuine kindness felt altogether foreign, it confused her. Stepping back, she felt numb and dizzy at the same time. Her throat grew thick as all the emotions of the past twenty-four hours came crashing down on her like a wave. As if the horror of being sold or the panic of drowning in the river, hadn't been enough. Now she had to contend with an outlaw proposing marriage and his mother's warm and hospitable embrace. Tears swam in her eyes and she fought hard to hold them back. Living as an unwanted child and then as an oppressed bondservant, Copper's life had been so devoid of love and acceptance that Ma Riley's motherly embrace simply overwhelmed her.

Just then Vernon put his hand on the small of Copper's back and gently pushed her towards his mother, "Ma you take good care of our girl while I put my horse in the barn." With a wink he added, "Don't worry Ma, I'm still honoring my promise—the preacher's on his way."

Copper's senses suddenly came back to her; somehow these strangers were already manipulating her into doing their will. Just like everyone else in her life always had. Another chill went down her spine as she remembered the lustful look Vernon had given when he said, that Percy would have sold her before her clothes were even dry, *'And I would have bought ya.'* he had quickly added. In the past year she had received a number of indecent proposals, and she supposed she should be thankful that he had at least offered marriage. But what was marriage anyway? In Copper's mind it was just another way for a man to own a woman—to have a socially acceptable mistress and maid!

Though it took all her gumption, she grabbed hold of Vernon's arm and stopped him from leaving. "Mister Riley," she said defiantly as she glared from the man to his mother and then back again. "I'm grateful that you saved my life—but—I am not a *gift* for your mother and I am not going to marry you." Shifting her gaze to encompass both mother and son she added, "So, before that ghost man and *the preacher* get back here we need to come up with another idea."

Copper knew Vernon would not like her words and she immediately braced herself, expecting him to lash out verbally if not physically. So it was a surprise when the man simply chuckled. "Red, if anyone can think of *another idea*, it'll be Ma." Then he turned to his mother and quickly told her all that he had seen and heard at the river. Then he reminded her about Dirk Culley and the gypsy's prophecy. Ma Riley paid close attention to her son's story but when Copper attempted to speak the older woman held up her hand to stop her.

"Young woman," she began, "I'm known fer lookin' on the bright side as well as the practical side of things. Right now you're frightened, cold and miserable. We can have our talk after I've put you in a nice hot bath. A clean body makes a clear mind, I always say."

Ma Riley clucked and fussed as she ushered Copper into her bedroom, muttering cheerfully, "Yer in fer a real treat, child. Bet ya've never seen one of these before." She pointed to the large soaking tub, and of course she was right; Copper never had seen anything like it. A large tub sat in the corner of the room and just behind it was a small potbelly stove with a water reservoir above the firebox. A spigot was down low on the reservoir and with a turn of a knob, hot steaming water flowed right down into the tub. Copper thought it was miraculous and from the look on Ma Riley's face, she thought so too. Just then the older woman let out a long sigh and said, "My boy is far from perfect, but I love him. He can be sweet as molasses, but there are other times when he's just like his Pa. I used to tell my late husband that he was half wolverine and half porcupine. Riley men can be mean and prickly. I've always told Vernon that he gets his *charm* from me, but his *ornery* comes straight from his Pa. Still, on one of Vernon's charmin' days, he bought me this here tub." The old woman ran her wrinkled hand over the tub's smooth surface and sighed. "And ain't it just a marvel?"

"Yes," Copper agreed politely, "it's very nice—but ma'am, you don't seem to understand what's happening here. Your son is forcing himself on me to protect me from another man—forcing himself on me. I need you to speak up and protect me from both of them. I think I'd just as soon jump back in that river than belong to either one."

Ma pressed her lips together and nodded her head sadly, "My dear girl, I suggest you not say that again. I must warn you that I wouldn't put it past either one of them to toss you back into that river if you don't cooperate." Ma Riley said no more allowing the girl to mull over her words while she pulled the blanket from her shoulders and helped her undress.

While Copper sank into the deep, hot water, the old woman went to the opposite corner of the room and opened up a brightly painted trunk. "I think I've got the perfect wedding dress for you, dear." She mumbled as she began laying things out on the bed.

"Wedding dress," Copper huffed. "Weren't you listening to me? Your son said you were a good woman. A Christian woman. So, why are you cooperating with this arrogant, high-handed idea of his?"

Keeping her back turned to Copper; Ma Riley shrugged her shoulders and said softly, "I think it was you who wasn't listening. Would you truly rather drown in that river than get married? Besides, Vernon's my son, and blood is thicker than water. I can't and I won't help you reject him."

Copper wanted to scream at the woman but soap was getting in her eyes. Holding her breath, she slid beneath the water to rinse her hair. When she came up it still felt dirty so she lathered it with the lemon-scented soap, rinsed it, then lathered it again. The fine river silt was proving as difficult to be rid of, as the mess she'd landed in. Finally, she let out a loud sigh and made her plea, "I think both those men will listen to you. I think you could keep them from tossing me back in the river *and* stop this wedding. Your son adores you and you saved the other man's life. Just tell them this is wrong. I can see you need help around here. If you talk them both into leaving me alone, I could stay on for a while. I'd work hard for just room and board."

Ma Riley refused to listen to the girl's pleading. She had prayed for years that something like this would happen. And now that it had, she was determined to see it through. Mumbling to herself the old woman sighed, "Oh, good, here it is. This color is just perfect for you."

Reverently she lifted the dress from the trunk, and then carefully laid it on the bed. It had been her favorite Sunday frock, a keepsake from happier times and much younger days. It was a soft pale green and though no longer stylish, the color would be beautiful on the little redhead and make her green eyes look even lovelier. Then she dug deeper into the trunk and found undergarments and even a pair of slippers she thought might fit.

After she laid the clothes out on the bed, Ma Riley stared out the window. Her hands moved quickly as she repositioned a few loose pins in her steel gray bun and without turning around she said wistfully, "I do understand how you feel. But, I haven't the power you think I do. I know that Vernon loves me and Dirk respects me, still, men rarely listen to women. Not unless it's something they want to hear. It has never been easy to be a woman—and don't I know it. The truth is I've been prayin' for a sweet girl like you to come into Vernon's life. I know all this seems unlikely but God's ways often are unlikely, and there's always hope."

"No!" Copper nearly shouted. "I don't believe in hope or God. I refuse to be owned by another man. I was a servant to my father and I've been a bondservant since he died in debt. I know I paid off my bond to Mister Barr, but he denied it—just so he could sell me to someone else. I never wished him dead but I'm glad to be free. And I am grateful to your son—I owe him something but not my life!" Copper wrung the water from her long hair, adding, "Missus Riley, I don't want to hurt your feelings...but I think your son and his friends are outlaws. I am nothing more than a trinket being fought over by two mean desperados—and shame on you for allowing it!" With quick angry movements Copper wrapped a towel around her hair and another one about her body as she stepped from the tub.

The old woman nodded slowly. "You're stronger than I first gave you credit for, my dear, and you're right about those two. They are thieves and robbers and—possibly even killers—I don't know." With a wistful shrug she motioned towards the clothes on the bed, "You can put these on after I've fixed your hair."

Though Copper tried to be defiant, she wasn't feeling as strong as she was trying to make herself sound. A look of concern clouded Ma's face as she pulled out a small stool for Copper to sit on. "You best sit before you fall. I don't know if it's from anger, fear or shock…but you're trembling like an aspen leaf. You rest while I brush out your hair and we can talk this through."

Copper glared at the woman, she wanted to storm around the room while she argued her point, but Missus Riley was right, her knees were already threatening to buckle. "All right," she sighed as she sank onto the stool. "But there is nothing to talk through. I've said all I'm going to say on the matter."

"That's what I had in mind, dear. I'll talk…you listen."

Ma Riley smiled indulgently when the girl let out a loud frustrated sigh and dropped to the stool. Ma slowly began massaging Copper's scalp then slowly worked the brush through the long cascade of silky bronze hair.

"Oh my, you are a lovely little thing." she cooed. "I'm not surprised that those two tom cats are in a tussle over you." Then Ma's voice took on a business like air, "Though I'm not one to gamble…I'd wager my favorite egg layin' hen that you've haven't any family nor a penny to yer name. Is that so?" When Copper looked away and shrugged, Ma Riley clucked her tongue, "I thought as much." She turned Copper around and looked her in the eye, asking: "So, what if there was no Vernon Riley or even an albino named Dirk Culley wantin' ya? Suppose I gave ya these clothes and a dollar or two, and sent ya on yer way. How far do ya think ya'd get before some other man or group of men took a fancy to ya? What do you think would happen then?"

Copper stiffened at the old woman's words. Then she wrapped her arms around herself and shook her head sadly. "Nothing good," she whispered, "I'm sure—nothing good."

Ma stepped back behind Copper again and continued to brush out her long hair, giving the girl time to think about her predicament. For a long while the only sound was that of the bristles gliding through the long amber-colored mane and the static crackle as her hair began to dry.

Finally, Ma broke the silence, "Oh—I know dear—trying to be a decent woman in a world full of unscrupulous men is like walkin' barefoot though cactus. Yer gonna get hurt, no matter which way ya turn. All I can do is pray that someday Vernon will become that good and godly man I've always wanted him to be. I know it's possible, with love and patience—and prayer. In the meantime, there's nothin' either of us can do, that will stop Vernon from takin' ya as his wife. I know my boy. He'll enjoy his time with ya fer a day or two and then he'll leave ya here, with me." Once again, Ma turned Copper to her and looked into her green eyes, "Try to be a good wife, and once this marriage is consummated, I'll treat ya like the daughter I've always wanted. Life here could be real good! I'll teach ya all I know about gardening and how to snare a rabbit. Best of all I'll introduce you to God. He truly does love ya child, and somehow I'll prove it to ya!"

A deeper understanding suddenly came to Copper and she decided to challenge the older woman. "How can you justify being a good Christian with the way you're using me? I saw it in your eyes just now. You weren't thinking of my snaring anything but your son. You're hoping I'll be the tender trap that will hold Vernon close to this farm and to you."

The old woman's gray eyes filled with tears. "I'm not quite that conniving but I suppose in a way—you're right. The truth is I don't know what else to do." She admitted sadly. "I didn't plan this, but I do think that God may very well have His hand in it. I'm so afraid my boy will die if he doesn't change soon and I honestly can't think of another way out for you. Oh, I know Vernon's desire to marry you is selfish. You're beautiful and he's justifying his lust under the guise of protecting you. I'd like to think there is a bit of nobility in his actions, for he also wants to provide me with some much needed help. However, what you must remember is that Dirk Culley will take you from here by force, unless you become a married woman—in every sense of the word. Vernon is your only protection from Dirk. But—not even I can protect you from Vernon. Only a miracle could do that."

Copper hugged her knees to her chest while she pondered Missus Riley's words. "I don't know why I'm shocked at any of this," she sighed. "It seems my fate is always to do what others want of me. I am afraid of Dirk Culley, but to be honest, I doubt that your son is any better." Finally giving into the inevitable, Copper stood and walked to the bed. Careful to keep the towel wrapped around her, she let her feelings be known as she modestly slipped into the clean undergarments. "I suppose it's six of one or a half dozen of another, I'm fairly certain that whatever Percy Barr had in mind for me was probably as bad or even worse than what Vernon and Dirk have in mind." Copper looked into Missus Riley's gray eyes, the older woman's expression was sympathetic and motherly. Copper couldn't help but wonder if this was as close as she might ever get to knowing a mother's love, or to having a home and family.

"All right Missus Riley," Copper said ruefully as she reached for the green dress, "with my luck, if I tried to get away, I'd probably run right smack dab into a Ute scalping party." Resigned to her fate, Copper asked, "Do you have any idea what Vernon does when he leaves here? And how often do you think he'll come back?"

Ma Riley sighed with relief as she helped Copper pull the heavily ruffled dress over her head. "I see I'm not going to be the only practical woman in this house." She gave Copper's shoulders an affectionate squeeze, then began buttoning up the dress while she attempted to answer the question: "Oh child...what does Vernon do? I fear when he's one hundred miles from this farm…he does exactly as he wishes. As I said, I try to look on the bright side of things, and my hope is that, with you here, he'll want to be home and work this farm. I pray that he will finally give his heart to the Lord and become a God fearing man. But to be honest, my practical side tells me that most likely my son will—die in prison or—at the end of a rope."

While Ma tied the sash on Copper's dress the women heard raised voices in the parlor. There were angry shouts and then Vernon stormed through the door, "You both are needed in the parlor," he demanded.

Ma hurried from the bedroom, pulling Copper by the hand. Vernon took her other hand and led her to the fireplace where a tall man, no doubt the preacher, stood with his Bible opened. He looked as nervous as Copper felt. Although she told herself not to look for the albino, her eyes betrayed her as they roamed across the room. He was sitting on a bench by the front door and looked as if he were mad enough to bite into a horseshoe and spit nails. His black holster was draped over the kitchen chair on the opposite side of the room. Dirk's glassy eyes met Copper's and then he sneered up at the young boy. Smitty looked scared to death and yet his pistol never wavered from Dirk's chest. "I'm sorry about this," he winced. "but you know I gotta do what Vernon says."

"Shut up kid." Dirk grunted. "I'm not mad at you." Then he turned towards Copper and folded his arms over his chest. "Listen to me, you were meant to be my woman—it was foretold. I'll marry ya, if that's what you want and I'll be every bit as good to ya as Vernon Riley. I promise ya Red, he's no better than me." When his glance fell on Ma Riley, he seemed embarrassed and then quickly looked away.

Vernon's mother was still holding Copper's hand. She pulled her closer and whispered, "Don't you believe him. Besides, if ya marry Vernon, you can stay here with me. If ya marry Dirk y'all have to go with him."

Just then Vernon cleared his throat and nodded for the preacher to begin. The man frowned as he looked at Copper, then said with a hesitant voice, "We—we are gathered here—to join Vernon Riley—with…uh…with uh?" His frown deepened when no one hurried to share the name of the bride. The preacher looked to the groom with raised eyebrows, "What is the name of your bride, sir?"

Vernon looked to the little redhead to supply the answer, but when she lifted her chin defiantly, he just smiled and shrugged his shoulders. "Reckon ya can call her Red—that's what I've been callin' her."

The preacher stared from the pokerfaced groom to the silent bride and slapped his Bible shut. "I think sir; you should become a bit more acquainted with this woman before I perform a marriage ceremony. This is a sacrilege, it's obvious she does not want to marry you and you don't even know the girls name. I will not do this."

The preacher spun on his heels, intent on heading to the front door, when Vernon's pistol suddenly leapt into his hand. The room was silent but for the sound of the gun being cocked. Then his voice rumbled, "Whatever her name is, she'll be sleepin' with me from now on preacher, so for the lady's sake you might want to rethink what you will and will not do."

Turning slowly around, the preacher gave Copper an apologetic look, "I'm very sorry about this Miss. I don't know how, but I believe that God will prevail." While Vernon holstered his gun the preacher asked, "Please dear, what is your name?"

Vernon squeezed Copper's hand, "Might as well tell us yer name, Red."

Copper didn't know why she was being belligerent; she'd already told Missus Riley she'd marry her outlaw son. Still, she was terrified of what was about to happen and just then she sent up a desperate prayer. *Oh God, if you're up there…help me.* Glancing about, Copper saw no help coming from on high or any other direction. Sighing, she shook her head and answered, "All right then, my name is Copper Delaney, sir."

The exchange of vows lasted only a few minutes, while Copper's heart hammered so loudly, that she heard very little of it. When the pastor asked her if she accepted Vernon as her husband, Ma Riley, a bundle of nerves herself, answered for her, "Oh yes Pastor, she most certainly does."

When the preacher insisted that the bride speak for herself, Copper glanced up at Vernon. He smiled and nodded his head, "You can trust me, Red."

Copper sighed, only a fool would trust a man that couldn't even remember her name. Suddenly she wondered if, even now, she should try to make a run for it. Perhaps she should just race back to the river and throw herself in. She didn't run though, instead, she heard herself whispering sadly, "I do."

For the young woman's sake, the pastor intentionally left out the part about kissing the bride. His ploy, didn't work, for the anxious groom instantly pulled Copper into his arms and pressed his lips to hers. Frightened and embarrassed, Copper put her hands on Vernon's chest and pushed as hard as she could but the man only became all the more aggressive. As her temper rose, she lifted her foot and kicked him in the shins. Vernon howled in pain then slapped Copper across the face. Ignoring his mother's gasp, Vernon grabbed Copper's arm and yanked her towards his bedroom, intent on consummating the marriage without delay. Suddenly a thunderous noise came from both the front and the back of the house.

It seemed the whole place shook with the sound of splintering wood and shattering glass. Vernon spun around in time to see a man wearing a silver badge, bursting through the front door and firing his gun at Smitty. The boy had already swung his pistol away from Dirk and shot towards the door, but he'd reacted too quickly and his bullet broke the glass windowpane while the sheriff's aim had been true. Copper watched in horror while a crimson stain blossomed across Smitty's chest. He was dead before his body crumpled to the floor. Vernon had also drawn and fired at the first sight of the intruder, but his shot also went wild when Copper rammed her shoulder into his side. The wild bullet that was meant for the lawman might have parted Dirk's snowy white hair, had he not already dropped to the floor, frantically making a grab for Smitty's fallen gun. He was just swinging it towards the sheriff, when the man kicked it out of his hand. Meanwhile, the deputy, who had crashed through the backdoor, raced towards Vernon and knocked him cold with the butt of his gun.

Ma Riley wept as they took her son away. She had hoped her boy would have this one last chance to change for the better. Copper wept too, but with relief. For the first time in her life she had been saved from someone's cruelty. She couldn't help but wonder if God had actually answered her prayer? She would have to ask Ma Riley.

Unfortunately, it took only one glance at the older woman's heartbroken face for Copper to know that she would never have her motherly, love and acceptance. The truth was, however, that they both needed each other and so perhaps they could at least be friends. Copper planned to work hard and in turn, she hoped Ma Riley would teach her all the things she'd promised. Especially about God, because now she was genuinely interested. If not, it would still be wonderful to have a solid roof over her head and a safe place to stay. Safe—she supposed it would be safe to stay on the farm—for a while at least. Until Vernon Riley and Dirk Culley were released from prison.

Chapter 3
Prison Cells & Hidden Treasure

One year Later - 1865
Mid-West Territorial Prison

"For we brought nothing into the world, and we cannot take anything out..." I Timothy 6:7

Vernon gazed into eyes the color of aspen trees in the summer. He was just leaning forward to kiss his bride's soft lips when the loud and gasping cough broke through his favorite dream. He rose from his cot, picked up his tin cup and threw it at the old man that shared his cell. Sleep was his only escape from this rat hole of a prison, and he didn't take his dreams being interrupted lightly.

A moment later, however, he softened a bit when he took in the ashen color and skeletal face of his cellmate. The old man shook his head and wheezed out, "I'm a dying—I tell ya. And don't be telling me I ain't."

O'Leary's face was gray, and as thin as the blanket that covered him. He'd been middle aged when he entered this prison, but after three years, six months and fifteen days in a cold dark cell he'd become an old man—old and sick. He was weak and gaunt and his voice was little more than a hoarse whisper, confirming that his prediction was most likely the truth. His weathered hand trembled as he ran it over his stubbly gray beard. "Listen up me bucko," he rasped breathlessly. "Got something big to tell ya."

While the old man spoke, his feverish eyes locked on the striped pattern on the wall. Cloud-shadowed moonlight shown through the barred window as it crept slowly across the small chamber. Even if he could stand, he wouldn't have been able to see outside, and the view wouldn't have been worth the trouble.

Yet, he looked forward to the daily trek of the sun by day and moon by night. Like welcome visitors, they slipped through the barred window, adorning the cell walls with changing patterns of darkness and light as they meandered across the room. It was at least something to look forward to in the colorless world of prison.

Vernon Riley sat across from the old man on his own small cot listening to O'Leary's dismal words and raspy voice. Vernon was young and strong, and had never been sympathetic to the plight of others; few inmates of prison were of that nature. However, he had become surprisingly fond of the old Irishman. Tar O'Leary was good company and with his fanciful yarns, he had made the past year nearly bearable. However, now as Vernon listened to the old man's labored breathing, it felt as if his own lungs were starving for air and his eyes grew suspiciously moist when he saw a tear rolling down O'Leary's wrinkled cheek.

The old man suddenly grew self-conscious and frowned at Vernon. "Don't ya go thinkin' me a coward. It ain't that I'm afeared to die—it's just that me Ma would surely be vexed to know that I'd ended me days in prison. She were a godly woman and I hate to think I'd let her down—that's all that bothers me."

"Will ya stop talking like that, old man," Vernon grunted. "Thinkin' like that is what kills ya!" He ran a dirty hand over his face as he leaned against the cold brick wall and sighed, "Still and all—I reckon I know what ya mean about havin' a godly Ma." Vernon felt a rare moment of contrition himself and he rubbed the back of his neck and thought of his own mother and her kind gray eyes. "Yeah, my Ma's a godly woman, too. But Bible teachin' didn't take root in me any more than it did in you. It's a sorry thing to disappoint yer Ma though. Always figured I'd settle down one day—and—take care of her—ya know? I got a wife that's taking care of her now, reckon that's something but—it ain't near enough."

"Well now, bucko." Tar grunted, "My ma's dead, but maybe you and me can take care a yer Ma and that little redheaded wife of yer's. Perhaps, between the two of us we might just finally do something right fer a change."

"Hush up old man," Vernon sneered. "Yer fever's doing the talkin' again."

"I'm as clear headed as you, me boy. Now, let me tell ya a tale that'll be putting the light back in her eyes." Tar motioned for Vernon to lean closer. "I stole somethin' big once. That ain't why I'm in here though. I'm here fer a bunch a little things, like bustin' up a saloon and punchin' a judge in the nose. Trouble was when they went and added up all them—little things—well—me prison sentence come to four long years. I've only six months to go but I'll not make it." Tar hesitated while he studied his young cellmate. He had never shared his secret with anyone, but it was obviously now or never. "Come closer me boy… and listen, I've got a little bedtime story fer ya and I think ya'll like it better than any I've told ya so far."

Vernon sighed indulgently, "Fine—talk if ya like, I'm listening, Tar."

"Do that now. Listen and remember. Not long before I ran my foolish fist into that old judge's nose and got meself arrested. I was trappin' up in the mountains near a small town called Otter Run. Fer a season or two I partnered up with a sorry cuss by the name of Ox Hennessey. He was the biggest scoundrel that ever drew breath—in mind and body both. On what was to be the last day of our acquaintance, we set up camp across the valley from the road that led from the lowlands up the mountains. I call it a road—but that's a mighty generous word, fer in some places it were no more than a narrow eyebrow that cut into the side of the mountain. There were long stretches on that road where a drop off the edge might take ya down a thousand feet—maybe more. We had camped just across such a treacherous place and just above it a wild fire had burned that whole side of the mountain."

O'Leary grew thoughtful as he stared at the shadows that moved across his cell wall and shook his head. "Ya know, all this happened years ago, but I remember it all like it were only yesterday. 'Twas raining pitchforks and pollywogs and we was bettin' whether or not there'd be a mudslide that would take out that there slip of road. Entertainment is scarce up there in the mountains and a mudslide was high drama. While we was talkin' over the possibilities, we heard the trace chains of the stage and the snap of the driver's whip."

O'Leary finally had Vernon's full attention and as he warmed to the story, the younger man leaned forward and asked, "So, what did ya do?"

"Ah, mores the pity…there weren't a blessed thing we could do—but watch. And…as sure as a hound dog has fleas…that whole side of the mountain began to move. 'Twas slow at first, like a crouching mountain lion stalking his prey. There were two teams pullin' the stage that day and them horses seemed to sense the danger and they was just a flyin'. They was moving out so fast, we thought for sure the stage was gonna make it. But then the whole side of the mountain gave way. 'Twas like it was reaching out for that coach, and all that muck and mire came down and took holt of the back wheels and then pulled that coach right over the side of the mountain. We heard a loud crack and the harness pole snapped and the trace chains broke. That were a blessing—fer the horses were free then and they kept on a runnin'."

Tar ran a shaky hand over his eyes like he was trying to rub away the vivid memory, and then he added, "The driver tried to jump free—poor man—but—him and the passengers was all carried right over the edge of the road and straight down the steepest part of the mountain. It all happened while the storm was still a raging, but I swear—I could hear their screams." Sighing, Tar grew silent for a while then added, "I can hear 'em still."

Just then the old man began to cough and Vernon handed him a cup of water. O'Leary drank deeply then continued with his story. "I turned to Ox and says, 'We got to get down there and see if we can help them poor devils.' But Ox, that sorry, lowdown cuss, he says to me, 'I ain't goin' down there and any man that does is a blazin' fool.' Ox packed his things right there and then and rode off in a huff. I never saw the scoundrel again and I was glad to be rid of the ornery beggar. After a while, the storm let up and I was able to ride part way down the mountain but it was powerful steep. When I got as far as I dare go on horseback, I tied three ropes together then dallied the end around me saddle horn. I held onto that rope and went down the rest of the way just a slippin' and slidin'. My old horse, Diggery, he was a brute of an animal, strong and well trained and I knew if I found anyone alive down there, he could pull them out and me with 'em."

Vernon leaned forward and asked, "Well, were they alive?"

"Sadly no… there were two men but they had both been thrown out of the coach. I never did find the driver." Tar muttered. "I started to bury the first fella I come to and to tell ya true, I went through his pockets. I hoped for a dollar or two, maybe a good knife or a watch. No sense in wasting such things. 'Twas then though, that I spotted something strange, he weren't a big man but he was powerful heavy, and when I touched his chest I wondered if he weren't wearin' some kind of armor. Sure enough underneath his fancy shirt and vest—was an undergarment unlike any I'd ever seen before. 'Twas made out of a sturdy canvas with dozens of little pouches sewn into rows all over the back and sides." Tar leaned closer to Vernon and whispered, "And what do ya think was inside them pouches?" When Vernon shrugged Tar grinned, "A solid gold eagle—that's what. Some pouches even had two or three of 'em. I was quick to check the other man and he was fitted out the same. I took both them vests and they was so heavy I could barely handle 'em." Tar paused to catch his breath and though his eyes were clouded with fever, the knowing smile that spread across his face, filled the younger man with excitement.

"So, how much gold was there?" Vernon demanded.

"Keep yer voice down." Tar grunted, but then his eyes grew bright, "Never took the time to count it, but there's plenty! Now, hush and let me finish me story. When I realized that I had stumbled upon me very own pot of gold, I'll tell ya true, that's when I got scared. Getting' away with that much gold could be as sticky as a broken barrel of molasses. Figured word would spread fast, and soon the whole territory would be gossiping about the stagecoach and about the two wealthy passengers and their gold. 'Course sooner or later I knew Ox would hear of it, he'd know I had it and then he'd demand his share or he'd turn me over to the law. The smartest thing I could think of was to hide the gold in a place where no one would ever find it, and then I'd just go on about my business, trapping and tanning me pelts—as if I didn't know a blessed thing. But when I went to the trading post to sell me pelts—there weren't no talk about passengers. No one seemed to know about 'em—nor their vests filled with gold eagles. Oh there was plenty of talk about the mudslide. Talk about the road getting' fixed and how it was too bad about losing the driver and the stage. But nary a soul came lookin' fer them two men, nor was there any talk of lost or stolen money. Looked like the whole kit and caboodle was mine to keep with no complaints."

"So, what fool thing did ya do to land in here?" Vernon scoffed. "Why ain't ya living the good life in Denver?" The younger man shook his head then he gave Tar a harsh look, "Where is it? And how do ya know it's still there?"

Tar was saddened by the greed he saw in Vernon's face, but he shrugged it off and then gazed up at the tiny window above them, "I hid it up there in a mountain valley so ancient and secret that God has forgot he put it there. It's been hid fer three years and it could stay there fer three thousand more and no one would find it. I was about to go fetch it and was celebrating my soon to be wealth when I sort o' ran into the man that put me behind these bars."

"You mean the judge you punched in the nose?" Vernon asked, "Even I know to steer clear of a *judge*."

"Well now, I'll be thankin' ya not to go criticizin' me for what I did to that overgrown baboon." Tar frowned with indignation then groaned. "And what would you do, may I ask, if a pompous oaf demanded that ya marry his homely sister? Fer that's what he wanted of me—and no less. Seems the lady in question and I shared a rather long stage ride together. And ya see Gertrude weren't what ya'd call a pretty woman. I must admit though, after sharin' a six hour coach ride and a whole bottle of whiskey...well...she got more appealin' somehow. Then before I knew what was happenin' the stage stops, the Judge opens the door to help his sister out and the woman grabs hold of me like I was her favorite bonnet and says, "Brother dear, this good man and I wish to wed. And we want you do the honors, this day, if ya please." Tar had made his voice sound high pitched as he mimicked the adoring Gertrude and Vernon had to laugh. Then the old man asked him, "So now tell me, what would you have done?"

Vernon leaned back on his cot shaking his head. He was anxious to hear about the gold but he knew O'Leary wanted to tell his story. And since it had been a pretty good yarn so far, Vernon replied, "Reckon, I'd do what you probably did... run for the hills."

"That I did, me boy—that I did. I snuck Diggery out of the livery and skedaddled back to the mountains where I belonged. Anyway, I figured I'd never see them two again and ya could have parted me down the middle with a feather, so surprised was I—when I saw the Judge six months later. Like I was saying, I was celebrating, before I went to fetch me treasure, when someone taps me on the shoulder. I turn around and there was the Judge—big as a mountain with a face as red as hot embers. And he says to me: 'My sister gets what she wants—and you are coming with me.'" Tar grunted in disgust, "Ya know how a bear wriggles its nose when it growls? Well, that's how the Judge looked, his snout was as wide as 'twas long and it kept wobblin' about as he spoke and—me being—rather deep in me cups at the time—well I threw me head back and laughed in his face."

"Huh-oh." Vernon grunted "That was a fool thing to do."

"True. Of course the madder that man got the more his nose wiggled and the funnier it was and before long the whole saloon was bustin' at the seams. 'Twas then that he picked me up right off me feet and shook me like a cat shakes a rat. Well—that got me dander up—and before I knew it, I landed me fist right smack dab on the end of that big wobbly nose. I didn't know 'til later that I broke the thing in three places. I also didn't know that he'd brought along his nephew, the Territorial Marshal of Colorado. Anyway, that and a few other trifles is why I'm not living the high life in Denver. And you should send Gertrude a letter of thanks, for things being the way they are… you, me bucko, have a small treasure waitin' for you in gold eagles, and I'm about to tell you how to find them."

Vernon suddenly let out a low whistle and blurted out, "Just one gold eagle is worth twenty dollars. There bound to be hundreds up there!"

"Shut yer gaub, ya fool!" O'Leary hissed, then fell to coughing. Vernon quickly helped him to another sip of water. When Tar was finally able to continue, he was considerably weaker, "Now listen hard boy," he wheezed. "The other day when you were on kitchen duty, one of the guards slipped in here and tells me that there's gonna be a prison break in three weeks. Says he can't tell me more but he's gonna forget to lock our cell that day. He'll even look the other way and let you and me both get away." When Vernon grinned, Tar grabbed his shirt, "Wait now, there's a big ugly fly in this mug o' honey. That guard was the spittin' image of me old partner Ox Hennessey…a nephew or cousin or maybe no relation at all. But it put me to wonderin'. Maybe Ox found out that there was gold on that stage and that led him straight to me. I fear they're settin' a trap fer us boy. They know I'm too weak to make it out o' this place without help. That's why they're lettin' you come too. I fear they'll try to kill you right off, once we get free o' the walls. Then—they'll torture me until I tell them where I hid the gold. Don't know nothin' fer sure—but it makes sense."

Vernon's dark gray eyes were suddenly ablaze, "I'm not an easy man to kill, but I think I'd rather die than live in this place for three more years. I'll take my chances." Just then an idea formed in his mind. "Listen Tar, next time you see that guard, tell him we'll need another man to help me carry you. We can trust Dirk Culley, not with my woman or your money but there's no better man in a fight." The thought of dying made Vernon's thoughts turn to his womenfolk and he said, "I think I know what you've got in mind. We'll send a message to Ma and Red, tell them about how to find yer money. If we make it out of here alive…fine…but if we don't. Anyway, I've told you about Ma's code, but there's even more to it. So now old man, you figure out the easiest way of giving directions to that gold while I get my Bible. I know you've wondered why I had one. Well you'll soon see. Looks like we've got some serious Bible studyin' to do.

Chapter 4
On the Run

"Send me your light and your faithful care, let them lead me: Let them bring me to your holy mountain, to the place where you dwell." Psalm 43:3

Remy stopped abruptly and Copper awoke with a start. She'd fallen asleep in the saddle *again* and—*once again* she was forced to remind her tired and foggy brain exactly why she and her oversized mule were riding, all alone, up and down treacherous mountain trails. It had been weeks since she'd left the Riley farm, but it still felt as if she were trapped in a nightmare.

The months that followed Vernon and Dirk's arrest had been the best in Copper's young life. Ma Riley had proved to be a very sweet woman and despite the sorrow she felt over her son being in prison, she made good on her promises and taught Copper many things. Most important of all, she explained to the young orphan that despite her hardships, God truly loved her! It had come as quite a revelation for someone who had never known love. Nevertheless, once Copper accepted that fact, she hungered like a starving beggar to learn all she could. The days and months that followed were joyful for both women, for Ma loved to talk about the Bible and Copper loved to listen. The two spent their evenings studying various Bible passages and their days working on the farm while discussing what they had read the night before.

Copper also made good on her promise to work hard—and as it turned out, the Riley farm was in sore need of hard work and diligence. There was plenty to do, and with tenacity and a bit of ingenuity, the two women managed to make quite a difference in the old place. Copper had even bartered some of her drawings in exchange for shingles for the roof and siding for the barn.

The women stayed so busy that before they knew it, a full year had passed. It was a very good year. Although it saddened Copper that her relationship with Ma Riley had not deepened into the mother and daughter bond, she'd hoped for. Instead, she still felt more like a servant girl—a beloved servant perhaps—but a servant just the same. She would always be an outsider, never truly belonging. In spite of this disappointment, Copper would not have traded this past year with Ma Riley for anything in the world. No, she may not have learned what it was like to have a mother's love, but what she had learned was far more precious. She leaned what it was like to have a Heavenly Father. One that would always want the best for her and never leave her.

It was a pleasant day in early spring when Copper and Ma Riley looked up from their gardening to see the sheriff riding into the yard.

Ma had just been telling Copper, "Always remember dear, that what God requires God provides." When the old woman took in the bleak expression on Sheriff Caldwell's face, she stiffened and her hand fluttered to her throat.

Unaware of Ma's reaction to their guest, Copper gave the man a pleasant smile, "Good morning, Sheriff, we're just getting our garden ready and…"

Ma suddenly touched Copper's arm. "Honey," she interrupted, "He isn't here for a social call—he's got bad news." Her gray eyes searched the man's face then said, "If it's my Vernon—then—just say it plain."

The sheriff stepped down from his horse as he took off his hat. Sighing, he fingered the brim slowly, "Yes ma'am, Vernon was killed two days ago in an attempted prison break."

Copper was expecting the man to offer words of comfort to Ma Riley but instead he turned his attention to her. The look in his eyes made her shiver and she knew immediately that once again her world was about to be turned upside down. Although life on the Riley farm hadn't been all she'd hoped for, it still had been better than anything she'd known before. Just then she thought of the words the older woman had just shared: 'What God requires….God provides.'

Oh Lord, you're about to require something of me—aren't you? Will you also provide for me as well? Copper suddenly realized that the sheriff was speaking again, explaining things she needed to hear.

"It seems there was a big fire inside the prison. A bunch of inmates tried to escape while the guards were busy putting the fire out. Vernon, his cellmate, Tar O'Leary and his old partner, Dirk Culley were three of the escapees. How the prisoners got guns I don't know, but there was an awful shootout. It seems a number of guards as well as prisoners were killed." He paused then added gently, "I'm sorry about Vernon, it seems he and O'Leary were both found dead, but..." The sheriff chewed on his lip then added, "The telegram I got said they didn't know if a prison guard killed them or… if Dirk Culley had done it. Unfortunately, Culley was the only prisoner that got away."

At the mention of the albino's name, Copper suddenly felt dizzy. Seeing her distress, the sheriff took her arm to steady her, "Miss Delaney, that marriage ceremony was never binding in my book, but now that Vernon's dead, even if you had intended to honor your vows, you're a widow now. My advice to you is, toss a few things in a bag and leave town, today." When Copper glanced at Ma Riley and then at the only home where she'd felt safe, she shook her head—no she couldn't leave. But the sheriff quickly added, "Ma'am, before now Dirk Culley was never accused of killing anyone, that's why he only got four years but if he killed his friend Vernon and O'Leary, who was old and sick…then he's more dangerous than ever. The wire I just got from the warden said that Culley somehow got hold of a horse right outside the prison. The posse chased him all the way to the Wyoming border. Where he stole another horse from a ranch outside of Laramie. If he's smart, he'll keep runnin' till he gets to Canada. I don't think he'll do that though. I'm bettin' that he's gonna come back—lookin' for you!"

The sheriff had just ridden away when Hyram from the J&B Mercantile came driving up in his buggy. He waved a letter in the air as he jumped down. "Missus Riley, I brought that chicken feed ya wanted and just before I left town the stage came in with the mail. You've got a letter from Vernon!"

Ma Riley quickly schooled her features; she glanced at Copper and shook her head. Hyram was a master weaver when it came to gossip and she didn't want him knowing or even suspecting that anything was amiss. "Thank you, Hyram," she said with surprising calm, "just put the feed in the barn."

"Yes ma'am, but don't let me keep ya from tearing into that letter. Reckon yer anxious to hear what yer boy has to say—ain't ya now?"

Hyram would win no prizes for subtlety, but Ma gave him credit for trying as she drew in a breath and forced a smile, "Actually Hyram, Copper and I like to save Vernon's letters till the end of the day...when we've finished our work. Speaking of work, we have plenty of it to do as I'm sure do you. Thank you and have a good day, Hyram."

When both women immediately returned to their gardening, Hyram unloaded the bag of feed. Then when they waved him goodbye, he reluctantly drove his buggy back to town. The moment he was out of sight, Ma Riley stood to her full height and locked eyes with Copper, "May the good Lord give us courage," she whispered then with quick movements she tore open the letter and began to read. It was almost as if she could hear her son's voice one last time.

Dear Ma and little Red,

Well, I have been locked up in this cage for over a year now and got three more to go. If I didn't know it before, I sure know it now that a cage ain't good fer man nor beast. Red, I dream about us being man and wife and I am remindin' you that we are married, all legal and proper. Remember too that I'm sufferin' here in prison fer my good deed. I am spending the prime of my manhood in this rat hole of a prison. 'Course I reckon I did it fer you too, Ma, cause marrying little Red was my way of living by the book. In three years, though I'll be free of this place and I plan to spend the rest of my long life takin' care of ya both. I have been thinkin' a lot lately and if something happens to me...I want ya to take care of each other. Red, Ma's getting' older and I want you to be good to her.

Tar O'Leary, my cellmate, is an old man and he keeps tellin' me that he's dying. I reckon he knows what he's talking about and he has made me think a lot about life and death. Tar and I have been talking about how God wants us to do the right thing by our families. Ma, I reckon me saying that is pleasin' fer you to hear, I hope so. Anyway, Tar helped me find some scriptures that have become important to me. Ma, I want you and Red to read them with care and let them speak to you as they have me. You've always been good at that. I ain't been much of a son and never got a chance to be a husband, good or bad. Still, this is a dangerous place and I just wanted you both to know that I spend my days here thinkin' good thoughts about ya both.

Yours truly,
Vernon Riley
(Loving son and hopeful husband)

Job 21:6:7, 1 Kings 7:2:12, Genesis 1:16:3, Matthew 23:17:3, Job 28:1:4, Hosea 12:1:6-10, Lamentations 3:2, Jeremiah 48:28:21-26, Proverbs 2:4:12-13

At the bottom of the page, Vernon had written down the chapter and verse of a number of Bible passages. This Bible code had been Ma Riley's idea. It protected Vernon's whereabouts from the law. More importantly, it forced him to read the Bible she'd given him, every time he wanted to send her a message.

The moment the old woman finished reading the letter, she grabbed Copper by the arm and pulled her towards the house. Once inside Ma took down her own Bible and began frantically looking up the scripture verses Vernon had written in the letter.

On a separate piece of paper she wrote down the code and the word it corresponded to in the Bible. When she'd finished her task, she turned to Copper, "Come here dear, let me explain. It's a simple code, just look up the chapter and verse. As you know a colon separates the chapter from the verses. However, in *our code* we add a second colon and the number written after it indicates what word or words we want to be used in the message. This isn't the proper way to refer to a Bible verse but at quick glance, you don't notice anything odd. You see this second colon after the chapter and verse? Well—this number indicates the word or words used in the message. When there's no second colon and number then you use the whole verse as part of the message. Using the code this is the message from Vernon."

Job 21:6:7	petrified
1 Kings 7:2:12	forest
Genesis 1:16:3	two
Matthew 23:17:3	fools
Job 28:1:4	mine
Hosea 12:1:6-10	chase after the east wind
Lamentations 3:2	he has led me—brought me into darkness, not into light
Jeremiah 48:28:21-26	by the mouth of a cave
Proverbs 2:4:12-13	hidden treasure

"Look here dear, the first verse is, Job, chapter 21, verse 6," Ma explained. "You see, after the second colon there's the number 7. We just count to the seventh word, which is *petrified*. In the next verse we look for the twelfth word, which is *forest*. Now, I know that there is a Petrified Forest way up in the mountains. You'll have to go by way of the Ute Pass, which begins just south-west of Colorado City. Ma suddenly took Copper by the hand, "I'm too old for an adventure like this. But you're not!"

Copper's eyes grew wide and she shook her head. "You mean for me to go to up into the mountains—alone? Surely you don't really want me to do that!"

"Actually—I'm afraid you must. Now listen carefully, this is the whole of Vernon's message: petrified forest—two—fools—mine—chase after the east wind—he has led me—brought me into darkness, not into light—by the mouth of the cave—hidden treasure."

"Humph," Copper muttered. "That's not a very clear message."

"It's not meant to be Shakespeare dear, it just a simple code. Now, we just need to reason it out. Somewhere in or near the Petrified Forest, there is a claim called the Two Fools Mine. I'll admit that chase after the east wind and brought me into darkness is a bit vague. I can only assume that means that you must walk inside the mine perhaps following a breeze of some kind that's going east, until you come to the mouth of a cave and that's where you'll find...whatever Tar O'Leary hid there."

Ma Riley stood and lovingly pressed the letter to her chest. Usually, whenever a letter came from her son, even if it were addressed to Copper, Ma would take it, read it out loud, then fold it carefully and tuck it into her corset. This time, however, she folded the letter and slowly handed it to Copper, "You must keep this—keep it someplace safe." Fighting back a sob she added, "My boy's last thoughts were to provide for us." Her chin quivered as she tried to smile. "He wasn't all bad—was he?" When Copper slid her arm around the older woman's waist, Ma sniffed and said sternly, "No—there will be plenty of time for tears. Right now, we must think clearly. I had hoped that your future was here with me but it's not. Your future is way up there in the mountains. Oh Copper, I know this is all very frightening, but that's where you must go!"

"Well, I won't go! Vernon asked me to take care of you and that's what I should do. It's dangerous for you to stay here alone. If I have to—I'll shoot Dirk Culley myself. I won't let him hurt either one of us!"

"Oh child, God doesn't want us killing anyone. Remember girl, you're a Christian now. And the Lord doesn't like it when we go around shootin' folks." When she pictured Dirk killing her beloved son she added coolly, "Even if they deserve it. No—we both must take ourselves out of harm's way. I've had a feeling something like this might happen." Just then Ma reached down the front of her dress and from her bosom she drew out a small roll of money. "I've been savin' up, and this is for you. I've already got enough for me to get to my brother's back in Maine, and once I'm there he will take good care of me."

"Then, can't I come with you? You might need my help getting all the way to Maine, and once there I'd help your brother, just as I've helped you. Not as a servant mind you—but as a friend."

The old woman smiled sadly, "You're a sweet girl, Copper, but you're not family. My brother is wealthy and somewhat eccentric; he wouldn't take in an outsider. You needn't worry about me. I'll be traveling towards civilization not away from it. I could have gone years ago, but I didn't want to give up on my son. I never told Vernon about his uncle's wealth because—well that doesn't matter now. Oh Copper, I hate to lose you, unfortunately, the sheriff is right. You must get away from here as quickly as possible. I just know that Culley will come for you. He may or may not know about this letter, but from the beginning he's thought you could lead him to treasure—and now—oddly enough—you can!"

"This is all happening so fast…I can't think what to do."

"You're a strong girl, Copper—no—you are a strong woman. First, we'll pack your bags and make sure you have supplies for the trail. Then we'll harness old Sam to my buggy, saddle Remy and tie her on behind. Sashay into town with a bright smile on your face! Tell folks that we said our goodbyes here at the farm. While you're purchasing your ticket for the stage, tell everyone within earshot, especially Hyram, how thrilled you are to be visiting your dear, sweet Auntie Ann and Uncle Ron, in Texas. Let folks see you boarding the stage and make a show of waving good-bye. Meanwhile, I'll drive to the Cherry Creek Crossing. I should have plenty of time to get there before the stage does. The driver's name is Fred Mullins, if you can, take him aside and tell him what we're both doing, all the better. He's a good friend and one that can keep a secret."

"Ma Riley," Copper groaned. "You make fooling everyone and getting to Cherry Creek sound easy, and maybe it will be, but what about the rest of the journey? The hard part is getting from Cherry Creek all the way up the mountains and finding the Petrified Forest. Once I'm off the stage, what in the world am I to do then?"

"Oh, my dear, I hate seeing you so afraid. I can't believe I'm sending you off like this...all alone! I wouldn't tell you to do this, if I didn't feel in my bones that this is the right thing to do. That doesn't mean that you should take chances though. If you can keep out of sight—do. I'm afraid all I know is that Colorado City is about forty to fifty miles south of Cherry Creek and the Ute Pass is just beyond it. I'm afraid you'll have to ask someone for directions to locate the forest and the mine. You be sure to look folks over carefully before you speak to them. In fact, that gives me an idea..." Ma Riley hurried to a trunk where she kept Vernon's things after he'd been taken to prison. She fumbled a bit then pulled out a long bronze expandable spyglass. Turning to Copper she smiled, "Vernon paid a lot of money for this, and if you use it wisely it might just keep you out of danger. As I said, look people over carefully—check them out from a distance before you ride up close. And—don't tell anyone more than they just have to know."

Ma Riley placed the spyglass in Copper's hands as tears filled her eyes. "I remember one of the first things I told you, Copper. It was that God's ways are often unlikely. Well, for a long while now, every time I've prayed for you, a verse in Psalms comes to mind: 'I will lift up mine eyes unto the hills, from whence cometh my help.' I know the mountains seem awfully dangerous—and they are! And yet somehow, I believe God is calling you to them. And since that's where Vernon said to go, I have to believe that you will be safe there."

Feeling dejected and scared, Copper finished packing the saddlebags with coffee, flour and beans, while Ma Riley flew around the house grabbing blankets and clothes all the while giving Copper last minute counsel and advice.

"That treasure is no doubt stolen money Copper—" she said. "But—find it if you can. Then, very carefully see if you can discover who lost it. If you cannot find the rightful owner, then I suppose it's yours to keep. Still, don't be showy about having money, for there are scoundrels everywhere, men and women alike who will gladly take it from you."

When everything was finally ready, Ma shoved the saddlebags into Copper's hands, and then picked up the bedroll she'd prepared and hurried them both out the door. “Now while I harness Sam to the buggy, you saddle and pack that silly beast of yours. Remy is as ugly as a mud pie but…she’s smarter than half the people I know.” A sudden tenderness crept into the old woman’s voice as she stopped and pulled Copper into her arms; then she raised her chin and said shakily, “I’ve become fond of that mule, and do you know why? Because I know that monstrosity would walk through fire for you! Between her and the good Lord—I know you’ll be safe. Now…you be sure to say yer prayers every night and keep your eyes peeled for outlaws and rogues. I know that you are slow to trust, Copper, and right now, that’s a good way to be—don’t trust anyone!”

Although it came as a surprise to Copper, everything worked out just as Ma Riley had planned. A special blessing was that…there were no other passengers on the stage. Even the driver, Fred Mullins had proved to be a true friend and a wondrous help. Fred not only promised to tell anyone that would listen about the pretty little redhead that was traveling all by herself from Colorado to Texas—but he had also given Copper the directions she so desperately needed. He even drew her a quick map from Cherry Creek to Colorado City, up the Ute Pass, and as best as he could remember, to the Petrified Forest. Everything went well, and yet when Copper saw the Riley buggy waiting at the crossing, all she wanted was to go right back to the farm, and take her chances with Dirk Culley. Ma remained firm, however, and insisted that Copper be on her way, for she was wasting precious daylight.

Copper felt alone and sick as she watched the stage heading south and Ma Riley turning her buggy back towards the farm. Gently she nudged Remy west towards the mountains for Fred had instructed her to skirt along the foothills as she rode south.

“What are we doing, Remy?” she moaned. “Everything was so pleasant and normal. Wasn’t it just this very morning that Ma Riley and I were working in the garden, singing hymns and discussing the Bible? Now, here we are, running for our lives and searching for treasure. It’s all so crazy.” Copper couldn’t remember when she felt so unsure of herself or so full of doubt. Remy on the other hand stepped out with confidence that was a bit extreme, even for her. In fact, the mule was so full of vigor; Copper was forced to smile. At least one of them was eager for this adventure.

The foothills of the Rockies and the lowlands beyond grew more beautiful with each passing mile. Copper sucked in a lung full of sweet mountain air and felt the wind tease the brim of her hat. Suddenly she had a thought...*I am truly free—for the first time in my life.* Then on the heels of that thought, came another, *I am also truly alone—for the first time in my life.* The realization was both exhilarating and terrifying.

The first night they made camp, Copper turned Remy lose to graze in a lush meadow. Suddenly, she realized that she hadn't packed any grain. Her mule would be carrying her for long hours each day and at night; she would need her rest. When would Remy have time for cropping grass? Or if she grazed all night when would she sleep? Furthermore, once they reached the high mountain passes, would there even be enough grass to crop? Remy was Copper's friend as well as her responsibility and though the mule was strong now, she wouldn't stay that way—not without food and rest.

At sunup the next day, Copper saddled her big mule and they continued south. Still, the longer they rode the more concerned Copper became. This country was beautiful but wild and unsettled. In two days she hadn't met a soul nor had she spotted one curl of smoke coming from a homesteader's chimney. Every time she reached high ground she looked through her spyglass, but saw only undisturbed prairie stretching towards the horizon. Seeing how empty this wilderness was, she now realized that if she were to happen upon a homestead, she wouldn't have the nerve to ask for a bag of grain. What she was to do—she didn't know.

Copper awoke on the third day to Remy braying out her distinctive call just as a glowing red sun was burning through an early morning mist. She guessed that they'd covered about fifteen miles in the past two days, and could only hope that the Colorado City wasn't too much farther. Copper started to call Remy and saddled up. However, when she saw her mule ravenously filling her belly on the lush growth of tender spring grass she decided to stay for another day. Copper smiled and shook her head when Remy stopped long enough to lift her head, her mouth full of grass, expecting to hear the whistle, telling her to come. "No girl, you eat and rest today—tomorrow we'll move on." Remy must have approved for she instantly returned to cropping the soft, sweet grass.

The following day, they had only ridden for about three hours when Copper thought she saw a cloud of dust in the far distance. Grateful again for the spyglass, she was able to make out at least fifty horses racing across the prairie with six, no seven riders following them. Moving the glass in the direction they were heading, she grinned when she saw what she hoped was a faint line of wood smoke.

"Well now, what do you think of that, Remy girl?" Hearing her name the mule's long ears swiveled back to listen. "That many horses with so many riders—maybe their driving their herd back to a big ranch. Big enough that maybe they'll even have grain to spare." When Remy snorted, Copper sighed, "I know—they could just as easily be rustlers I suppose."

They continued to ride along slow until they crested the top of a hill, where once again, Copper took the spyglass from her saddlebag. What she saw was impressive and for the first time in days, she almost allowed herself to relax. Then a sudden feeling of apprehension tied a knot in her stomach. "That's a prosperous ranch sure enough, but I'm still just one girl all alone and there are an awful lot of men down there—and men, more often than not mean danger." She could almost hear Ma Riley's last words, "Don't trust anyone!"

The name of the ranch was painted in large letters on the side of the barn—The Bar 61. It seemed, for all appearances, a well-to-do place. The group of horses she'd seen earlier was only a small part of a larger herd. Altogether, there were over a hundred horses. The cowboys were milling about cutting some of them from the larger corral and moving them into smaller ones.

"Maybe they're going to take part of this herd off somewhere to sell." Copper mused hopefully. "We'll watch and wait Remy. I don't want to take any chances and I don't like being around that many men. Still, it's quite a place, though—isn't it?"

Some of the ranch hands were unbuckling their gun belts as they stepped inside a long log building, Copper assumed that was the bunkhouse. When she spotted what had to be the main ranch house, she drew in a breath and sighed. In her school days her father had taught that people around the world live differently and their houses were unique to their country. The house below she recognized as a Mexican hacienda, an almost square building, complete with a courtyard in the middle and a covered porch that circled the entire house. The thick adobe walls would keep the family warm in the winter and cool in the summer. Moreover, this hacienda had been built like a fort. Perfect should Indians or outlaws attack. What an excellent choice, she thought and longed to peek inside. Of course, after watching the ranch activities for a time, she soon realized that there were no signs that any women or children lived there.

"No, Copper Delaney, you best keep your distance. That is no place for a young woman."

For the next two day's she concealed herself in a dense outcropping of scrub oak and boulders. From her high lookout, she was entertained by all the daily activity of the Bar 61. Each morning the ranch hands would feed the animals and clean the barns, and then they would head for the hacienda. Where she assumed they enjoyed a hearty working man's breakfast. The scent of wood smoke floated towards her on the morning breeze carrying with it the tantalizing aroma of bacon and coffee. Copper's mouth watered and her stomach rumbled as she bit into her stale biscuit and drank tepid water from a canteen.

After breakfast, she watched as the men seemed to burst from the hacienda and head straight for the largest corral. Copper watched closely as cowboys with their lariats twirling in the air slowly strolled among the horses and swung their loops. When the men caught their mounts, they led them to another corral and began to saddle them. It seemed these horses were all in various stages of training; some were docile and cooperative, while other's recoiled at the idea of being saddled and ridden. The wilder ones reared and fought and tried hard to pull free. When a horse began to show improvement, it was unsaddled and the cowboy would lasso another and begin all over again. It worried Copper when a few of the men took their horses outside the corral, but when they didn't come near her hiding place, she sighed in relief. This was all so thrilling for her to watch and she didn't want to hide and miss all the fun. She was after all, a young woman. Although she was afraid of these men, she still couldn't help but be fascinated by them. The ranch hands all seemed to be so strong and agile. Copper thought them brave as well, for some of the horses put up quite a fight. They bucked and spun and some even tried to bite...while others seemed to enjoy the attention.

The spyglass enabled Copper to see all the horses and the cowboys, almost as if she were leaning against the corral fence. She couldn't hear their words but saw the frowns of determination on the men's faces as well as their smiles. However, the artist in Copper wasn't content to simply watch. This was an exhilarating experience for her, and she just had to get all this wild action down in her sketchbook. Hour after hour, she watched through the glass—then holding the images in her mind, she would put the glass down and sketch what she'd seen.

Copper had almost talked herself out of purchasing the very sketchpad and pencil she now held in her hand. After all, Ma Riley had only given her a small roll of money. The stagecoach fare had been unfortunate, but it was necessary. That extravagance however, made her all the more careful with her remaining funds. As she looked about the mercantile, she thought of other things that could prove useful. Her first purchases had been the boy's shirt, overalls and boots she was now wearing. They were not only practical, but if anyone saw her from a distance, she hoped they might think her a boy and be more likely to leave her alone. The purchase of two sketchpads and six pencils might have seemed frivolous, but Copper had come to view her drawings as a form of currency. Her hope and plan was that, from now on, she would save her money and whenever possible, barter for what she needed. Soon, her plan would be put to the test. Hopefully the owner of the Bar 61, whoever he was, would be content with a few drawings in exchange for a sack of grain.

That night, Copper scrutinized her work, adding a bit of shading here and there. "Oh my…these are turning out so well I wish I could keep them." She'd made her camp about a mile north of the ranch. It was a secluded spot at the bottom of a deep ravine where a creek cut into the prairie. The surrounding pine trees dispersed any smoke that might rise from her small campfire. Copper bent over her sketchpad and studied each drawing by the light of a moon that was not quite full.

In her lap lay the results of three days of watching the activities of the ranch. On the first page, she'd drawn the ranch grounds as she'd seen them in the early morning from her high lookout, all peaceful and serene. The second drawing was dramatic and chaotic, with men chasing the herd of horses down the hill and into the large corral with swirling dust clouds churning all about them. The third drawing celebrated the excitement and frenzied activity of the ranch. One man was spinning a wide loop while another had his rope secured around a mare's neck as she reared high. In the same corral, three men were trying to saddle a twisting horse while two others rode mounts that bucked wildly.

Her last drawing, however, was Copper's favorite. Every afternoon, regardless of whatever else was going on at the ranch, an elderly man, tall and black came from the barn, leading an old sorrel stallion to a small stream behind the hacienda. Both the man and the horse walked with a pronounced limp. When Copper used her spyglass to get a closer look she also saw that both man and horse had once been powerfully built, handsome and proud. And yet, as it always does, time had taken its toll. Copper watched the old man bathe and groom the stallion with care. Then hes gently rubbed the animal's sore legs with liniment. As she watched this daily ritual, an idea came to her, a sweet light filled her eyes and her hand moved skillfully as the idea took shape. There would be two sketches drawn on the same page, depicting both sunrise and sunset. On the upper half of the page, she drew the head and shoulders of the man and the horse standing side-by-side, facing east towards the morning sun, just as it broke over the horizon. Copper studied the old man and the horse very closely, imagining how they both had looked while in their prime; magnificent, strong and confident—and that's how she drew them. Their faces were youthful and eyes bright, eager and alert—because everything was ahead of them. When the first drawing was complete, she once again lifted the glass to her eyes and studied them both carefully. As before, Copper sat the glass down and her hand began moving quickly across the lower half of the page. This time she drew the same profile of the man and the horse, only facing in the opposite direction, towards the setting sun as it slipped behind the mountains. In this drawing, she drew them as they were now. And yet, it was not at all unflattering. The man and the stallion were still quite handsome for they both had maintained their dignity and their pride. To Copper the most notable difference was that in the second drawing, there was a deep serenity in their gaze. They seemed happy, even content, to see the day was coming to an end.

The morning of the fourth day, Copper climbed to her lookout. Even from that distance she could feel the exhilaration in the air. Something important was happening today. All the ranch hands were rushing about, tying bedrolls to their saddles, whistling, shouting and laughing. Then she saw two very tall men walking from the hacienda. She'd seen the tall blonde man before, the ranch hands seemed to defer to him and she had thought him to be the owner of the ranch. However, now she realized that he must be the foreman instead. For as she looked at this new man, she realized that this one had to be the owner of this impressive ranch. He was tall and dark with very broad shoulders and his clothes, though not fancy, spoke of quality and wealth. He was more polished—more confident. There was also something powerful in the way he carried himself—yes, she had no doubt—this man was—the boss. Still, as Copper watched him, a cold shudder rocked her frame. Of all the faces she had focused on these past few days, his face was the most intimidating—and yet she felt sorry for him at the same time. She didn't know why she thought this…but this man had unseen wounds. As she watched him however, she realized that his wounds did not make him weak or vulnerable, but like a wounded bear, he was all the more dangerous. Perhaps neither the foreman or the boss would be a threat to her, and yet they both looked like the sort that would insist on getting their own way. Somehow, Copper knew that if she showed herself to anyone on this ranch, they would keep her. Either because they wanted her, like Vernon had wanted her or because they wanted to protect her. Still, she knew instinctively that they would never allow her to leave.

Studying each man again through her spyglass, Copper gritted her teeth, "That settles it. I'll stick to my plan." Still, Copper hated the idea of being a thief and she felt terribly guilty about what she had to do. "Lord, please forgive me." She whispered, "I know it's wrong to take something without asking, but it's also wrong to put God to a foolish test. Me going down there among all those men, that's not wise and I don't think you want me to do that. So, please, Lord, let them be satisfied with my payment for their grain."

Suddenly, there was a ruckus of loud shouts and shrill whistles, as all the ranch hands exuberantly mounted their horses. A long legged and powerful chestnut horse was brought out for the boss and Copper smiled when the big man grabbed the horn and gracefully swung up into the saddle. Just then, she recognized the old black man, and watched as he limped to the corral gate and opened it wide. At first, the horses just looked at him, unsure of what to do. Then one by one or a few at a time, the horses timidly approached the gate, snorting and blowing. Then once they'd stepped beyond the confines of the corral, they burst forth, bucking and kicking up their heels as they raced across the yard. Immediately, a dozen mounted cowboys gathered around the herd, whooping and hollering as they bunched the horses together and headed them east.

Copper let out a great sigh of relief as she watched them heading away from her. Once again, she focused her glass on the ranch yard. Another older looking man, one she hadn't seen before, came from the hacienda and climbed onto a small chuck wagon. He had a swarthy complexion with snow-white hair and a bushy white mustache. He grinned broadly and shook hands with the old black man and a young redheaded boy then slapped the reins and followed at a quick pace behind the herd.

"What a blessing." Copper breathed, "Looks like just about every man on the ranch is leaving except for the old man and the boy. She nearly laughed. "Thank you, Lord. You led us to the right place and at just the right time!"

The following morning, the old man, Joseph limped into the barn; he stopped, frowned and then sniffed the air. Then he glanced over at the old stallion and saw that he was bobbing his head up and down.

"Somethin' don't feel jes' right in here—ya feels it too, don't ya, Echo?" When the stallion lifted his head and snorted, Joseph shrugged and ran his hand over his scratchy chin whiskers, "Always feels like a regular old ghost town around here—until all them boys come home. Kind o' lonesome… ain't it?" He muttered as he shuffled into the tack room. When he bent to open the trunk, where he kept broken bridles or reins to be mended; he was surprised to find a stack of papers there, weighed down with a horseshoe. Picking the papers up, he read the note that was on top.

To the owner of the Bar 61,

Please accept these drawings in exchange for one sack of oats and one feedbag. I apologize for just taking them but I have good reason and I hope you will understand and forgive me.

Gratefully yours,

C. Delaney

Joseph slowly sat down on the trunk and began looking through the drawings, each of them signed in the lower right corner with the same name as the note, C. Delaney. "Well now, if these don't shave the hair off a tick." He whispered as he gazed down in wonder, for it was evident that a true artist had been watching the ranch hands for the past few days. Joseph stood and went outside so that his old eyes could see more clearly.

"Here now—Shep, come on over here, son." he called to the red haired boy that was busy cleaning out the large corral. "Put that shovel down, boy and bring yourself on over here. We done had us a—a secret visitor."

When the boy saw that Joseph was holding a set of drawings, he shook his head, "Man o' man, where did these come from?"

"Well now, it appears somebody's been spying on us, from…" Joseph turned and pointed his crooked finger to the hill just beyond the barn. "From up yonder, I reckon, in that stand of scrub oak." His bushy eyebrows rose high as he added, "And we can thank the good Lord it weren't Injuns, cause we sure never knowd we was being watched."

Shep looked closely at the drawings and pointed to one of the cowboys riding a bucking bronc. "These almost look like tintypes. That one there is Rusty, plain as day and there's Hitch, barkin' orders!"

The two scrutinized each picture until they finally came to the last one. Joseph suddenly had to catch his breath as unexpected tears filled his eyes. "How—how'd they know?" A knot rose in the old man's throat and he shook his head, "How'd they know what Echo and I looked like back yonder? How'd they know we was together all them years ago? Still and all—there we is—thirty years younger. I was a slave back then, started out being a stable boy. Wasn't long though before, old Mr. Grainger made me the Stable Master. He never would let nobody train his plantation horses but me." Joseph pointed to the lower drawing adding, "And just look at us now—old Echo and old Joseph. That there artist was being kind, I reckon, looks like we still got us a *little* pride left. Tell me true Shep; does we really look like that to you?"

"Yes Sir, ya surely do!" The boy answered truthfully then added, "Whew-ee, that's some real good drawin', ain't it?" Then he looked up at the stand of scrub oaks, "I want to know who done this. Think I'll ride up there and see what I can see."

Joseph only chuckled, "They's long gone, boy—and it's clear, they don't want to be known." Then he handed Shep the note and said, "Reckon they didn't want nobody to see 'em so they got what they needed and skedaddled. Only took one bag o' grain and a feedbag for all o' these. Whoever done this felt right bad. I wish we could tell 'em that we got the best of it." Suddenly Joseph took his hat off and placed his large hand on the boy's shoulder, "Take yer hat off son, we gots us some prayin' to do."

Joseph and Shep stood side by side in the big corral, as the old man's deep bass filled the air. "Dear Lord," he began, "whoever left us these here pictures has a good heart. I'm thinkin' maybe they gots a long road ahead and maybe they gots troubles too—I 'spect they do. We ask that ya keep 'em safe and guide 'em on their way." Then the old man lifted his arm and pronounced a blessing, "May the Lord bless ya and keep ya. May the Lord make his face shine on ya and be gracious to ya. May the Lord turn his face toward ya and give ya peace."

Now that Copper had secured a good supply of grain for Remy, she began to relax a bit. It was beautiful country and she enjoyed the sound of the breeze gliding through the pine trees as they rode through a dense pine forest that began just south of the Bar 61. Suddenly, the forest ended and as they crested a hill the land opened up to a long valley, and there before her was the mighty Pike's Peak. The imposing mountain stood like a sentinel, centered in ranges that spread out on either side like arms open wide, as if to welcome her. It was truly a majestic sight and grander than she could have imagined. Her view of the Rockies from the Riley farm, east of Denver, hadn't seemed all that impressive. The mountains were simply part of a jagged and distant landscape. Now that she was up close so to speak, she thought they were magnificent. And yet—for a young woman all alone they were also quite intimidating.

Hiding her mule in a stand of trees, Copper hiked to a high bluff that overlooked the small town of Colorado City. Using her spyglass, she spotted a number of businesses built on either side of the main street. It was a young town and though not as busy as Denver, it still felt too busy for Copper's liking.

Slowly she made her way back to Remy. "There are just too many men down in that town," she grumbled. "That means another cold camp again tonight—which may not bother you—but it sure is a disappointment to me!"

After Remy was groomed and given her oats, Copper reached into her saddlebag for one of her dried biscuits. When she found only a few pieces of dried apple, a few crumbs and an empty coffee bag—she panicked. Suddenly she was desperate to check her supplies.

For the past few days she'd eaten very little. Instead, her focus had been entirely on making her drawings worthy of a sack of Bar 61 grain. When she'd packed up the food from Ma Riley's pantry, she remembered grabbing two sacks of flour, but one was only half full and she'd used up *the last of it* two nights ago. Now as she rummaged through the other side of her saddlebags she found only clothes, her Bible and some soap. At the very bottom her fingers brushed over the second flour sack and she sighed in relief, but then she realized it didn't feel just right. Sure enough when she yanked open the draw string and peeked inside, rather than flour she found, "Sugar? Oh—Copper Delaney, you dolt—you grabbed the wrong bag!"

Furious with herself, Copper kicked at a rock and groaned, "Now I'll have to buy supplies." Of course, she knew she'd have to sooner or later, but she'd been able to avoid people so far and hoped to do so for a while longer. "Lord, I don't know if I should risk being seen. If Dirk follows me here and asks about me, someone is bound to tell him. Between my red hair and Remy being—well Remy—anyone that sees us will remember us!"

Early the following morning Copper saddled up and carefully skirted around Colorado City and headed for the Ute Pass. Fred Mullins had mentioned that there was a small settlement and trading post nearby, where she could purchase supplies. However, when she looked the place over with her spyglass, she saw a number of rough looking men lounging around the front, passing around a jug of whiskey. Keeping well out of sight, she watched the place for a whole day. Although a variety of men came and went, there was always at least one man sitting or lying on the covered porch, either getting drunk or sleeping it off. In any case, she never felt safe enough to chance it.

Staring up the trail that lead up the mountain, Copper felt as if a horde of bats were terrorizing her stomach, "Ohhhh—dear. This has to be it, Remy girl. You have your grain but I have almost no supplies. Still, it is springtime, after all. Surely, there will be some small game up there, that I can hunt or snare, and there's bound to be wild plants I can eat. There must be wild onions, or asparagus, or pigweed, or sorrel. All I have to do is provide for myself—just long enough to find the gold."

The 'Ute Pass' was just a sandy trail leading up and up, even as it followed the stream that came down the mountain. The fact that it was just as Fred Mullins had described wasn't all that encouraging. Copper wanted to turn back--but—turn back and do what? There was no turning back. Ma Riley was well on her way to Maine by now and Dirk might be right behind her. Once again, Remy seemed eager to be on her way, but Copper pulled back on the reins.

"Not yet girl," she chided. "Before you set one hoof on that trail, we have to remember all of Fred's warnings. We have to keep our wits about us or we could get in a lot of trouble up there. We could be captured by

Indians or wild mountain men. He said to watch for bear sign and wolves and mountain lions. He also mentioned flash floods and late spring snowstorms." Then with a shudder she added, "The only thing he didn't warn us about was Dirk Culley—but we're scared of him already—aren't we girl?"

Thinking of the countless dangers that lay ahead, Copper suddenly felt like she might be sick. She slid from Remy's back and staggered to the stream that ran beside the trail. Dropping to her knees, she splashed cold water on her face. Soon she was crying so hard she could barely breathe.

"Lord, I'm scared." she sobbed. "I'm trying to be brave, to trust and believe. It was easier to be a faithful Christian when I was living with Ma Riley. Right now, all I have is a sack of grain and a...*bag of sugar*. This is too much for me—I can't do it!"

God hath not given us the Spirit of fear; but of power, and of love, and of a sound mind.

It wasn't that she heard the words, and yet they came to her as gently as the breeze that brushed against her cheeks.

Slowly, Copper sat back and dried her face on her sleeve. "Lord," she sniffed, "was—was that you?"

Ma Riley had given her a number of verses about fear to memorize, but they never seemed to take root in her mind. God had to have helped her. Copper found herself smiling, "That was nice, thank you Lord! You don't want me to be afraid, do You? Maybe...Remy and I...aren't as alone as I thought." Copper washed her face and drank from the bitingly cold stream before she stood to her feet. Climbing back into the saddle, she continued her dialogue with God. "I haven't had an easy life Lord, but now as I look back on it, I can see how, even when I was miserable, You still had a plan for me. You loved me, even when I didn't know it—even when I didn't believe in You. You knew that someday I *would* come to trust in You. Oh Lord, I don't want to disappoint You. What God requires...God provides. So, I'll trust You Lord, for everything."

Chapter 5
Something Good

"It will be a shelter and a shade from the heat of day, and a refuge and hiding place from the storm and rain." Isaiah 4:6

The following days, the oversized dapple-gray mule eagerly carried her mistress up a slender trail that curved and wound back and forth, as it rose higher and higher. The altitude made the journey more difficult, the air grew thinner as the climb grew steeper. Though the trek seemed harder on the girl than on her mule, they stopped often to rest.

Copper had often imagined what the mountains would be like and was not disappointed, for everything she saw outdid her expectations. Sometimes it felt as if she and Remy were the only inhabitants in this sky-high-country, for they hadn't seen another human since leaving the Ute Pass Trading Post. She had read everything she could find on The Rocky Mountains and knew they were home to multiple tribes of Indians. The Utes, Arapaho and Cheyenne fought over these treacherous peaks and valleys. Now trappers, miners, ranchers and farmers were seeking to make a living in this high-country, while outlaws used this wild land as the perfect hideout. Long before any men, either white or red had settled in these beautiful and often unforgiving mountains, they were already a sanctuary where eagles soared, bears rambled, coyotes sang, wolves howled, and mountain lions shadowed herds of deer and mountain goats. Here moose, elk and bands of wild horses grazed on the rich meadow grasses. It seemed that wherever she looked there was life—and it was there in all its wild abundance.

The first time she reached a high plateau and looked out over the expansive mountain ranges, she marveled at how anything could be so large and wondrous. They seemed to go on forever. Her heart beat furiously while her eyes searched, first to the north, then to the south and west. This high-country was another world. A fathomless panorama of jagged peaks spread out before her, like a thousand stony waves on a rough sea. She made out what must be the side of Pike's Peak with its high dome of gray granite, and even though it was late May, it wore a cap of white snow. The lower peaks were dressed in cloaks of evergreen, and groves of delicate white-barked aspen dotted the hillsides. Wild flowers covered the meadows and valleys far below. Sunlight reflected off a distant waterfall and turned the river that sprung from its mouth into a shining thread of silver. It seemed as if the universe were laid out before her, encompassed by a wide canopy of cloudless sapphire blue. At such times, the cynical words of her father, Jarvis Delaney, would come to mind. How he would laugh at his daughter, if he could see her now. "Never underestimate the unknown." That was one of his favorite phrases, but Copper had never understood it—not until now. This raw beauty defied description and yet two words came to mind as her eyes took it all in...*wild* and *dangerous*.

The further they rode the more treacherous the mountain trail became. Thankfully, Remy had proved to be sure-footed and hadn't missed a step, even though half the time, her mistress couldn't keep her eyes open. Copper's weariness was partly due to the altitude and partly the lack of food and rest. So far, Remy was doing well with her ration of grain morning and night, and she'd been able to crop grass from time to time. Copper, on the other hand, was nearly starving. Despite her earlier optimism, she hadn't snared a thing nor had she found many mountain greens that she knew were safe to eat. Although she felt like a thief for eating Remy's food, she finally yielded to hunger's siren call. Reluctantly she took one handful of grain each evening and made herself some hot porridge. Since she had no coffee she was forced to settle for a hot pine needle tea. Practically speaking, what Copper needed most just then was meat. And yet, as a young woman all alone, what she longed for most of all, was the feeling of being safe. The nights were terrifying and she was desperate for a night of sleep with a solid roof over her head behind a barred door!

Copper curled her right knee around the saddle horn and allowed Remy to drop her head and crop grass while she once again studied the map. It had finally become clear that; either Fred Mullins had no idea where the Petrified Forest was or she was reading the map wrong. Leaning over, she patted Remy's neck, but it was more to comfort herself than the mule. Blowing out a frustrated breath she shook her head, "We're lost you know! This is the third time we've ridden through this same meadow. There's only one direction, we haven't tried." Nudging Remy forward she lifted her voice heavenward, "Lord, we really need your help right now."

It was the steepest climb they'd made so far and Copper tried to make it easier by zigzagging their way to the top. Even so, the mule's breathing became more labored with every step. Finally, Copper slid to the ground, wrapped Remy's long tail around her hand and huffed, "You're the one doing all the work, girl—pick the way you like best."

Remy finally made it to level ground, sucking in great gulps of thin mountain air. Copper instantly staggered to the mule's side and hurried to loosen the cinch. "Oh, Remy, I'm so sorry to put you through this." As if in reply, the mule looked straight at Copper, pinned her ears back and snorted loudly.

Knowing that she'd been justly reprimanded, Copper winced, "We'll stop and make camp here—I promise. Ma Riley said you were smarter than most people, and now more than ever, I'm sure that includes me. I know—I've been pushing us both too hard." Reaching up to scratch the mule's ears she added, "I just hate stopping for the night! I'm ashamed to say it, but I'm a downright coward from sundown to sunrise. The days go by so quickly but the nights, they just seem to last forever."

Thankfully, they were on level ground, for the sky was already turning a pinkish-red as the sun made its western decent. With slow stiff movements, Copper began untying her saddlebags. Remy swung her large head around and touched her moose sized muzzle to the feedbag that hung from the saddle horn. Copper had to chuckle as she playfully pushed her away. "You always think it's time to eat—don't ya girl? But there will be no grain for you—not yet—you have to cool down first or you'll get a mountain sized belly ache." Pressing her fingers to her pounding temples, Copper winced, "It might even rival the mountain size headache I've got. This altitude makes my head throb and my feet feel like lead weights."

Just then the mule reached around and nipped at the stirrup, as if to say, if I can't eat, the least you could do is pull that saddle. "All right, a little patience if you please." Copper huffed. "I know you've had a hard day but don't I always take care of you first? I am moving as fast as I can." Groaning she yanked the heavy saddle from the mule's back then began rubbing her dapple-gray coat with handfuls of dry moss while she checked for ticks or cuts.

Naturally, the highlight of Remy's day was when Copper finally poured oats into her feedbag. Instantly, she'd shove her large head inside and began munching loudly. Then and only then did Copper take care of Copper.

As she made camp, her stomach grumbled in complaint. Gazing off in the distance she shook her head. "I could probably shoot something with my rifle but—I bet noise carries for miles up here." Picking up the sack of grain, she glanced at her mule apologetically, "Sorry girl, but I'm going to have to take another portion of your grain tonight." Feeling guilty, Copper took a handful of precious kernels, then dropped them into a small pan of water. She'd soak the oats for a while then make porridge with lots of sugar. Copper thanked God over and over for the blessing of that bag of grain but she had always prided herself in being honest, and taking it from the Bar 61 the way she had still troubled her conscience.

As each day passed, Copper realized that she was growing weaker and the importance of finding the treasure paled compared to the increasing need for food. Tonight she even lacked the strength to set out her snares. So far, she hadn't caught anything anyway. Instead she gathered pinecones, ate any pine nuts she found and kept the cones for kindling. Still, her stomach protested at being teased by such a meager offering. Just then, she remembered her favorite Sunday dinner and her mouth began to water—roasted rabbit covered in choke cherry sauce and sprinkled with pine nuts. It seemed like a lifetime since she'd felt content and safe. Now, the fear of starvation, along with Dirk Culley's cold glassy eyes, haunted her day and night.

"Oh Lord," she whispered, "I don't think Ma Riley realized how hard this would be when she sent me up here—all alone. Sometimes it looks so beautiful and peaceful, but danger prowls around every corner." Easing herself down on a rock, Copper listened to the pleasant sound of Remy's large teeth grinding her oats, as she breathed out a long sigh, "I'm sorry, Lord. I know I'm being a flibbertigibbet," she moaned. "You tell me that you don't give us a spirit of fear and I trust you—then I forget what you said and I'm afraid all over again. One minute I'm truly grateful that you've brought me through so much. The next I'm worried that you've forgotten all about me. The truth is, I'm weak—half starved—and completely overwhelmed!"

Feeling disgusted with herself, Copper didn't finish her talk with the Lord. Instead, she wandered into the woods. Every night as she gathered dried branches and twigs she always debated whether or not it wise or foolish to build a fire, and if she did, should it be large or small? A big fire would frighten away wild animals, like bears and wolves. However, it would also be an invitation to the kind of trouble that came on two legs, like a mountain man or outlaws and Indians. Danger was always out there, but what kind was closer to her at the moment, the kind that walked on four legs or two? Just now, Copper was concerned with the four-legged variety. On the way up the steep trail, she had seen some strange marking on the trunk of a large pine tree. She remembered the Barr's camping alongside an old trapper once; he had spent the evening telling stories of how he hunted for bear. By the glow of the blazing fire, he had explained how a male bear marks his territory. 'The great beast stands up on his hind legs, reaches up as high as possible and then—with his razor sharp claws he gouges deep lines in the trunk of a tree. When another bear comes along…if he doesn't measure up to the first bears markings—he knows he better move along. Copper guessed the marks she'd seen were at least six or seven-feet high. The animal had also left tuffs of black fur behind. Knowing that she was in a black bear's territory rather than a grizzly's wasn't all that comforting.

Finally, she decided to take a chance on a small fire. Nights always turned cold in the high-country and she desperately felt the need for her hot porridge and tea. Her head was still pounding and her hands trembled as she pulled the shredded paper and the flint and steel from her pocket. It took her four tries before the spark became a flame and then ignited the small mound of dry moss and pinecones. Soon, her face and hands grew warm as the flames licked hungrily over the pine branches that she added one by one.

Warming herself by the fire Copper ate her humble dinner. Knowing that she was being watched, she turned and smiled at her big rawboned mule. Remy seemed to think she was her guardian.

"I'm fine now, Remy, you go on!"

The eccentric mule would never leave Copper to graze or sleep until she was content that all was well with her mistress. Then and only then would she go about her own business. Remy was always hungry, she was a large animal and needed more than just the grain. There was little to no grass to crop in their heavily wooded campsite, but Remy was resourceful and she made her way to a stand of young saplings. Copper smiled as her mule sunk her teeth into the tender, sweet bark and chewed contentedly. Copper didn't have to hobble or picket Remy for the mule never went far and always came when her mistress whistled.

Suddenly, Remy stopped chewing and lifted her large head and scented the air. Instantly, Copper grabbed her rifle, leapt over the fire, and quickly placed her hand over the mule's muzzle before she could bray out a warning. Still, she could be alerting to just about anything. Ma Riley had often jested that, "Remy could most likely hear an ant sneeze."

Copper doubted it was anything so harmless. So far she'd managed to stay clear of both man and beast and she'd like to keep it that way. Just then she heard the sound of a tree limb breaking and then came the unmistakable breathy grunt and growl. Remy tossed her head up and down, but Copper tightened her hand over her muzzle while her own heart hammered in her chest.

Copper Delaney; leave it to you to set up camp in a black bear's parlor.

Fortunately, they were downwind of the animal, and at least for the moment, he was unaware of their presence. His next growl was louder and closer than before and it caused Remy to side step but Copper managed to keep the mule from making any noise while she breathed out a silent prayer.

Glancing up longingly at the tall pine trees Copper couldn't remember...*do bears climb trees—or not?* Just then she didn't care, knowing she'd feel safer in those branches than she would on the ground. Her options were few; it was too dark to attempt escaping down the steep mountain trail. This was the only level ground; they'd have to stay here for the night. Copper and Remy waited and listened until the bear headed off, thankfully, in another direction. Copper decided to put the fire out and quickly covered it with dirt. Then she hid her saddle and tack under some bushes. Grateful that her rifle had a sling, she draped it over her head and left shoulder and her lariat over her right. Standing there in the evening dusk, she looked tough and capable but she was as frightened as she'd ever been.

Never having played much as a child, Copper had never climbed a tree before, and finding one with branches low enough to climb up was proving to be a difficult task. Finally, she came across a large boulder with a sturdy pine growing just beside it. Once she managed to climb onto the boulder, she was quite proud of herself, for she made quick work of climbing through the branches until she found a suitable spot to make a bed. Then she tied herself in place. Pleased with her accomplishment, Copper began to relax as she watched the sun slipping away and listened to the melody of the evening breeze as it glided through the pine branches like invisible satin ribbons. On the wind came the strong scent of evergreens and that of early spring.

Feeling much safer now, Copper lifted her eyes to the sky, "Me again, Lord." she whispered. "Thank you. I don't think that bear ever got wind of us. Ma Riley was always telling me to be thankful for all things. 'Ya never know when a hardship or even a nuisance might turn out to be a blessing.' Well, I'll admit now that I haven't exactly been thankful for my lack of supplies. But now, I realize that if I'd been dishing myself a plate of food a little while ago… that bear would have probably eaten Remy and me for the main course and had my dinner for his dessert. Ma was always telling me that I could trust in You even if I didn't understand Your ways. So, I'm thanking You for everything—even though I can't say I understand. And oh…thanks for giving me the good sense to buy these overalls. I never could have climbed this tree in a skirt. Lord, you've helped Remy and me make it through another day…I am so very grateful…and…I…."

If Copper finished her prayer, it was in her dreams. As unlikely as her sleeping quarters were, she slept soundly through the night—better than she had in weeks. In fact, she didn't wake until the morning sun felt warm against her cheek. When she opened her eyes, she instantly felt the need to hurry down from her perch. However, it proved to be a challenge, for her poor body felt like it had been tied in triple knots and it took real effort to straighten her back, unfold her legs and then climb down from the tree without falling on her head. When she finally set foot on solid ground she suddenly remembered why she spent the night in a tree—the bear!

"Ha. As grumpy and hungry as I feel this morning—that old bear better watch out for me!"

The ridiculously bold words brought a smile to her lips. For many years, she had longed to be free—but now that she was, she realized that freedom didn't mean that life became easy. So far, freedom had proved to be frightening, difficult and lonely. These mountains were beautiful—oh yes, but they were also rugged, untamed and deadly. A misstep on a steep path could kill a person just as quickly as the swipe of a bear's paw or a bullet. And yet, what she feared most was even more unpredictable than a wild mountain or the creatures that dwelt on it. Most of all she feared running into the most untamed creature of all, the mountain man. Again, Copper hoped that with her wearing overalls, men would assume that she was a boy, at least from a distance, and leave her alone. Still, the best and safest place for her was someplace where there were no men.

Oh wouldn't that be heaven," she thought. "*No one to tell me what to do or take a whip to me or blame me for their failures or want me, like Vernon and Dirk wanted me. Yes indeed, that would be freedom, at its best!*"

Gazing about her, Copper suddenly realized that her mule was nowhere in sight. That had never happened before. Weak and miserable, she began muttering to herself as she walked around the camp.

"Remy where are you?" she whimpered, "You know I'm not strong enough to search for you."

Just then, she stumbled on a pine root and fell to her knees. Sharp pine needles gouged the palms of her hands and suddenly a cloud of tears filled her eyes. "Lord," she cried, "please don't let me lose Remy, too. My head is pounding and I feel so weak and confused. I'd be ever so grateful if I could find some food and any kind of safe shelter, even for just a little while! All I need is just a few days of not being scared or hungry or cold. Couldn't you let something nice happen to me? Something not terrible or frightening. Couldn't you—please—couldn't you open just one door for me—even a little?"

Suddenly, Copper realized that she was acting like a sniveling little coward; she quickly stood to her feet and stamped her foot in disgust. "Copper Delaney, you've had tougher times than this—stop feeling sorry for yourself and find your mule!" She swiped the tears away with her shirtsleeve, and then put her fingers to her lips. Her shrill whistle always brought Remy on the run. Fortunately, her common sense stopped her just in time.

"Now wouldn't that have been a fool thing to do! Whistling up here would have brought Remy all right. Along with every Indian and crazed mountain man within earshot. Might have brought that bear back too—you ninny."

Being angry with herself seemed to clear Copper's mind and it came to her what she needed to do. It would be no problem to track her mule. After all, Remy had hooves the size of a fry cook's skillet. The trail down was as steep as the trail up had been. She wasn't strong enough to carry her things, not for three feet, but since it was downhill all the way…she could drag them. She cut a large pine branch with her hatchet and she tied her saddle and gear onto it, making something of a bouncy travois. Then she added a loop that went around her shoulder. Although Remy left a clear trail, Copper was worn out by the time she reached the meadow below. And what she found there was completely unexpected. Her legs gave way and she sank to the ground while tears of relief filled her eyes. She'd heard of people seeing mirages in the desert, seeing what they wanted to see rather than what was real. Well, she was seeing what she wanted to see all right. After all, hadn't she prayed for a safe shelter, for something nice and this was—so much more. This was—a little bit of heaven!

Actually, it was just a simple mountain homestead, but if ever a place was fashioned with love—this was it. The cabin and barn and out buildings were laid out just so. The log cabin—was just that—and yet, it truly was beautifully built. The honey-colored logs were stripped of their bark and joined together so skillfully, they reminded her of a tightly braided whip. The cabin on the left and the sturdy barn and corrals on the right were both built into the base of two opposing hills, with a long stretch of valley beyond them. In the distance was the sound of a rushing river.

Suddenly Copper laughed, for wonder of wonders, Remy herself came walking out of the barn, with her mouth full of hay. The mule gave her a puzzled look as if to say, 'Now—why did you sleep up in a tree last night—when you could have spent the night here—like me?'

Copper quickly glanced all about. Surely, they were intruding on a family about to begin their morning chores. She waited, but there was only Remy. No cow bawled to be milked, no rooster crowed, nor did a human voice break the silence. There was not one sign that said that this was home to anyone.

The corral gate and barn door were both open wide. That didn't surprise Copper for the mule was notorious for opening latches and peeking into places where she did not belong.

Just then Copper noticed that the cabin's doors and windows had been carefully boarded up. She was thankful for that, because if they hadn't been, she probably would've found Remy stepping out the front door of the cabin instead of the barn. Copper couldn't imagine why anyone would abandon a place like this. And yet, that's exactly how it looked—abandoned. Perhaps she had never been lost at all; perhaps God had heard her prayers and led her to this wonderful place. Hadn't she asked for something nice and for a door to be opened?

"Oh Lord, this is so wonderful. Please let me stay here—at least for a while. I know—the owner could come back and be even worse than Dirk Culley. I'll not worry about that though; I'll trust You and I'm going to enjoy this blessing for every second You allow me to stay. I don't care about Vernon's treasure in the mysterious Petrified Forest. As far as I'm concerned this is all the treasure I want!"

Looking more closely at the cabin, she realized that it was really one long roof over a main cabin and a slightly smaller one, with a wide dog run or breezeway in between. Finding a pry bar hanging in the barn, Copper loosened the boards covering the beautifully carved front door of the larger cabin. Her breath caught in her throat as she stepped inside. It was just one long room, and in the center of one wall was a wide stone fireplace with an ornately carved mantel. A large four-poster bed stood in one corner. Diagonally across from it was the kitchen, complete with a small but real metal cook stove, and a skillfully made table with four matching chairs. The cabin had indeed been built by one who knew the trade of joinery and carpentry. The floor wasn't dirt but instead she stood upon wide wooden planks that had been carefully scraped smooth. Real glass windows graced each wall, and though they were quite small and covered in soot, Copper knew what a luxury they were.

"Oh yes. This place really is a little bit of heaven!" Copper whispered the words as she reverently ran her fingers over the intricately carved mantelpiece. Oak leafs and acorns were perfectly detailed as they spread from one side of the mantle to the other and in the center a fancy letter 'M' was carved with a distinctive flair.

Copper's stomach grumbled reminding her that there might be some food in this place. Probably not but maybe. Crossing the room, she stepped into the kitchen, "My goodness, is that a pump?"

The wonderful contraption was attached to a wooden table under the back window of the cabin. It had a wide spout jutting over a wooden sink, and a jug of water sat beside the pump. Copper smiled, if she hadn't lived with Ma Riley she never would have known the secret of *priming the pump*. She could still hear Ma explaining, 'You have to give the silly contraption a drink first—if you want it to do the same for you.' Lifting the jug, she carefully poured water down into the handle mechanism. She waited a few moments, then pushed the handle up and then down, when nothing happened she gave it another drink, then tried again and that time she was rewarded when a gush of water splashing down into the wooden sink below. It was a bit rusty at first but soon it was clear and clean and she washed her hands and face then drank her fill.

Greatly refreshed but still weak from hunger, Copper wiped her face on her sleeve. To her right was the cook stove and beside it, the back door of the cabin. To her left she noticed something she thought quite odd. A huge buffalo hide hung from ceiling to floor and had a bar across it, as if it were a door. The hide was stretched onto a frame that was attached at the top to a long horizontal pole, which was hinged into solid rock.

Obviously, there was a cave behind that buffalo hide and the realization triggered one of Copper's oldest fears. Though she was un-nerved by this discovery, it did make sense. The cabin had appeared to have been built into the side of the mountain. Though Copper detested dark closed in spaces, she forced herself to light a lantern and peek inside. To her joy and relief, she saw shelves built into either side of the cave walls. She'd found—a pantry. Timidly she stepped into the shadows; her mouth went dry and she suddenly envisioned thousands of spiders, or worse, waiting for her, lurking there in the darkness. At first glance the shelves held only empty glass jars and Copper was just about to rush back to the safety of the cabin, when her light reflected on at least a dozen unopened tins. She couldn't quite make out the labels but it looked like carrots and green beans. Instantly, she snatched up a tin of each, spun on her heels and raced out of that loathsome cave, as if the hounds of hell were nipping at her heels.

As the hide door closed behind her, a whoosh of air sent another shiver careening down her spine. She sat the lantern and tins on the table with care, then twirled around and dropped the bar back over the door with amazing speed. It didn't take long to forget her fear, for her stomach growled loudly reminding her of its empty state.

What a day this had been. A day of fear mixed with miracles, and there before her was—food—real honest to goodness—food! On the wall behind the sink, there was a nail with string twined around it, and on the other end of the string was a sturdy knife. Grinning, Copper took that knife and eagerly opened the tin with a picture of carrots. Prying the lid up she plucked out three slices with her fingers and popped them into her mouth.

"Mmmm." her tongue and empty belly instantly celebrated the sweet and juicy offering.

After swallowing her second mouthful, she mumbled, "Oh, sorry, Lord." Bowing her head, she sank to her knees beside the wooden table. "Lord, how can I begin to thank you for all of this? I've been so frightened and discouraged but you've been leading us here—all along—I know it! If we had managed to stay on our own course—we never would have found this wonderful cabin. You've more than answered my prayers. There is even a bar over the door and food in the pantry. In the Bible You promise Your people a land flowing with milk and honey, but right now, I'm just as grateful for water and carrots."

As it happened, the cabin held even more treasure for Copper to discover. When she opened the large metal trunk that stood beside the stove, she found sacks of flour, cornmeal and buckwheat. There was also a tin of lard. Copper squealed in delight at each discovery and praised God for the bounty!

Lacy cobwebs fluttered in every corner of the cabin, there were large muddy footprints all over the floors while a thick layer of dust covered every nook and cranny. The state of the cabin was pleasing to Copper, for it certainly hadn't been cared for—in a long while.

"Abandoned." she whispered joyfully, and prayed it was so. Her plan had been to find the gold and leave the mountains before winter set in. Now, however, all she wanted was to stay right here. Still, if she stayed, she had much to do in order to survive a winter all alone up in this rugged high-country.

"I think I could make it, if I could just store up enough food for myself and Remy and cut enough fire wood. Of course, I'd need some warmer clothes too. Still, if I could do all that before the heavy snows come—I'd be as happy as mouse in a corncrib." The thought of being completely alone was a bit daunting, but she convinced herself that being alone was for the best.

Copper feasted that day on biscuits and vegetable stew and when night settled over the valley she snuggled down in the comfortable big bed with its elegantly carved posts and headboard, and felt like a queen. Her own night gown had been in the wash when she'd heard about Vernon, so Ma Riley had given her one of her newest gowns and though it nearly swallowed her up, wearing it made her feel less lonely. The next morning, she awoke to Remy's loud braying. The mule was in the habit of welcoming the sun's first rays the moment they split the horizon. Laughing, Copper ran outside to greet the silly creature, but she didn't tarry for she had much to do.

Hard work had always been a part Copper's life, but never before had she been this happy to do it. Every hymn Copper could remember, she sang over and over, as she praised God for this blessing. No one had ever been more joyful as they scoured and scrubbed. Copper washed the grimy windows until they sparkled. She brushed down the log walls, ridding the cabin of every speck of dust and every cobweb. The beautiful plank floors were no longer caked with dirt but shone like golden-honey. The cabin had a small loft, and when Copper climbed the ladder, she found the first signs that a woman had lived here. She found a large sewing box and in the corner, two large bolts of sturdy beige fabric. When she unrolled one bolt, she found what looked like curtains for the windows. The fabric had been cut but never sewn.

Tears suddenly came to Copper's eyes. She had seen a grave for an older woman named Maudy up on the hill. Perhaps it was her grieving husband who had abandoned this place. Speaking into the air as if the couple could hear her, she made them a promise, "I'll finish your curtains and keep your home polished and clean, Maudy. And to you sir, whoever you are, you built a wondrous place and I'll do my best to take good care of it."

Every morning Copper was afraid to open her eyes for fear that she was still lost and that the cabin was nothing more than a dream. Then she'd reach up and trace the carving on the headboard of the bed and—thank God! A moment later she'd bound from the big four poster-bed and become a whirlwind of industry. There had once been a garden behind the cabin and although it took courage, she searched inside the cave for seeds. Sure enough, hanging from the ceiling, she found a basket with carefully marked papers containing seeds for planting. Knowing that the growing season would be short in the high-country, she eagerly prepared the ground and planted each seed with care.

Thankfully, it seemed to rain nearly every afternoon and soon rows of tiny green sprouts were peeking up through the dark brown earth. Smiling, Copper sat down on the back porch of the cabin to look out over her very own garden while she enjoyed the glory of the orange-red sun as it began its final decent. The onions were sprouting first and she anxiously awaited the arrival of carrots, green beans and corn. However, just as she was admiring her sprouting vegetables, a movement in the grass caught her eye. It was a bold little rabbit, for it didn't hesitate to leave the green grass it should have been feasting on and make a beeline for her neatly planted rows of tender green shoots.

"Oh, no you don't!" Copper shouted as she picked up a rock and hurled it at the furry trespasser. When she missed, the little stinker simply hopped to the next row and continued to nibble away. Copper watched in horror as another rabbit followed the first into the yard and audaciously brought along a friend.

"I'll starve this winter if they have their way." Then she thought of something Ma Riley had told her, 'Hardships are sometimes blessings in disguise.' Of course, these rabbits were a blessing—to be sure. Yes, she needed these vegetables to make it through the winter but she also needed meat and warmer clothes. From that night on, Copper slept on the back porch to protect her garden, while dozens of snares were set around it borders. While her vegetables grew, she was busy tanning soft furry pelts. Copper thought she might just burst with happiness—for once—life didn't seem to be her enemy. Instead, everything was going well. For the very first time that Copper Delaney could remember...she was happy. A bit lonely perhaps, but happy!

Chapter 6
Meeting the Boss

"Delight yourself in the Lord and He will give you the desires of your heart." Psalms 37:4

"Pray that I will be given the message to speak and that I may fearlessly explain the mystery about the good news." Ephesians 6: 19

Shadrack McKenna was as miserable as he had ever been. Usually when he rode his powerful appaloosa stallion along his favorite mountain trail, he felt alive and free. This past winter, however, had taken its toll. In fact, the big man hadn't felt this wretched since the war. That's why he had left Tennessee and come to the Colorado Rockies in the first place. For these mountains did not bear the ugly scares of war and the meadow grasses had not been painted red with the blood of brother against brother or father against son. McKenna had loved the Rockies even before he ever saw their jagged edges slicing through the western horizon, but he hadn't prepared himself for the loneliness. He had just lived through his second winter and it was the longest and the loneliest experience of his life. At the first hint of spring thaw, he saddled his stallion and headed for Canyon City.

"Get along Boone," he mumbled, as his horse carried him down the steep mountain trail. "Thought I'd never tire of the high-country but right now, I'm near sick to death of it. If I don't get hitched before next winter boy...I think I'll go plum crazy!" When the stallion twitched his dark tipped ears, the man added, "No offense old pard, but I reckon yer getting' as sick of my company as I am of yers. 'Cause when a fella spends as much time as I have, talkin' and even readin' to his horse—well it just ain't good—ain't good a'tall!"

The dark eyed stallion seemed to agree for he picked up his pace. The horse was named after Shadrack's boyhood hero, Daniel Boone of Tennessee.

He had traded a fine thoroughbred mare in foal and his sharp shooter medal to a Ute brave for the stallion and was surprised he'd gotten him that cheap. Boone was a buckskin appaloosa with a blanket of snowy white draped over his hindquarters from the point of his withers to just above his hocks; the blanket was heavily dotted with quarter to fist sized suede colored spots. The stallion was a powerhouse of an animal, sure-footed, deep chested, the perfect mountain horse.

However, after such a long winter, both man and horse were sorely weary of each other's company and longed to mingle with their own kind. Now as they rode towards Canyon City, Shad contemplated the things that he wanted to accomplish once they arrived. One thing he was determined to do before the end of summer was find a wife. He was so desperate on that score, that he knew that he'd pretty much marry any woman that would have him. Beyond that, he planned to purchase some new reading material. He possessed a total of three books: Ivanhoe by Sir Walter Scott, Moby Dick by Herman Melville and the Bible. The latter had belonged to his mother and until recently, he had only touched it to move it out of his way. However, the other two books he had all but memorized. After this past winter McKenna was certain that if Boone could speak, the horse could have explained in detail the struggles between the Norman's and the Saxon's as well as commiserate over the frenzied hunt of the white whale and the ill-fated sailors of the Pequod.

Still, it was more than just loneliness that troubled McKenna. He was quite proud of the homestead he had built, for he had worked incessantly to make it more than just a cabin. It was a very special place—and yet there was still something missing—after two years—it just didn't feel like home.

Why this past winter had bothered him so much, Shad really didn't know. He had come West hoping to put the war and all its memories behind him. So far, it hadn't been an easy task, for he was often hounded by gruesome nightmares and a full night of sleep was a rare blessing. On the nights when sleep eluded him, the big man found himself heading to the barn for a talk with Boone. The barn was built halfway into a cave and warmed by an underground spring. The cabin and the barn were both comfortable in the winter but loneliness made him prefer spending time in the barn, with Boone.

He had survived what some called: The War of Rebellion and still others called the War of Northern Aggression. History would remember it as the Civil War. He generally spat when he heard that description of a conflict that killed so many.

There was nothing civil about war; neither that nor any other war should ever be referred to as…civil.

As soon as possible, Captain Shadrack McKenna left the battlefields behind and hurried home to Tennessee. He found his mother, still in good health and packed what few belongings they had and headed west. Maudy McKenna had been the sweetest little mother any man could ever have and he wanted to take her away from all the sorrow that had filled their lives.

"Come west with me Ma." he had cajoled. "Can't rightly explain it but… whenever there was a moment of calm in the fightin', I found myself dreaming of the mountains. I'd close my eyes and see a beautiful cabin set way up in the high-country. I'll make us a home Maudy McKenna! I'll find me a sweet little woman to marry and we'll give ya a passel of grandchildren to spoil!"

It was a sweet promise, but one not meant to be kept, for the chinking on the cabin walls was barely dry when his mother took sick and died, leaving Shadrack McKenna—all alone in his beloved mountains. His happy dreams had faded away like autumn leaves, trampled underfoot and forgotten. Still, Shad knew that he'd go mad if he didn't stay busy. In spite of his sorrow, he pressed on to put the finishing touches on the cabin. Day and night, he labored—carving his mother's designs into the mantel on the fireplace and a beautiful mountain scene onto the headboard of his big four-poster bed. Shad always liked working with wood. This, however, he did for his mother and because he desperately needed to use the hands that had been trained for war and put them to better use. Still, Maudy drew all the designs for her son's carvings, knowing this work soothed him. She saw how the war years had filled her son with bitterness and anger and she had tried to tell him that God could heal all the unseen wounds that festered inside him. Sadly, when Shad refused to listen, she felt the need to draw as many sketches for him as possible before she died. Her last words were, "Keep on making beautiful things, son. But put your trust in the Lord. Carving is good for you—yes—but only God can heal your soul."

Shad wondered if perhaps this past winter had been so burdensome because he had finished carving every one of his mother's drawings. Shad had one odd weakness, if you could call it that, he disliked carving the same pattern twice. He felt he did his best work only when challenged with a new design. When carving something for a second time, he was never satisfied with the quality. When he and his mother had moved to the mountains, the plan was always to make their living selling the pelts he trapped as well as the woodwork he made from Maudy's drawings. However, when he had nothing new to carve, he turned all his energy into trapping and curing pelts. Even though by spring he had an impressive stack to sell, that kind of labor was not a balm to his spirit in the same way that carving and carpentry had always been.

As Shad road away from his home, he was beginning to wonder if he truly belonged in these mountains. He had boarded up his beautiful cabin and as far as he was concerned, it might be best if it stayed that way. Right now he was filled with doubts and regrets. He should never have brought Maudy up to those rugged mountains. He regretted not listening to her when she tried to speak to him about her Savior. Shadrack McKenna was a strong man, and strong men don't need to be saved—or so he had thought until the war. That was when he'd seen firsthand how death came as easily to the strong as it did the weak. Now, Shad recognized his own arrogance in not allowing his mother to speak to him about her faith in God. Looking back, he saw how desperately she had tried. While he was building the cabin, he had even promised himself that when it was finished, he would take the time to sit with his sweet little mother and hear all that she had to say. Sadly, she died before that was possible. Now, after the war and these past years of loneliness, he began to fear that perhaps there was no meaning to life—no God—no hope—nothing that mattered. Could it be that the kindhearted Maudy McKenna with her loving spirit had simply returned to the dust, from whence she came? Then Shad looked around him at the majesty of the mountains and saw the perfection all around him. From the lumbering grizzly bear to the tiny bees that pollinated every plant and flower. Everything had a purpose…a need…an important role to fulfill. There had to be a powerful force that had created all living things with wisdom and foresight, giving them order and setting them in motion. God had to be real, and it was high time Shadrack McKenna stopped fighting his mother's teachings, and stopped fighting God! It was time to surrender to his creator and get to know who He really was.

As Shadrack McKenna walked up the steps and through the open doors of the small church, he felt as nervous as a mouse in a barrel full of cats. He drew in a steadying breath, intent on finding the first seat and planting himself in it until the services were over. It was a bright and sunny Sunday morning and he was thankful that all the windows were wide open. He felt less hemmed in with a gentle breeze filling the room. Just then, he awkwardly remembered to take off his hat and for the first time in his life, he wished he weren't such a big man. It wasn't that he was given to fat, in fact he ran a little on the lean side. Still, there was a lot of him—six feet, three inches to be exact and his arms and legs were thickly muscled from tramping up and down mountains and chopping down trees. His shoulders were broad, and his feet and hands had often been compared to the paws of a grizzly. He had jet-black hair, eyes the color of the forest and a jaw that looked like a battle-ax couldn't break it. No, it certainly wasn't easy to be inconspicuous, especially in a room that was overflowing with people.

Sweat began to trickle down his back as he lumbered down the aisle looking for an empty seat, thinking…*There sure are a lot of people in here and they sure do sit close together. Maybe this was a bad idea. No,* he assured himself, *it was a good idea—just not easy to do!* When he stepped past an old man who gave him an amused look, he wondered if the old codger had read his thoughts. It felt like every eye in the place was turned towards him, watching his progress. He surely was glad he'd taken the time to stop at the bathhouse, shave off his winter beard, and change into his town clothes, which consisted of a pair of brown wool pants a clean white shirt with black string tie, a wide brown leather belt and brown knee high boots.

He continued down the center aisle answering whenever anyone greeted him with, "Good morning ma'am, sir—good morning." His voice sounded unusually low and gravely, but he'd spent the winter longing for the sound of human voices, and it was pleasing to his ears. He was even pleased when some only smiled their welcome. A few of the men stood and shook his hand as he passed.

Services hadn't started yet and he was relieved that at least a few of the folks were talking amongst themselves instead of watching his progress. Although it seemed the majority of them were curious to see if this big man would actually find a place to light.

"Shoot" he whispered a bit too loudly, then winced, for he wasn't sure if these church folks would consider that a swear word or not. Now the sweat had gone from sliding down his back to sprouting over his forehead, and if he didn't find a seat soon, he'd have to turn around and walk all the way back up that aisle and have to look into all those same faces again.

"Finally," he grunted with relief when he spotted an empty place on a bench, but then he grimaced and muttered, "Well, if that don't beat all." The one and only seat available in this whole building was smack dab in the first row—front and center. He wished he'd just been content to stand in the back but it was too late now, people were already sliding over to make more room for him—he had to sit down. The wooden pew made a loud groan as he added his weight and Shad felt exactly like a bull moose at a tea party.

Fumbling with his hat as he held it between his knees, he pulled on his collar and gazed around hoping to see the familiar face of his friend, Preacher. Reverend Quincy Long was about Shad's age, he was educated and had been raised in a well to do family back east. Although they didn't know each other well, Preacher had visited Shad's cabin a number of times and they had struck up an easy friendship, for both men were humble and down to earth.

Just then, an elderly gentleman stepped to the front of the church. "Good morning to you, one and all." he said with a smile, "We shall begin our worship today by singing 'How Sweet The Name of Jesus Sounds.' If you all will remain seated, I believe it will be easier to see the words printed here on the blackboard." The man started everyone off, his voice a little shaky but for the most part, he was on key.

How sweet the name of Jesus sounds in a believer's ear.
It sooths his sorrows, heals his wounds, and drives away his fear.
It makes the wounded spirit whole, and calms the troubled breast.
'Tis manna to the hungry soul, and to the weary rest.

These words struck Shad so powerfully that he felt a lump rising in his throat. How many times had his mother used similar words, "Son, war has wounded your spirit, and it's troubled your soul. But God can heal those wounds—if ya'll just let him."

He had ridden down the mountain in search of many things—companionship—entertainment—but what he needed most was to find God! Now, the words to the very first song were piercing his heart like a bayonet. Was this just a coincidence or was God truly speaking to his heart? The words of the song and the blending of voices all around him touched Shad in ways he could not describe.

The next song was "Rock of Ages". After the first few verses he got himself under control and blended his rich baritone with all the tenors, altos and sopranos. Shad had always loved singing and hearing the voices all around him lifted his spirits. He was disappointed when the singing stopped but quickly changed his mind when he saw his friend's familiar face, as he stepped up behind the podium at the front of the church.

Pastor Quincy Long was a bear of a man, even bigger than Shad. In fact, he'd always reminded Shad of the Viking warriors his mother used to tell him about, for Quin stood at least six feet and six inches tall with blonde hair and intense blue eyes. And like his mighty ancestors, his body was strong and muscular and his face and hands were a leathery brown like any man who worked to survive in a harsh land.

The last time Shad had seen this man, they both had full beards and wore buckskins like most of the other mountaineers. Just now, however, Quin's strong face was clean-shaven and he wore an expensive and finely tailored black suit with starched white shirt and collar. Although his clothing made him seem every inch the proper Reverend, Shad could tell that the man was nervous, for Quin raked one large hand through his thick golden hair and pulled at his fancy starched collar with the other. When he gazed out at the congregation and saw that every seat was filled and there was even a group of men standing in the back, he seemed to look even more ill at ease.

Just when Shad feared his friend might be thinking of making a hasty exit, the big man suddenly bowed his head and closed his eyes in silent prayer. Most everyone went still but some became restless and muttered amongst themselves. Preacher, however, was unfazed, and continued his prayer, and when he finally raised his head, he looked like a different man. His face was a picture of tranquility, and his blue eyes sparkled with pleasure as he graced the congregation with a broad grin. The few single women in attendance stared up at the handsome young preacher giving him their sweetest and most pious smiles.

"Good morning and welcome!" his deep voice sounded strong as it resonated throughout the small building. "My name is Quincy Long. I've been the circuit preacher to the mountain folk of the Rockies for five years now and most folks generally just call me, Preacher. I'll be filling in all summer while Reverend Craddock and his wife visit their relatives in Virginia. Come autumn my horse Flint and I will head back to our mountain church. We have no fine building up there, but its people who make up a church and mine is wherever I find folks who want to hear God's word. Be they miners, trappers, ranchers, farmers, Indians or anyone else who chooses to live in the high-country. The good news for all of you is that—if you don't cotton to my preaching—you won't have to put up with Quincy Long—for long!"

When most of the congregation at least smiled, Preacher seemed to relax a bit more. "Now, I'm very fortunate, for I truly love my job and I have the best Boss in the world. Still, I am on duty every time I get up to preach, so I always check with The Boss first! "What would You like for me to talk about—I ask. This week His answer to me was: begin in the beginning. Now, He didn't mean the book of Genesis, He meant my beginning."

Preacher stood quietly as he looked out amongst the congregation. His piercing blue eyes seemed to be inviting the people that filled the pews to come with him on a journey. Drawing in a long breath he said solemnly, "The first twenty years of my life, were what you might call—smooth sailing—almost idyllic. I had two loving parents who were devoted to God, to each other and to me! My father knew shipping, my mother knew business, and together they owned and managed a shipping company out of Boston Harbor. Although I graduated from college, most of my education as a boy was acquired aboard one ship or another. While I traveled to distant ports, my instructors were my parents, a tutor, the crew and the sea itself. By the time I was sixteen, I had twice sailed around the world. Since I spent a good part of my life aboard ship, I often relate to the world around me in nautical terms: forward, aft, port, starboard, mast, deck, and anchor. Anchor. The Boss wants me to tell you when I finally found my anchor. Do you all know what an anchor is or what it does? It's a heavy iron hook that grabs onto the sea floor and is attached to the ship with a thick rope or chain. It holds the ship in one spot and keeps the current, the tide or the wind from blowing the ship off course or…into trouble!"

Working to make his voice sound even, he said, "Seven years ago my parent's decided to take a romantic voyage to Paris in celebration of their twentieth anniversary. I stayed in Boston as I was finishing my final college exams. The plan was that when they returned, I was to begin working full time for the company. Tragically—their—their ship went down and—all souls were lost." Preacher swallowed back the pain those words always caused him and he took a moment to collect himself before he was able to continue. "I'm ashamed to say that I lost my anchor that day! I was so—so devastated that for over a year it was as if—well—it was as if I had perished right along with them. During that time I rarely saw or even spoke to anyone. I was in a rage against God! After their memorial service, I refused to go to church or pray and I shunned my Christian friends. I had run into the biggest storm of my life—without an anchor." Preacher's blue eyes looked beseechingly out amongst the people. "Please, stop and think. Do you have an anchor? Is it strong enough to keep you secure when the next storm comes your way?"

He swept his eyes over the church full of people who were listening with rapt attention, then continued, "I had called myself a Christian for ten years but I suddenly realized that I had always relied upon my parents' faith in God. Their anchor was God and my anchor was them—their faith—their trust—their dedication. I ask you again, are **you** prepared to stand alone through the next storm that comes your way? Or for that matter are you prepared for the day when you take your last breath? Where is your faith? In what or in whom are you placing your trust? Because I can tell you this, there is no other personage but Jesus Christ, who promises to equip us and to sustain us through hardship and death. In Hebrews six, verse nineteen, it says, 'This hope is a strong and trustworthy anchor for our souls.' And in chapter eleven, verse two, it says, 'Faith is being sure of what we hope for and certain of what we do not see."

"As I said, seven years ago, both my parents drowned at sea. And I'm ashamed to say that, I was drowning in self-pity." Preacher suddenly gave a self-mocking shake of his head. "I might still be living in that sorry state, but for my best friend Tim Grainger and three of his strong and very determined sparring partners. They were all good Christian men and on one fine Sunday morning, they broke right into my room, rousted me from my warm bed, and quite literally shoved me into my clothes. They ignored the string of colorful names I called them, that now—I am truly ashamed of—and they carried me straight to church. At first, I folded my arms and refused to listen. 'Not so much as one word was going to get through to me!' I boasted. "Then, I looked around and I saw widow Thomas, she was sitting in the front row as always, Henry Franks was sitting with his four children, his wife had died of consumption four years earlier. I was ashamed and quite suddenly—right there and then—my frozen heart melted. Not only had I been wrong but completely selfish. For over a year, I had arrogantly shaken my fist and shouted at God. I buried my face in my hands—and wept. Finally, with a shamed and broken heart, I begged God to forgive me." A gentle smile spread across Preacher's face and his voice filled with awe as he said, "And do you know what happened? The mighty God of the universe bent down and listened to my prayer. I know he forgave me, because a warmth came over me as if He had put His arm around me, and at that moment, a memory flooded my mind. It was of my dear parents hand in hand, kneeling in prayer. They were devoted Christians who adored each other but—God had first place in each of their lives. Who was I to say when the days had been accomplished for them both to be called home? How could I be so selfish as to wish them back? Of course I missed them terribly, but I also knew that they would have considered it a blessing to step through heaven's gate—arm and arm."

"After that day, I knew God had something specific He wanted me to do—I just didn't know what! I immersed myself in God's word and listened intently to every sermon, hoping for direction. Then one day the pastor was preaching from the book of Mark. In the later verses, Jesus told his disciples what He wanted them to do after He returned to heaven. He said simply, "Go into all the world and preach the good news to all creation." Of course I had heard that verse many times before, but that day I knew that God was talking to me!"

"Our Pastor reminded us that this vast nation that spreads from sea to sea is quickly filling up with people who have never heard the name of Jesus Christ, and many who have still don't know what He has done for them or what He offers them. They've not heard or understood that God offers love, forgiveness, mercy and salvation to all who will give their hearts to Him. Many people rely on the notion that if they believe that God or even a higher power exists, then they will surely go to heaven when they die. That makes no sense. It's like expecting an anchor that has never been fastened to your ship to keep you from crashing into the rocks. After all, the devil believes in God—but he's certainly not a Christian nor will he ever walk through the gates of heaven. The truth is that to become a Christian we must have a Father/child relationship with God and put our faith in all that He is. The bond He wants to have with us is as vitally important as the chain that runs from the ship to the anchor. Without it, we like the ship, will find ourselves adrift in a storm tossed sea."

"That day, it occurred to me that there are thousands of people who are drifting heedlessly into troubled waters because they have no anchor. After what I experienced, I knew that I must at least try to share what I learned. As I listened to the sermon that day, I felt God asking me this question: Quincy Long will you turn everything over to me and allow me to be your Boss? Will you go where I send you? Will you be a friend to those in need? Will you tell them about me?"

As Preacher gazed out over the congregation of pioneers that had traveled to this small town from all over the world, it was easy to see what his answer had been, for his eyes were shining, "I guess I don't have to tell you how I responded," he said with a broad grin spreading across his face. "I said—yes Sir! Because when God takes the trouble to tell you something that plainly—it's best you just surrender and go where He leads."

Shad found himself leaning forward as he listened to the simple but powerful message. All the mountain folk seemed to respect the man they called, Preacher, and it was plain to see that the big man had followed the direction God had given him. Though Shad considered Quincy Long a friend, he still didn't really know him all that well. Now, he looked forward to becoming better acquainted with this man—because now—he was the one needing direction.

After the service ended, Shad waited by the hitching rail and watched patiently as the people left the church. It seemed nearly everyone wanted to share a word or two with the young pastor. Finally, when the building was empty, Preacher looked over and grinned broadly when he spotted Shad. The two men met each other half way and clasped hands in a hearty greeting.

Shad was first to speak, "That sure was a fine talk, Preacher. I remembered you sayin' that you'd be sermonizin' down here all summer. I had you in mind when I packed my pelts and some of my best carvings and come here, instead of Colorado City. Sold everything—made me a tidy sum. What I'm trying to say is that...I have the time and the where with all to stay all summer. Last winter was mighty hard and lonely—and I had a lot of time to think about God. And, uh...well...I've come to meet your Boss!"

Preacher couldn't have been more pleased and Shadrack McKenna had meant what he said; he attended every church service, soaking up every word.

Each evening he would read his mother's Bible until the letters blurred and he was forced to put out the light and go to sleep. Finally, one Sunday, a month later, Preacher finished his sermon and asked if there was anyone there who wanted to ask Jesus Christ to become the Lord of their Life…their Boss? Shad stood and unashamedly walked towards Preacher saying, "Yes Sir, its past time I put Jesus Christ in charge of my life. Let's get it done!"

After Shad got things straight with God, he decided it was time he found a wife. He couldn't abide the idea of living through another lonely winter. There were a half a dozen single women in town that attended the church services. One by one, Shad proposed marriage and, one by one, they turned him down. Of course, they all thought McKenna was a handsome enough suitor; with his jet-black hair, green eyes and muscular build; he could easily turn a lady's eye. Most of them even enjoyed the eloquent way the man had of describing his cozy cabin with its breathtaking views that only a mountain paradise could offer. They just couldn't see the need of suffering through a long, cold winter. Not with only this big bear of a man for company. In fact, three of them agreed to marry him, but only if he would build them a pretty little house, and live in town. They just knew he could make a fine business for himself building furniture. The truth was that though they might be interested in what a man like Shad could provide, none of them cared what was best for Shadrack McKenna.

When he'd first ridden down the mountain he thought he might never go back. He didn't know if it was the war years or just his nature, but life in town was a burdensome thing for a man like Shad. Living in the lowlands was slowly suffocating him. He thrived in the high-country, he could breathe up there and he could be himself. Finally, the day came when he'd had enough of female rejection and of Canyon City in general. He longed for the peace of his own little valley and the tranquil and raw beauty of his mountains. The plain and simple truth was that he had become a mountain man—and with or without a wife—it was time to go back to those mountains.

Preacher too had become discouraged. He had hoped to start up a special ministry there for women who had no place to go and for those who had suffered from abuse. However, since it was to be a ministry to help women it would need to be run by a woman or married couple. When he could not enlist the help of anyone in the entire town with what they all considered a controversial ministry, he became anxious to return to his mountain congregation. One blessing that had come of the summer was that a deep and abiding friendship had grown between him and Shadrack McKenna. They both decided that the journey back up the mountains would be more enjoyable if they went together. It was a steep two-day ride from Canyon City to McKenna's homestead, and when the trail permitted the two men talked easily, and found that even though their backgrounds couldn't have been more different, they still had much in common. They spoke briefly of their past experiences, but mostly they talked about God, for Preacher had a passion for sharing and Shad had a hungry soul.

Chapter 7
Home

"Two are better than one, for they can help each other succeed. If one falls the other can reach out and help." Ecclesiastes 4:9 & 10

As Shad and Quin reached the high plateau, they stopped their horses to rest but mostly so they could take in the view. Stretching out before them was a wild and seemingly endless panorama of mountaintops. They stood in dark relief against a blazing sunset sky, streaked with clouds of crimson and magenta.

Preacher crossed his hands over the saddle horn and breathed deeply of the crisp air. "I know it seems strange to say but when I'm up here like this, it's almost as if I were back on the ocean. As if I were steering a ship through a choppy gray-green sea," he chuckled slightly adding, "and of course red sky at night—sailors delight! That should mean that tomorrow morning will break clean and clear."

"Well, I know next to nothing about sailors and the sea, Preacher," Shad grunted as he reined Boone alongside Flint, "But I reckon that's why we men take to the mountains like we do; we see what suits us. You see a fitful ocean while I see a sharp, saw-tooth mountain range, cuttin' into a blood red sky. Sights like this always make me wish I was an artist, like my Ma. Yep, Maudy McKenna could have done justice to a sight like this!"

The two mountain men may have felt different things as the rugged trail led them through the wild and untamed high-country…but it was pure tonic for both of them. The higher they climbed the more alive they felt. In the evenings around the campfire they remained vigilant while they talked quietly of many things, during the day, they spoke very little. For rough and dangerous trails are best traveled in silence. Yet, as they looked out across vistas cloaked in the variegated greens of pine and fir or forged glacial streams that were icy cold, yet shimmered like molten gold in the sunlight, they were not silenced by caution but by the wonder of it all.

Even though the men had taken great pleasure in their journey, as they approached McKenna's homestead, they were both anxious to step down from their mounts and looked forward to a shave and a hot bath. However, just before they rode into the yard sudden mayhem exploded from the barn door. Like a blast of buckshot—out came the biggest as well as the ugliest mule either man had ever seen. The silly beast lifted her oversized head and began braying out an alarm call if ever there was one. Both horses spooked and although the men were quick to settle them down, they were baffled as to why or how this strange animal came to be there. For strange it surely was! The creature seemed to be the product of the impossible mating of opposing species. It was a female mule, a molly, at least of *that* they were certain, but she was the size of a Percheron with a large bulbous nose resembling that of a moose and ears that stood out comically, like two flags flapping in the breeze. Her back was too long and her legs seemed far too short for her skillet-sized hooves. It was if this animal had been assembled from a variety of equine scraps and end pieces, from draft horse to pony, with moose and mountain goat thrown in for good measure. Flint snorted and blew, his nostrils flaring and ears pricked forward as Preacher coaxed him back towards the barn, even as the mule continued to bray.

"Stop that—you bag of leftovers!" Preacher scoffed, then looked over at Shad and only half jesting asked, "Is that a big mule or a little mastodon?"

Although Shad had never heard of a mastodon, he was inclined to go with that, whatever it was, rather than call that thing a mule. He didn't bother answering however, because he suddenly alerted to movement in the cabin. Slowly he drew the pistol from his holster while he chided himself for becoming distracted. The barrel of a rifle was protruding through his cabin door. Glancing down he noted that the only tracks around the yard were those of the mule and one pair of small boots. He figured that maybe a runaway boy had happened upon his cabin. Child or not, at least the kid could hunt for two skinned rabbits were lying on the large stone he always used for cleaning game.

"Hello—in the cabin!" Shad shouted, intentionally making his voice sound deep and threatening.

While Copper hid behind the door, her heart pounded so loudly she couldn't think. All she wanted to do was make these strangers leave. But how? Thankfully, she had stepped inside to fetch a bucket of water before the men had ridden up. When she heard Remy's warning she had immediately grabbed her rifle, double-checked the chamber then opened the door a crack and slowly slid the barrel through.

Trying to hide her fear, she lowered her voice and demanded, "Go away! We don't like strangers. You aren't welcome here—so go on back where you came from."

The men raised their eyebrow and exchanged knowing glances. They could tell by his voice that it was a scared kid hiding behind the door, young enough that his voice hadn't even changed yet. Still, they had to give it to the boy, for he was doing his best to sound menacing.

"You best move on now—or you'll end up like those rabbits out there!"

Shad gritted his teeth and prayed for patience, "Listen young'un, my name is Shadrack McKenna. I've been on a—well a holiday you might say—but I'm home now. And you are trespassin' in my cabin!"

Preacher held his hand up, "Now Shad, trespassing might be too harsh a word." Speaking to the partially closed door, he said kindly, "My name is Quincy Long. I'm the circuit preacher in these parts. I can vouch for this man. He's telling you the truth, this cabin does belong to him."

Copper cocked the rifle, "Anybody could say that. I've been here for months. The place was as dirty as a mud-wallow when I found it. I've cleaned it up one side and down the other, and I've planted a garden. This place was abandoned—I tell ya—it's mine now!"

When Shad looked like he might be close to losing his temper, Preacher spoke again, making sure to keep his voice as gentle and unthreatening as possible. "Sounds like you've worked mighty hard, but the truth still remains, this is not your cabin. I'm sure you've seen the finely carved initial 'M' on the mantle and the front door, it stands for McKenna—Shadrack McKenna."

Shad turned his stallion so his saddlebags could be seen. "That's right. See, they all look the same, just like this one." He ran his hand over the tooled initial emblazoned across the leather flap.

When Copper saw the familiar, 'M' with the same distinctive flourish that matched all the other carvings she had thought so beautiful, her heart sank, "I should have known." she moaned. "It was all just too good to be true."

Her life was about to take another one of its familiar downward turns—only this time it felt more like she was being thrown off a cliff. Tears gathered in her eyes as she un-cocked her gun and watched as the two large men stepped off their horses. Still speaking from behind the door she said gruffly, "Didn't mean to trespass—just figured the owner must be dead—" Then she added sarcastically, "'Cause only a *fool* would leave a place like this—for months on end."

The men couldn't help but hear and turned away to hide their amused glances. When the boy made no move to come out and greet them, Preacher said gently, "Tell ya what young'un, Mister McKenna and I are dirty, and saddle weary but—most of all—we're just about as hungry as two men can get. We're gonna unpack our gear then head down to the hot spring and wash off some of this trail dust. Those rabbits sure look good! Why don't you rustle up whatever kind of supper you had in mind and add a little more to it. We'll break bread together and the three of us will figure this thing out. Does that sound all right with you?"

Still hidden behind the door, Copper mumbled, "Sure—guess the least I owe you is a cooked meal." She closed the door, but hurried to the window and peeked at the men as they unsaddled their horses.

"I'm losing my little bit of heaven—and I didn't even know it had a hot spring." She whimpered as tears slid down her cheeks. "And—why are you surprised Copper Delaney? Isn't this how things always go for you? You've lost your beautiful home to a stranger, and that big old bear is going to reap all that you've sown." Copper wanted to curl up in a corner and weep over her luscious garden, not to mention her beloved cabin. Then she went to the carved mantle over the fireplace and traced the smooth acorns and oak leaves with her fingertips. Then she looked closely at the initial M carved in the center. "I guess that big oaf must love this place too—he must or he wouldn't have worked so hard to make it so perfect."

Suddenly, flooding back into Copper's mind came the memory of the days and nights she'd spent lost, starving and terrified, before God led her to this cabin and she lowered her head in shame. "I'm—sorry, Lord. I'm acting like a spoiled child. You led me to this wonderful place just when I needed rest and shelter. It was arrogant and just plain foolish to think I could stay here. I know Ma Riley said not to trust anyone, but I need help! Those men could have ordered me to leave and be quick about it…but they didn't.

Help me know if I can trust them, Lord. I was lost and in trouble when I found this place and I'll be in trouble again if I just strike out on my own. I need help and I have to assume that, that's why you sent me here. And Lord, thank you for these past few months. I had a wonderful home for a while—" then she added stubbornly, "and for this summer at least—it was all mine!"

The moment the men were out of sight, Copper hurried outside to fetch the rabbit meat. When she came back she realized that her overalls were covered in blood and mud from a day spent hunting and skinning. Still, clean or dirty, she had no intention of shaming herself by letting a preacher see her in men's overalls. Quick as lightning, she washed and then slipped into her Sunday dress. It was a soft shade of green with tiny stripes and flowers of dark brown. She also had two work dresses but she reasoned that at least for one more night, this was her home and she would greet these men as if they were guests, and she'd serve them dinner—like a proper lady. Just then, Copper remembered that the preacher had referred to her as—young'un. Well, she wasn't a child, nor was she a beggar. Her hands moved quickly as she undid her braids and brushed out her long hair, then headed for the kitchen. When those two mountain men returned, they would find a clean cabin and would be served a fine meal. Afterward, she would show them her bountiful garden and then perhaps they might be inclined to help her find a safe place to spend the winter.

While Copper fried up the rabbit meat in a heavy skillet, she couldn't help but think of how large both men were. They could hurt her very badly. Part of her wondered if she shouldn't be using this time to run rather than prepare supper for those two giants. She never met a man she trusted, so why wasn't she searching for a safe place to hide? Deep down she knew why, she just couldn't make herself leave. She'd been so happy here and those men, even if they were giants, didn't seem to frighten her, not like most men did. Perhaps they might even help her find the Two Fools Mine. She didn't know if that was wise or not. She'd almost forgotten about the mine and the promise of gold. It wouldn't hurt to make a few friends up here—if that was even possible. What was it Ma Riley used to say? 'Satisfy a man's appetite and you'll be surprised how helpful he can be.'"

With that in mind, Copper began flying about the kitchen like a whirlwind. She cooked up a half dozen sliced onions on the stove and when they had turned sweet and golden-brown, she added water, fresh sliced carrots and green beans from the garden. Thinking that they might be even more reasonable if she fixed dessert, she fetched the basket of mountain berries she'd picked the day before. Instead of drying them for winter, she decided to bake two pies with them instead.

The sun was just about to go down when Shad and Preacher stepped across the threshold of the little cabin and yet they hardly recognized the place. It was as clean as a mountain stream. It smelled of the wild flowers and herbs tied in small bundles, hanging upside down from the rafters. The beautiful wooden floors were scrubbed and polished to a honey-gold. The curtains Maudy McKenna had planned to sew now fluttered at every window.

A knot lodged in Shad's throat, he'd been in bad shape when he'd left this place. It had been a mud-wallow all right…but now the place was more than just clean and neat. It had frustrated him that it had never felt quite like *home*. Now as he gazed around the place, he realized that whatever it was that it lacked before—was no longer missing. He couldn't stop the grin of pleasure that spread across his face. The homey atmosphere was enhanced even more by the sweet and savory aroma of a fine dinner.

Just then, the back door of the cabin opened and the men waited to get a closer look at the boy that had threatened them earlier. Instead, a lovely young woman stepped inside with a small tin cup of flowers in her hand. Both men found themselves rooted to the ground and speechless. They had discussed the fact that there was only one set of tracks, well two if you included the big mule. Still, they thought it was a boy living there all alone—but it wasn't a boy. It was a woman, a young and lovely woman, who quietly placed the tin of flowers in the center of the table, then stared at them with inquisitive clover-green eyes. Her silky amber hair had fallen over her shoulder and absent-mindedly she tossed it back behind her.

Finally, Copper decided she might as well be the first to speak, she blinked up at them with a cautious yet dignified smile, and said, "Dinner's ready." Before she could think better of it she dropped into a polite curtsy. Her smile suddenly turned to a frown, she was acting like the bondservant she had always been and although it angered her, she wasn't sure how else to act.

The men, however, simply raised their eyebrows and exchanged glances. They had talked while shaving at the spring about what to do with the *boy*. They had decided that they would give *him* the choice of staying with either one of them through the coming winter. Now the thought embarrassed them, and the realization robbed them of words and planted uncomfortable smiles on their faces as they headed for the table.

Shad was the first of the men to speak as he stepped forward. "Ma'am, this place sure is a surprise. I've always been proud of my little cabin, but even I never imagined it could look *this good.* It was a sorry mess when I left it and I can see how hard you've worked—mighty hard to have done all this. I know you didn't do it for me—but I sure would like to thank you in some way—just the same." When Shad noticed that the young woman was hiding her trembling hands behind her back and that she looked terribly pale he quickly added in a gentle voice, "Preacher and me, we probably look a little scary, but—ya needn't be afraid. We're both Christian men and neither of us would ever harm ya—not in any way. But I got to ask, you said 'we don't like company', but yer all alone here—ain't ya?"

Copper eyes traveled from one face to the other, as if she were trying to read their expressions, hoping to see if she should trust them or not. As if defying them to reproach her, she replied gruffly, "Except for my mule, Remy—I am quite alone—I'm a Christian too but I was afraid you might be—well—dangerous men. I'm sorry for lying and for trespassing. I—I'll pack up my things and leave right after I clean up the supper dishes." Not wanting these strangers to see how miserable she felt, she swallowed back her tears, lifted her chin and gracefully reached to pull out her chair. However, she stopped in confusion when both men tripped over each other to do it for her. Frowning she sat down and watched self-consciously as each man took the seat on either side of her. Glancing at the blonde headed man, who said he was a preacher she asked softly, "Sir, would you mind asking the blessing?"

"I'd be pleased to Miss." Preacher bowed his head, hesitated a moment then began, "Well Lord, we three find ourselves in what seems like an odd-predicament. I've always known You to have a plan though, especially where Your children are concerned. So, please, help us to figure out just what it is You want us to do here. I ask a special blessing on this hard working young woman who has labored here all summer and who has prepared this fine meal. We thank you for it. In Jesus name, amen."

As they passed the steaming bowls of food around the table, Shad found it hard to take his eyes from the 'hard working young woman', as Preacher had called her. She seemed calm and poised right now; however, earlier as he passed the cabin window, he thought he had heard muffled sobs. Had this girl wept when she realized that this place was no longer hers? He was sure there were probably women who were more beautiful than this one. Nevertheless, she had his heart pounding and his tongue tied in knots. This girl fascinated him. It wasn't just that her hair was the color of sunset or that her skin looked like fresh cream, nor was it the band of freckles that dotted the bridge of her nose. Although all those things made her very appealing. He thought perhaps, it was her bright and expressive eyes that held him captive. They were heavily lashed, large and green as a spring meadow. Shad couldn't seem to stop himself from staring at her—then around his cabin—than back at her again. This girl had turned these four log walls into an inviting home. She had succeeded in giving this place just what it needed. Most of all, what kept rolling through his mind was…she loved the place! The women in town didn't want him because of his mountain cabin but this woman loved it. He gazed at her again and realized that she had indeed been crying. She'd been heartbroken at the thought of having to leave—and right now, the last thing he wanted was to see her go.

Preacher suddenly shook his head, "Please forgive our poor manners ma'am. I just realized we don't even know your name. We'd also like to know; what hardship has brought you to these mountains? Surely you wouldn't have worked this hard if you hadn't hoped and needed to spend the winter here."

When the girl remained silent Shad nodded his own encouragement and said gently. "I hope ya'll feel free to trust us with your story, ma'am. This place isn't all that easy to find. Seems to me God led ya here—maybe so we could help. Please speak plainly—for we'd both be proud to assist ya in any way."

Copper had studied these two giants all through dinner and the dark haired one was right. She too had believed that God had led her to this special cabin. Glancing from one man to the other she slowly answered them. "My name is Copper Delaney, and yes—I do have troubles. I've been a bondservant most of my life and truthfully, I have never had any reason to trust men—not any man—not ever!" Biting her lip, she narrowed her green eyes, as she slowly considered the two men sitting beside her. Finally, she shrugged her shoulders, "Still, I know it would be pure folly to go back to wandering in these mountains. I was in a bad way before I found this place. I could surely use some help but I wouldn't want you to risk your lives. You see, I'm running away from a man I believe to be very dangerous. His named is Dirk Culley. You two just came up from the lowlands. I don't suppose you happened to see an albino, a tall man, in his late twenties?"

When the men shook their heads she added with a shrug, "I honestly don't know if he's still looking for me or not. The last time I saw him he had a long white braid down his back. He escaped from prison a few months ago. The sheriff told me that a posse chased him all the way to the Wyoming Territory, but he believed Dirk would turn back, and come looking for me. Naturally, I don't want him to find me. It's a long and extremely complicated story but that's the heart of why I'm here."

Shad exchanged glances with Preacher then said, "Miss, if there is a dangerous man lookin' for ya it would be best if we knew exactly what yer up against."

His words made sense and although Copper needed their help, she still struggled with the idea of telling them everything. After all, they were not only men—they were strangers. Even though they claimed to be honorable, it would take more than one shared meal for her to trust them. Then again, how could they help her and not put themselves in danger if they didn't at least know most of the story. Finally, Copper told them briefly of her years as a bondservant. Then she explained how Vernon Riley had lassoed her and pulled her from the river.

"Vernon had only just tossed his blanket over me when his partner, Dirk Culley rode up. The minute he saw my red hair he claimed that I belonged to him. He spouted some nonsense about a gypsy telling him that he would meet a redhead and that she would lead him to treasure. I soon realized that both men were outlaws. At the time, they were heading to the farm that belonged to Vernon's mother and they took me with them. While we rode to the farm, Vernon sent Dirk on ahead and then he told me that I had to marry him—because that was the only way to protect me from Dirk. I told him to think of another way, but then Ma Riley warned me that I had better do what Vernon said. Then a preacher came to the farm and married us. The next thing I knew Vernon had thrown his arms around me and was kissing me and then…"

"Hold on there—you're married to that outlaw?" Shad's asked, his words sounding like a sigh and a groan combined. He knew he had only just laid eyes on this girl but the jolt of disappointment that pierced his heart at hearing that she was married felt like a firebrand.

Copper misunderstood his reaction. Thinking he was just as confused as she had always been, she frowned and shook her head, saying, "It's hard to say if we were or we weren't? Ma Riley and I talked and talked about whether or not it was legal and binding. Naturally, she and Vernon always said it was. Of course now it doesn't really matter one way or another—like I said—start to finish—the whole thing was just so very—complicated."

Shad frowned and this time his voice sounded both irritated and dejected, "What's complicated about it? You're either married to the man or you're not."

When Copper leaned away from Shad with a hurt expression on her face, Preacher interfered. "Now, Shad you're not giving Miss Delaney or is it Mrs. Delaney—no you said Vernon's name was Riley? Shouldn't you have told us your name is Copper Riley?"

Copper suddenly lost her timidity; now she was becoming irritated as well. "Please, if you men will just allow me to finish my story—I'm sure you'll be able to understand." Narrowing her eyes at Shad, she added sternly, "And it most certainly *is* complicated. Now, where was I?"

Shad folded his arms over his chest and said through gritted teeth, "Vernon was kissing you."

Copper blushed and frowned, "Actually, he was trying to and while I was busy giving him a good kick and pushing him away—everything happened all at once. It was miraculous really, and one of the reasons that I finally started to believe that God might truly care about me. I knew I was in real trouble but just as Vernon and I were struggling, the sheriff and his deputy stormed into the house. Sadly, a poor young man was shot and killed. Vernon and Dirk were arrested and sentenced to four years in prison.

I had no place to go and since Ma Riley was getting old and needed help, I stayed with her. I lived with her for a little over a year. Everything was fine until the sheriff came one day and told us that Vernon and Dirk had escaped from prison and that Vernon had been killed. The sheriff wasn't sure but thought that Dirk might have done it. He thought they might have been fighting over me. That's why both the sheriff and Ma Riley told me to run! It was her idea for me to come up here, but I don't think she realized how dangerous the mountains are." Copper was quiet for a moment, wondering if she should ask them about the Petrified Forest and the Two Fools Mine. When she decided against it, she continued, "Remy and I got terribly lost and

I was nearly starving. But God *was* watching over us because one night He led Remy down the mountain to this valley and the next morning I followed her to this little bit of heaven." Copper gazed down at her clasped hands, "When I saw this beautiful cabin all boarded up—I thought—well I thought it was the answer to all my prayers. Now I—well I'll admit to being a little worried. Still, I know God hasn't forgotten us. Everything will work out."

Shad blew out a relieved breath and said, "So, you were either never married and you're single now…or you were married but you're a widow now."

Nodding her head Copper shrugged her shoulders, "Now, do you understand why I said it's…"

"***Complicated***."

Both men ended up saying the word along with Copper. Then their eyebrows rose as they looked at each other as if to say, 'Well now that we know the story…what are we going to do with the girl?"

The bemused look on the men's faces caused Copper to suddenly stiffen with pride; and she lifted her chin, "Listen to me, I realize that I'm young and I've already admitted that I got lost up here—but that was because I lacked proper directions, not because of my age or lack of abilities. I'm not asking that either of you take care of me, for I do not wish to become any more indebted to you than I already am. I have complete faith that God led me here and He'll lead me to the next place." Despite her bravado, Copper was at a loss to know where that next place might be so she quickly added, "Of course, if either of you happen to know of a truly abandoned cabin or even a cave—although I loathe caves. That would be the kind of help I wouldn't mind accepting!"

Shad's heart went out to the girl, "Ma'am," he said gently, "I admire your courage, and you are not indebted to me at all, but I am to you for doing so much work around here. You could ask a lot of me and it wouldn't pay what I owe you. My cabin will be warmer 'cause of the curtains you made and I'll have food all winter cause of the garden you planted and tended. I'd be honored if ya'd be my guest fer as long as ya like." When Preacher gave him a cautionary look, Shad quickly added, "Course me and Preacher will help ya all we can but for now, we men will be content to bed down in the barn and I'd be pleased if you'd continue to make yourself at home right here in this cabin—just as ya have been."

Copper surprised them when she shook her head vehemently, "I'll do no such thing! I will not impose upon your hospitality, Mister McKenna. I know now that I've been trespassing—and I refuse to continue, not even for one more night. I'll be the one to sleep in the barn—and I'll not only be grateful but content to be there."

Shad frowned and countered with his voice sounding so low it resembled the rumble of a bear. "Miss Delaney, if ya think it proper that a woman should sleep in the barn while two able bodied men stay in the cabin, then I don't wonder that you've have so little regard for men! Now, the three of us have just prayed about all of this. And—we've agreed that God led ya to this place. The only sensible thing to do now is for ya to stay right here, until God tells us what to do next. Until then, I insist that you stay right where you've been comfortable and safe all summer!"

When Copper stiffened and Shad clenched his jaw, Preacher feared these two might soon be embroiled in an all-out but foolish argument. "Now stop right there you two. You're both about to find yourselves in a ridiculous fight trying to out-polite each other. As I see it, you are both beholden to the other but I think it's The Boss that should get the thanks for all of this. Shad needed to be away from this cabin for a while. Miss Delaney, you were in great need of food and shelter and this place fulfilled your needs. Shad came back thinking he had a lot of work ahead of him but instead found that you had things well in hand. Shad owes you and you owe Shad but mainly it seems that God should get the credit for putting all this in place and I think we should continue to trust Him. We've asked for guidance but some things we already know. Such as, we know that God would want us to harvest the garden He blessed." Spotting the pile of soft rabbit furs on the settee, he added, "Looks like you've been making yourself some winter clothes from the furs you've tanned. There's always a lot to do to prepare for winter and thanks to your efforts, Miss Delaney, we're well on our way. Still, the work will be lighter if we three work together. So, let's have no more fussing and get on about the business of doing what needs to be done!"

Looking at things that way Copper no longer felt like she was imposing. "That does sound reasonable. If I stay in the cabin, it will be easier for me to prepare all the meals. In the evenings after you two have bedded down in the barn, I can stay up and work on making my winter clothes, and during the day I can help harvest the garden." Glancing up at the rafters overhead, she added,

"As you see, I've got a good start on stringing the beans." Both men followed her gaze and realized she hadn't just hung flowers and herbs from the rafters but she had wreaths of beans drying up there as well.

While the men smiled at the girl's ingenuity, Copper turned to Shad and asked shyly, "The bean crop has been more than bountiful. Mister McKenna, would you consider trading me some of those beans for labor? When I leave here, they'll pack in my saddlebags as easily as jerked beef and they're almost as nourishing."

Preacher watched Shad nod his agreement to Copper's humble request, only to have his expression slide into a concerned frown. The very idea of this special young woman packing her saddlebags and traipsing around this high-country all alone wasn't setting well on the mountain man's tender heart.

Believing he knew what the Boss wanted him to do before he got back to doing God's business, Preacher began thinking of ways for Shad and Copper to become better acquainted. Just then, he smiled to himself; if The Boss was telling him to do some matchmaking, then he didn't need to get back to God's business. Matchmaking was God's business. Trusting that his next idea was inspired, Preacher said, "Miss Delaney as delicious as your pie was, I think Shad and I can show you a more practical use for those berries." Turning to his big friend he said, "You know we'd planned to make a big batch of pemmican and split it? Now that Miss Delaney is preparing to spend the winter up here…I think we should make an even bigger batch and divide it three ways. In fact, let's pick berries tomorrow and tackle that garden later. They're ripe and thick down there by the hot spring, but if we don't hurry—the bears will get them instead."

"Pe—pemmi—can…what's that?" Copper asked.

Shad's thoughts were far away. The idea of this sweet girl preparing for the harsh winter was filling him with dread. He imagined her and that big mule struggling through a snowdrift and not being able to find decent shelter or food. Winter in the lowlands of Colorado could be difficult but winter in the mountains was an entirely different beast. He couldn't help but admire her determination to take care of herself but he knew what she was up against—and she didn't!

"Shad—Shad, Miss Delaney wants to know what pemmican is?" Preacher asked the question for the second time. "I've always traded for mine. I've never made it so you'll have to explain."

When Shad realized he was being spoken to, he frowned, "Huh? Sorry, my mind was on all the things a body needs to do to prepare for winter in this high-country." He muttered as he turned to Copper adding, "If you expect to be alive come spring!" It shouldn't have, but somehow it was a relief to him when the young woman's green eyes grew wide. He frowned for a moment longer then answered her question, "Pemmican is—well—its Indian food, but an old trapper by the name of Black-Eyed Jack taught me how to make it. You mix together ground up jerked beef, dried berries and pine nuts with bone marrow and honey. I have plenty of honey but we'll need to hunt down a big elk or a moose, so we can get enough meat and enough marrow from their bones. There never seems to be enough pemmican. You still need to hunt every day ya can, all through the winter. I save mine to keep me strong while I'm out huntin' and for when game is scarce or if a blizzard or the cold makes huntin' downright impossible. You might get a little tired of it sometimes, but it ain't half-bad and it's real nourishin'. For many a soul it's made the difference between livin' and dyin'."

The following morning Remy, the crowing mule, brayed so loudly that both Shad and Preacher thought they were under attack. They jumped from their bedrolls, grabbed their guns and rushed from the barn. When they realized that they were standing in the middle of the yard, barefoot, still half asleep, and staring at nothing but an ugly mule...they couldn't help but laugh!

Shad shook his head and grunted, "Ya know, I traded Black-Eyed Jack three wolf pelts for some chickens and a rooster. He's supposed to bring them to me in a few weeks, but if that crazy mule stays around I don't reckon I'll need the rooster."

Preacher grinned and slapped Shad on the arm, "Do I need to remind you that—if you're going to *raise* chickens...you're gonna need a rooster! They do more important things than crow...or didn't you know that?"

Shad rolled his eyes and grunted at Preacher's jest, but just then, Copper stepped outside. The men were still not quite awake. They stood in the yard with prickly, bewhiskered faces and tousled hair, silently watching the pretty young woman make her way across the yard to the stack of firewood.

"Good morning, gentlemen." she called, her voice sounding soft and a bit timid.

Although both men nodded their heads in greeting, neither of them spoke nor did they offer to help. Instead, they simply enjoyed the pretty picture she made as the morning breeze blew her silky amber hair away from her face and caused her skirt and petticoats to press against her slim body and flutter behind her.

With her arms full, Copper hurried back to the cabin, calling over her shoulder, "Breakfast will be ready soon!"

Shad hadn't realized that he was holding his breath, but when the cabin door closed he released a lung full of air and groaned, "Ohhh, Preacher! I don't need to be reminded that a hen needs a rooster or that a rooster needs a hen. In fact—you remember how I spent all summer—trying to get a woman—pretty much any woman to come up here and be my wife. I wanted so badly for just one of them to like me. I just now realized that I wasn't much impressed with any of them, but she's something though, ain't she? That—*sweet girl*, I couldn't stop thinkin' of her all night. It took a heap o' gumption for her to run from that albino and come way up here all by herself. She must have been weak and hungry when she found this place, but she just jumped right in and tried to make a go of things up here. Every time I think of her or look at her, my mind turns to mush. I should o' spoken up just now, should o' helped her carry that firewood, but I'm as awkward as a schoolboy or a new colt whenever she's around. Why does she have to be so dad-gum sweet and pretty and worst of all a dozen years too young?"

Preacher smiled patiently. "I doubt that it's a dozen years, my friend, but so what if she is? I knew a man and wife that were fifteen years apart and I've never known a happier couple. Besides what you need to find out is, did God lead that *sweet girl*, here for *you*? Haven't you been praying for a wife, for someone that loves you and wants to live up here in these mountains?"

Shad frowned as he ran a hand through his shaggy black mane and pondered his friend's words as they gingerly returned to the barn, brushed off their bare feet and pulled on their boots.

Later, while the men finished their breakfast of porridge and biscuits, Copper set out baskets and pails. Soon the three were filling them with the wild berries that grew abundantly all over the hills that surrounded the cabin.

As the following days went by, each morning Remy called up the sun so passionately; it was as if the day could not begin without her help. At first, the mule's morning antics were amusing but it wasn't long before the men were complaining about the persistently vocal mule. Copper only laughed at their irritation, and insisted that Remy was an intelligent animal; she was not only a good rooster but a proper watchdog as well! The men were not impressed and continued to view the ugly beast as nothing but a nuisance. That is...until late one night when they were all sound asleep and Remy set up such a racket that Shad jumped from his bedroll intent on inventing the first mule muzzle. However, just then, something caught his eye and he turned to see a streak of tan race across the yard. The following night the men sat up and waited. They had just about given up when a mountain lion jumped onto the cabin's porch and headed for the open window. They shot the lion and from that day on—Remy, the watchdog, had their respect!

While the men's regard for Remy grew, so did their appreciation and esteem for young Copper. Every morning they fed the animals, washed up, then hurriedly made their way towards the cabin. As they stepped inside their senses were assaulted with the heavy aromas of wood smoke mingled with fresh coffee and biscuits. Copper was always busy when she greeted them, wearing either a blue or a green work dress. The later was Shad's favorite for it enhanced the color of her eyes. Sometimes they would catch her with her tawny hair flowing long and loose about her shoulders. Although, most often her silky locks were twisted into a no-nonsense braid that fell down her back like a bronze rope.

Each morning Preacher would greet her with a hearty hello and a broad grin but Shad was often tongue-tied, and would simply stand and watch her as if he were savoring the treasured vision of a pretty woman bustling about in his kitchen. He drank her in even as she handed him his morning coffee. As the three of them shared the work, the days were pleasant and their friendship grew as they gathered in the food and filled the cave beside the kitchen that Shad referred to as his pantry. Though the men tried to spare Copper the hardest of the work, she would have none of it and insisted on doing her share.

Harvesting the garden had been hard work, but when the men began digging up the last two rows of sweet potatoes, Preacher happened to glance back at Copper and saw a very melancholy girl. She was staring at the cabin, as if she trying to memorize every log and shingle. He knew she must have been remembering her promise that she would leave when the harvest was over—and—it nearly was. Wanting to put a smile back on her sweet face, he caught her attention and winked. Then he turned his back on her and slapped Shad on the shoulder, saying gruffly, “McKenna, you sure are slow. I’m a city boy—born and raised but—I bet even I am faster than you are!”

Shad stopped and frowned, but when Preacher gave a slight nod in Copper’s direction, Shad realized what he was trying to do and growled his reply, “Well now reverend, I’m thinkin; that you’re just mighty long on talk—Quincy—Long.”

A slow grin spread across Preacher’s face as he reached into his pocket, “Is that a challenge I hear Shadrack McKenna?” With an air of confidence, he handed Copper his watch, “Here Miss Delaney, you can time us. Three minutes should be long enough for me to show this poor fellow the most efficient way to dig up a row of potatoes. When you’re ready just—uh—yell go!”

Copper quickly wiped her hands on her apron before she took the fancy watch. However, she was completely baffled at the notion that these grown men were suddenly acting like—well—like two boys—who were both determined to see who was king of the hill. A moment later, she found that their playfulness was contagious and she began enjoying this rare moment of fun. Realizing that neither man was ready, a spark of impish delight filled her eyes and she shouted, “Go. You said, just yell go. So…GO!”

Both men were startled but Shad was the first to drop to the ground. Preacher was right behind him and instantly the dirt began to fly. Copper giggled and goaded them on. “Oh, come now—even old Ma Riley could dig faster than that!” she teased.

Though the men grunted their protest, they both picked up the pace. Copper couldn’t stop laughing as she watched these two giants scrambling down the rows and realized that neither man intended to play fair. Shad grabbed a fist full of dirt and shoved it down Preacher’s back collar. Preacher retaliated by pushing Shad over. They tossed clods of dirt and did everything possible to get in each other’s way while they struggled to fill their own sack. There was so much laughter, grunting and dirt flying, that Copper doubted if either of them managed to harvest anything. Anything but dirt—that is.

“Times up.” she called. “Stop you two—stop. Hey, no cheating—STOP!”

Covered in dirt from head to heel, the men finally stopped their digging and groaned loudly as they sprawled out on the ground, panting and chuckling. They blinked the grit from their eyes and shook the dirt from their hair all the while struggling to catch their breath.

Preacher grimaced as he rose easily to his feet. His shirttail had been neatly tucked in but when he pulled it out…clods of dirt fell to the ground. When both Shad and Copper laughed, he rolled his eyes, "Shadrack McKenna, you scoundrel, I feel like I'm wearing this garden—and—I think you put an ant hill down my back…along with the dirt!" The big man frowned but he looked amused as he wriggled uncomfortably, "Miss Delaney, I'd appreciate it if you'd hurry up and count those potatoes. Once you declare me the winner, I'll take myself, along with the dozen or so new friends I've acquired, and head down to the hot springs for a bath. Then I'll come back and collect my prize!"

"You silly men." Copper said with a bemused grin. "You never said what the winner gets!" While clucking her tongue she stepped over Shad's long legs then reached down and grabbed both sacks. "While I'm counting you two better hurry up and decide what you want for a prize!"

As she suspected both sacks had more dirt than potatoes but when Copper added them up, there was a winner. Walking over to Shad, who was still lying on the ground, she held out her hand. "You're the winner by two potatoes. Congratulations!" she beamed.

When Shad and Copper reached for each other's hand, it had seemed like such an innocent thing to do. However, the moment they touched, a lightning bolt of awareness passed between them. It was so obvious that they both looked at each other—and their eyes locked. Still holding her hand Shad got to his feet while Copper stuttered, "Con—congratulations, M-Mister McKenna."

"Thanks!" Shad grinned, "but—uh—you already said that."

Copper's stuttered words and blushing cheeks filled Shad with a joyful hope. He had feared it was a one sided attraction. As he studied her now though, he could see it in her beautiful eyes. They changed from a soft clover green to a dark velvety emerald. What did he want for his prize? Now Shad's face grew rosy and warm. All he could think of was a kiss for the winner.

When Preacher saw the longing in his friend's eyes, he loudly cleared his throat. Suddenly aware that she had been standing there in a near trance, Copper quickly looked away and withdrew her hand. Keeping her eyes down cast she said self-consciously, "You know—I—uh, I supposed I could be talked into cooking the winner whatever he wants for supper. Would that be an acceptable prize?"

No, Shad thought, kissing Copper was still foremost in his mind and he couldn't seem to think of anything else. Finally he muttered, "Preacher—you started all this, if you hadn't been so slow, what would you have chosen?"

It was all Preacher could do to keep from laughing at these two. The attraction was so obvious. Shad was thrilled and Copper was frightened and perplexed…but it was happening just the same.

In answer to Shad's question, Preacher grinned, "You wouldn't have to ask me twice. I know exactly what I'd want." He picked his hat up off the ground, slapped it against his leg and said, "I would have asked this fine lady to bake me a sweet potato pie."

"Well now, I think we can make that the prize for second place." Copper announced, hoping the men couldn't hear the slight tremor in her voice. Glancing back at Shad and being careful not to look the man in the eye she asked, "So, Mister McKenna, what's the prize for first place?"

Shad's expression was sad, something special had just passed between them but now she was pulling away from him again—and he didn't like it. He studied her for a long moment then said with a tender gaze and gentle words, "First of all, I'd like to think that we've become friends in the past few weeks, I sure would like for you call me Shad. And allow me to call you Copper. As for my prize—it may sound silly to you, but I really like those little fried corn cakes you made the other day. So, I'd like to have a big batch of corn cakes with honey."

Copper surprised the men, when her green eyes suddenly grew glassy with tears. Biting her lip, she shook her head and dabbed at her eyes with the back of her hand. "I certainly would like to meet the women that raised you two." she mused. "Both of you are so kind and so—undemanding. I never would have guessed there were any men in this whole world as nice as the two of you. Mister Mc…I mean Shad," she said awkwardly, "are you sure that's all what you want? I think you're just trying to make it easy on me. I'd happily make anything you like!"

"I know you would, but even so ma'am, that's what I want." The look Shad gave her just then, and his words were spoken so tenderly, Copper felt almost as if the man had hugged her. She was still wondering at that when Shad added, "Speaking of the woman that raised me at least, those little corn cakes remind me of Maudy McKenna. You would have liked my Ma and she surely would have been proud to meet you. Ma would have taken one look at ya and said, "Why little darlin' yer as pretty as a bug's ear and twice as sweet!"

Chapter 8
Hope and a Future

"A wife of noble character who can find? She is worth more than rubies." Proverbs 31:10

Copper sat on the back porch of the cabin and looked out over the now empty garden. Thinking of what Shad had said, she chuckled and shook her head. "Well, Maudy McKenna, I wish you were sitting here with me. I wonder if you really would look at my straight, red hair and proclaim that I was as pretty—as a bug's ear!"

Actually, Shad's words had pleased Copper. After she discovered the woman's grave, she had felt a kinship with Maudy McKenna. In fact, on lonely days, before Shad and Preacher had come, Copper had often talked to the old woman for whom this wonderful place had been built. She spoke to Maudy while planting wild flowers at her grave, while she scrubbed her floors and hung her curtains. When Shad had returned to his cabin, he had placed a tintype of his mother on the mantle and Copper thought the old woman had the sweetest face she'd ever seen. Now she had just finished helping Maudy's son harvest a bountiful garden and had stocked his cavern pantry for the coming winter. It was all so bittersweet. It was obvious that Shad loved this place and that he belonged here. Copper tried not to feel sorry for herself, but after a summer full of hard work and preparation, her future was still as bleak and uncertain, as it had been when she'd left the Riley farm.

I'm sorry Lord. I know you've been providing for me all along. I had a wonderful summer and Shad and Preacher's friendship is a gift. I know worry dishonors you. I am trying to believe and trust that even though things look bad just now...that you're still going to work everything out.

Shaking off her fears, she purposely tried to think of something more positive. Gazing about, she noticed the patch of Evening Stars that grew along the garden fence. The flower didn't have much to recommend it. At least not during the day, its stems and leaves were scraggly and as rough as sandpaper. Each evening, though, as the sun faded in the sky, their pointed petals of white satin would open wide. At night the humdrum plant became a romantic flower; Copper suddenly wondered if God hadn't made it especially for lovers strolling in the moonlight.

Whatever made me think of that? I'm like Ma Riley. I look at the practical side of things. I have no time or desire for romance. Besides there is a practical purpose for the Evening Star. Ma said to pound out the yellow juice inside the stems, and then boil it for a poultice to ease a fever.

Copper sighed, the afternoon was fading and soon the sun would be swallowed up behind the jagged horizon, but as she walked to the fence and examined the night blooming flowers, the thought of cutting them down made her sad. "They should probably grow a while longer," she told herself. Of course if she had another project it would be another excuse to stay a few more days. It seemed she could only justify her presence here if there was work to be done. "I'll never be anything but a servant girl." She huffed.

Her stiff back was a reminder that she *had been working*—pretty much non-stop since she'd first spotted this cabin. Leaning against the fence, she stretched her tired body and stared up at the sky. What she saw brought a gasp of wonder, for floating above her were dozens of thin, feather-like clouds.

When Shad stepped out the back door, Copper grinned and pointed towards the sky, "Come and look—with the sun shining on those clouds they almost look like an army of golden angels flying through the sky."

Walking across the now empty garden, Shad nodded in agreement, "They surely do. I don't recall seeing clouds like that before." Then he grinned adding, "Maybe they really are angels—just stopping by to say hello."

A pained expression clouded Copper's face, "Just another sign that this place really is a—little bit of heaven!"

Shad caught the emotion in her voice and drew in a deep breath as he stepped closer, "Yeah—it sure does seem like it—especially since you've been here." When Copper walked away from him, Shad followed, "Ya know," he said gently, "this was the best harvest I ever had. And—I have the good Lord and *you* to thank for it." Just then, they glanced at each other but this time they both quickly looked away. There was a feeling of unspoken sadness that hovered between them. Copper had said that she would leave when they finished the harvest but no one had spoken of it since.

They turned their eyes back up at the sky, only to see that the delicate clouds were melting away and in their place flew three buzzards. The dark birds stretched their wings, spanning nearly five feet with white tipped feathers that fluttered like fingers. Expertly adjusting their course, they floated smoothly on the high-mountain current. Shading her eyes Copper smiled as she watched the birds gracefully circle and circle again, in an ever-expanding search for food.

Following her gaze, Shad hissed bitterly, "I hate those things! Ought to get my gun and take care of 'em. Saw too many when I was in the war—wicked, dirty creatures."

Copper had never heard anger in this man's voice before and she was surprised that it didn't frighten her. Instead, she felt the pain in his voice and without thinking; she gently placed her hand on his arm. "I can only imagine how you feel," she said softly. "But…since I've become a Christian, I've come to see things differently. I've come to realize that God has given all of His creations specific jobs to do. Not all jobs are pleasant. The Bible says that, we are to walk humbly before our God. I think the buzzard must be a humble bird. He's the ultimate tracker but he doesn't hunt down and kill his food." Copper smiled softly as she stared at the birds but Shad couldn't take his eyes from her sweet upturned face as she continued to speak. "You see the buzzard must be content to live on what other animals leave behind or on those who have died from sickness or age. He's given buzzards the unpleasant task of keeping the world clean. He doesn't ask for more than his due. Yet look at how gracefully he does his job, and without complaint."

Shad soaked in Copper's words. He'd been just a boy when he lost his father, the war years had taken their toll and then he came up here only to lose his sweet mother. He'd been lonely for years and felt as if he had been living his life in darkness. From the beginning he'd thought of Copper as special. Now, she seemed to him like the first rays of sunshine breaking through a bleak and moonless night.

Shad turned away when he felt his eyes clouding. Finally, he swallowed and said gruffly. "Thank you for that. Seeing those dark creatures has always stirred up—dark memories for me. But now I—well I think I'll always see them—in the way you've just described." Shad leaned towards her, "Miss Delaney—Copper, yer so young, but even so, yer quite a woman too—do ya know that? Just as pretty on the inside as ya are on the outside…

and…I…" Words suddenly failed Shad and he lowered his head, even as Copper lifted hers.

The tender moment vanished when a loud, happy whistle came from the path that led from to the river. Shad quickly stepped away and Copper felt confused. Soon they saw Preacher's tall form ambling towards the back garden.

The man couldn't stop a slow smile from spreading across his face, for he knew that he had most likely interrupted the prelude to a first kiss. Silently he lifted up a prayer. *Well, Boss, things seem to be progressing rather well between those two. It hasn't been easy playing, both cupid and chaperon. Nevertheless, it's time for me to be moving on. So, please help me—help them—take the next step.*

Holding up his stringer of rainbow trout Preacher grinned, his white teeth a sharp contrast to his tanned face, "Miss Delaney," he said with mock formality, "these fish have requested the honor of joining us for supper. I don't know what you had in mind but—I sure would like to oblige them!"

Feeling terribly self-conscious, Copper managed to force a smile then say, "If you clean them…I'll cook them. I'll go fetch you a bucket of water."

Hoping that the men hadn't noticed her burning cheeks, she hurried into the cabin, went straight to the pump and then splashed cold water on her face. It took a few minutes before she even remembered why she'd come inside. Finally, she began pumping water into the bucket, but her mind was reeling. Had Shad truly meant to kiss her? What surprised her most of all was that she felt an aching loss when he had stepped away. Somehow she'd become infatuated with the big mountain man. It was then that Matilda Barr's solemn warning rang in her ears, "It's a fact of nature that women are drawn to men just like a moth is drawn to a flame. The results are the same—most the time—all ya get is a bad burn. You be especially wary of the handsome man or the one that tells ya pretty lies. And don't ya never forget, it's in a man's nature to lose his temper and when he does—his woman and children will suffer for it!"

Matilda's words tormented Copper, she wanted to be near Shad and she wanted to run from him at the same time. In her heart, she believed that he was a cut above all the other men. Then again, if he truly was a better man then what would he want with her? After all, Copper Delaney was nothing but a penniless orphan with ugly, carrot-red hair and a freckled face. How many times had Percy Barr told her that she was not the kind of girl a decent man would want to marry? "Men only want a girl like you as a servant or a whore—nothin' more." Then he had always laughed at what he thought a clever rhyme. Still—his words shamed her.

While working the pump handle, Copper's mind filled with fear. The only men she'd truly been acquainted with, from her father and Crookshank to Vernon and Dirk…had only wanted to use her or hurt her, one way or another. Still her thoughts kept turning to the kind-hearted and handsome mountain man. Shad wouldn't have tried to steal a kiss from a girl he didn't care about—would he? No—she was certain, that he would not, so then perhaps Shad had marriage on his mind. The thought at first made her heart soar…but then it fell. What would she do if he turned out to be like all the others? Copper shook her head at the idea—that she just could not bear. Suddenly, her past fears took over and she knew that it was time for her to leave. Finally, she had her freedom and she would not give it up. Glancing about the cabin she loved, she realized that she would not stay long enough to harvest the blossoms of the Evening Star—nor would she allow herself to dream of romantic moonlight walks. With stern resolve Copper reminded herself that she had come to these mountains to find gold and when she'd found it, she could be independent. That's what was best for her. Tomorrow, she and Remy would pack up and be on their way!

When Copper brought the bucket of water outside, the men couldn't help but notice that her face was pale and her eyes were red rimmed. They said nothing when she forced a smile and said, "I hope you two are both hungry. Tonight we'll have a party! We'll have fried trout with onion, beans, corn cakes with honey and sweet potato pie for desert." She wavered for just a moment then added, "It will be a harvest celebration and a—fa—farewell dinner." Copper tried to sound light hearted, but when both men frowned, she simply stared over their heads at the high mountain ridges and said softly. "I've been thinking. It's time for me to get on about my business. We've finished the harvest and last night I even finished my winter coat." She tried again to look at them but when she couldn't she stared at the ground, "It really is past time for me to be on my way. Remy and I will be leaving—first thing in the morning."

Shad felt like he'd been sucker punched. He couldn't imagine why Copper was in such a hurry to leave. He knew she loved his cabin and these mountains, not to mention that the girl had no place else to go. Maybe it was just the mountain man she didn't cotton to. Shad rubbed the back of his neck and struggled for something to say. When nothing came to mind he shrugged, "Well—I reckon—I'll just go feed the stock."

Preacher blew out a sigh as he watched Shad walk away. Of course he also couldn't help but notice Copper's chin begin to quiver, just before she spun on her heals and disappeared inside the cabin. When he entered the barn and found Shad leaning on a pitchfork with a look of pure misery on his face, he hefted a grain sack over his shoulder and poured equal amounts into three buckets for Boone, Flint and Remy. He had to pry the pitchfork from Shad's hands, so he could fill their mangers with hay. Still, Preacher couldn't help but be amused when his big friend began pacing back and forth—and each time he passed the barn door, he'd stop, gaze at the cabin, then mutter, "That poor little thing. That poor, foolish, head strong, stubborn little thing! Reckon I can't blame her for not wantin' a rough-cut man like me, but what's to become of her? She told us she got lost and was nearly starvin' when she found this place. A few minutes ago…I thought…and now she says... Oh Preacher, she ain't makin' a bit of sense."

"Yes, there's a lot of that going around." Preacher grunted. Holding back a smile he added, "Listen my friend, I see God's hand at work here but you still have to do your part. Shadrack McKenna—you're as smitten as a bull moose in autumn. You asked every female in all of Canyon City to marry you this past summer, so why haven't you bothered to propose to this one? And just what makes you think 'that poor little thing' doesn't want you? The way you two look at each other, it's downright painful to watch. You could be a blessing to her and she to you."

Shad shook his head, "I don't know Preacher. You heard what she said, sounds like she's downright anxious to—be on her way!" Shad suddenly turned to his friend, "What do you mean—how does she look at me?"

"Well, you know that sweeter than molasses smile she gets when she's polishing the mantle? Well, it's like that. Every time you do or say something nice, and then walk away, those big green eyes follow you and they get all misty."

"I don't believe it." Shad grunted. "I won't argue that she loves m' cabin. Wish I could believe she thought half as much o' me."

A rare frown marred Preacher's face, "McKenna." he said sternly, "If you care about this woman, you are going to have to look at things through her eyes. That woman has been taught to serve and expect nothing in return. What's more, it seems every man she's ever known has been abusive and cruel. We've both noticed the terrible scars on her arms and we both know she has other wounds that can't be seen. I truly believe she has strong feelings for you but she's afraid to trust them—to trust you. I've prayed a lot about this and I believe God approves of this union. Still, I must warn you that a true marriage with Copper is going to take more than just a wedding ceremony. You my friend are going to have to be incredibly gentle and have Job's own patience to be able to overcome her fears."

Shad scratched his head, "Yer worryin' me Preacher. I know I can be gentle but patient—that'll take some doin'."

Copper nervously opened the trunk Preacher had carried down from the attic. Once again, her life was about to take another one of its turns, but she honestly didn't know if it was a turn that went downwards, upwards or sideways. Just last night she had agreed to Shad's proposal of marriage and now she struggled to remember exactly how it had all come about.

Their big farewell dinner had turned out to be awkward and painfully quiet. Feeling miserable, all Copper could do was push the food around her plate. Actually, they were all behaving strangely. Shad kept stealing glances at her but he never said anything—Preacher wasn't much better. So much for their celebrating the harvest and farewell dinner. No one was talking nor was anyone eating.

Finally, Preacher sighed and cleared his throat, "My dear Miss Delaney," he began, "this is a lovely meal, but none of us have an appetite tonight. I'm afraid it's because we all have more important things on our minds—don't we?" When Copper kept her eyes downcast and nodded sadly, he continued, "Now, ever since we met, we three have been praying that God would reveal His plan. These past few weeks I've watched you and Shad—and well—I believe that The Boss has given His answer. You see Shad here has asked me to help him—speak to you. He's concerned that you might feel coerced into making a hasty decision because I need to be leaving soon to tend my mountain ministry. Still, neither of us wants to rush you."

Copper's soft green eyes looked especially bright as they slid from one man to the other. "Rush me? Preacher, I'm—confused. What are you trying to say or is it what is Shad trying to say?"

Shad ran his hand over his thick black mustache and sighed, "Oh, never mind Preacher. I reckon I should be the one to speak after all."

Copper was suddenly petrified. She couldn't manage to look at either man. Instead, she stared at her hands. When they began to tremble she clasped them tightly together then pushed them firmly into her lap. She felt Shad turning towards her, heard him say something, but could barely hear him over the pounding of her heart.

"Miss Copper," he began, "I mean Miss Delaney…no…I mean… Copper. We've only known each other a short time but…I've been prayin' real hard and I think that God would bless the idea of Copper Delaney and Shadrack McKenna joining forces."

She didn't understand what he meant, keeping her eyes downcast, Copper asked softly, "Join…forces?"

Shad suddenly remembered all the past rejections he'd suffered from the women in Canyon City and he couldn't tell if Copper's pale face was a sign of confusion or just plain disgust. Blowing out a breath he groaned, "Woman. What I meant was…will you marry me? Preacher needs to leave tomorrow but he could marry us before he goes. I know I'm not much but I can take good care of ya. What do ya say?"

Preacher winced at Shad's impatient tone and clumsy words. He saw Copper's head snap up defensively and her eyes grow wide. He knew that Shad was afraid of another rejection but Copper was dealing with a much greater fear. Still, he believed whole-heartedly that these two would make a good match.

Not really believing Shad meant what he said, Copper frowned and turned to him, "Mister McKenna," she asked softly. "Your life is so wonderful and free up here—why would you want to marry? I always thought men preferred freedom over marriage."

Despite his earlier clumsiness, Shad very gently took Copper's hand from her lap and held it in his. "It is a free spirited life in the high-country—that's true. But take my word on it—it's not nearly so nice when yer up here all by yer lonesome. I've been hankerin' fer a special gal to share my cabin with for a long time now. I think yer as special as they come. I'm older than you, maybe ten years or so, and I reckon I'm a bit rough around the edges. Don't mean to brag but I can be pretty handy. I'd be a good provider." Shad rubbed his chin then his green eyes looked imploringly, "I've been prayin' for a wife and I think yer the one. As you've already learned, stayin' warm and fed ain't always easy up here. The fact is you need a husband. A man that would hunt for ya and keep ya safe. I'd sure like to be that man. I'm thinkin' that we both might just be God's answer to each other's prayers. So—please—will ya marry me?"

Just then Copper turned to see what Preacher had to say, but was surprised to find that he had quietly slipped away. Shad smiled and leaned towards Copper, hoping to convince her with a kiss. However, Copper frowned, moved her chair back and stood to her feet.

"Mister McKenna," she asked, sounding a bit like her schoolmaster father. "Would you mind asking Preacher to come back inside? I need to speak to him—alone."

Although Shad tried, he did a poor job of hiding his disappointment. Sighing, he managed to nod in agreement and then head for the barn.

When Preacher entered the cabin, Copper was standing by the fireplace, her hands clasped in front of her. With her chin lifted, almost defiantly, she stared right into the man's dark blue eyes and asked, "With God as your witness, will you answer two questions with complete honesty?" When he nodded his head Copper asked, "First, does Shadrack McKenna *want* me to be his wife or does he feel sorry for a poor unwanted waif—who has no place to go? And more importantly—is Shadrack McKenna the kind of man who when angered or upset would yell and threaten or especially hit or mistreat his family?"

Preacher's face took on a somber expression as he stepped close to Copper and rested one hand on her shoulder, "To the best of my knowledge, Shadrack McKenna is an honorable man and is sincere in his devotion to God. I believe he cares deeply for you and with his whole being wants you to be his wife. I think it will break his heart if you say no. He is just a man though, a flawed human being, just as I am. I won't promise that he will never lose his temper and yet if there was ever a man that I would trust to always be kind to women and children…it is Shadrack McKenna."

Copper pondered his words while she paced back and forth, shaking her head and muttering to herself. Preacher was convinced that her answer was no. Then she surprised him when she suddenly looked up at him and said, "I know you've stayed here longer than you intended—but—could we please wait until morning to have the wedding?"

Preacher let out the breath he hadn't known he was holding and grinned, "Yes ma'am—I'll go tell Shad! But first the groom wanted me to give you a gift." He climbed the ladder to the attic and quickly returned with a small trunk on his shoulder. She'd seen it before, but it was locked and she hadn't tried to open it. The wooden box had beautifully scrolled letters spelling out the name: *Maudy Duncan-McKenna*. He pulled a key from his pocket and unlocked it, saying, "Shad told me that if you said yes, I was to give this to you. His mother's wedding gown is inside, among other things he thought you might find useful. He said the trunk and all that's in it belong to you, now. Whatever you wish to do with it—is—fine with him."

As Copper dressed the following morning, her feelings ranged from moments of outright panic to a state of overwhelming peace. It was a beautiful day and it seemed as if the sunshine fairly danced through the windows. As if God himself were saying, trust me, this is right! Just now though, she didn't want to think about marriage. To Copper, the blessing was that she could stay here, in this little bit of heaven. Of course her thoughts would inevitably turn to Shadrack McKenna and when they did—she would instantly stiffen her spine and tell herself: "That big mountain man is the perfect answer to all my troubles—and—I will work harder for him than I have for anyone else—nothing has to change—everything's going to be fine."

Maudy McKenna's trunk had turned out to be a gold mine. It held not only a lovely dress, but a corset, petticoats, and even a dainty pair of satin slippers. Copper wondered if this gown had not only been worn by Maudy but perhaps her mother and grandmother as well. Still, everything was lovingly wrapped, awaiting future generations and wedding days to come. On a sentimental whim, Copper ran to the mantle and took down Maudy's picture. She set it on the bed, as if allowing her mother-in-law to keep her company. "Oh, Maudy," she whispered, "Thank you for raising such a fine son!"

Copper knew she was being a bit silly, but somehow the woman's kind face was a comfort to her, and she smiled at the picture as she gracefully stepped into her wedding gown. Maudy must have been a bit taller but other than that, it was a perfect fit—and absolutely lovely. Copper had never before worn anything as fine or as elegant. The fabric had probably been a pale buttery-yellow when new, but the years had deepened the color to a rich tawny-gold. If there had been a matching hat or veil, it had not survived the years. Copper was disappointed for she had hoped for something to cover her head, for she knew in the sunlight her hair looked like it was on fire. Just then however, she spotted the pitcher that sat on the kitchen table. As a decoration, she had filled it with aspen branches with variegated shades of autumn leaves ranging from olive green and pale yellow to a golden russet. Searching again through Maudy's trunk, Copper tore some beige lace from an old petticoat. Her hands worked quickly as she fashioned a dainty wreath for her head, using the lace to tie the branches together. Then with long, firm strokes, she brushed her thick hair until it shone, and trailed down her back, nearly touching her small waste. Finally, she peered into Shad's shaving mirror while she settled the wreath on the crown of her head.

Smiling at her reflection she whispered, "Just one more thing to do!"

When Copper finally appeared at the top of the hill, she stopped to gather her courage and steady her nerves. But when the men saw her, neither one would have guessed that she was afraid. Their only thoughts were of how poised and beautiful she looked. Maudy McKenna's dress shone like spun gold in the sunlight and with the lovely wreath upon her head, Copper looked more like an enchanted forest sprite than the frightened young woman she was. Shad's mouth went dry as his bride slowly made her way down the hill. Copper described her hair as straight, ugly and carrot-red but to Shad, it was nothing short of sun kissed bronze. And he loved the way it spilled over one shoulder, all silky and long.

"Thank—you—Lord!" Shad sighed, and then he grinned when he heard Preacher respond with a hearty, "Yes Boss—thank you indeed."

The romantic vision didn't last for long, because in the next instant, both men began to laugh. For closely following the beautiful, blushing bride, was her dearest friend, her oversized dapple-gray mule, Remy. The beast's forelock was even adorned with a lacy ribbon.

Preacher slapped Shad on the back, "I had wondered about witnesses!"

Shad was amused, but the distraction was short lived for he quickly turned his full attention back to his bride. An unexpected thrill passed through Copper when she saw the big man's appreciative smile, his dark green eyes sparkling as he held out his hand to her. "I've pictured this day for a long while now, but Copper Delaney, soon to be Missus McKenna, yer more beautiful than anything I ever dreamed up!"

The men were standing on a large petrified stump just behind the cabin and Shad carefully helped his bride stand next to him. Grinning with happiness, Shad curled his large hand around her much smaller one and teased, “I see you’ve invited a guest.”

Lifting her eyes from their joined hands, Copper shyly gazed into Shad’s handsome face, “She’s been my best friend for a long time—you don’t mind do you?”

Copper’s face was so radiant and her voice so utterly innocent and sweet, Shad could only smile and shake his head. At that moment he couldn’t imagine objecting to anything this woman ever said or did. He would have allowed her to invite a grizzly bear, if it would have kept that same sweet smile on her pretty face.

As they settled into their places, a reverent hush fell over the meadow. Surely, there were other forest sounds but Shad and Copper heard only Preacher’s deep voice as he began to speak.

“In Proverbs is says, ‘In everything you do put God first and He will direct you and crown your efforts with success.’ A Christian marriage is the joining of three, God, a husband and a wife. If your relationship with God is strong—He will keep your marriage strong. Although you two are starting your life together, almost as strangers, the vows you are taking today are no less valid or binding. I wholeheartedly believe that God led you here Copper, just as I believe that God sent Shad down the mountain to become a Christian and then sent him back here so that you two could be together. You’ve become friends in the past two weeks and you’ve a life time ahead of you to learn to love each other as God intends.”

Preacher smiled when he glanced up and saw that Shad and Copper were both blushing. His smile broadened when he noticed Shad giving Copper’s hand a slight squeeze. Clearing his throat, he continued. “Honor God first and then make every effort to be respectful and kind to each other. Those are the tools that will help you build a successful marriage. It won’t be as easy as it sounds. I know, I’m just a bachelor, but I learned this by watching my parents. My prayer is that you two will have the kind of happy marriage that they enjoyed. A successful couple learns to experience the challenges of life through each other’s eyes. Men and women look at the world quite differently but if you try to see things through your partner’s eyes, you’ll not only show them respect but you will begin to understand who your mate really is. Again, this advice sounds so simple but relationships everywhere are destroyed due to the lack of basic kindness and respect!”

The mountain preacher stopped to allow the couple to think on what he'd just said. He never really sermonized at weddings, reasoning that enough was as good as a feast. Then he led them in saying their vows.

At first, Copper was overwhelmed by the beautiful ceremony. Then, being the practical girl she was, she remembered that she was marrying Shadrack McKenna, because it made the most sense—for both of them. Before going to sleep the night before she had prayed and read in her Bible that...*God would supply all her needs.* This marriage to Shad was God providing what she needed. He had led her to this place and to Shad—hadn't He? She couldn't deny that she had feelings for the handsome mountain man. Even now strange little bubbles of happiness welled up inside her, simply because he was holding her hand. Her groom had sounded so sweet and so very sincere as he promised to love and cherish her. A moment later, it was her turn to promise to love and—*obey.* They didn't know each other well enough for a deep heartfelt love but physical love would be expected. Was Shad anticipating a wedding night—and if she refused, would he remind her of her vows and order her to obey? Copper's heart began to pound. She just couldn't—not yet—not until she knew for sure that he wouldn't use her promises against her. It was all so confusing. As a new Christian, she knew she should honor her vows and trust that God was in control and that Shad was a good man. And yet, the girl that had never trusted men looked at him and saw a man she didn't really know all that well. A big man—a very—strong man. She wanted to believe that he would never hurt her but sooner or later, everyone loses their temper. And when a bear of a man like McKenna lost his temper—what would he do? He could do a lot of damage to a girl like her, a lot of damage.

Preacher couldn't help but notice that both the bride and groom were growing paler by the minute. He wished he or Shad had thought to pick a bouquet of flowers for the bride. It seemed that with nothing to hold, Copper had begun to nervously rub her free hand up and down her side. Even though the woman looked radiant throughout the first part of the ceremony, the moment she promised to love and obey she began to lose her composure. When Shad noticed Copper's discomfort, he too began to fidget and frown with concern, which seemed to frighten the already anxious bride. Fearing that Copper might suddenly change her mind, Preacher quickly chose to omit the part about sealing the marriage with a kiss, choosing instead to end the ceremony with a fervent prayer, "Heavenly Father, by your grace and the promises these two have made, they are now husband and wife. We are trusting that you will sanctify this union between Shadrack and Copper. And that you will bless them as they begin a new life together, and please Lord, with each new day, give them a special understanding and a deep and abiding love for You first and then for each another. In Jesus' name. Amen."

Grinning broadly Preacher shook Shad's hand and hugged Copper. "Well now, congratulations Mister and Missus McKenna. I think we should declare a—holiday. Why don't we celebrate by having a picnic down by the river?"

In no time at all the small wedding party was back in the cabin. In his easy way, Preacher soon had the new couple relaxed and laughing as he told them of his most amusing adventures at sea, while they packed what Copper proclaimed to be a banquet. Soon they paraded down to the river with baskets and blankets in hand. The animals were even invited. Boone and Flint were hobbled in the lush meadow that flanked the river. Remy on the other hand roamed freely. Ever-faithful, she stayed close, keeping a vigilant eye on Copper. The equines cropped grass while the humans lunched on roasted venison sandwiches and potato salad with sugar cookies for dessert. It was a glorious autumn day, and somehow Copper pushed away her fears and every thought of marriage or of Shad as her husband. Instead, she reminded herself over and over—that her life was good. For she was home—at long last—she was finally home!

Later that evening, as he had on previous nights, Shad brought out his chessboard. Both men were surprised when Copper admitted, after all this time, that she knew how to play chess as well. She further surprised them when she made her bold challenge, "I'll play the winner…unless you men are afraid to lose!"

Most of the time it was Preacher who won these matches, but that night, Shad was the winner. Patting the nervous groom on the back, Preacher yawned and explained that he hoped to get an early start for Otter Run in the morning.

Though the chess matches between the men often took hours, Copper was surprised at how quickly she won her first match against Shad. Just as she checkmated his King, the man stood up awkwardly, "Uh, why don't you go ahead and get ready for bed. I always like to check on the stock before I go to sleep. I know Preacher's out there—but I can never rest unless I check things out for myself. So—I—uh—I'll be back in a little while."

When his young wife gazed up at him and blinked her large green eyes like a deer staring into a shotgun, Shad tried to give her what he hoped was a reassuring smile before he quickly left the cabin. It was then, that Copper remembered, for the first time in hours, that this was Shad's wedding night. "Oh Lord, help me—" she breathed, then she put her hands to her burning cheeks, "At the very least he'll expect to sleep in his own bed—but not with me!"

Copper had never moved so fast in her life. She ran towards the bedroom and changed into her nightgown with neck breaking speed. Racing around the cabin in her bare feet, she yanked one of the pillows from the bed and pulled an old quilt from Maudy McKenna's trunk. Just as Shad was coming through the front door, she leapt onto the parlor settee and covered herself with the blanket, tucking it up under her chin.

Slightly flushed and out of breath from her sprint around the cabin, Copper glanced at her new husband with a look of wide-eyed terror. Shad stopped in the doorway and tried to make sense of what he was seeing. His new little bride was staring at him, her expression held both the look of fear and of challenge. He tried to hide his disappointment as he closed the door behind him.

"Well—I'm back—now." Shad said, feeling like a complete fool. She could see that for herself, and it was obvious that she wasn't overly pleased about it. Rubbing the back of his neck he tried to think how best to handle this. Copper was obviously terrified. He could tell that she was as happy to see him, as she would have been to see a grizzly come walking through the door. Frankly, he was a little nervous himself—but not so nervous that it would have deprived him of his wedding night. Just then, however, he remembered what Preacher had said, try to look at things through your spouse's eyes. *I've got to be kind and respectful*, he told himself, then he waved his thumb at the massive pine bed with its four carved posts and peaceful forest scene. "You know…I made that thing big enough for two." Then he added gently, "I guarantee you won't be comfortable on that little settee. It wasn't made for sleepin'—" he ran a hand over his jaw and gave a slight chuckle, adding, "fact is—that thing isn't all that comfortable fer sittin'."

Copper straightened her blanket and stared at Shad. "You don't have to worry about me…this is better than anything my previous owners provided for me. The Barr's had me sleep in a hammock under the wagon, most nights and…"

Shad's face suddenly grew hard as he stopped her from saying more. "Hold on there, I know a little about what your past has been like, but—you are Missus Shadrack McKenna now. I am your husband. I've promised to protect and cherish you. I am—I am not your owner!"

When the big man's green eyes grew dark and he raised his voice and stepped closer to prove that he meant what he said, Copper's face paled and her eyes grew wide and wary. She knew every man had his breaking point, and when his temper reached it, he would strike out with whatever was his preferred weapon. When she saw that his hands were clenched into fists, she glanced towards them and then towards the back door to gauge how many steps it would take her to reach it. Her heart raced faster and faster while a voice seemed to whisper: *No man can be trusted. Run, Copper, run while you can!*

Following his bride's terrified gaze from his eyes to his fisted hands, then to the back door. Shad realized that he was scaring the woman he wanted only to comfort. It was their first hour alone and he was already doing everything wrong. He drew in a calming breath and then slowly blew it out.

Preacher warned me about this. Ain't gonna be easy.

Softening both his stance and his tone he said, "I'm sorry, sweet girl, please forgive me for frightening you. You never need to be afraid o' me! You are my cherished wife. I promised to care for you and I don't in anyway think of you as my property. It makes me sick to think that there have been so many that have treated you as such, but you've got to know that I will never hurt you!"

When Copper still looked fearful and her breathing was still coming too fast, he said, "Hey now, this is all new to me too. There is no need to be scared. I know we don't really know each other very well. But like Preacher said at our wedding, I plan to always respect you and be kind to you." Shad lowered his head and held out his hand as his eyes locked with hers, "Come to bed, so you'll be comfortable. I won't hurt you. I won't even touch you if you don't want me to."

Biting her lip, Copper stared at the man's out stretched hand. In the firelight, her green eyes were glassy with tears and she shook her head and frowned. "If—if you truly respect me—and if you want to *be kind* to me—then please—allow me to choose where I sleep!"

Again, Preacher's words came to Shad's mind, 'Even if Copper agrees to become your wife you'll have to be patient. She's never trusted a man before.' Realizing that this is what Preacher had been talking about, Shad gave his new wife the most understanding look he could muster and said simply, "That's all right, sweet girl. Before I turn in though, I want you to know that you made me very happy today. I'm honored to be your husband. I want you to come to trust that I truly meant the vows I spoke today—I meant every word. And right now, I'll add another—I'll never ask more of you, than you're willing to give. I'm looking forward to us having a good life together. We had a pretty fine day today and tomorrow will be even better!"

Shad turned out the light before he stripped down to his long johns. As he climbed into his big bed he called softly, "Good night Missus McKenna, sweet dreams—sweet girl!"

Chapter 9
Desperate Days

"The LORD examines the righteous, but the wicked, those who love violence, he hates with a passion." Psalms 11:5

"It's been fourteen days, Victor Kent. Have you finally made good on your threat to run out on me?" Mariah spoke into the crisp autumn air as she gazed down the trail that led from her small mountain shack towards the town of Otter Run. A storm was coming and she kept a wary eye on the wall of charcoal clouds that rolled and clashed in the distance. The wind that blew the pale hair from her face had a sharp bite to it, and yet the chill that ran down her spine wasn't just from the impending storm. Nor was it the promise that winter was just around the corner, but from the tempest that had become her life. She wrapped her arms around herself thinking that if her husband had finally abandoned her, it would be a blessing on one hand but quite possibly a death sentence on the other.

Their provisions had run out a month ago and Mariah had given her husband one of her last pieces of jewelry, hoping he could trade the small pearl and sapphire pendant for winter supplies and return before the first snow fell. Usually displays of Mariah's past wealth brought derogatory words from her husband, but this time he slipped the delicate thing into his pocket without a word, saddled his horse then headed for town, leading their pack mule. Otter Run was only a two hour ride away, so when the man returned a full week later, with no food and no mule, Mariah didn't think, she just foolishly blurted out, "What kind of man are you? I've given you everything I had to claim this land and purchase good stock. If you had just stayed here and worked, we could have a start on a decent life. Instead, little by little you're gambling everything away. How do you suppose we'll live this winter?"

Even as the words flew from her mouth, she knew it was foolhardy to speak that way to a man like Vic, but her frustration had been fueled by months of disappointment, fear and hunger. Usually she was able to block his first few blows, but this time his fist just came too fast. The next thing she knew her face was throbbing and Victor was bending over her. Instinctively, she rolled into a ball but he wasn't trying to hit her again. Instead, he yanked the small band of gold from her finger, jumped back onto his horse and spurred him back down the mountain.

That had been two weeks ago and still Victor hadn't returned. Last winter had been their first in the mountains and they had barely survived. Having both been reared in the flatlands of Texas, they were ill prepared for such a harsh winter. Vic knew next to nothing of carpentry but somehow he and Mariah managed to put together a rickety shack that swayed when the wind blew, leaked when it rained and had a fireplace that smoked incessantly. Mariah knew that if they were to survive their second winter, there was much to be done. Beyond reinforcing their shelter, they desperately needed a winter supply of firewood but most of all—they needed food. Winter was a harsh taskmaster; summer was over and autumn in these mountains could last for months, weeks or days. Winter might easily catch them unprepared and Vic didn't seem to care. Mariah cared a great deal, but being reared in a family of wealth and privilege, she lacked the necessary skills to know exactly what to do. Still she ventured out early each morning and searched the meadows and hillsides for anything she could find to eat, like berries to dry or wild onions to dig up and she gathered and stacked all the fallen branches she could find in the forest. It had been Victor's choice to live in this wild high-country, but Mariah was afraid that this was where they both would die!

Victor Kent had seemed so handsome and charming, like a dream come true when Mariah had first met the man. As it turned out the only thing he was good at was manipulation, and it had been easy for him to worm his way into Mariah's fragile heart, for she had always been love-starved and lonely. Although she had recognized signs of the man's irresponsibility and self-indulgent ways, she chose instead to focus on the fact that Victor always seemed so kind and gentle, while her own father had always been demanding and overbearing—even cruel at times.

Her father, Ruxton Hunter was what folks called a self-made man. He had built up his Candlestick Ranch until it was one of the largest and most prosperous ranches in all of Texas. When Victor Kent heard of Mariah's beauty and more importantly, that she was the sole heir to a fortune in land

and cattle, he had hired on, as one of the ranch's many cowhands. Vic hated manual labor, but forced himself to work hard, especially when the ranch foreman or Mariah's father was watching. Then he waited for just the right moment to befriend the woman he considered a walking gold mine. He was certain that the old man would deny his pampered daughter nothing, including the husband of her choice. His plan was to overwhelm her with kindness and entice her into eloping with him—which he did quite easily. However, despite Victor's plan for a life of wealth and ease, he underestimated the cold and calculating ways of Ruxton Hunter. He was not the type of man to be tricked—or used. When the young couple returned to the ranch after a two-day honeymoon, Mariah's parents met them on the porch of their lavish ranch house with their daughter's two matching carpetbags packed and ready.

Ruxton barely glanced at his daughter before he motioned to one of the hands and told him, "Tie these satchels onto that woman's saddle."

"Father," she cried. Her Texas drawl, soft and pleading. "I'm not *that woman*; I'm your own flesh and blood! You honestly aren't gonna turn me away—are you? You've always insisted that I stand up for myself—I thought you were just testing me to see if I'd accept a man of your choosin'. You're going against everything you've ever taught me."

Ignoring Mariah's words Ruxton turned to Victor and said calmly, "Young man, two days ago, Miss Mariah Hunter was one of my many assets, an essential part of my plans for the future. However, now that she is Missus Mariah Kent, she has no more value to me—no worth at all." When Mariah's mother started to protest, Ruxton seized her by the arm and glared her into compliance. Then he turned to his ranch foreman, "Victor Kent is no longer employed here and we no longer have a daughter. You and the men escort these people off my land." Though he wasn't speaking to her, he did finally look at Mariah adding, "Neither of them, either together or apart, are welcome to return."

Instantly a group of hired hands encircled them as if they were cattle to be herded off the property. As she rode away Mariah called out, "Mother, please say something!"

Though her mother made no move to speak, Mariah thought she saw tears in her eyes, but her own were so clouded she couldn't be sure. As she left the only home Mariah had ever known, Victor suddenly turned on her,

"You knew he'd do this, why did you allow me marry you? You tricked me—this is your fault. What do I want with a penniless wife?"

Shocked by her husband's outburst; Mariah suddenly saw that Victor was not only immature but perhaps even unbalanced. Later, when she found that her mother had hidden every piece of jewelry her father had ever given her in the bottom of her carpetbag, she quickly showed them to Victor, hoping to calm his rage.

For a time, Victor did become more reasonable. Still, his plans and schemes were more often than not outlandish and ill conceived. Although he knew nothing about living in the mountains, he insisted that they claim a homestead in the Colorado Rockies. It had always been his belief that he would make his fortune overnight. Surely, if there was gold in those mountains he would find it. Mariah on the other hand knew that success came from hard work, and though she didn't know how to cook or sew, she did know ranching and she convinced Victor that mining was hard work and hard working men would pay well for beef.

Hoping to light a fire under her lackadaisical husband, Mariah reminded Victor that her father had built his ranch up from nothing. "Surely you are as good a man as Ruxton Hunter." she challenged. "All it takes is hard work and diligence—and we could do as well as he did."

At first, her words played well to Victor's ego. However, it wasn't long before he would tell Mariah he was heading out to check the cattle, but went instead to the poker tables at the Long Shot Saloon. The quality stock Mariah had carefully selected became nothing more than collateral for her husband's wagers. Sadly, Victor Kent was as poor a card player as he was at everything else.

The greatest challenge married life asked of Mariah, was that she never knew who her husband would be when he returned home. Would it be the Victor Kent who was so hung over that all he wanted to do was sulk? Or the humiliated man who had lost yet again at the poker table and needed to take his fury out on someone who couldn't fight back? She never knew if she would have to comfort a crying drunk, placate a disgruntled tyrant, or just roll herself into a ball and hope that the man that had promised to cherish her wouldn't hurt her too badly.

Outside the storm was coming closer and the wind was pushing against the flimsy shack walls as they creaked and swayed. Feeling the familiar despair welling up inside her, Mariah studied her reflection in the silver plated hand mirror—a token from another life. In the time that Victor had been gone, the fist size bruise had run the gambit of colors. Now it was a pale shade of yellow. Seeing her puffy and discolored face always irritated Victor. Somehow, he always managed to forget that he was the cause.

"Ya used to be so beautiful." He would jeer, "Folks used to say that Mariah Hunter was the prettiest girl in all of Texas. Ha—just look at ya. Yer ugly and ya used to fill out that dress, now yer nothin' but skin and bones. I'm forced to go to a saloon if I want to see what a real woman looks like. The reason I don't take ya to town is 'cause I'm ashamed to be seen with ya. Yer mighty lucky I don't run out on ya, woman. What other man would even bother to come home? Only me Mariah—only me."

The sound of the wind and the distant thunder rumbled through the tiny shack. Like Victor's cruel words, they seemed to echo in her ears. They had been married for fifteen months. Looking back into the mirror she found herself remembering what she had looked like on the day they were married. Her life had changed so drastically in such a short time. Victor used to lavish her with kindness and words of praise. Now he called her ugly. How strange that sounded when all her life people had remarked how unusually lovely she and her mother were. Mirror images, folks would say, "You two look more like sisters than mother and daughter." People often said, they were what they had imagined angels to look like, with their hair all shiny and pale, the color of flax. Both of them, tall and graceful and when they smiled their teeth were a glossy white and rounded like a row of pearls. Everyone especially remarked about their unusual large violet eyes—oh yes, they were rare beauties indeed. Or so everyone told them. Oddly enough, neither Mariah nor her mother had ever paid much attention to these overly generous praises, for beauty had not kept either of them from a life of misery. Although they looked alike, they had never been close. Olivia was elegant, quiet, and so exceedingly reserved that she rarely spoke, not even to her own family. There were times that Mariah even thought she hated her mother, not just for her cool and aloof manner, but because she was weak—too weak willed to stand up to her tyrant husband and protect her own children!

Mariah hadn't realized at the time that her mother had no choice but to acquiesce to her husband's demands. After all, Ruxton Hunter was often compared to a gale force wind. He was big, powerful, and never hesitated to inflict his will upon others. Outwardly, he was the picture of self-control, distinguished and handsome. He could even be exceedingly charming, when it suited him. Onlookers thought the Hunters' were the perfect family and that was exactly what Ruxton intended. Publicly he referred to Olivia and Mariah as his 'sweet beauties'. And most people thought that if anything he spoiled his womenfolk, for he often made a show of sending away for expensive gifts and jewelry and when his purchases came into the mercantile, he would collect these gifts himself and make a show of having everyone in the store exclaim over his generosity.

"What do you think?" He would ask the crowd that gathered, "Do you all think these little baubles worthy of 'my sweet beauties'?"

Everything Ruxton did was contrived, part of a grander plan. He often gave lavish parties, entertaining bankers and politicians at his large and ostentatious ranch house. Olivia and Mariah were always on display as the perfect hostesses, always impeccably dressed and bejeweled. Ruxton viewed both women in the exact same way he viewed the furnishings of his home, they were visible proof of his accomplishments. They were simply a part of the image he wanted to portray of the perfect man with the perfect family.

The proverbial skeleton in the closet was Olivia's son by a previous marriage. The boy was different. Ruxton believed he bore the mark of Cain and refused to claim him. Instead, on Ladd's twelfth birthday, he was sent to live in the bunkhouse with the rest of the hired hands. That was the first and the last time Olivia ever tried to challenge her husband. The beating she received that night was proof that Ruxton would never yield to her in any way.

Oddly enough, the following day, a very angry three-year-old Mariah walked up to her father, grabbed him by the pant leg and said, "Papa, you be nice!" Only Olivia and the cook were witnesses to this act of defiance and they both feared for the tiny girl. However, to their surprise, the man laughed and the two women cringed when he roughly picked Mariah up by her shoulders so he could look her in the eye.

"So, it appears my pale little flower has some of me in her, after all." He growled. "If you want me to listen to you then—show me that you've got some worth." When the child didn't flinch, he was pleased and he narrowed his eyes and added, "When you can ride a horse and learn what I teach you... then maybe someday, I'll listen to what you have to say."

Little Mariah had her first riding lesson that day. Olivia breathed a sigh of relief when anything and everything that had to do with running the Candlestick Ranch came naturally to Mariah. Olivia silently watched as her daughter spent her days in Ruxton's shadow. It was then, she decided to distance herself from both her children, hoping that Mariah might soften her father's heart. However, believing that her mother had rejected her, Mariah hid the hurt in a mask of anger towards Olivia, and yet her father's heart never softened—not a bit. Oh, he was pleased with the girl, but he only saw her abilities and her appeal as potential assets that he could use for his own purposes. He enjoyed reminding Mariah he would have preferred a son and no matter how well she did, he never offered her a single word of praise.

Mariah stared out the door of her poorly built shack, watching and waiting for her own brutal husband to return. Now she understood things that just a few years before she never could have imagined. As she touched her own bruises her mind went back to one day in particular. She'd returned home from a long ride to find that her father had just horse whipped his stepson, her half-brother and then ridden away. Filled with anger, Mariah stormed into her mother's bedroom, "Why won't you do something to protect your own son? Don't you even care that Ladd is lying out there in the barn, bruised and bleeding?"

Staring out the window, tears glistened in Olivia's eyes as she listened to her daughter's angry outburst, but as always, she said nothing. Disgusted by her mother's cold heart and constant silence, Mariah groaned and was about to stomp from the room when her mother suddenly spoke, "Oh, daughter, don't you think I would do more if I could? I promise you that I am more of a buffer than you know. Right now, you are too young and much too innocent to understand how powerless a woman can be. We are at the mercy of the men in our lives and if those men have no mercy—what can we do?" Mariah saw her mother's hands shake as she twisted her handkerchief, trembling as she watched out the window, waiting for her husband to return from his ride.

It wasn't until now, years later, that Mariah suddenly remembered that whenever her father whipped his stepson, he would ride off for a few hours. When he came back, he would demand that everyone in the house leave and allow him privacy with his wife. Mariah knew full well that her father had a vicious nature and her mind went back to that dark day, and she remembered how her mother had turned to her and said with tears in her eyes, "Your father will be back soon and you know he—will want to—to be alone with me. Before he returns, you need to gather up the bandages and salve and go to the barn and take care of your brother. Stay with him—sing to him—comfort him. You've always been able to sooth my Laddy. Your father was always jealous whenever I—well you know you can comfort Ladd better than I ever could." When Mariah seemed hesitant to leave, her mother nearly screamed, "Go Mariah! I've said too much—and so have you!"

Now, it was Mariah who trembled as she waited for her husband's return. "Oh Mother," she whispered. "I'm so sorry. The girl I was just couldn't understand, but the woman I've become—she understands—only too well." Nervously, she looked about the tiny room. She had swept the dirt floor, but there wasn't much more she could do to make this place look more presentable. Still, she knew Victor would find something to punish her for, and as her mother had said, some men have no mercy—and Victor Kent was a man without mercy.

The sound of galloping hooves coming up the mountain path shook Mariah from her thoughts. Her stomach clenched, her heart began to pound and she hurried outside to greet her husband. The wind was harsh and she put her hands up to protect herself from the dust that spun around her in circles. Suddenly, two horses appeared before her, it was almost as if the storm had blown them into the yard. Two horses but only one rider.

When she was finally able to see, she was both surprised and relieved—it wasn't Victor. The man in the saddle was Jimmy Todd, the sheriff of Otter Run. Since she'd only been to town a few times, she hardly knew a soul in these mountains. The only reason she knew Todd was because he had brought Victor home a number of times when he was too drunk to ride. Still, something was wrong. As usual, the sheriff was riding his black and white paint gelding and leading Victor's horse. However, this time her husband wasn't in the saddle or even draped over it.

Just then, the wind picked up and she stared down the mountain path only to see a steal gray wall of rain steadily moving towards them, even as fingers of lightning danced across the sky. Mariah wrapped her shawl tightly about her shoulders, "Sheriff Todd," she called over the churning air, "where's Victor?"

The man frowned then glanced back at the approaching storm and swung down from his horse. Trying to make his voice heard over the increasing wind, he shouted, "Ma'am, I've just about killed these ponies getting' up here before that thing hits. Let me take care of them and then we'll talk." He turned away then stopped abruptly and yanked a bundle from his saddlebag, handing it to Mariah he yelled, "Figured you might be low on supplies. Sure could use a cup of hot coffee and any kind of vittles you can make with this."

Frustrated Mariah wanted to insist he tell her—why Victor wasn't with him. An instant later, she conceded that this was not the time for explanations. Lightening was flashing in the distance and a toad strangler downpour was headed their way. Nodding her agreement, Mariah swallowed back her questions took the bundle then hurried inside.

Instantly, she tore into the package and nearly cried when she saw the bounty hidden within. There was coffee, flour and even some of Sephora Castle's special sausage. After weeks of living on little more than a handful of berries or a few fried onions, Mariah's mouth watered at the idea of real food. Still as she looked forward to a good meal, she wished fervently that she knew how to prepare such a thing as a 'good meal'. The ranch had employed an excellent cook but the eccentric Frenchman would not allow her or even her mother in **his** kitchen. After becoming Victor's wife, she did her best to prepare their meals. Unfortunately, with no one to teach her, it seemed she just learned all the ways a woman could ruin good food. That was about the only thing she and Victor agreed on—she was a terrible cook. Still, Mariah was starving so she set right to work. Of course, her mind was spinning while she boiled coffee, kneaded the biscuit dough and fried the sausage. Where was Victor? Had he finally left her? If so, then why would the sheriff have his horse? Had Vic shot someone over a hand of poker? Was he sitting in jail? A thousand questions went through her head, maybe it was something she'd already thought of—or—maybe it was something worse!

When the sheriff finally came inside, the food was ready and they sat down and ate in silence. Of course, the coffee was weak, the biscuits were as tough as jerky and the sausage was burnt on the outside and raw in the middle. However, Mariah, like the starving woman she was—ate every bite.

Jimmy Todd wondered how anyone could ruin such a simple meal and he was quick to turn down Mariah's offer of more. As he pushed his plate away, however, he turned his attention to the woman sitting beside him and said slowly, "Ma'am by the way yer finishin' off that plate, a body'd think ya hadn't eaten in a month!"

Embarrassed, Mariah quickly sat her fork down—she'd fallen on the food like a poor beggar. Then she pushed aside her pride and decided she might as well tell the truth. Shrugging her shoulders, she said softly, "That's about the way of it; I've been living off berries and anything I could scrounge in the forest for well over a month now. Twice Victor's headed for Otter Run to purchase our winter supplies—but—well—you know what he's like—" She was quiet for a few moments then finally she turned her questioning eyes to the sheriff, "Don't you think it's time you told me where my husband is?"

Todd chewed on his lip for a few moments, pondering how to begin. He was a handsome man, not tall but muscular, he had dark hair with hazel eyes that were so intense that they sometimes bothered Mariah. The way he stared at her often seemed far too bold. However, just now, she stubbornly held his gaze until he began to speak.

"The news I have for ya ain't good. Like always, Victor thought he had a sure fire hand of poker. He bet everything—and then he lost—everything!"

Mariah's heart nearly stopped, "Everything?" she asked. "You mean this homestead and the last of our stock? Then what? Did he just run away?"

Frowning, Todd ran his hand over the rough tabletop and said slowly, "I reckon at first that's what he had in mind. 'Course, he'd been drinkin' pretty hard by then and when he signed over the ranch and last of yer cattle…well… he jumped up and hurried out of the saloon then he swung up on his horse. Actually, he had signed his horse away too and the man that won him told me to go out and fetch him back. I felt sorry for Vic and I thought I'd give him some time to think, so I just trailed along behind him. I had no idea what he had in mind or I sure would have stopped him. He rode right up to the edge of 'Widow's Lookout'. He stepped off his pony, drew his gun and emptied a couple of shots in the air. Then—well—he turned it on himself! I spurred my mount and tried to get to him but his body just slipped right on over the edge. That drop is a couple hundred feet straight down. I know the shot killed him but if by some chance it didn't—then the fall did!"

The sheriff watched Mariah as he spoke. She was staring out the door of the shack, watching the torrent of rain as it fell in sheets. She made no sound, she looked puzzled at first, then her eyes clouded. When she blinked, a single tear rolled down her cheek, but she didn't bother to wipe it away—in fact, she didn't move at all. Finally, as if coming out of a trance she whispered, "So—Victor is dead?" Her expression was one of complete bewilderment and she shook her head. "I've been so scared, so very scared of his coming home and now—I'm so very scared because—now he never will. It sounds terrible but I've dreamed of being free of him, but—now that I am—what do I do, Sheriff?" When he didn't answer her, she frowned and asked again, "Go ahead and tell me, I take it I own nothin' at all, not even this poor excuse for a home. What does a woman with no husband, no money, no family or friends—what does she do?"

Jimmy Todd knew exactly what he wanted her to do, but now wasn't the time to speak of it. He'd never seen anything to compare with those large violet eyes of hers. Even now as they filled with tears, they shone like pale amethysts. She was rail thin just now and her hair was dull and dry. Oh, but he remembered how breathtaking she'd been the first time he had seen her. This year in the mountains had been hard on her, but she was still very young, and soon—with a little care—she'd be as stunning as before.

Feeling the man's eyes on her, Mariah jumped up to pour more coffee, even as she squirmed under his blatant perusal. All her life men had looked at her like that and she hated it. Self-consciously she set the pot back on the stove and wrapped her shawl more tightly around her thin body.

Jimmy Todd smiled at her discomfort. The woman had been married well over a year and yet she was still such an innocent. "Well, I reckon the only thing I can tell ya to do right now is to pack up yer things. Sam Pettigrew pretty much owns this whole mountain now. Everything on it, in it and around it belongs to him. I hate to rush ya, but he wants ya out today. His men will be coming up here tomorrow to tear down this pile of rubble and build a decent cabin before winter sets in. Once you get yer things gathered we'll leave just as soon as this rain stops.

Just then Mariah noticed that the cans she'd placed to catch the rainwater were about to overflow. Carefully she emptied them out the door then returned each one to its proper spot. When she turned and saw that the sheriff had been watching her every move, she blushed crimson. There was an uncomfortable tension between them until a sudden loud crack of lighting split the air just outside the shack.

Mariah jumped and Todd let out a long whistle, "I reckon we'll need to wait a spell before we head down the mountain." When Mariah began nervously pulling the threads from her worn sleeve, he took pity on her and decided to ask a question that had bothered him ever since he had first met Victor and Mariah Kent. "Ma'am," he asked, "something's befuddled me for a long time. Would ya mind telling me how a refined, beauty like you ended up with such a weak-minded, drunken, poor excuse of man like Victor Kent?"

The man's cutting words seemed offensive at first, but the Sheriff was right…Victor was a poor excuse for a man. He had used her and abused her from the first. Because of him she had lost everything and now he'd taken the coward's way out and left her to survive all alone.

Finally, Mariah sighed and answered the man's question. "I married Victor Kent because…because I'm a stupid woman, Sheriff. I wanted to escape from a controlling father. Although I lived in luxury, I was lonely and unhappy. I thought my life—quite difficult." Shaking her head, she added scornfully, "Now I know what difficult really looks like. Vic said he would be better to me than my father was. He lied of course; my father only bruised me with his words, while Vic bruised me with both his words and his fists. Vic was one of the hired hands on my family's ranch. One of his daily chores was to saddle my horse and bring it up to the house. I'd thank him, he'd tip his hat and we'd exchange a word or two but not much more than that. Then one morning, my father explained that a Hunter must always own the Candlestick Ranch of Texas. Naturally, since I was just a girl and my mother had failed to give him a true son to carry on the name, he had to do what was necessary. He told me that my cousin, who was a 'city boy' but had been trained in business, was moving to Texas. He would inherit the ranch with the stipulation that he live there permanently and that he marry me. You see, Father made sure I knew how to manage a ranch while my cousin knew how to manage a business. Father considered it an acceptable match. I did not. I was furious and I guess everyone on the ranch knew it. When I went for my morning ride, I found a note in the gullet of my saddle. It was from Vic, it said simply, 'You don't deserve to be treated like this. I'm your friend, if you want to talk, meet me at the creek at midnight. Of course, I met him that night and every night for a week. I had never had a beau before and of course, he said all the things an unhappy and foolish young woman needed to hear."

Jimmy Todd raised his eyebrows and shook his head, "It's pretty easy to sweep a sheltered girl off her feet!"

Mariah rolled her eyes, "Oh yes, I was certainly naïve. You see Mother and I weren't allowed many friends. Those midnight rendezvous with Vic were very special. They were exciting and romantic. Still, I thought it just a lark. I knew that in the end I'd obey my father. Oh, the idea of marrying my cousin was repulsive but no one ever fought Ruxton Hunter and won. Still, Vic was very persuasive and he talked me into eloping with him. He assured me that since Father was such a public figure, if we married and stayed away for two days, what could he say? I was his only child and it would be a scandal for him not to accept my marriage. I tried to tell him that no one had ever backed my father into a corner, but Vic had a way of making you think that he knew best. He told me to trust him and foolishly, I did. Mostly he kept telling me that my parents did not love me but that he truly did. He promised that my life with him was going to be like a holiday compared to what I'd known before and that he was going to—cherish me, just like it says in the wedding vows."

With an unladylike groan, Mariah stood and took down a large carpetbag hanging on the wall. Slowly she began packing her things, "You know," she said sadly, "I used to think my mother was the most foolish, weak willed woman in the world for marrying a cruel tyrant like my father." Shaking her head, she turned to the sheriff and asked, "So, tell me, sir, if my mother was stupid and foolish and weak, then what does that make me? She married because she was a widow and desperately needed a way to provide for her newborn son. I married because I wanted to have my own way. I was a fool who married a bigger fool! And in the end...I probably deserved what I got."

Chapter 10
Mountain Ministry

"The Spirit of the Lord is on me, because he has anointed me to preach the gospel to the poor; he has sent me to heal the broken-hearted, to preach deliverance to the captives, and recovering of sight to the blind, to set at liberty them that are bruised." Luke 4:18

Preacher sadly shook his head as he took in the condition of the young man sitting at the bar of the Long Shot Saloon. "Clem, how many times have you promised Celia you'd stop this foolishness?" Groaning he half carried his hungover friend from the bar to a sun drenched table by the window.

Glaring at the rotund bartender, who was also owner of the saloon, Preacher almost growled, "Ox Hennessey…the least you could do is bring that pot of coffee and a big mug over here."

While Ox shuffled towards them with coffee in hand, Clem Talbott buried his head in his hands and moaned. "Go ahead on, Preacher, but ya can't make me feel any worse that I already do. What am I gonna tell Celia—and my three good boys? I'm a decent man, you know that, until I set foot in town. Always say jes' one little drink. But when I drink, I gamble and when I gamble, I drink. And—I always think I'm smarter and better at everything—especially at cards."

Preacher blew out a breath as he glared at Hennessey, but his words were for the poor young fool that sat before him. "How much this time Clem, how much did you lose?"

Clem lowered his eyes with shame as he admitted, "Celia's gone to hiding our money. Only come to town with two dollars in my pocket. But—this time I had me a real winnin' streak—honest I did! Don't rightly know what happened though." Shaking his head in confusion, he tried to explain: "Just like clockwork, I always win the first three hands. Naturally, I celebrate a little—drinks are on the house when yer winnin'. Then the bettin' got higher than

I could go…so…I bet my Sharps rifle. I tell ya, Preacher, I thought sure—I had me the perfect hand. So, then I bet Rebel too—you know that mustang stallion I caught last year." With a defeated moan, Clem buried his head in his hands again.

Preacher gritted his teeth and rolled his eyes, wishing that it were possible to shake sense into someone. "You worked night and day breaking that horse. So, now how are you going to raise horses without a stallion, Clem? And how will you hunt game or protect your family without your gun?" Again, the pastor's words were directed towards the young rancher but his eyes were shooting daggers at Ox Hennessey.

Ox was aptly named and the beady-eyed, beer-bellied Irishman sucked on his back tooth while he poured Clem another cup of coffee. "Now don't ya be lookin' at me that-a-way, Preacher. I know ya told me not to be servin' the lad whiskey. But ya'd best be rememberin' that we work for different bosses. Yours is in the business of keeping folks out o' here—while mine is in the business of drawin' 'em in. And I'll not be throwin' a payin' customer outta me door—at least not while there's a penny in their pocket." Hennessey turned and walked back behind the bar, adding, "Still and all—don't I give him coffee the next mornin' and sober him up before sending 'em home? But ya best be rememberin' that when the lad comes back again…and he will. I'll be sellin' him whatever he wants. And if he's of a mind to gamble, he can put up: his gun, his horse—or his wife as far as I'm concerned."

Preacher frowned at the owner of the saloon as he tossed a coin on the table, "Give him some breakfast to go along with the coffee. And your right Ox, we do work for different bosses. But you need to think on the fact that in the end, you'll have to answer to mine." Preacher turned his back on Ox and put his hand on Clem's shoulder. "While I go see what can be done about all this, your job is to get as much of that coffee down as you can and some food too!"

Preacher strolled out of the bar and glanced up and down the dusty main street of Otter Run. As the story goes, the town came by the name because a French trapper and his Indian wife built a cabin on this spot. The squaw believed that otters were strong medicine and she spoke a warning over her husband's traps and no otter ever came near them. Soon multiple families of mountain otters made their home in the nearby river. When the couple died, their children opened a mountain trading post. When a small town grew up around it, they named it Otter Run. A common jest regarding the town's name is that: 'Once a body rides into Otter Run—they generally see real quick—that they Otter Run right out again!'

Actually, the town itself could have been a very pleasant place to live. Unfortunately, it was full of people like Ox Hennessey. Preacher worked at not hating Ox but he had no misgivings about hating the Long Shot Saloon. In fact, he hated the way all saloons fed off the weaknesses and vices of its patrons until it destroyed them. He often wished he could light a match to every saloon in the world. Of course, he would never do such a thing for he knew that wasn't the answer. Even if the whole town burned down—the first thing the men of Otter Run would rebuild—would be the saloon. No one in town had even thought of building a church, but that was something that Preacher hoped to change.

Quincy Adams Long, III, was a bit more than the simple mountain preacher that folks knew him to be. His family had amassed a fortune in the shipping trade, importing silks and spices from the orient. Only the bank knew of his wealth and they had been instructed to keep it quiet. Preacher was content to live a simple life, although he did use his money freely wherever and whenever those in his ministry needed it. Mostly he helped these mountain people by using his strength, his compassion and his desire to make a difference. Although Preacher was unhappy with Clem Talbott. He would buy back the man's stallion, his rifle—and whatever else the poor fool had lost. Hopefully for the last time.

The bell jangled as Preacher stepped through the bank's glass door. Hank Wyatt, the young curly-headed teller, welcomed him with his usual grin, "Howdy, Pastor Long." Lowering his voice he said, "Figured you'd be headin' in this mornin'. Heard about Clem Talbott—reckon you'll be needin' twice your usual withdrawal today?"

Preacher nodded indulgently, knowing that a man's ruination was the tastiest of all gossip. He watched as the young man spun on his heels, and nearly tripped over his own feet as he raced towards the banks floor safe. A few moments later Hank was carefully counting out the money. Time's like this, when his wealth was so obvious, made Preacher uncomfortable and he rubbed the back of his neck self-consciously, wishing Hank would hurry it up. Just then, the bell over the bank door jingled again and he turned to see the most striking young woman he had ever seen, step inside. Tall and graceful, she was dressed from head to foot in black. Immediately he breathed a prayer, she was much too young to be a widow. Her dark bonnet made a stark contrast against her pale blonde hair, coiled into a bun at the nap of her neck. Still, a dozen soft curls peeked out from her bonnet and caressed her delicate oval face. Her posture was serene and dignified. By chance, she stared up and locked eyes with Preacher. Even though she quickly looked away—it was almost as if, in that brief moment, she had told him her life story, for he saw her strength as well as her sorrow and her fear. He had never seen eyes like hers before. They were a deep shade of lavender, as lovely as a mountain columbine and yet their intensity spoke of a depth beyond her years.

This brief encounter suddenly left Preacher's mouth dry and he felt his heart beating in his chest like a torn sail slapping against the mast. As discreetly as possible, he watched the woman as she walked across the lobby. She held her head high and back straight as she slowly made her way towards the president's office.

Quincy Long was a healthy, red-blooded man who enjoyed the sight of a beautiful woman as much as any other man, but never before had he felt so intensely drawn to a woman. Still, he had always believed wholeheartedly that having a wife and a mountain ministry were just not compatible. Perhaps when he was too old to traipse through these mountains, there might be a sweet wife in his future but for now? No. It was best for him to stay married only to his ministry. Believing this as strongly as ever, he still found himself fighting down the almost tangible fascination with this woman. Instantly, he refocused his attention on Hank as he laid down the bank notes, one by one.

Normally, whenever Preacher saw a widow he always inquired if he might be of any help to her. Now he found himself debating if it was wise for him to even speak to this woman. When he realized what was happening he nearly laughed.

I just need to get my thinking straight again. I've been praying for romance to blossom between Shad and Copper—and—I've allowed myself to get caught up in it. Now that I'm back on the job, looking for those that need my help and instead of a dirty old miner, it's a lovely young woman. I'm acting like a schoolboy. God has called me to help anyone in need. Therefore, if this woman needs my help...then I'll help her... simple as that!

Feeling more like himself, he watched as the woman lifted her hand to knock, but finding the president's door ajar, she peeked inside and spoke with an educated and yet decidedly Texas drawl.

"Pardon me, Mister Krane. I saw that your sign is still up. I just had to inquire if you might have had a change of heart? I truly am excellent with organization and bookkeepin'. I know I could do a good job—if you'll just give me a chance!" She paused for another moment then added, "However—if you're still against hirin' a woman—I'm certainly not too proud to scrub floors or—wash windows."

Theodore Krane, the middle-aged bank president, smiled appreciatively as his eyes traveled over Mariah Kent in such a way that she felt like turning on her heels and running for the door. Biting back her revulsion, she lowered her eyes and said softly, "I am an honorable woman Mister Krane. I would certainly work hard at any appropriate job."

Krane raised his eyebrows and said arrogantly, "My dear Missus Kent, is working out in the public, really appropriate—for an unattached young woman—if she truly is, as you say, an honorable woman?"

Preacher couldn't help but hear and he dawdled as he straightened the bank notes and tapped the money on the counter. Slowly he rolled the bills and slipped them into his pocket. He needed to hurry and buy back Clem's stallion before its new owner left town. However, he also felt an urgency to protect and to help this woman. He just didn't know how he could, not without intruding into her business. Especially since they had never met.

Almost without realizing it, Preacher had wandered away from the teller's window and found himself staring at the woman as she faced the pompous bank president. He couldn't help but see the dejected look on the young widow's face, as she slowly backed away. Suddenly he blurted out, "Oh come now, Krane!"

When the woman jumped at the sound of his voice, Preacher felt ashamed for startling her. "Forgive me ma'am, I didn't mean to frighten you." Then Preacher turned on Krane. "You've got a 'help wanted' sign posted, Theo, why not give the lady a chance?"

When the widow looked up with gratitude sparkling in her eyes, Preacher felt as if he had just be given a gift. He needed to get Talbott's stallion and his rifle; he needed to return to his duties as a mountain Preacher, but most of all—he needed to stop staring. The woman had the face of an angel; her hair was pale and as shiny as sunlight. And her eyes truly were—the most perfect shade of lavender. Forcing himself to look at Krane, he managed to say, "Everyone deserves a chance."

Suddenly, the woman stepped forward, offering her hand, "Might I ask, are you Pastor Long?"

Preacher drew in a breath as he took his hat from his head with one hand and her hand with the other. He managed to smile though inwardly he chided himself. He'd met beautiful women all over the world, so why did just touching this one make him feel as off balanced as the ships deck in a hurricane.

"Yes ma'am, my name is Quincy Long." He managed to say. "I'm Pastor to all the mountain people. Might I be of any service to you?"

"My name is Mariah Kent, I'm the widow of Victor Kent; we only moved here about a year ago. Victor came to town but I always stayed at home. I'm afraid I don't know many people." Her words trailed off as her eyes clouded, but she gave a quick shake of her head and brightened. "I'm looking for work, Pastor. Do you happen to know of any ranchers or farmers around that need a cook or a housekeeper? Or even a wrangler…" She asked with a slight smile and a shrug. "I was reared on a ranch in Texas; truth be told I'd probably make a better wrangler than cook. And I'm certainly not too proud to clean barns."

A tender expression covered Preacher's face; he was surprised that such an elegant woman was so brave and especially that she was so down to earth. "I'm pleased to meet you Missus Kent …and you have my deepest condolences for your loss." Preacher thought for a moment then shook his head, "I wish I knew of someone that needed help, but I'm afraid that mountain folk tend to take care of themselves or do without." Thinking not to embarrass her, he motioned for her to step towards a quiet corner of the bank for he didn't want anyone to hear what he said next, "Ma'am if you have any family or friends you can go to—I would be pleased to help you get to them. I assure you that the Lord has provided for me in such a way where helping you would not be a burden. On the contrary, I would count it a blessing. Please, allow me to assist you."

Mariah's sad eyes warmed at his kind gesture; however, she had been raised that to seek pity or take charity was to sink as low as one could get. It wasn't that she was averse to borrowing money—that is—not if she thought there was any way of repaying the debt. The trouble was that she had no talent for what was deemed—'woman's work'. How many times had Victor complained that her meals wouldn't tempt a starving coyote and that her house keeping skills weren't any better. On the other hand her father had taught her to ride horses and balance ledgers. She was suited for a 'man's work', but no man would allow her to do it. The sad truth was that the only thing that Mariah still possessed were the last remnants of her pride and dignity.

"You are very kind, Pastor Long," she answered, her voice both gracious and firm. "And I do thank you. But you needn't worry about me. I am young and strong and I am sure I can take care of myself!" When the tall preacher looked unconvinced she added, "I have sent a telegram to my family in Texas. I should be hearing from them any day now." Mariah winced inwardly. It wasn't a complete lie; she had sent a telegram but had very little hope that her parents would reply favorably, if they replied at all. Feeling terribly awkward and self-conscious, she moved towards the door, speaking softly, "Pastor Long it was a pleasure meeting you. Thank you again for your kindness—and—I bid you a good day, Sir."

Preacher couldn't keep from watching Mariah as she opened the bank's glass door with her gloved hand then gracefully moved down the boardwalk. He felt an inward rebuke for ogling her, especially when he turned around and realized that he wasn't alone in his admiration. Every man in the bank was watching her, too. Although Preacher was known as a man of great patience and an unruffled manner, the way these men were looking at Mariah Kent filled him with anger. He slanted a frown of disapproval at them as he walked back to the teller's window.

"Listen Hank," he said, keeping his voice low. "I need you to do me a favor. I have to see that Clem Talbott gets back home, and then I have to take supplies to Slim and Jozy Warner. They've both been down with a fever, may even have to stay with them for a while. I don't know how long it will be before I'm able to come back to town. I need you to make sure that Cyril Castle has enough funds to cover Missus Kent's room and board at the hotel. If she decides to return to her home in Texas, then I authorize you to pay for her ticket on the stage and give her a hundred dollars to cover any other traveling expenses. And be sure to wire for extra funds from my Denver account."

A short time later, while Preacher was paying nearly double the price for Talbott's stallion and his Sharps rifle, he couldn't help but notice the beautiful widow once again. She was going from one business to another, never stopping in any one place for long.

While Preacher tied Rebel to the hitching post outside the saloon, Ox Hennessey was sweeping the boardwalk, but mostly the man was watching Missus Kent. When he headed back into the saloon, he had an odd grin on his face, as if he knew a secret.

"Hey, Ox." Preacher called, as he followed the older man through the swinging doors, "Do you know that woman or anything about her late husband? His name was Victor Kent."

"Well now, don't know near as much about *her* as I'd like." he said with a lecherous grin. "But to be sure, I knew that worthless husband o' hers. They bought a ranch about a two hour ride from here. It's no wonder he never brought that gal to town—ain't she somethin'! There's not a man alive that wouldn't like to be knowin' a woman like that a whole lot better."

"Ox Hennessey." Preacher growled, "Missus Kent is a fine and decent woman. Don't ever talk about her like that again!"

When Ox's eyebrows lifted, Preacher forced himself to tamp down his anger. A man like Ox could never understand the protectiveness he felt towards Mariah Kent, especially since he didn't quite understand it himself. Blowing out a breath, he rubbed the back of his neck, "All widows should be shown mercy, Ox. Do you know how her husband died?"

"Sure preacher, I know plenty. Victor Kent was a regular here at the Long Shot. He was—well he was like—this one here." The bartender pointed his meaty finger at Clem Talbott. The young rancher shifted uneasily at the insult, then tossed back another gulp of coffee while Ox Hennessey continued. "Kent was a fool; he was always comin' to town with a piece of his wife's jewelry. He nearly always lost and then he'd get rip-roaring drunk. They had a nice heard of find beef critters when they come up here. Then one by one, he gambled 'em away. A while back, he come in with that little gal's weddin' ring. I'll tell ya the man was jes' that worthless. He bet the ring, and then his homestead. Finally, the poor fool bet his horse. 'Course he lost like always, his horse weren't his no more but he ran outta here and jumped on him all the same. The sheriff followed him up to a high place called 'Widow's Lookout'. Kent must o' thought he was gonna be arrested, he pulled his gun and Todd had to shoot him. His body went right over that steep cliff. They don't call it 'Widow's Lookout' fer nothin'. 'Course he's down there still—'twasn't worth the trouble o' pullin' his sorry carcass up, just to be puttin' it under the ground again. Besides, that canyon is said to go all the way to China."

Preacher, thought of the woman he'd just seen, then asked, "So she couldn't even bury her husband?"

Hennessey laughed, "Now who would be fool enough to climb down into that hell hole—fer the likes of him? Still and all, Sheriff Todd rode straight to their ranch and broke the news to the woman gentle-like." Then Hennessey scratched his head and shrugged, "Course the man who won their ranch was keen on rebuilding the place. She had to get out in a hurry." Hennessey turned to Clem and poked his dirty finger in his chest, "Mark me words Talbott. It'll be your wife next. You're as big a fool as Victor Kent ever was! Just like you bucko, he had good land, fine stock and a beautiful woman. Yep, soon all the men in town will be watchin' yer wife walkin' down that street!"

Clem was horrified at the strange glint in Hennessey's eyes. He felt like a tub of cold water had just been dumped over his head—and in that instant he was fully sober. Clem stood and joined the other men as they watched the young widow leave the café. She quickly dabbed a hanky to her eyes, then straightened her shoulders as she preceded down the boardwalk. Hennessey tapped Clem on the shoulder then gave him a sly wink and pointed his beefy thumb towards the upstairs rooms where the saloon's girls slept.

Preacher didn't see the exchange but Clem understood the vile man's meaning and shuddered. Suddenly he could think only of getting home to his own sweet Celia. What would she have done, had he lost everything the night before? And what would they do now without his stallion and his rifle? He and Celia had three sons—three fine boys that needed a father to teach them how to grow-up to be better men than he'd been so far. Clem remembered how tempted he had been the night before—to put the deed to his ranch on the table in hopes of getting everything he'd lost back and coming home with extra money as well. What he had lost was bad enough but—like Kent—he could have lost everything he owned. Tears of shame filled the young rancher's eyes, as he glanced out the saloon door. It was then that he realized that the horse tied to the hitching post was none other than his stallion Rebel. It was his saddle on the horses back and the scabbard held his Sharps rifle.

"Ain't that—Rebel?" Clem asked, keeping his eyes on his stallion but reaching a trembling hand towards Preacher's arm. "I figured Grady would have him half way down the mountain by now." Clem ran his hands through his hair, feeling confused, "I did lose him and the gun last night—didn't I?"

Preacher's eyes turned the color of steal and his voice sounded just as hard, "You lost them, all right, Clem. But—since The Boss had me in town—I figured He wanted you to have another chance. They are yours again by God's grace. More importantly, Celia, the boys and the ranch are still yours—for now at least." Preacher grabbed Clem's arm and turned him so the young man was facing him. "Clem, if you don't get yourself straightened out—Ox is right—you will lose everything! How about I take you home and you start making things right with your family. Are you man enough to face your weaknesses—and be the kind of husband and father they deserve?"

Clem ran his hands through his curly brown hair and he swallowed hard. "Yes sir—Preacher, I see it's time I let God take the lead in my life. I'm not sure how to begin. Will you stay with us fer a spell and show Celia and me how to put together a godly family? I never want to dishonor God or Celia and my boys ever again. I want to be a good man and I want my boys to be good men."

Preacher was nodding his agreement when Sheriff Jimmy Todd sauntered down the steps of the saloon and joined the men as they watched the young widow heading down the street, making her way towards the livery.

"Mmmm," the sheriff groaned. "There goes the prettiest woman in the territory!"

Preacher found the man's words irritating, but then he chided himself. These possessive feelings he had for a woman he had just met were out of place for a man who was not meant to marry. Maybe The Boss wanted him to do some more match making. Mariah Kent seemed like an intelligent and discerning woman, especially after being married to a man like Victor Kent. He knew very little about the sheriff, but believed Mariah was the type to recognize if the man was worthy of her or not. The truth was women alone didn't fare well. If she didn't return to Texas, then it would be best if she remarried.

Mariah Kent—from the moment he'd set eyes on her angelic face and heard her honey sweet drawl; he knew he'd sailed into rough waters. He told himself that once he knew the woman was well and safe, he could get himself back on an even keel. He could once again be content with his mountain ministry. Forcing himself to believe that this was best for all concerned, he said, "You know Todd—that's a good woman and she is in need of a good husband. After some gentle courting, the town Sheriff could end up with the prettiest woman in the territory, as his wife."

When Jimmy Todd lifted his eyebrows and seemed to be considering the idea, Preacher quickly added, "Naturally, a fine woman like her, being a widow and all—will probably require a very long courtship. I'll be back here in about a month. You can tell me then if you've been fortunate enough to make any plans for the future." A sweat suddenly broke out across his brow. Wishing he hadn't even started this conversation, Preacher added, "Of course it's not wise to rush these things—marriage is a big step!"

Sheriff Todd grinned broadly, he lifted his hat, finger combed his hair, then resettled it back on his head. "Well, Pastor, reckon I'll just go talk to that little lady." As he pushed out of the saloon doors, he added. "Might just be my lucky day!" Tipping his hat he added with a wink, "Good day gents."

Preacher was the only man that didn't smile as they watched the sheriff following the beautiful widow Kent down the street.

Chapter 11
Black-Eyed Jack

"A mirror reflects a man's face, but what he is really like is shown by the kind of friends he chooses." Proverbs 27:19

Peeking out the window, Copper watched as jagged, white-hot veins of lightning burned across the sky while thunder resounded throughout the valley. Storms like this always terrified her and it seemed as if the wind might just sweep the cabin right off the mountain. Stepping away from the window, the hair on the back of her neck began to prickle and gooseflesh rose on her arms.

Just then came a loud pounding on the door. Assuming that Shad had his arms full of firewood, Copper sighed with relief and hurriedly flung the door open. To her horror, it wasn't Shad standing there. Instead, outlined by flashes of lightning stood the albino—Dirk Culley. He was just as she remembered. He was dressed in black and his pale skin made him seem as if he were a ghost who had appeared from the midst of the storm. She was paralyzed when she saw the anger flaring in his glassy gray-green eyes. Then when his white hands reached out for her, the sound of her scream split the air as she spun away from him!

Copper awoke the moment she landed on the cold wooden floor. At first, she was frightened and confused. Then she realized it was the middle of the night, and indeed a terrible storm was truly raging outside. Inside, however, all was well.

Rubbing her shoulder, Copper moaned, "Guess it was just a nightmare—and fell off the settee."

"Ya surely did darlin'!"

Copper looked up and saw Shad standing over her. "I'm sorry I woke you—hhhhey." she yelped, when Shad bent down and with one smooth motion, scooped her up off the floor and lifted her into his arms.

"Are you all right?" he demanded. Though his voice echoed his concern, his face looked somewhat fierce in the flickering light of the fireplace. "I knew you'd tumble off that sorry little thing one of these nights. I keep tellin' ya—it wasn't made for sleepin'." When Copper's eyes grew wide he blew out a sigh, "Sweet girl, how long is it gonna take for ya to finally trust me? A minute ago, you screamed as if the devil himself was after ya and flung yerself right onto the floor. I'd wager ya'll be sore fer a week after that fall. Now, I promise not to bother ya none but yer gonna start sleepin' in the bed—with me!"

Not since they'd held hands on their wedding day, had the couple been this close. Copper bit her lip nervously as Shad carried her across the room and gently set her down on the end of the bed. Copper knew she should protest. And yet, with the storm raging outside and the vision of Dirk Culley still so vivid in her mind…it was comforting to be so near this big man. Still, her large green eyes watched warily as he pulled back the quilt and then tucked her in as carefully as if she were a child.

"There ya see yer all safe and snug." He muttered as he shuffled back to his side of the bed, "and you'll sleep like a top, I promise."

It was a bit unnerving when she felt the bed sag and creak while the big man climbed into it. He fumbled a bit making sure they both had the heavy quilt pulled over their shoulders. Copper held her breath waiting for Shad to do something—she wasn't sure what, but the man didn't so much as pat her hand. Instead, he yawned out, "Sweet dreams—sweet girl."

Copper lay awake for a long while. Each time the lightning illuminated the room she studied the plains of her husband's face. A swatch of dark hair fell over his forehead, his high cheekbones and his chin bore the heavy shadow of his beard. In the morning, he would shave off his dark bristly whiskers, but not the black mustache that lined his upper lip. That, she doubted he would ever shave—and for the hundredth time she wondered if it were scratchy or soft. Soon Shad's breathing became even and deep. Copper smiled in spite of the storm that continued to pound the mountain, she couldn't remember ever feeling so protected and warm. It was just as if Shad had slipped her into his pocket for safekeeping. Soon, she was sleeping better than she had in ages.

On Shad's part, he feared he would never be able to sleep with his 'sweet girl' so near. However, the knowledge that his little wife had suffered a fright helped him keep his thoughts chaste and his hands to himself. Well, his hands to himself at least. A further blessing was that the typical night terrors that had also plagued him since the war—quite miraculously—never came.

Shad awoke the following morning, just at daybreak. The wild storm had played itself out in the night and now only a dark reddish glow spilled through the window. He was lying on his side and realized that his little wife was nestled against him. They lay together like two spoons—like newly-weds should! He thought to himself.

The pup tent Copper wore for a nightgown, a hand-me-down from her ex-mother-in-law, was many sizes too big. The neck opening was so large that it eventually pulled to one side, exposing her neck and shoulder. Shad smiled sleepily as he realized that her bare shoulder was a breath away from his lips. Her skin looked as smooth as fresh cream, and not being quite awake himself, Shad simply leaned forward, just to find out if her skin was truly as lusciously soft as it looked. Trying not to awaken his sleeping beauty, Shad very gently touched his lips to her shoulder. *Oh yes—soft—very soft!* He didn't stop to think—just ever so lightly kissed his way from her shoulder all the way up to just under her ear. As he expected, she was sweeter than honey and as smooth as velvet. He was enjoying himself so much and—since Copper seemed to be in a deep sleep, he decided to make a return trip.

He was halfway back to her shoulder when Copper stirred, "Hummm." she moaned. *That's nice—and—it—tickles.*

Suddenly, she realized exactly what—that something was—Shad's mustache! Her bright green eyes flew open and instantly, Copper sprang from the bed as if she'd been catapulted from a cannon. She stood grounded to the floor with her hand touching her shoulder, where she could still feel the tiny sparks his kisses had ignited. As a bewildered frown spread across her face, she asked, "W—what were you doing?"

At first Shad feared he'd made a terrible mistake but then he realized that he needed to show Copper little by little that being near him was a good thing. Therefore, with a look of complete innocence he locked his hands behind his head and said nonchalantly, "Just saying' good mornin' sweet girl. That is the polite way for a husband to say good-morning to his wife, ya know. Remember what Preacher said 'bout be kind and respectful? Well, bein' po-lite is both and it sure is a nice way to start the day—don't ya think?"

Copper wasn't sure how to answer that? It was nice, but then she wasn't always sure when Shad was jesting with her and when he was serious. Their mutually green eyes locked as she asked, "Do—do married people really say good morning—like that—all around the world?"

When Shad kept a straight face, nodded then shrugged his shoulders, Copper decided that it must be true. After all, she'd never known a man that was more *polite* than Shad. Besides, he was older and knew a great deal more about the things of the world. Still rubbing the strange tingling that spread from her neck to her shoulder, she gave him a tentative smile.

Shad saw her confusion and smiled back. Still looking the picture of innocence he asked, "Want me to try it again? May not have done it just right."

"NO! I-I mean you did w—well enough, I'm sure." Copper stuttered, feeling terribly uncomfortable, she hurried towards the kitchen muttering, "My goodness, it's way past time I started breakfast."

Leaning back against his pillow, Shad folded his muscular arms across his chest and whispered, "Thanks Ma, ya always did say that being' polite would come in handy someday!"

Shad and Copper continued to be kind, respectful and very polite. Although they weren't in every sense husband and wife, their days were pleasant and busy. Winter was licking at their heels and having a plentiful supply of firewood was of great importance. Each day Shad and Boone would drag up logs that he had chopped down the year before. Time had cured the logs and now they were ready to be cut and stacked. Shad was skillful with his axe and cross cut saw and Copper quickly learned to be the perfect partner to handle her end of what Shad called a 'misery whip'. She also was efficient at stacking the wood neatly. By the end of each day, they both were bone weary. They spent their evenings taking turns reading to each other from the Bible or from one of Shad's new books he had purchased in Canyon City. They both liked, "The Last of the Mohicans" by James Fenimore Copper. However, their favorite was, "The Pilgrim's Progress" by John Bunyan. When they were too tired to read they would play chess. Copper had won only a handful of times since their wedding night, but she was getting better and their matches sometimes lasted for hours.

After they had finished their winter preparations, Copper expected Shad to return to his woodworking. When he didn't she finally asked,

"Shouldn't you be starting one of your carvings soon? I can't wait to see how you take knives and chisels and turn a plain block of wood into such realistic renditions of leafed out tree branches and winding rose vines."

Shad surprised his young wife when his expression became sad and he muttered, "Oh, kind o' reckon my carvin' days are over." When Copper tried to question him, Shad waved her off saying, "Sweet girl, I really don't want to talk about it right now—if ya don't mind."

As much as she wanted to see Shad return to his carving, what was more important to her was to see him when he was truly upset. So far, he was always even tempered. However, Copper knew that there had to be another side to this man. Everyone had moments of anger and she desperately needed to see what Shad was like in that moment. Finally, one morning she decided she would make it happen. Biting her lip nervously, Copper watched the bacon turn black, then she lifted the lid off the porridge and decided it looked just about right. Right that is, if you were hoping for lumpy, grey and completely disgusting. Shad should be in for breakfast any minute and she hoped that at long last she was going to see what the man would do when he lost his temper.

Copper wrung her hands as she watched out the window, "Lord," she whispered, "is it wrong of me to provoke him like this? Not to mention, waste food. I can't help it; I'm falling in love with that big mountain man. He's been so patient but I know he's anxious to begin our…honeymoon. I think—I am too. I like being near him and I love the idea of having a sweet little baby with dark hair and green eyes. But—what if I learn that Shad has a terrible temper? What if he turns out to be like every man I've ever known? I don't want to bring a child into a home like that. I can't imagine that dear man hurting anyone. Still, he's pretty much been courting me from the start, so he's always on his best behavior. Please forgive me if this is wrong; but I just can't go forward with this marriage until I see what he's like when he's on his worst behavior."

When she heard Shad's voice as he came through the cabin door, Copper quickly set the plate on the table when she heard him exclaim, "I hope you made plenty this morning, sweet girl. I'm so hungry I could eat a buffalo—pick my teeth with his horns and ask for another!"

Shad was chuckling at his jest as he tossed his leg over his chair. He stopped cold the moment he saw what was on his plate. His usual grin instantly turned into a look of complete shock. There were shriveled up black strips of something that he assumed had once been bacon, and next to it was a bowl of… well…he really wasn't sure what it was supposed be. It might have started out to be porridge or mush or gravy—but it was as unrecognizable as it was unappetizing.

Copper held her breath, waiting to see what Shad would say or do. It seemed the man was too stunned to say or do anything. He just stared at his plate. Staying well out of reach, Copper decided to explain, "I got busy and I think breakfast got a little over cooked. Guess you'll just have to eat it anyway; it would be a shame to let that much food go to waste." Not knowing what else to do she turned her back on him and began taking clean cups off the shelf, wiping them and then putting them back.

Shad ran his hand over his jaw as he glanced at Copper and then eyed his breakfast once again. She had always been a good cook. Not everything was always perfect but there was no way he could eat this just to spare her feelings. In fact, it made him a little sick just looking at it! Even so, his stomach growled, he really was hungry. He went over to stand beside his little wife and said gently, "Ain't ya feeling well, sweet girl? Maybe I've been workin' ya too hard. Why don't you lie down fer a spell—I can fix our breakfast this mornin'!"

Copper couldn't believe it and before she realized what she was doing, she swung around and punched Shad's arm, just as hard as she could. When the man only gave her a puzzled look and rubbed his arm—she stamped her foot and shouted: "Shadrack McKenna—what does it take to make you mad? What kind of lily-livered mountain man are you anyway? I burned your breakfast! Do you know what else? I did it on purpose AND I made it just as revolting as I could—I *wasted* good food—don't you have anything to say about that? Doesn't it make you mad?"

Shad contemplated her strange outburst for a moment, then a deep scowl spread across his face, "So, you wanted to make me mad did ya?" He growled. "I can do that—I'm as hungry as a two headed bear. And I'm mad enough to peel the bark of a tree just by lookin' at it." Shad grabbed his plate and bowl, then dumped the nasty contents back in the skillet along with the pot of porridge or whatever it was supposed to have been on top. Then he stomped out the back door and emptied the whole mess on the ground. Leaning his head back, he bellowed for all the world to hear: "If there are any varmints that are fool enough to eat my wife's lousy cookin'—then yer welcome to it!" Still frowning Shad tramped back inside the cabin and slid the large skillet into the wooden sink.

Copper's heart beat in her chest and she watched warily to see what the real Shadrack McKenna would do next. When he stepped closer, Copper just barely managed to hold her ground as she lifted her chin, almost defying him to strike her.

"Copper Delaney-McKenna." His deep voice boomed while his dark eyebrows formed a 'V'. "I don't want you to ever burn my breakfast on purpose again…do ya hear me?" A scant instant later, Shad's green eyes lit up and a broad grin spread across his face. "How was that, darlin'? Was I mad enough fer ya?"

Feeling utterly defeated, Copper slapped at Shad's arm half-heartedly, then she flopped into the nearest chair. "Shadrack McKenna…" she whined. "What am I going to do with you?"

With a tender look on his face, Shad squatted down beside Copper's chair, then he took her hand in his, "Lots of things—sweet girl. We'll make lots o' happy memories. Once you've finally learned you can trust me!"

That night it was impossible for Copper to sleep. Instead, she thought of all the things she did and did not know about the man who was now her husband. His melancholy response about not wanting to carve anymore was a mystery and so was his silly reaction to her burning his breakfast. The following morning she made sure everything was as perfect as she knew how to make it. Later, while she swept the dog run, she noticed that Shad was building a fence. Knowing that he'd be hungry soon, she hurried back inside. It hadn't been long since they'd eaten—but if she'd learned anything about that man…it was that he was always hungry. Even as she worked over the small stove, she found herself imagining how much better her cooking could be with luxuries like eggs and milk. Still, she wasn't about to complain.

When Copper walked outside she felt her heart beat quicken when she caught sight of her handsome husband. It seemed odd to think it, but she was married to a beautiful man. It was an unusually hot fall day and he had taken his shirt off. It never ceased to amaze her that Shad could be so big and powerful, and yet he was never clumsy. On the contrary, his movements were graceful, almost catlike. When he grinned at her, she marveled at how white his teeth looked against his tanned face. When she came closer, he gave her that playful wink of his that always set her stomach to fluttering like two hummingbirds fighting over the same flower.

Shad loved it when Copper came looking for him and he loved it even more when she turned a rosy pink as she handed him a cool cup of water in one hand and a plate of fried corn cakes in the other. That simple blush gave him hope for their future. To Shad, Copper was all the women he had ever dreamt of, bundled into one sweet package.

Taking the cup from her hand, he saluted her with it, saying, "My thanks, sweet girl." After he gulped the water down, he wiped his mouth with the back of his hand and winked, "You are proof that God blesses fools and answers prayer!"

Copper lowered her eyes and shook her head at his kind words. This dear man never complained, instead he continued to say such lovely things when she so blatantly didn't deserve them. He had prayed for a wife and she hadn't truly fulfilled that role—not yet. He was always a gentleman, patient and kind. The only time he was the least bit forward was when he politely said good morning to her with kisses on her shoulder. The way husbands everywhere said good morning to their wives. Though Copper had never heard of that ritual, she had to admit she'd come to like it—very much!

While the big man munched on his corncakes, he stared at his pretty wife and couldn't remember every being this happy. Just being near Copper—pleased him beyond measure. He knew he probably looked like a moonstruck boy most of the time and was glad there was no one around to tease him. Then he remembered how lonely he had been—and didn't care if the whole world saw. He had God to thank for this treasure. Being patient wasn't always easy but then he reminded himself that he and Copper had just met. These early months should be a time for courting. These were the days and weeks when a couple should work on their friendship and on their combined faith in God. Shad fully believed that day by day, things would get better until one day his sweet girl would look up at him and see a man she completely trusted. And then…she would give him her heart!

While Shad wolfed down the corncakes, Copper examined the strange looking fence he was building. It was just outside yet another cave opening, next to the barn. Every two feet there were thin posts set vertically into the ground. For the horizontal part of the fence, Shad split long saplings into thin bendable strips, then he wove each strip in and out of the posts.

"What is this for?" she asked, "You're weaving this fence so tight; it looks like you're making a basket."

Shad raised his dark eyebrows and grinned mischievously as he popped the last bite into his mouth. When Copper frowned, he handed her the empty tin cup and plate. "It's a surprise sweet girl. 'Course, if yer good at riddles, maybe you can guess. It hops about on four legs, flies and sounds a little like Remy at sunup."

"It can fly and it has four legs—there's no such thing." Laughing, she shook her head, "I can't even imagine…give me another hint."

"Nope, no more hints. The man whose bringing yer surprise is a good friend of mine. His name is Black-Eyed Jack and should be here any day now. Guess I ought to warn ya though, he's an ornery old bird and he takes some gettin' used to but—he's harmless." When he saw a look of worry on Copper's face, Shad quickly added, "It's just that Jack—well he's Jack—there's nobody quite like him. Fer one thing he had a load of buckshot blow up in his face—he's a little scary lookin' but he's a good man." Ignoring Copper's frown Shad rubbed his hands together. "Now, if yer anxious to know what yer surprise is, just step inside the cave, maybe you can guess."

"Oh no—you won't get me in there. That's one of the first things I told you. Remember, I hate caves!"

Shad did remember, but he needed her to get over her fear because there was another cave and another surprise to come. "I'll go with ya." Shad coaxed. "Hold onto yer hand every step of the way. It's real nice inside."

Copper shook her head as the color drained from her face. "Please—I just can't." she said softly, "You've used these caves to good advantage, I know. It's just, I don't like dark places like that. When I was little, some boys dragged me into a cave and left me there in the dark for hours. Finally, one of the older boys felt bad about it. He brought a lantern and led me out. I'll never forget how scared I was. My schoolmaster father made many enemies among the bigger boys in town. Little did they know that being mean to me didn't bother him in the least. Still, I'm afraid I'll always hate caves."

Shad had a sudden desire to line those boys up and escort them to the woodshed. He never did have any use for bullies. In fact, Shad thought he'd like to have a word or two with her father, that is, if that sorry ogre were still alive. Then he looked at Copper twisting her hands and said gently, "You know you really shouldn't allow fears to boss you around like that. These caves are a blessing and one of the main reasons I built my cabin in this spot. And if you peek inside this one—you might be able to guess your surprise." He teased. When Copper shook her head emphatically, Shad's green eyes softened and he smiled. "That's all right, we'll forget about the cave for now, but ya know Jack could come any time; I could sure use your help!"

Copper brightened instantly, "I'd love to help—I can do more than just woman's work, ya know."

"I do know, sweet girl. I'd still be cuttin' and stackin' firewood if you hadn't helped me. So, would ya mind draggin' some of those small poles over here?"

Shad chuckled when Copper's face lit up and she spun on her heels and skipped across the yard, like a little girl.

"Lord help me." Shad muttered softly. "Sure have fallen hard fer that little gal. Seems every blessed thing she does pleases me right down to m' toes!"

The tender expression remained on Shad's face as he watched his sweet little wife stopping for a moment to rub Remy's ears. The big mule had her large legs curled under her as she dozed in a patch of warm sand between the stack of poles and the new fence. Like Shad, Remy watched Copper dragging a thin pole across the yard and then return for another one. Each time Copper walked passed her mule, she gave her a little pat. It was a fact that Remy had a moose sized head, but it was also a fact that it housed an unusually keen mind.

It wasn't long before Remy decided that naptime was over and she got to her feet. Neither Shad nor Copper noticed the mule's actions for they were both working together weaving the split saplings into the fence. However, when Copper felt something nudge her in the back, she jumped. At first, she wasn't surprised to see Remy, assuming she wanted her ears scratched. Then Copper began to laugh and so did Shad. It seemed that Remy had decided to continue where Copper had left off, for she had one of the thin poles held in her teeth.

"Oh Remy, you big sweetheart." Copper cried as she hugged the mule's neck. "Isn't she clever, Shad?"

"Well. She sure beats all I ever saw. If I hadn't seen it I wouldn't have believed it!"

As far as Shad was concerned, Remy won the prize of being the ugliest critter he'd ever seen and now it seemed she'd win a prize for the smartest. Shad ran the back of his hand down Copper's cheek, "She's clever all right, but then again I think you could charm anybody to do just about anything. Kind o' worries me a little."

Copper blushed at his touch and then asked, "Why would that worry you?"

"Well," Shad groaned, "if ya can get that beast to do something like that—without even askin'. I fear it won't be long before ya've got me actin' just as silly. Yep, it's kind o' worrisome for a man like me."

Shad looked truly vulnerable just then and wanting to reassure him, Copper gently squeezed his arm and said, "You don't have to worry, Shad, 'cause I'd do anything for you too." Suddenly thinking of some things she wasn't doing for Shad made her cheeks burn. Instantly, she spun around and continued working on the fence as if her life depended on it.

The big man smiled gently, wishing he could somehow convince her not to worry. Right now he'd be satisfied with the same kind of hug she'd just given that crazy mule. Of course, a kiss would have been even better, for he was still waiting for that first kiss! They had been married for weeks now and it was downright disturbing for him to watch his *sweet girl* throw those tender arms around that ugly old mule. Especially with her un-kissed groom standing right there.

Still, it was a happy day, filled with laughter as the three of them worked together. Each time Remy brought her a pole, all Copper had to do was hug the oversized pet, by way of thanks, then simply point towards the pile and say, "One more please." Once the mule decided not to move. Copper giggled and gave her ears a good long scratch and when she made her request a second time, the mule trotted back to the pile. Remy seemed happy if Copper was happy. Shad couldn't help but smile because...he felt the same way.

The following day, just as the sun was slipping behind the highest mountain and the moon was a thumbnail on the eastern horizon, Shad closed the gate on the fence and latched it. Feeling tired but proud of their efforts, Shad took Copper's hand as they headed towards the cabin.

Copper was just taking down her bowl to mix up a batch of Shad's favorite corn cakes when she turned to find the big man himself ladling lard into the large cast iron skillet and stoking the fire beneath it.

"Shad, you don't have to help with this…this is my job. You've worked hard today! I'll call you when dinner's ready."

Shad's eyebrows shot up and he laughed. "And—who—was that sweet girl that was workin' beside me all day? I reckon it's my turn to help you—we're a team—right?"

A lump formed in Copper's throat but then she grinned and nodded her agreement. This mountain man was always surprising her. She still feared that he was too good to be true and kept waiting for the angry, demanding husband to show himself. And yet, these past weeks of married life had proved that Shad was polite, pleasant, patient, and he made her laugh. Now that Preacher was no longer there to chaperon, Shad was no longer tongue-tied. He complimented her, teased her and flirted with her outrageously. She was embarrassed by his praises and always changed the subject by asking him questions about his childhood or his plans for the future. Each day she came to know Shad a little better and she liked him more every day. In fact, as she watched this mountain of a man lumbering about the kitchen helping her prepare supper, she suddenly realized that these days spent with Shad had been the happiest of her life!

Shad grunted as he held Boone's hoof between his legs. "Wish ya'd quit leanin' on me pard, I ain't no footstool ya know!" Lifting the hoof Shad pushed the big stallion's weight off his back and onto the brute's own stout legs, then sighed in relief. He trimmed the last hoof with his nippers. Then moving the flat side of the rasp in circular motions, he smoothed the surface of the hoof, making sure it was even. "Come winter, you'll be happy we did this son. When you don't have to walk on snow and ice wearin' metal shoes."

Sensing that he and Boone had an audience, Shad lowered the stallion's hoof to the ground, stood upright and stretched. When he saw Copper watching him, he gave her his usual ear-to-ear grin. When he noticed a new expression on her face he narrowed his eyes, "Yer a wearin' a look I don't believe I've seen before. Yer up to somethin', ain't ya sweet girl?" Then he leaned down and whispered, "Don't want me to get mad at ya again—do ya?"

"No!" Copper huffed, "You aren't any good at it!" Then, looking as innocent as possible, she said in a singsong voice, "I've made you a ***luscious*** berry pie!" When Shad murmured his approval and licked his lips she added, "But

I've hidden it—you can't have even one bite—not until you tell me what my surprise is."

Loving the idea that his cautious little wife was feeling bold enough to tease him, Shad grinned as he stepped close and put one finger under Copper's chin and asked, "So, you made me a ***luscious*** berry pie—did ya? Not a blue berry or black berry but a ***luscious berry* pie**. Not knowing what yer surprise is—is doin' ya in darlin'!" He wiggled his eyebrows at her and said, "All right—you win. The best way to tell ya though…is just to show ya. Come on, peek inside the cave and you'll see what it is."

Ignoring Copper's frown, Shad turned and took off Boone's halter, allowing the horse to wander back inside the barn. Then the big man headed for the new enclosure they had just finished and disappeared inside the cave. Shad wasn't playing fair but Copper followed as far as the gate, then she stopped and stamped her foot. She thought sure her plan would work. Now what was she to do? No one had ever given her a surprise before and she couldn't contain her excitement or her curiosity. Still, she wasn't about to step inside that cave.

Suddenly, Remy trotted out of the barn braying out her alarm call! As noisy as she was, she couldn't compete with the wild cacophony of bleating and squawking that was coming down the path and into the yard. Shading her eyes with her hand, she saw that it was a man with two heavily loaded pack mules. He looked exactly like the mountain men she heard tell of; for he was surely the fiercest looking character Copper had ever seen. He was dressed in buckskins, dark and well worn, with long fringes fluttering from his sleeves and the outside seams of his leggings. His face was nearly as dark and leathery as the clothes he wore. The skin around his right eye looked almost like a black patch. This had to be none other than Black-Eyed Jack, she told herself, remembering the man's mishap with exploding gunpowder. Adding to his fearsome appearance was a long, steel-gray beard braided into rows. As if this fellow's appearance wasn't eccentric enough…on top of his head, was another head. Copper found that she had to look twice to make sure…but her eyes hadn't deceived her. It was indeed—the smooth white skull of a skunk with what looked like the rest of the animal's furry body still attached! Copper had seen coonskin caps but—skunk? She couldn't help herself; she leaned forward and sniffed. Fortunately, there was no pungent smell, but still it was quite a cap! The white skull protruded over the man's forehead, the body of the skunk formed the cap and of course, the fluffy, black and white striped tail fell down the old man's back.

Rendered mute by the man's appearance, Copper slowly backed away. Oddly enough, the mountain man found himself almost as dazed. The sight of this pretty, bronze haired girl had whisked his old heart back to another time and to another redheaded beauty. One who had for a while given meaning to his life. Finally, he shook himself out of his reverie and in a low and raspy voice, he growled; "McKenna—get that sorry carcass o' yourn out here, I'm a scarin' yer woman!"

When Copper remained transfixed by the sight of him, the odd little man chuckled as he swung down from his saddle. Putting his gloved hand over his heart, he said kindly, "Please ma'am, no need to be afeared o' me. 'Cause even though I've known grizzly bears to swoon at the mere sight of me, I'll make ya a promise—I'm as much a friend to you as a waggle-tailed pup!"

It was the strangest thing. Despite her fears, there was just something about this outrageous old man that Copper suddenly found completely endearing. Her lips curved into a smile as Shad came and slipped a protective arm around her shoulders, "That's right, sweet girl. Like I told ya, this old goat is as harmless as a baby chick."

Narrowing his eyes, the mountain man puffed out his chest, "I said I was *friendly*, ya no account young buck, *not harmless!* And I'll not stand fer a cub like you defamin' m' character. It ain't that I mind being called old…'cause I'm as stubborn as a rock to make up fer it. I don't want yer woman to be afeared o' me, but she should know the truth! I'm the best shot—the worst liar, and the most humble man in all the Rockies. I've sailed from Maine to Spain, and I've trailed a million buffalo from Mexico to the North Pole." Giving Copper a wink he waived his thumb at Shad and said, "Given my illustrious credentials, the boy should treat me with a bit more respect—ain't that right, ma'am?" When Copper giggled and nodded her agreement, Jack softened his voice adding, "One more thing, I got eyes like an eagle. And you, dear lady, are the prettiest thing on either side of the great divide!"

Shad smiled proudly at the old man's appraisal of his little wife. Then the two men stepped towards each other with broad grins and clasped their right arms together while they pounded each other on the back with the other. Without a word, the old man turned away and pulled what looked like a bundle of white fur from one of the pack mules. He strolled towards Copper with a sheepish grin and sat the small animal at her feet.

Laughing with delight, she fell to her knees beside the snow-white nanny goat. Then her eyes wandered back to the crates tied to the two pack mules and understood all the noise.

"Oh, Shad this is a wonderful surprise! Chickens and goats…eggs and milk. Oh thank you!" She cried, but she hugged the goat. Then she looked up at Shad and laughed, "Now I understand your riddle. It hops about on four legs, flies, and sounds like Remy at sunup? Goats hop, chickens fly and tomorrow morning the rooster will crow, like Remy. AND…I bet there's a chicken coop inside the cave—isn't that right?"

Shad grinned his reply then took Copper's hand, prompting her to stand beside him as he said proudly, "Jack, let me introduce ya to m' wife! This is Copper Delaney-McKenna."

When Copper smiled, Jack took a step closer and doffed his hat. The fluffy skunk tail brushed the ground as he bowed at the waist in a courtly greeting.

"Missus McKenna, Preacher should a warned me, and that's a fact. He told me this scoundrel had married up—but he plum forgot to tell me that you were as pretty as a Rocky Mountain sunrise!" The old man straightened as he held his skunk cap dramatically over his heart then added, "And sayin' that ain't half enough, ma'am—ain't half enough!"

Suddenly wishing that he'd fetched these critters himself instead of allowing this smooth talking old buzzard to bring them to *his sweet girl,* Shad frowned as he mumbled, "Copper…this here is…Jack."

Still holding his hat in his hand, the old man shook his head, "Forgive me ma'am, but this here reprobate yer married to, he don't know how to make a proper introduction. Ya see he don't know my rightful name, but I'd sure admire fer you to know it—dear lady. My name is Josiah Alfonzo Jackson, the third. At yer service."

Shad's eyebrows nearly lifted to his hairline as he stammered, "A-Alfonzo? The…the third?"

Had the old man's eyes not been narrowed into a permanent squint, the couple might have noticed that they sparkled with mischief. Jack couldn't remember when he'd enjoyed himself so much. Copper was as sweet and pretty as a spring meadow. And McKenna? Well, he was quickly becoming as green-eyed jealous as a tree frog and as sour as an unripe apple.

Intent on goading the younger man further, Jack stepped closer to Copper and said sweetly, "Since me and Pa shared the same name, everyone called Pa, Jo and me Siah. Haven't been called that in—well, too many years ma'am. I surely would be pleased iffen you'd call me, Siah instead of Jack."

To her husband's consternation, Copper didn't seem at all afraid of the black-eyed mountain man. Instead, she gave their guest her sweetest smile, as she replied, "I am very pleased to meet you, Siah." Then turning towards Shad she said, "By the time you gentlemen make the chickens and the goats comfortable in their new home—I'll have dinner ready!"

Shad sighed as he watched Copper gracefully making her way towards the cabin. He frowned, however, when he turned to see the old codger was also watching, *his little wife*, with a wistful smile covering his darkened face. "Yep, Preacher should a warned me. She sure is a little darlin'!"

Shad's frown deepened, "Just so you remember ***whose*** little darlin' she is. Come on—***Siah***…" he groaned, exaggerating the old man's proper name. "We've got to make these critters—comfortable."

The ole man instantly bristled. "Now—hold on there, boy. I'm still Jack to an ornery polecat like you. I'm Siah only to that little red-haired angel." Jack's gaze turned tender as he stared towards the cabin. "She's just like a touch a springtime on a winter's day. I tell ya boy iffen I was just a mite younger…"

Shad glared at Jack but when he saw the teasing look on the older man's face, they both began to laugh. "Come on you skunk-topped, moth-eaten Romeo!" Shad grunted, "Grab one of those crates and we'll introduce these chickens to their new home."

That night, to Shad's irritation and Copper's delight, Jack announced his plan to stay and teach them how to tend the goats and make cheese. Shad couldn't keep from clenching his jaw every time he heard his pretty young wife giggling at something the old man said. He felt left out. Oh, he knew it was ridiculous to be jealous of Jack. The old man had been a good friend to him and he was kind and respectful to Copper. But dog-gone-it—she was only just beginning to trust *him*—and they were married! Then here comes this ornery old mountain man and his timid wife takes to him like he was Saint Nicholas himself. Of course, Jack took to Copper the same way. He treated her like the sweet daughter he never had. He praised and complemented every blessed thing she did, and Copper couldn't do enough! She fixed his favorite buckwheat pancakes nearly every morning, she prepared a special poultice for a boil he had on his shoulder. She made him a little footstool to put his sore leg on. And what bothered Shad most of all? She listened hungrily to each and every crazy, braggadocios story the old scallywag told.

"Yep, it were Chief Colorow," Jack explained while Copper lifted the old man's leg onto the stool. "He's the one who gave me this here wound."

"Chief…my foot." Shad mumbled under his breath. "Probably some squaw thinking she was getting rid of a skunk!"

Jack pretended not to hear and said dramatically, "Don't like to complain about my wounds, ma'am, even if they do pain me somethin' fierce." he lamented, then leveled a frown in Shad's direction when the younger man rolled his eyes. "Yep, the tip o' that arrowhead is still lodged in the bone. "'Course me and Colorow are blood brothers now."

"Oh my, Siah—I'm sorry it hurts." Copper soothed, "But, I'd love to hear that story! We'd both love to hear all about it, wouldn't we Shad?"

"Sure…" Shad mumbled sarcastically, "I can hardly wait."

Copper smiled as she listened with rapt attention to Jack's stories while Shad continued to mumble and groan throughout each tale. Of course, Shad couldn't really fault the old man for enjoying Copper's attention. He was lonely and Shad understood loneliness—only too well. He even understood and appreciated that Copper had a tender heart, and yet understanding didn't ease the resentment he felt over the growing friendship between his lovely young wife and the rough old mountain man. It felt like a splinter under his thumbnail, a splinter he couldn't get rid of.

Finally, after a full fortnight, Josiah Alfonzo Jackson, III, saddled his horse, packed his mules and said good-bye. Shad had always been fond of Jack and he always would be, but that didn't mean he wasn't down right thrilled to be saying good-bye. And yet that's when it happened, the one thing that nearly did Shad in. He watched miserably as his own sweet girl rose up on tip toe and placed a good-bye kiss on the old man's leathery cheek.

"We'll miss you." she said softly, "Remember, Siah, you promised to come back soon for another long visit! "

Shad gave Jack a solemn closed mouth grin, and although he shook the older man's hand he did not second his wife's invitation. Jack had been a good friend and had taught him many things. Over the course of his visit, he taught Copper a lot about raising goats and chickens in the high-country. Together they made the first batches of butter and cheese, which would certainly liven up their mealtime. It was a pure fact that the old codger had been a godsend and a good friend. And yet, hang-it all, Shad couldn't seem to tamp down his jealousy, even though he recognized it as a sin. He longed for Copper to be truly his, and the sight of his sweet girl—placing a kiss on that old buzzard's cheek—was more than Shad could bear. Especially when his bride had yet to give her groom—even one kiss!

Chapter 12
Learning to Trust

"Above all...put on love, which binds everything together in harmony." Colossians 3:14

Sure as shootin'...sparks are gonna fly, if I don't put some distance between me and Copper... I'm gonna say or do somethin' I'll regret!

Shad kept silently warning himself, even as his irritation grew—he just needed to get away for a while. He knew his attitude was wrong—his feelings were uncalled for and ungodly. He told himself that once he was alone, he'd ask the Lord to take away this hurt and jealousy and help him find a way to earn Copper's trust and love.

He managed to stand quietly beside his wife until Jack had ridden out of sight. Then Shad blew out an exasperated sigh, turned to Copper and muttered, "The trout ought to be bitin' down at the river about now. Reckon I'll go fishin'."

Copper blinked up at him, wanting to ask what was wrong, but something warned her not to. Everything about Shad was suddenly unrecognizable to her: his stance—his tone. Still, Copper couldn't imagine why he was acting this way. Normally, when he went fishing, he always asked her to go with him. Not knowing what to say or do she gazed awkwardly around the yard. It was then that she spotted a problem with the cabin's roof.

"Oh—Shad—look!" she called to the man's back as he headed for the barn. "There are some shingles missing from the roof. If we don't fix it before it rains it will ruin your beautiful floors!"

Almost violently, Shad spun on his heels and nearly shouted, "Hey now, they're not *my* floors they're *our* floors." He knew he was being a fool to act like this around Copper. But—the truth was—he was fresh out of patience today. That girl seemed to care more for the dirty buzzards in the air and old buzzard's like Black-Eyed Jack. And she most certainly cared more for his cabin—than she did for him. As he reached the barn, he grabbed his pole off the wall and growled, "The roof can wait. Right now—I'm goin' fishin'."

As he left the yard, Shad hesitated for a moment as he glanced at Copper. Her mouth was pursed and she was frowning at the ground as if she were trying to figure out a complicated puzzle. She was such a pretty little thing and her lips looked so soft and pink. Just then he remembered seeing them on Jack's weathered and scratchy jaw. He knew he had better walk away before his smoldering jealousy made him do something stupid. Like wrapping his arms around his 'sweet girl' and giving her the kind of kiss that might just—set the mountain on fire! Of course behavior like that would probably make Copper want to run from him, just like she'd run from that outlaw, Dirk Culley.

Before leaving the yard, Shad grunted. "I know what I need to do…and right now…I need to go fishin'."

Shrugging, Copper tried to tell herself that his behavior wasn't hurting her feelings. "That's a good idea." She called amiably, "You catch them—I'll fry them up!" Thinking he would be pleased by her willingness to help, she added happily, "I'll have the roof fixed by the time you get back with your catch."

Snapping to a halt, Shad turned his head and scowled at her, "Ya'll do no such thing! You stay *off* that roof—ya hear me?"

The man's rough tone and blatant order startled Copper at first, but then she straightened, "I'm not a craftsman like you, but I know how to nail shingles on a roof. I fixed Ma Riley's roof more times that I can count, and it was much steeper than the cabin's. I can do more than women's work and you know it!"

Shad could no longer tame his irritation, he lowered his voice and emphasizing each word he said, "I'll not have *my woman* doin' *my work*. I'll fix the roof—in my own way—and in my own good time!" Sounding more like Captain McKenna than the loving husband he had tried so hard to be, he added forcefully, "Do I make myself clear?"

They stood there and stared at each other. Copper was confused and Shad didn't know why he was so annoyed. Then again, maybe he did. He had fallen hard for Copper, he'd come to love her dearly—he needed her. Copper, on the other hand, didn't seem to need anything but room and board—she didn't love him—she didn't need him. Apparently, not even for his carpentry skills and—that was what he did best! Since the night she'd fallen off the settee, she shared his bed. Of course she clung to her side, that is until she fell asleep, then she clung to him. It had been an exquisite form of sweet torture but it was the only sign that maybe they had a future as husband and wife. Then this morning, as if to add insult to injury—she had kissed that ornery old—Black-Eyed Jack. Shad had dreamt of their first kiss; be it good morning or goodnight or anytime in between he'd take any kiss she offered and be glad of it! But there had been no kiss. How much longer must he wait? He hadn't even received a kiss on the cheek—but that ugly mule got hugs and Black-Eyed 'Siah' Jackson received a sweeter than honey kiss good-bye. Shad figured he must be doing something wrong...but what it was...he sure didn't know!

When Shad frowned at her, and then stomped away, Copper couldn't help but wonder if perhaps she was finally seeing the real Shadrack McKenna! The day had started well enough. He had awakened her with sweet kisses on her shoulder, as he did every morning. She hadn't done anything to make him mad—had she? No—she felt certain that she hadn't. Still, there was no mistaking his bad mood. Had his even temper thus far been just a ruse? She had almost come to trust him—almost told him that she loved him. Now Copper reasoned that it had been wise for her to hold back.

Never in Copper's life had a day passed so slowly. The sun seemed to meander across the sky like a lazy turtle while she waited for Shad to return. Frowning and biting her lip, her gaze went from the meadow that led to the river then back up to the changing sky. That morning it had been cornflower blue and the day had been filled with buttery warm sunshine. However, as the hours passed, she watched as angry, steel-bottomed clouds churned and rolled in the distance. Inside the clouds, she saw the soft bursts of light slowly followed by deep rumblings. The storm was still far away but the wind was growing more restless as it blew the bronze strands of hair across her freckled face. The rain she had feared would be arriving soon and still, Shad hadn't come home! Quickly, she picked up a feed pan and called to her precious chickens. Clucking nervously, they followed her through the fenced yard. She hurried towards the opening of the cave, still too afraid of dark places, she flung the feed inside, then locked them in so they'd be safe. Putting her fingers to her lips, she whistled for Remy. When the mule came running, she locked her in the stall next to Boone. Then she poured grain into their mangers, and when she returned outside, she had to fight the wind to make sure the barn doors were latched securely.

Once again, her eyes searched in the direction of the river. "Shadrack McKenna." Copper chided. "Can't you see that a storm is coming? Where are you?" Her heart wavered between fury and fear, while the wind grew steadily stronger. "Are you in trouble? Is that why you haven't come home all day? Oh, Lord, should I go looking for him or should I stay here and fix the roof? And if I fix it—what will he do to me?"

Troubled thoughts swirled through Copper's mind in the same way the wind was spinning dust devils across the yard. "He was in a foul mood when he left this morning! If he decided to walk off his angst…those long legs could have taken him miles away—and in any direction. He may just be too far away to get back here in time." Just then, a fearful thought came to her, "What if he's watching right now to see if I'll obey him. Maybe when he sees me climbing the ladder, he'll come after me with his belt!"

One last time Copper looked towards the river and then searched the sky. Shad was nowhere in sight but she did see crooked fingers of lightning stretching out across the darkening horizon. Then from a distant cloud, she watched as rain began to fall in a wide silvery curtain.

"It has to be done now," Copper grimaced. "I'll be working in the middle of that storm if I don't hurry!"

As she gathered the tools and pulled the ladder across the yard, she tried to speak comfort to herself, "Shad's going to be upset…but I think he'll also be happy if I can show him that the shingles are on and the cabin is safe. Shad won't hurt me—I have to believe that—he won't hurt me!"

Glancing back up at the sky, Copper realized that there wasn't even enough time to change into her overalls, so she bent over and grabbed the back of her skirt, pulled it up between her legs then quickly tucked it into her waistband. In the next instant, she was on the roof, replacing the missing shingles as if her life depended on her speed—and quite possibly—it did!

When the storm finally hit, it was like a wild creature—all fangs and claws. To keep from being blown off the roof, Copper was forced to lie down as she nailed the last shingle into place. When a bright arrow of lightning arched through the sky, Copper breathed a prayer for Shad's safe return and added one more nail for good measure. Again, she wondered if she shouldn't have gone looking for him rather than fixing the roof. "Oh please Lord," she begged, "bring Shad home and let him be all right! And…please don't let him be angry at me."

"COPPER DELANEY-MCKENNA!"

At first, she wasn't sure if she was hearing her name or just the screaming wind and rumbling thunder. Then she realized that it was unmistakably her husband's deep voice with her name on his lips and from the sound of it, God had answered her first prayer, Shad seemed whole and well. Unfortunately, it was obvious that God hadn't paid attention to her second prayer—the one about Shad not being angry. For the man sounded even more dangerous than the storm that was attacking the mountain.

"You get yerself down off that roof!" he bellowed. "Before ya break yer fool neck!"

Shad's booming voice coupled with the raucous storm was terrifying. Copper's hair blew wildly about her as she jumped to her feet and scrambled to gather her tools. When she reached for the ladder, a sudden gust of wind blew it out of her hand and she quickly stepped away from the roof's edge. Then another blast of wind slammed into her and threw her off balance. Her feet went out from under her and she began to slide.

Shad couldn't believe that he'd slept the day away. Then again, he hadn't slept well in weeks, so it shouldn't have been a surprise when he drifted off beside his favorite fishing hole. So deep was his sleep that he failed to notice the changing weather until he awoke to the rumble of thunder and the wind blowing harshly through the pine trees. When he looked up to find the churning clouds were a menacing shade of gunpowder gray, he jumped to his feet and headed for the cabin. Not until the first drop of rain hit him right between the eyes—did he remember the roof!

"Copper was right, it's gonna come a floodin' through that roof and ruin her, 'little bit of heaven.'" Shad said each word through gritted teeth even as he started to run.

Just as Shad bounded into the yard, he looked up and in the midst of this violent rainstorm, he saw Copper on the roof. The site shook him so hard he thought his knees might buckle and that his heart would surely stop. Before he could think straight, he allowed his fear to override his common sense. Growling like a crazed lion, he shouted her name—he knew he'd done the wrong thing when he saw the alarm in her eyes. She was being careful before his foolishness, but when he yelled, she panicked! His mind refused to work but his legs tripled their stride, even as the wind fought against his every step. Whatever it took, he had to get to Copper!

A blinding, gut wrenching terror gripped Shad as he watched the ladder being ripped from her hand and then his precious 'sweet girl' was sliding helplessly towards the edge of the roof. It seemed to him that one minute he was watching a nightmare unfold and then in the next moment—miraculously—Copper was in his arms! They were both soaking wet and breathing hard as they stared at each other in amazement. Without a word, Shad carried her to the cabin and kicked the door closed. The moment they were inside, Copper wrapped her arms around him while Shad buried his head in the crook of her neck. Panting and trembling they clung fiercely to each other, while outside lightning struck and thunder splintered the air with such fury—that it shook the cabin.

Struggling to catch her breath, Copper smiled up at Shad and whispered her thanks. The fall had terrified her but then, Shad, that dear wonderful man, had caught her! Just then that's all she could think about, and he was holding her so tenderly that she could only assume that he had forgotten his anger. However, when the man didn't return her smile, but instead, lifted one dark eyebrow and scowled down at her, she wasn't so sure. Suddenly, feeling the need to do something, Copper wriggled out of Shad's arms and hurried to fetch them both a towel.

Handing one to Shad, she patted her face with the other and said softly, "I've been so worried. I'm so glad you got home safe!"

When Shad just stood there without saying a word, Copper became desperate to see her dear Shadrack McKenna again. That special, sweet man who laughed when all other men would be angry. Although she'd never attempted using her feminine wiles before, she decided she'd do just about anything to break this awful tension. Stepping closer to the fire, she tipped her head slightly and pulled all her hair around to one side. It fell long and lose over her shoulder as she shook it and ran her fingers through it, allowing the warmth of the fire to dry it. Shad loved it when Copper dried her hair this way; he always stopped whatever he was doing so he could watch the way the fire light reflected against the amber colored hair. This time, however, her obvious ploy didn't work. When Shad folded his arms over his chest and narrowed his eyes, Copper knew that he had seen through her trick. It was plain to see that nothing would pacify the man but a full explanation and—it had better be good!

Finally, Copper let out a sigh, "I'm sorry you're upset, but you have to understand. I waited for you, but when you didn't come back and then I saw that the storm was coming…I just had to…"

Copper stopped in mid-sentence for she could see that her words were rolling off the man as quickly as the raindrops were rolling off his thick black hair and down his face. He was holding the towel she gave him but not using it. More importantly, he was still breathing hard, his nostrils flaring and his powerful chest heaving but it was no longer from exertion. Now, she could see it clearly, the big mountain man was angry! This time—he was mad to the core!

"I—I know I didn't do what you said. But—you didn't do what you said either." Pretending a confidence she didn't feel, she added, "And I did a good job." Then she pointed up to the ceiling and said happily, "See…no leaks!"

Normally, when she put that happy tone in her voice, Shad couldn't help but grin, but this time he wasn't amused. He wasn't sure anything would ever amuse him again. Copper had scared the living daylights out of him—probably ten years off his life. He kept telling himself *"she's all right"*, as he watched his 'sweet girl' walking about the cabin and talking as if nothing had happened.

Shad listened to the rain and hail as it continued to pummel the cabin and thunder boomed all around them. He gripped the towel in both hands while agonizing images played out in his mind. *What if she'd been struck by lightning? What if I hadn't caught her?* As visions of what might have been, consumed his thoughts, he could no longer hold his tongue, "Woman," he growled. "Did ya lose all your good sense today? Or were you just tryin' to make me mad again?"

Startled by the fury in Shad's voice, Copper stepped back, "I—I wasn't trying to do *anything*—but fix the roof!" she insisted. Then she stiffened, "And I didn't just try—I fixed it." Now Copper was becoming angry and she added with a deep frown of her own, "Everything would have been fine if you hadn't yelled at me! The roof had to be fixed. The storm was almost here and—you weren't. So I fixed it—that's all."

"That's ALL?" he roared, as his countenance grew dark. "Didn't I tell you that I'd fix the roof?"

"Yes, you told me…but you didn't do it, did you?" Instantly Copper lowered her head, her bold words frightened her. She sounded arrogant and defiant—she'd gone too far! Her face blanched white and her green eyes grew wide with fear. Believing that now punishment was sure to come, she tried to calm herself:

Maybe if I don't say another word, he won't hurt me too badly. I've been waiting to see what he's really like. Now that I have...I won't stay. I'm no more Shad's wife than I was Vernon's. Tomorrow—I'll run away!

As lightning, wind and thunder continued to roar around them, it was as if the storm outside was somehow in step with the storm that was silently raging inside. They stood like two statues in the middle of the cabin. Copper waited for the punishment that was sure to come. Shad trying to purge the realization that Copper could have easily been killed or badly injured. The big man's hand shook as he ran it through his wet hair. It was a miracle that God had allowed him to get to her in time. Somehow, he had to make her understand that nothing—absolutely nothing was worth her taking that kind of risk.

Although his voice sounded gentle at first, by the time he finished what he had to say, it sounded more like a thunderous growl, "You will listen to me, Copper Delaney-McKenna. You will do what I tell ya from now on—and you stay off the roof! You will not put yourself in danger—ever again!"

Copper remained silent but her eyes went from his hands to the heavy belt at his waist.

"Woman," he continued sounding a bit more in control. "It seems like the only thing around here you care anything about—is—this—blasted cabin. I fear what would become of our marriage if this pile of logs blew away. Would ya leave me, if I couldn't build ya another just like it?"

No words passed Copper's lips, but her heart pounded like a drum in her chest, tears stung the back of her eyes and her throat felt like it was closing. She couldn't see that Shad's angry words were born of worry and hurt. All Copper could think of just then was that she'd stood before angry men before and she knew what came next. Warily she watched Shad's large and powerful hands flex and tremble as he once again ran them through his wet hair, shoving the black curls from his eyes. Since he hadn't unbuckled his belt that might mean that, he planned to use his open hand or maybe even his fists! Copper's knees threatened to buckle, the room was getting smaller—the walls seemed to be closing in.

Shad saw the color draining from his wife's face. He had wanted to frighten her—but from doing dangerous things—not from him! Sucking in a huge breath, he released it slowly then asked in a truly gentle voice, "Do ya even remember that ya fell off the roof? Even though I caught ya—ya landed mighty hard." Suddenly, the thought struck him, perhaps she was pale because she'd been hurt—inside. His mind suddenly relived the injuries he'd seen in the war. "Hey…you look like you're about to faint! Where does it hurt?"

Copper jumped, when Shad lunged forward and reached out for her. Then she screamed as if the man had suddenly turned into a monster. Spinning on her heels, she ran for the door that led out to the garden. Outside, the tempest was still raging like a wild beast, and all Shad could think of was that, the little fool was heading right back into the storm—he had to stop her! Copper jerked the door open only to have Shad slam it shut with the palm of his hand.

He stood there and waited for Copper to turn around. This was their first fight and he figured it was about to become a real barnburner. He had seen snippets that suggested that his little redhead might have a temper, and for a while, she acted as if she was going to stand up for herself. However, after he slammed the door shut, she didn't cry nor did she fight. Sadly, there was no fight left in her. The moment she saw that she couldn't get away, she covered her head with her arms and slowly slid to the floor protecting herself from the beating she obviously believed was sure to come.

Copper's reaction told Shad more than her words ever could—why trusting men was so very difficult for her to do. Seeing her small form huddled on the floor like this was like being dropped into icy water. His temper cooled in an instant, and he fought to catch his breath as he knelt beside her, wishing with all his heart that he could start this day over. All the *'should haves'* suddenly came to mind. He should have fixed that blasted roof the minute she mentioned it. He should have helped her pack a picnic and taken her fishing. He should have spent the day courting his wife, instead of feeling sorry for himself. Preacher had warned him, that earning Copper's trust wasn't going to come easy. Now he understood. For her to be this afraid, she must have known a great deal of cruelty. How could she ever trust any man?

Trembling, Copper held her arms over her head as she waited silently. Not knowing what form the punishment would take was almost as bad as the attack itself. Her heart pounded in her ears as she wondered if the first blow would be a kick, a slap or a punch from his powerful fist. What she feared even more was that perhaps the man's patience had finally been exhausted.

Would he now allow his heightened emotions free rein, would he force himself on her?

Copper flinched pitifully when Shad knelt then sat down beside her. She didn't cry. This was when she needed to keep her wits about her. She never wept while she received a beating. There would be time enough for tears when he was finished with her. However, as Shad stared down at her huddled on the floor, **his** green eyes were the ones that filled with tears.

Lord, I could use some wisdom here. I've been trying so hard to earn her trust—but now—what am I to do?

When Copper realized that the big man was only sitting quietly beside her, she cautiously peeked up at him. Shad's head was bowed and his eyes were squeezed tight. Then to her amazement, she saw a tear making a track down the dark stubble of his cheek. Confused, Copper turned away from him while her head and heart struggled to reason this out. Her past experiences told her that angry men become brutal—and Shad had truly been angry! And yet, her heart reminded her that Shad wasn't like any man she'd ever known. He wasn't mean spirited like her father nor cruel like Percy Barr. Shadrack McKenna was strong and powerful, not the kind to shed a tear easily. And—until today—he had been the most patient and the kindest of men.

Shad was sitting cross-legged beside Copper, and in an especially gentle voice he said, "Darlin' I—I wasn't gonna hurt ya—I never will. Just wanted to make sure yer insides didn't get bruised when I caught ya. Just now, I ran after ya 'cause I didn't want ya running outside and gettin' struck by lightnin'." He stopped and ran his large hand over his face, then groaned. "Ah, sweet girl, I beg ya to forgive yer poor fool of a husband—that ornery—no good—Shadrack McKenna. All day long he's been doing everything wrong."

Copper was confused, he sounded so sincere, but a moment ago she saw fury in those green eyes of his. Then as she huddled by the door she glanced up at him and realized that shame had replaced the fury.

Shaking his head sadly he muttered, "Ya don't believe me, do ya? Well, don't reckon I blame ya, but the truth is…I'd rather cut off my right arm—than ever use it to harm ya."

He reached his hand out, but paused when Copper shied away from him, and yet very slowly he persevered. As lightly as a feather, he laid his hand on her still damp head, then ran it slowly down her back. When she shivered, Shad took the towel she had given him and draped it around her shoulders, then very carefully pulled her thick hair out from under the towel.

"Oh…my sweet girl," he crooned, "I hate that ya've had reason to fear men. And I'm more ashamed than I can say that I have caused ya to fear me. I've behaved badly today but ya never were in any danger! Not from me! The fact is—well—when I saw that ladder fly out of your hand—and then the wind knock ya down—it just about scared me to death!"

Copper tightened her arms around herself again, then somehow found the courage to speak, "You weren't scared. You were angry!"

Shad frowned but nodded his head in agreement, as he continued to run his hand slowly down her back. "Well now, yer right and yer wrong about that. I *was* angry—I'll admit it—but I was angry 'cause—well I don't think I've ever been so *scared!* I knew I should stay calm and speak gentle, but I kept seeing ya fallin' off that roof. You could o' been killed! Sweet girl, ya just don't know what you've come to mean to me." Shad shook his head mournfully, "Probably shouldn't tell ya this but—from that very first day, I walked into this cabin and took one look at ya—it felt like—well like sunshine was breaking through everything that had ever been dark in my life. I started lovin' ya before I even knew yer name. Then as I came to see what a little sweetheart ya were, I knew you were the answer to my prayers."

Wariness was evident in Copper's eyes as she looked up at Shad and asked, "If what you're saying is true…then why were you angry with me this morning? You were upset with me, long before I climbed onto that roof!"

"Yep, reckon I was at that," Shad agreed. Feeling his face-growing warm, he added with disgust. "Dog-gone-it—always thought I had skin as thick as a buffalo…but…I'm ashamed to say, I stomped off to the river this mornin', cause my feelin's was hurt. Then I just plain—fell asleep. The storm woke me and I ran full tilt for the cabin, cursin' myself with every step. Then I saw ya up there—with the wind screamin' and lightnin' flashin'. God alone knows how my clumsy feet managed to get to ya in time. Your landin' right in my arms was God's doin'—not mine! Still and all, 'sweet girl', ya landed mighty hard." Are ya sure ya aren't hurtin', anywhere?"

"I'm not hurt." Copper said softly, but she noted the look of concern and then relief in Shad's eyes and that told her more eloquently than his words that he meant what he was saying.

When she seemed to be getting over her fright Shad moved a little closer. "Darlin', you're cold and wet and if you keep hunched over like that your muscles are gonna seize up on ya. Now, I know it's hard for you to give yer trust. I understand, but it's time you let me prove myself to ya. I'm gonna make you more comfortable and show you that you've got nothin' to fear from me."

When Copper nodded and sat up a bit, Shad opened his arms, "Come here, darlin'." Slowly and with infinite care, he maneuvered them both around so that he was leaning his back against the door and Copper was seated on his lap.

"W—what are you going to do now?" She asked.

"Easy now." he soothed, "It's high time that you learned that there is such a thing as a gentle touch—from a gentle man. I could tan the hides of every man that has put that look of fear in your eyes—including me. If I could figure out a way to give myself a good wallopin', I'd do it—I surely would!"

The sincere and sorrowful look on Shad's face and his ridiculous words about walloping himself, amused Copper, and her lips lifted in a brief smile.

Shad felt a glimmer of hope and breathed out a sigh, "Hey, if you forgive me for stomping around like a loco polecat and scaring you, I'll forgive you for scaring ten years off my life." As he slowly rubbed Copper's back he said, "Ya know I think we can have a happy life together, if ya can find it in yer heart to forgive me and learn to trust me."

Although Copper allowed herself to sit on Shad's lap, she didn't relax. Nodding sadly, she said, "I know you are a good man Shad. Forgiving you isn't the problem. It's giving you my complete trust. That's what's hard for me to do!"

Shad nodded, "I know, but I intend to honor my promise to love and protect ya till the day I die. I'll never be perfect though and I can't promise that I won't do something ignorant again! But this fear of yours is a problem that we're gonna have to work on together." When Copper frowned in confusion, Shad gently ran the back of his hand down Copper's cheek, "We're gonna have our first lesson right now." Applying only the slightest pressure, he guided her towards him, "Just lean back and rest your head on my shoulder."

When Copper stiffened, Shad was reminded again that it was not easy for her to comply, for even though she was sitting on his lap, she sat there like a block of wood. She was still too unnerved to do what he asked.

Knowing he must not rush her, he once again placed his large hand on the top of Copper's head then with a touch so light it felt like the caress of a butterfly; he moved his hand in slow circular motions down her back.

"It's all right sweet girl. We've got all the time in the world." Leaning back the big man settled his head against the door. With his eyes closed and a contented smile hidden just beneath his black mustache, he looked like he might be asleep. Instead, he was beseeching God to heal his wife's wounded heart. They had come a long way, but just now, he felt that they were at a crossroad.

Little by little, Copper began to relax. First, she placed her fingertips on the soft suede of his shirt. Then she pressed her palm against his chest, it felt hard against her hand and then finally she leaned her shoulder against him, his face just inches away.

Since Shad was sitting calmly with his eyes closed. Copper felt brave enough to study his strong jaw, perfect nose and the clef in his chin. His cheekbones where high, his skin was tan, smooth and leathery. The dark shadow of his beard stubble made him look dangerous. Her life up until now had taught her that dangerous, angry men—hit. That is what she'd come to expect. She had no doubt this man had been furious a few moments ago, but now...instead of beating her...*this* is what came next!

Finally, Copper found the courage to rest her head just under Shad's chin and she felt him smile. When she heard the loud thumping inside his chest, she drew back and frowned. "Are you alright? I think I just heard your heart beating!"

"Yep—that's my—hard old heart, all right." He said gruffly.

Immediately, Copper put her head against his chest again, amazed that she could actually hear another person's heartbeat and when he spoke, she smiled for she could also feel the vibration of Shad's deep voice.

"Sweet girl—" he asked softly. "Has—no one ever held you close enough to hear their heartbeat before? Surely your parents did—didn't they?"

"Not that I can remember." Her reply held no self-pity, only wide-eyed wonder, and she snuggled closer thinking this was such a miraculous thing. Finally, she said, "I suppose my mother must have held me this close when I was very little. I only remember when it was Father and me, and I don't recall him ever holding my hand or hugging me goodnight or anything of the kind. I saw a little girl sitting on her father's lap once and I asked him if I could sit on his lap?

I never asked him again, he told me that it was a ridiculous notion, and it was not only improper but would ruin the creases in his trousers." Copper shrugged, adding flippantly, "The only time Father ever touched me was with the flat side of a ruler or a switch."

Her words broke Shad's heart and infuriated him at the same time. He had to force his jaw to unclench, then he asked calmly, "What would he punish you for?"

"Oh, I don't know…" she sighed, "I guess it was mostly if I didn't make the best marks in the class. He said it reflected poorly on him, being the school master and all."

Hearing her words, Shad's large hand instinctively rolled into a fist and he wished that he had been around to *teach* Jarvis Delaney a thing or two. Just then a loud bolt of lightning hit just beyond the cabin and Copper jumped. However, instead of moving away from Shad she wrapped her arms around him and snuggled even closer. When he heard her contented sigh, Shad thanked God for the storm. His wife was discovering how reassuring it was to be held within the strong arms of someone who truly cared.

Feeling the need to explain her actions, she muttered, "I've always been afraid of storms."

Ever so gently Shad wrapped his arms around Copper and said, "Nothin' to be ashamed of, Ma was scared o' storms too. It may seem odd to you, but I've always liked a good loud storm! I like to hear rain on the roof and the crack of thunder—see flashes of lightnin' across the sky! I've learned somethin' tonight though. It's a whole lot more enjoyable…listening to a storm ragin' all around while yer holding someone special in yer arms."

"Mmmm—it certainly is!" Copper admitted, even though her words made her cheeks burn she added. "You know this is the second time you've made me feel safe in a storm. The first time was when I fell off the settee."

As if on cue, another bolt of lightning shook the cabin, and somehow Copper managed to wriggle a little closer, as she hid her face against Shad's neck. While he thanked God that somehow this horrible day was ending like this!

They silently held each other for a long time…and then Shad decided he had something he needed to say, "It really is something the way God came into both of our lives and then brought us together. I'm not meanin' to rush ya darlin', but I think with a little effort on both our parts we could have a truly happy marriage."

Copper ran her hand down the sleeve of Shad's deerskin shirt, enjoying the feel of the tanned leather against her fingertips. Finally, she replied, "I've always believed that everyone has two sides to them: a light side and a dark side. I've been so afraid that when I met the dark side of Shadrack McKenna, he would be like all the other men I've known. I finally met your dark side today, Shad. You were truly angry with me—but even so, you didn't hurt me!" He looked down with understanding and their green eyes met. Then she said softly, "But I've hurt you—haven't I?" Softening her tone, she pleaded, "You were upset about something before I even mentioned the roof. You said you had hurt feelings. What did I do?"

It was an embarrassing thing for a man like Shad to admit but finally he groaned, "Well—I reckon—I stomped off like a dad-burned fool today 'cause—I've been as jealous as a green toad." When Copper gave him a disbelieving look, he continued, "It's true. Just didn't cotton to the way you befriended old Jack, or Siah, as you call him. Oh—I know—you think of that old rapscallion as if he were yer favorite uncle and he thinks of you like the daughter he never had. Doggone-it, it's just happened so fast for me. I fell fer you like a rockslide, tumbling down a steep mountain! And I know it ain't been the same fer you and truly—that's all right."

Shad's heart plummeted when Copper lowered her head and said nothing. Somehow, he had hoped that she'd argue and declare that she loved him too. Trying not to sound as vulnerable as he felt, the big man nodded thoughtfully, "It's all right sweet girl—honest it is. God doesn't force us to love Him. And even if you never love me, I'm gonna make ya a promise: I'll always protect ya with my life and, I'll always love ya, no matter what!"

At the man's tender promise, Copper sat up and stared into Shad's eyes as her own were becoming glassy with tears. Her expression was so intense that Shad frowned back at her in confusion. Then, in the next instant, her sweet face crumpled and she flung herself back into his arms and held him tight. At first, she made no sound but she trembled violently in his arms. Then a soft keening suddenly rose up from somewhere deep within Copper's very soul. Shad had never heard anyone cry like this before. It was not mere weeping but choking, heartbreaking sobs. Unintentionally, the man's words had laid bare a great open wound, deep within her—never before had anyone told her that they loved her—not until now!

Copper was ashamed of her tears but she couldn't seem to stop them. Still she expected Shad to tell her to hush. Ma Riley had told her that a woman should only cry when she was alone. Instead of rebuking her, Shad whispered against her ear, "It's all right, sweet girl," he crooned, "l—let it out." Shad's deep voice cracked and he sounded as if his heart were breaking, right along with hers. "Ma used to say sometimes a body just needs a good cry. Ya've needed this—haven't ya darlin'? Get it all out my love—let it go."

That's exactly what Copper did—she wept until her tears were spent. She released all the pent up fears, heartbreak and loneliness her young life had stored up in life of silence and servitude. Shad rocked her and crooned soothing words while he stroked her silky hair. His embrace was unbelievably gentle. Never had anyone treated her as if she truly mattered more to them than the things she did for them.

Her own father had been cold and indifferent. Mrs. Barr had taught her many things and Copper had thought her a good woman, just because she had never struck her. Ma Riley had led her to God, and for that alone, Copper would always be grateful. And yet, even with that good, Christian woman, she had never felt completely accepted. It was always the things she did for the older woman that mattered, it wasn't Copper herself. Now for the first time in her life, she realized that she was truly loved! Every other person in her life, from her father to Ma Riley would have been upset with Copper had she *not* fixed the roof. Shad on the other hand, had been furious, yes. But it was because she had endangered herself. Shad loved his beautiful cabin—but he cared even more—for her! She would never forget the wounded look in his eyes, and the sincerity she saw in them as he promised to love her—even if she never loved him. It was just about impossible to believe…but God had led her to a man that she need not fear—even when he lost his temper. And—oh, the sweet joy of it—he actually, genuinely—loved her!

Resting his chin on top of Copper's head, Shad felt her body finally relaxing. Her weeping had ended but still she shuddered from time to time. "There now, sweet girl, are ya feelin' better?"

Copper answered in a shaky almost amused voice, "I am feeling better but I bet your legs are falling asleep."

"Don't ya go worryin' about me." Shad assured her as he handed her his huge red bandana. "Right now, I'm as content as a mouse in a cheese factory. I could hold ya like this fer hours—or all night—if ya want me to."

In a shy voice Copper whispered, "I want ya to." Glancing down at the long legs and huge boots of the man sitting on the hard wooden floor, her heart sang as she thought of him promising to sit there all night, just to comfort her.

As she wiped her face and blew her nose, Copper wondered if Shad wasn't nearly as lonely now as he had been the year before. He had given her so much and she had given him so little. Remembering what he'd said about Siah, she peeked up at the man she was snuggled so closely to and asked, "When you said, you were jealous as a green toad…you were teasing me, weren't you?"

Shad shrugged then looked away. "Wasn't teasin'. Ya—kissed that old goat this mornin'." Then he mumbled, "Ya never have kissed *me*—not even on our weddin' day or the day I gave ya yer surprise! You and Jack was thick as thieves from the start. What if I just hauled off and kissed another woman? Ah, never mind—that probably wouldn't even ruffle yer feathers."

A surge of warmth spread all through Copper at the idea that Shad had been truly jealous. Of course, she hadn't meant to hurt his feelings. Then she imagined her handsome husband kissing another woman. Suddenly, she felt pain—a real physical pain stabbing her heart. She was jealous too! Then her thoughts turned to what he had said about falling in love with her—how it had happened so quickly. The truth was, it had happened quickly for her as well. She was in love with this big, mountain of a man! He loved God, he was a man of integrity, kindness and humor and she loved him for all that he was. Just now she loved the way his powerful arms wrapped around her; loved the deep timber of his voice. Her whole body grew warmth as she thought of how much she always enjoyed—that very special way he had of saying good morning. Then she looked into Shad's strong face. He truly was a bear of a man, with hair as black as night, and eyes as green as the mountains he loved. It was plain to see that she had hurt this dear man, and now, she needed to be brave enough to make things right!

"I'm so sorry that I've hurt you, Shad." Copper spoke the words as she stared boldly into his eyes, willing him to see her sincerity. "I couldn't tell you before, not until I saw what you were like when you were truly angry. Now that I have, it's all right for me to finally tell you. I love you too—very much!"

"Ah, sweet girl ya don't have to be sayin' that…I…"

"Oh hush!" Copper whispered as she took Shad's face in both her hands. Then she kissed his cheek, then the tip of his nose, then his forehead and then very lightly, like a promise, she kissed his lips. As her face blushed a rosy red, she added shyly, "I thank you for your patience but…don't you think it's time we began our honeymoon?"

Shad feared that he hadn't heard her right. Then he looked down into Copper's beautiful clover green eyes. When she gazed up at him so sweetly, he bent close. When she boldly closed the distance between them, he covered her lips with his.

For both of them it was much more than just their lips touching in a kiss that finally sealed their wedding vows. No—something more profound was happening with that first kiss. It was more like the joining of two wounded souls, finally being made whole. They both felt as if they were being caught up in the storm that blew in a wild frenzy just beyond the cabin walls. At first Shad's kiss had been heartbreakingly gentle, for he was being mindful not to frighten his wife. Copper was no longer afraid. Instead, she slid her hand around Shad's neck and she was the one who deepened the kiss. When it ended, they stared at each other in wonder. Shad smiled at Copper's wide-eyed expression, then he laughed out loud when her green eyes sparkled happily and she said, "I liked that very much! Can we do it again?"

"Bless your heart! Yes ma'am…we surely can—again—and again." Shad lowered his head, but just then a gust of cold air came under the door and it made both of them shiver, for they were still wearing damp clothes from the rain.

"You know…" Copper said softly, feeling surprisingly bold, "If that storm quiets down soon, maybe we could go take a dip in the hot spring to warm up. We're going to catch a chill if we sit here like this much longer."

A spark as bright as hot green flames lit Shad's eyes and he stood to his feet taking Copper with him. As he set her down, he asked, "Can ya finally trust me, Copper?" When she nodded shyly he said, "Listen darlin', I've planned on takin' ya someplace special whenever we—had—our—a—honeymoon, as you say. Yer gonna have to trust me, though. I mean ***really***

trust me, but I promise it'll be worth it. So again, I'm askin' ya, do you trust me sweet girl?"

"Of course, I trust you Shad, but no place is as special as right here—right now!"

"Ah, ya don't know how it pleases me to hear ya say that, but it ain't far darlin' and it means a lot to me. I've been plannin' this fer ages. Ya can't ask any questions—ya can't argue—just trust."

Although Copper shivered, she nodded her head and gave Shad a nervous smile.

Heaving out a great sigh, Shad lit two lanterns then said gently, "All right then, go fetch yer robe and slippers and wait right here. I'll be back before you can miss me." To Copper's complete dismay, Shad didn't head for either the front or the back door. Instead, he gave her a roguish wink, grinned from ear-to-ear, then he opened the buffalo hide door and disappeared—inside the pantry of all places.

Copper gathered her things, then stood trembling in the kitchen. She wasn't really sure if it was due to her wet clothes or her nerves. Finally, Shad poked his head out of the pantry door. He held a lantern in one hand, and the other he held out to his bride saying, "Your honeymoon hideaway awaits, Missus McKenna."

When Copper stepped back and bit her lip, Shad quickly reminded her, "Ya said you'd trust me."

It took all her effort but Copper swallowed down her fear. As she placed her small hand in his, she whispered, "All right Shad, I'm trusting."

Clinging tightly to Shad's hand, Copper allowed him to lead her past the shelves of canned goods and then he made a sharp right turn and by the light of the lantern, they made their way down a narrow corridor she hadn't even known was there. Suddenly Shad stopped and said, "Hope ya don't mind me not tellin' ya about this place before—but ya had to get over yer fears—and I wanted it to be a surprise!"

Offering up a desperate prayer, that Copper would not be afraid and that she would like his surprise, Shad made one more turn, and then ushered Copper into another world.

"Oh my." She whispered. Her voice was filled with awe, for although she knew that Shad had taken her into yet another one of his special caves—she never could have imagined anything as special as this! At first glance, she couldn't quite grasp exactly what she was seeing—for both the walls and the floors seemed to sparkle and shimmer.

It was a small cavern, only about sixteen feet in diameter. Four lanterns shone brightly as they hung from spikes driven into the rock walls and Shad quickly hung the one he was holding on a spike near the entrance. Adding additional light, dozens of candles flickered as they sat on stony shelves, scattered all around like twinkling stars on a dark night. As her eyes adjusted, Copper began to understand what made this cavern so remarkable. The floor shimmered because of the bubbling pool that took up nearly half of the room. The walls sparkled because scattered everywhere were deposits of mica, as well as pale white and pink quartz. The effect was dazzling, for every flame, both large and small reflected against the walls and across the surface of the pool.

Shad watched Copper's expression as her eyes looked about and filled with fascination. That is until she noticed the soft bed made of plush buffalo hides with a quilt on top.

Sensing her blush more than seeing it, Shad quickly pulled on Copper's hand. "Come over here darlin'. See how this little stream of water runs down the rock wall and into the pool."

Copper touched it with her fingertips and shivered, "It's ice cold!"

Shad grinned, "Yep, but over there, where its bubblin' up. That water is plenty hot. Over the years, I've chipped away at the rock—here and there—and right in this little nook, the two waters mix and it's always just right. Yer bath water is never too hot and it never gets cold on ya neither. Plus the fresh clean water comes in from the top and pushes the dirty water out of the cracks in the bottom."

When Shad saw only wonder and delight in Copper's eyes, he released her hand and bent down to grab a jug of apple cider sitting in the spot where the water was hottest. Then he opened the metal box at their feet. Inside were towels, soap, and two tin cups. He filled the cups then handed one to Copper, "Here Missus McKenna, this will warm us up!"

Smiling shyly, Copper savored the warmth of it in her hands while she took her first sip. It was tangy and sweet as it rolled over her tongue and down her throat, spreading a delicious warmth all through her body. It was then Copper felt herself truly relaxing, it was all so wonderful. Still, as she glanced from Shad to the pool, she felt a bit bashful, but then she remembered how much she loved this man and she smiled up at him and said with a bold and playful tone, "Mister McKenna, I see I'm going to have to keep my eye on you. You are a much more calculating man that I realized." When Shad innocently raised one dark eyebrow, Copper continued, "You said you built the bed big enough for two, and here you've got two cups and towels all ready. And now you tell me that you've chipped away at that pool in certain places. Shadrack McKenna—did you make this pool big enough for two as well?"

At first Shad wasn't sure what to say, but then he saw the playful sparkle in Copper's eyes and grinned, "Well, ya might as well get used to it, Missus McKenna. You've married a man—who thinks ahead!"

Neither Shad nor Copper knew who moved first but in the next instant they were caught up in a kiss that was even sweeter and more passionate than the one before. When they finally drew apart, Copper kept her eyes closed, savoring the moment. It was a strange feeling...like something cold and dark hidden deep inside her was now melting away. Finally, she opened her eyes and saw that Shad was nearly as dazed as she was.

"Oh, Shad—are all kisses like that? I had no idea something so simple could be so—powerful."

Shad shook his head, humbled by the love he now saw in Copper's beautiful face and touched by her innocent confession. "No, darlin', this is special. Kisses like this only happen when the right two people come together!"

Chapter 13
Copper's Gift

"A tree from the forest is cut down and worked with an axe by the hands of a craftsman." Jeremiah 10:3

"I have put wisdom in the hearts of all gifted artisans, that they may make all that I have commanded." Exodus 31:6

A silvery shaft of moonlight filled the room while Shad dreamt that he and Copper were lying in the soft grass beside the river. As he floated between the worlds of sleep and wakefulness, he smiled and reached for her. When he found the place beside him cold and empty he frowned himself awake then scanned the room for his little wife. In the darkened cabin, the small sphere of light was easy to find for it was coming from the lantern on the kitchen table. Rubbing his eyes, he padded silently across the floor with a sleepy smile on his darkly shadowed face.

Copper's tawny head was bent over the table, as her hand moved quickly over Maudy McKenna's old sketchpad. It was larger than the ones she had purchased, and especially for this drawing, she didn't think Maudy would mind. So intent was she on her work that she didn't hear or even sense Shads approach, until he gently caressed her head and whispered, "Hey—darlin'!"

Copper let out a yelp and jumped from the table, taking the sketchpad with her, she tried to hide it behind her back. Looking terribly guilty, her other hand flew to her chest where her heart was beating like a frightened rabbit. "My goodness—you—you really shouldn't sneak up on me like that."

Her shamefaced expression troubled Shad. Since they had begun their honeymoon—he had never been happier. Now as he studied the paper in her hands and the frown on his wife's face, he couldn't stop his mind from fearing the worst. Was she unhappy, was she writing him a note—maybe—to say good-bye?

"Dear Lord," he breathed. "Are you leaving me?"

"Shadrack McKenna!" Copper fumed. "Shame on you! How could you even think such an awful thing? If I ever decide to leave you—" she blustered, "I'll just make you come right along with me—do you hear?"

Shad blew out a breath, then grinned sleepily; "I hear ya sweet girl, kind o' sounds like you might care fer me a little. And ya got that right—where you go—I go. And since I'm goin' back to bed that means you're comin' with me—right?" Shad reached for Copper, but she sidestepped around him and frowned again. That brought the worry back, and Shad's face grew serious, "Hey darlin', what's wrong—what are ya doing up in the middle of the night?"

Copper put her free hand on her hip and stamped her foot. "Shadrack McKenna, you are spoiling my surprise." She studied him for a moment then she gave him a hesitant smile, "I've been desperate to show it to you—and—scared all at the same time! Oh well, I guess now is as good as later. So sit yourself down here in the light, where you can see. Only, please remember I'm not a true artist, not like you and Maudy."

Shad kept his eyes on Copper, patiently allowing her to push him into a kitchen chair. Her expression was vulnerable and bashful as she slowly took the sketchpad from behind her back. She sat it down on the table in front of him, then adjusted the kerosene lamp so he could see her drawing without any shadows.

His expression was filled with tenderness as he kept his gazed on Copper, "Ah sweet girl—you didn't have to do anything for me. Yer lovin' me is more than enough—you're all I've ever wanted." He reach out to pull her onto his lap but she quickly stepped out of his reach, "No Shad. If I let you touch me…you know what will happen. So, I'm not getting anywhere near you—not until you look at your present."

Shad slanted a mischievous wink at Copper then said, "I'll look if ya tell me ya love me more than this here cabin."

Copper rolled her eyes at the question. Shad had needed to be assured that her love for him was greater than her love of his cabin a dozen times a day at first, now he only asked her half as many times.

"I love you a thousand times more than this cabin! In fact, I love you so much that I made you a surprise. So please stop looking at—me!" She chided, even as she blushed at the smoldering gleam in her husband's eyes. "Look at your gift!"

Shad wink again then slowly he turned and gazed down at the sketch-pad lying on the table. At first he couldn't quite believe what he was seeing. Then, he rubbed the sleep from his eyes and looked more closely. When he realized what she had done, he found he had a lump in his throat, "W—why haven't you told me you could do this?"

Seeing how her gift had moved her bear of a husband, she bit her lip and shrugged, "It's not much—I've just always—loved to draw. I used to sell little sketches like this for the Barr's. Even so, they both always said my scribbles were poor at best, nothing at all compared to what a real artist could do. Not like you and Maudy. I hope you don't mind my using her sketchpad, it's bigger than mine!"

Clearing his throat, Shad shook his head, "If yer other drawings were half as good as this one, yer talent isn't poor, sweet girl, it's incredible! I've seen tintypes that aren't as clean and real as this."

The sketch that Shad was now staring at was a perfect replica of his cabin, barn, corrals and surrounding mountains. It was perfect and true in every detail, right down to the individual shape of the trees in the yard, even to the graining of the wood on the logs and the leaves in the trees.

Copper wrapped her arms around her husband's neck. "It's all I had to give you, Shad. I've wanted so badly to give you something. It's just a simple drawing, but I hope it tells you how I feel about my life here with you. You've made me happier than I thought possible!"

Shad didn't trust himself to speak when she kissed his cheek and then pointed to the couple standing in front of the cabin. "This is you and me on our wedding day. See, I drew myself wearing Maudy's dress." Her words were unnecessary; the likeness was incredible. The fabric of the dress as well as the silky strands of Copper's bronze hair seemed to flutter in the mountain breeze. What Shad loved most about this drawing was that Copper had drawn them with their arms around each other and they were looking up with happy, hope filled faces.

Though the scene needed no explanation, Copper continued to clarify each detail. "I wanted to show that we love each other, very much, and that we keep our eyes on God. Does it look like that to you—can you see it?"

Still not trusting his voice Shad only nodded as he curled his arm around her waist and pulled her closer.

Copper hugged him back, then added shyly, "I've adding something special, Shad. Look closely at the oak tree, do you see? I hope it doesn't offend you. If you don't like it, I'll understand. If you think it's strange or irreverent, I can erase it. Ma Riley never liked my little trick of the eye drawings. I've always thought it added something special. It may take you a moment to see it—sometimes you have to look at a picture a long while before it becomes clear."

At first Shad didn't know what she was talking about, but then something out of place caught his eye. Everything in the picture was accurate, except for one thing. Copper had drawn a large oak tree just behind the cabin. Oak leaves and acorns were Maudy's favorite things to draw and that's why they appeared in so many of her son's carvings. However, oak trees don't grow at this altitude. The thin air of the high-country is better suited for aspens or evergreens, like pine, spruce and fir. Still Copper had drawn a magnificent oak tree that gracefully sheltered the cabin. Then he noticed the tintype of Maudy McKenna. It usually set on the mantle but now it was on the table. As Shad glanced at his mother's picture and then studied the tree more closely—his breath caught in his throat. He hadn't seen it at first, but now he couldn't miss it. Somehow, Copper had drawn the gentle features of Maudy McKenna's face using the branches, leaves and acorns of the elegant oak tree. Each leaf, curved branch and shadow recreated her kind smile and delicate brow. It was an amazing likeness, for even the laughter and love in her eyes were plain to see.

Shad was so moved it was difficult for him to speak. Finally, he managed to say, "You called me an artist and a craftsman—but you—sweet girl—you're not only a true artist—you're a magician." He pulled her onto his lap and nuzzled her neck, then he looked up and their eyes met, "God surely must have gone to a lot of trouble to put you and me together. And...I'm sure glad He did!"

In reply to Copper's questioning look he said, "Ya've given me more than you realize darlin'. And I hope ya don't mind but ya've gotten yerself another job." he added playfully. "Ya asked me when I was gonna start carvin' again. Well, I've been worried that my carving days might have come to an end. I can't draw a lick—but I can carve anything someone else draws. Ma used to do the drawin'—but now, sweet girl, if you'll keep on drawin' then—I can keep on carvin'! The minute I laid eyes on you—I knew you were a gift from God—seems I'm still learning just how much of a gift. We were meant to be together Copper McKenna! And I'm as sure of it as I am of the sun rising' in the mornin' and settin' at night."

Chapter 14
No Escape

"I look for someone to come and help me, but no one gives me a passing thought. No one will help me; no one cares a bit what happens to me." Psalm 142:4

There was a brisk knock on the door, but Mariah didn't have to open it to know who was standing on the other side. She also knew what words were about to be spoken. *You can't stay if you can't pay!*

The day the sheriff had brought her to this little town, the first thing she did was rip open the hem of her old work dress and retrieve her last three pieces of jewelry she'd hidden away from Victor. Holding them up for the sheriff to see she asked, "Is there any place I can get a good price for these? They are all I have left!"

That was the day she'd met the bank president Theodore Krane. He didn't give her as much as she'd hoped, but both men assured her that no one else, in this town at least, could give her more. Mariah knew no one in these mountains but Sheriff Jimmy Todd and she was grateful when he was kind enough to carry her bags down the street to the Castle Café, Hotel and Mercantile and help her make arrangements for a room.

Mariah was surprised to see three businesses under one roof, but Cyril Castle's idea had been a good one. He constructed the largest building in Otter Run and then divided it down the center with a wide staircase. On the left was a good-sized café, above which were five small rooms, making up the entire, 'Castle Hotel'. On the other side was the Mercantile, above which were the living quarters for he and his wife Sephora. Like the ill-humored tyrant he was, Cyril kept a watchful eye over all three-business ventures from one large desk at the bottom of the staircase.

When another knock sounded against the door, Mariah jumped, for it was considerably louder and more insistent than the one before. Feeling miserable, she stared into her small hand mirror and grimaced. Her face looked as pale as her hair and her eyes were red-rimmed from crying herself to sleep the night before. Still, she wasn't about to give this man an excuse to gloat over her predicament. Giving her cheeks a hard pinch, she breathed in a lung full of air, blew it out slowly then opened the door.

"Good morning, Mister Castle. How are you today, sir?" Mariah managed to produce a pleasant expression on her face as she greeted the man. However, as she had expected, Cyril Castle only stood there and stared. The man was rude beyond measure. Each time he saw her, he had the annoying habit of silently scrutinizing her from head to foot. He never spoke until he had looked her over thoroughly. Mariah fought the urge to slam the door in his face, but unfortunately, she was already beholden to this vile little man. Fighting down her irritation and embarrassment, she lowered her eyes and waited. Castle was bald, slightly pudgy, his eyes were dull and small, and he had no chin whatsoever. What annoyed her most of all was that whenever the man wasn't speaking, his mouth always seemed to twist into a lecherous smirk.

Mariah kept her eyes turned away until, finally, Cyril answered her questions, "I can tell ya how I am today, Missus Kent. I'm a businessman and I expect payment for this room. You did just fine the first two weeks but ya haven't paid even a widow's mite since, and we ain't running no charity."

"No sir—of course not. However, I do all I can to compensate you. I take care of my own room and I help your wife clean the others. I wash the dishes in the café whenever they allow me to help. I'd call that more of a barter than charity. Besides, you have another room that has been empty for well over a month. It's not as if I'm keeping you from a paying customer."

"Maybe not, but if some folks came in and I needed two rooms...it would make me look bad when they saw me throwing ya out. That'd be bad for business! Besides you know sooner or later yer gonna have to get a real job. Now, Ox Hennessey tells me that he offers you a job every day. There's no need in me allowing ya to stay here free when ya can go over to the Long Shot and move right in. I'll thank ya kindly to vacate the premises today and that's final. No more charity for you!"

No more charity—we ain't running no charity. We don't care if you mind hard work or not. So stop askin'.

Even in her sleep, huddled in the corner of the stable, hidden under a stack of hay, Mariah heard these same words over and over. The dignity and pride she'd strived so hard to maintain didn't seem all that important anymore. Daily she swallowed down her pride and begged for work—any kind of *decent* work! The answer was always the same. 'No—we don't need you—can't help you.'

Life had changed so drastically for Mariah. The beautiful young heiress had gone from picking over the delicacies prepared by the French chef her father had imported from Alsace-Lorraine to picking through the garbage heap just outside of town. When she wasn't begging for work, she walked through the forest, searching for anything edible. Then by the cover of darkness, she searched through the town's garbage. Sometimes she found a crust of bread or a bone that hadn't been picked clean. Although the livery owner had turned down her offer to clean the stables in trade for a place to sleep, the very last thing she did each night was sneak into the livery anyway—where she made a bed in the hay. The Rocky's were enjoying an Indian summer, but still the autumn nights were quite cold and even though the warm sunny days seemed to deny it—the truth was—winter was coming! Each day seemed harder than the day before and she became more and more desperate. Foolishly, she'd assumed that people would be kind to a young widow. However, it had turned out to be just the opposite. No one but the handsome golden haired preacher had offered to help her. And oh, how she wished she hadn't turned him down. She had learned so many things since that day, the most important was that, pride is a luxury beggars can't afford!

Mariah awoke with a start when she heard the horse in the stall next to her pawing the ground. She'd been dreaming that the maid had brought her breakfast on a tray. When she awoke, however, there was no silver tray with buttered toast and tea served on her favorite hand-painted china. She wasn't lying on a feather mattress in an elegant room with blue and white wallpaper and mahogany furnishings. No, she was hiding in the livery, covered in horse blankets and hay. She was no longer a wealthy girl of privilege, but a penniless widow.

Mariah ran her parched tongue over her peeling lips, a sure sign that she was running a fever. "Well, that might just be the best thing to happen to me in weeks." she muttered scornfully. "Maybe I'll catch pneumonia and die in my sleep. The way things are now—any escape from the life I have—would be a welcome relief."

When she heard another horse moving about in his stall, Mariah slowly rose to her feet and pushed the barn door open a crack, allowing a ray of moonlight to stream inside. Knowing that she must be gone before anyone saw her, she swept the hay from her clothing, then she brushed and fashioned her pale hair into a long braid. Though she was trying to hurry, the headache and fever made her fingers clumsy and slow. Somehow, she managed to wind her braid into a tight bun and pin it into place. When she had done all she could to make herself presentable, she forked the hay back into a pile and carefully shook out the blankets. When everything looked as if no one had been there in the night, she slipped from the back door of the livery and hid herself in the nearby woods.

A few hours later, once the storekeepers opened their doors, Mariah lifted her chin and strolled into town where she would repeat her daily ritual of asking for work. At first, she had not wanted anyone to pity her. Now she wished that *someone* would!

"Top of the mornin' to ya, ma'am."

Mariah winced at the sound of Ox Hennessey's voice as he called to her from across the dusty street, as he did every morning. "Mornin' Mister Hennessey."

A year ago she would not have even acknowledged a man like him. However, a few nights before, he had brought a blanket and a sandwich to the livery. He hadn't shamed her but had simply whispered, "Here's a blanket and a bit of food, should anyone be wantin' it."

Mariah knew the man had ulterior motives for he had been the only one to offer her a job. Even now as she walked down the opposite side of the street, Ox hurried across to block her way.

"I've got somethin' fer ya, lass!" Ox panted as he held up a delicate gold band. "That last time Victor was in me place, he gambled this away. Said, 'twas yer grandmother's. I want ya to have it, no strings attached. Now, ya see, I ain't all bad." Then he added, "Besides, it's so small, there ain't that much gold in it no how."

Hesitantly, Mariah took the ring and placed it back on her finger. It *had* been her grandmother's, and she had vowed never to sell it! "Thank you Mister Hennessey."

"Yer a lookin' mighty thin, gal. Working fer me ain't as bad as ya think. Ya'll get room and board and I'll even let ya keep half yer earnings." With a wink he added, "Come now—pride is all well and good but it's time ya give up. Let me and the men of Otter Run take care of ya."

Tears rushed to Mariah's eyes and she nearly stumbled over her skirts as she backed away from the man. "I thank you for the ring, sir. Thank you for the blanket and the food—good-day."

As Mariah stepped into Castle's Mercantile, tiny bells jangled their welcome and she tried to forget Ox and remember the life she used to have. Oh how she had always loved stores like this. The tinkle of the bells, followed by the aroma of coffee beans, leather, pickles and molasses. There were always colorful dress goods and ribbons on the shelves and jars filled with candy. Of course, she had learned that it wasn't nearly such a happy place when you had no money to spend. Sadly, Mariah's pockets were as empty as her stomach.

In answer to the bells, Sephora Castle hurried from the back room, but she sighed when she saw it was only Mariah Kent. Sephora was not a friendly woman but she did respect the young widow. After all, she had paid what she could, and then worked hard to help out until Cyril had insisted that they were only prolonging the inevitable. It was all too obvious that he wanted the young beauty to give up and become a 'saloon girl'. Although she risked her husband's wrath, Sephora continued to provide Mariah a place to keep her large carpetbag. Each morning she also gave Mariah a pan of warm water so she could wash up in the ladies changing room.

After washing and putting on a clean dress, Mariah approached the older woman. "Missus Castle, I have truly appreciated your helping me as much as you have. I know we're havin' an Indian summer, still the nights are already quite cold and winter is comin'. I'll do any kind of labor—" Lowering her head she asked softly, "If I could just sleep in your storage room at night?"

Before Sephora could speak, her husband came down the steps and cleared his throat, "Wife. We've discussed this—have we not. Tell her what she needs to hear—tell her the truth." He didn't even look at Mariah, just glared at his wife as he stomped out the door, causing the bells to jingle again.

Just as he was leaving a few men wandered in. While they seated themselves on the café side of the building, they made no attempt to hide their lustful perusal of the young beauty standing at the counter. Frowning at them, Sephora quickly pulled Mariah well away from their shameless stares.

"Missus Kent," she began, "I am not indifferent to your plight, but—Cyril and I have, as he said, discussed this. The truth remains—if I help you today—you will be just as cold and hungry tomorrow and—the day after. You told me that your family has disowned you—and—it's obvious by now, that no one in town will employ you. You will never be able to pay us back for any kindness we give you." In a rare motherly gesture Sephora placed a hand on Mariah's arm, "It's a horribly harsh thing for one woman to say to another but—we both know there are only two things a woman in your position can do. The first is to find a man—any man that will marry you! The second is—well—I loathe to say it but—the other is to give up and become one of those women who work upstairs at the saloon. I know it sounds cruel—but with your own family treating you this way; I have to assume that you are now reaping what you've sewn. I'm not as heartless as I sound. I ran away with Cyril Castle and you ran away with Victor Kent. You must pay for your own sins and foolishness—just as I continue to pay for mine!"

Mariah hadn't the strength to respond to the older woman's words and what did it matter? Her head was spinning, and just then she was fighting down both tears and nausea. She simply nodded her head, and once again listened to the happy bells chime as she left the store. She hadn't the heart to beg anyone for a job just now, and if what Missus Castle said was true, there wasn't any use in it anyway. The throbbing in her head was getting worse, and a constant shiver seemed to be taking over her body. Her throat felt as if it were on fire as she headed towards the town well. It took all her strength to turn the crank that lifted the bucket and her hands shook as she retrieved the tin cup from her small satchel.

"At least this doesn't cost anything." she shuddered, as she swallowed down the ice-cold water. Although it felt good on her burning throat, it sent a tormenting chill sliding down her already trembling body.

Sitting there beside the well, Mariah puzzled what to do next. She felt so small and alone. She had no friends for Victor never allowed her to accompany him to town. After all, what man would want his wife along to interfere with his carousing? Ox Hennessey, however, made a point of telling her that Vic didn't only gamble but that he had enjoyed all the delights his saloon offered. The man needn't have bothered, for she was well aware of her young husband's vices. That's how she'd become acquainted with the sheriff. How many times had the lawman brought Victor home, drunk and smelling of cheap perfume? It was a waste of time thinking of how Victor Kent had let her down. And yet now, if she was going to survive, she must swallow what was left of her pride. Sephora Castle told her that she had two choices, but in Mariah's mind, there was only one.

As if she had summoned him with her thoughts, Sheriff Jimmy Todd came trotting into town on his high stepping black and white paint. "Finally!" she sighed. He was the one man she had hoped might help her, but he had been out of town for two full weeks. "Surely," she whispered, "he will help me. He's always been kind to me before."

Even as she breathed the words, she admitted that there were some things about the man she disliked. For one thing, he was much too flirtatious to be considered a gentleman. He was also a bit of a dandy and dressed more like a professional gambler than a sheriff. As a horseman's daughter, she hated the large Mexican spurs he wore, believing them unnecessarily severe. Although she had never seen his horse with bloody sides, his wearing spurs like that bothered her just the same. Instantly she shrugged off her misgivings. They just didn't matter—she had no other choice. Mariah watched the man dismount and tie his horse. Then she waited for him to notice her—but when he finally looked her way, it seemed as if he looked straight through her. Then with an odd smirk on his face, he strolled into his office and kicked the door shut with the heel of his boot.

Knowing what she had to do, Mariah stood, lifted her chin and slowly made her way towards the sheriff's office. As she walked, she reminded herself that Todd had often said that he thought she had married beneath her and that she should find a man that would treat her as she deserved. At the time he had looked at her so tenderly and when he smiled, he had seemed so very charming. She remembered blushing and looking away. Being a married woman, she hadn't wanted to encourage the man but now these thoughts gave her reason to hope. What concerned her was that Todd had only spoken to her twice since Victor's death. The first time had been to tell her that her husband had killed himself and to move her to town. The second and the last time she had talked with the sheriff; their encounter had been quite strange. It was after she'd spoken to that mountain preacher, and had asked him if he knew of anyone that needed a cook or housekeep or even a wrangler. It was then she'd realized that she hadn't asked the livery owner if he might give her a job. She liked the idea for she could keep his books, clean stalls and even exercise the horses. The owner wasn't there, and while she was waiting, Sheriff Todd came in to the livery. They exchanged the usual pleasantries, then she asked him if *he* knew of anyone that needed a cook or housekeeper. She'd been hurt and insulted when he had actually thrown his head back and laughed at her.

"You—a cook or a housekeeper?" He scoffed, "Not a chance! I'm afraid your late husband complained much too loudly about your lack of skills. I doubt if there's a soul within a hundred miles that would be foolish enough to hire you."

Mariah hadn't known how to respond to the man's offensive manner and cutting words. She could only hope that his lack of compassion was simply due to a bad day. After all, her father, brother and certainly her husband had all been moody men. "Today will be better." Mariah assured herself. "It just has to be!"

Surviving meant working at the saloon or finding a husband. The first option was out of the question—that left—getting married. Before reaching the door to the sheriff's office, Mariah reminded herself that this is what she must do. It wasn't that she hadn't had her share of proposals since her husband's death. But only one proposal of marriage. The man was terrifying to look at, and he smelled as if he were terrified of soap and water. Sadly, all the other offers were of an indecent nature. Mariah was horrified at how many lewd propositions she'd received, and not just from single men. Theodore Krane and Cyril Castle had offered to build her a cabin on the outskirts of town if they could visit her whenever they liked. She hadn't realized just how vulnerable a woman alone, could be. Even being married to a man as worthless as Victor Kent had provided some protection. Although Sephora's words that morning had stung, the woman was right. She had to find a husband and Sheriff Jimmy Todd was the only man she thought she could consider marrying. As she stood outside his office door, she pinched her cheeks, raised her chin, drew in a deep breath, and then slowly turned the knob.

Todd had his feet propped up on his desk and his hands clasped behind his head. Looking like the cat that ate the canary, he said smoothly, "Hello beautiful, what took ya so long? I've been waitin' for ya!"

Mariah couldn't help it, his words and attitude upset her. Still, she forced a smile as she entered his office. "You have?" she asked. "And why is that?"

Todd's face grew serious as he slid his feet to the floor and quickly stepped around his desk. Mariah silently chided herself for instinctively taking a step backwards, away from the man as he stepped closer.

He backed her against the door and leaned towards her, "I know what you want. Ya want to talk about—you and me—right?" His voice was seductive and low. "And the answer is—sure. You can be my woman!"

At first, his words embarrassed Mariah, but then she felt relieved. She wouldn't have to try to work marriage into the conversation. Maybe now she wouldn't even have to make her carefully planned speech. Actually, she'd do anything rather than become a saloon girl. Now perhaps the humiliating words needn't be spoken.

Jimmy Todd didn't give her time to speak, for he lowered his head and covered her mouth with his. The kiss was possessive even ravenous, and it frightened her. Mariah wanted to push him away but she forced herself to remain calm and not protest. After all, when they were married she'd have to let him do what he liked. He might even be testing her to see if she would be the type of wife that would be cold and unfeeling. She tried to return his kiss, all the while fighting down the urge to run away.

Finally, he leaned back and laughed. "Well, it's a good thing that you're beautiful, 'cause you're not any better at kissin' than you are at anything else. That's all right; we'll work on it. You can move your things into my cabin right away and uh—you can spend the rest of the day giving it a good cleaning. I'll come get ya around five. We'll have dinner at the café 'cause darlin' there's no way I'm eatin' your cookin' until you've had some lessons. You know where my place is—don't ya?"

Mariah's pale face had turned crimson, but she nodded eagerly, "Oh, yes—thank you Jimmy. I promise—I'll work hard to make you a good wife. Will you stay at the hotel or here at the jail until the Pastor comes back? Do you know when that's supposed to be?"

Todd ran his hand over his smoothly shaved face. "We won't need a preacher." Then he added with an amused grin, "And—why would I sleep anywhere but my own home? Especially when I've got a beautiful woman to come home to!"

Confused, Mariah shook her head, "But—it wouldn't be proper for us to live together, under the same roof, until we're married. Of course, if the Castle's know it's just temporary, then maybe now they'll let me have a room at the hotel or at least let me sleep in their storeroom. You're right you shouldn't have to leave your own home. I'll find someplace until the preacher gets back."

"It's time you stop bein' so innocent!" He scoffed, "I want ya, sure. But I'm not the marrying kind. I'll feed ya and cloth ya until we both get tired of each other. Surely, what I'm offerin' is better than sleepin' in the livery and eatin'—garbage—ain't it?"

Quick tears filled Mariah's eyes. "I thought you were my friend but you've known all this time of my suffering and shame! Now you're using my misery for your own selfishness!"

When the sheriff saw the hurt and anger in her violet eyes, he laughed. Mariah's hand flew out on its own accord and she slapped Jimmy Todd across the face, just as hard as she could! Todd touched his cheek, grinned, and then he slapped her back. Her head cracked against the door then she slid to his feet.

Bending over he took her chin in his hand. "If ya want to play rough, I can oblige. Now, darlin'—you just learned your first lesson. I don't believe in chivalry, so don't give it out if you can't take it. Lesson number two: this dirty little town isn't civilized, and that's just how I plan to keep it. Now, I've wanted you since the first time I saw ya. Yer husband stood in my way, fer a while, but now you're all alone. As I see it, ya have two choices: you can belong to me on my terms or you can be a whore at the Long Shot. Then you can belong to me and every other man in town that's noticed what a pretty woman you are. We'll all get to spend a little time with ya. Best you think on that for a while."

The sheriff made no effort to stop Mariah when she silently got to her feet and hurried from his office. Todd had been her last and only hope. Feeling desperate and weak, she staggered into the forest. By the end of the day, she was nearly blind with fever.

"With any luck…" she scoffed. "It will get cold enough tonight that I'll be dead by mornin'."

The thought of death was frightening, and yet just now it seemed to be her only escape. She welcomed the fever, hoping that it would consume her—and then—free her. Both Sephora Castle and Jimmy Todd had spoken of two choices, but neither of them seemed to realize that there was a third choice—she could die!

Fearing that Todd might come looking for her, she hid under the fringed, low hanging boughs of a huge spruce tree. Throughout the long, cold night, her fever raged on and her body trembled uncontrollably. Yet every hour she kept promising herself that soon, her suffering would be over.

In spite of her pledge, when the first blush of dawn rose in the eastern sky, Mariah's eyes fluttered open to behold it. "No—oh—no!" She moaned."

If she wasn't about to die, then Mariah hoped at least to escape her misery within a deep sleep. Unfortunately, not even that wish was granted. As the sun rose higher and hotter, her parched body and burning throat begged for a drink of water. Unable to bear the torment any longer, she crawled from her hiding place, and once again made her way towards town, only to collapse within a few feet of the well. The next thing she knew, the world tipped oddly and she felt herself being lifted up and carried away.

Her first feverish thoughts were fanciful: *Maybe I finally died; maybe I'm being carried to heaven!*

The pleasant thought was short lived, for in the next instant her nose was assaulted by the scent of cigar smoke and the odor of whiskey and unwashed bodies. Obviously, this was not heaven, but she was relieved when she open her eyes for a moment and saw that it was Hank Wyatt, the nice young bank teller, who was carrying her up a flight of stairs. As they reached the landing it was too dark to see, but she heard whispering voices and the soft rustle of petticoats. The scent of strong perfume floated about her as a soft, cool hand touch her forehead and cheek.

"My—my, she's burning up, Hank! Poor little lamb! Just lay her over there on the bed. Reckon this here room belongs to her now."

Struggling to remain conscious, Mariah thought that she felt a mattress beneath her. Though she didn't recognize the woman's voice, she did recognize her speech as being from the hill country of Tennessee. Mariah didn't understand, however, why the woman sounded so angry.

"Wish I could take me a buggy whip to every man in this town," she sneered. "They'd see me a comin' and know they—Otter Run—ya can bet on that!"

"Now Shotsy," Hank warned, keeping his voice low, "you're takin' a big risk talkin' that-a-way. You know the Sheriff and the Highlanders are behind this. They wouldn't allow anyone to help her cause this was their plan all-along. I wouldn't put it past any one of them to take a whip to you if they heard what you just said. Now, you know she wouldn't have made it through another night if we'd left her out there. They just want you to get her well, then she'll be treated every bit as good as you 'n Velvet!"

"Hah! As if that were somethin' to brag about. You listen to me Hank; ya still have some good left in ya. But iffen ya don't get away from

Jimmy Todd and that 'Highlander's Association'—they'll make ya as evil as they are—and iffen they cain't—ya mark m' words—they'll kill ya!"

While Mariah struggled to remain awake and listen to what these two were saying, her fever made their words float around her like mosquitos she couldn't catch. She had just drifted to sleep again when she felt the woman's cool hand slip beneath her neck, "Drink this hon. Yer half-starved and ya've got a high fever. Ya may not thank me for it, but I'm going to do everythin' I can to get ya well again."

A spoonful of warm tea touching Mariah's dry lips. Sighing with relief, she eagerly accepted the tea mixed with honey, even though it hurt each time she swallowed. "Thank you." She finally managed to say when she was able to get words past her parched throat, "I didn't think anyone would ever be kind to me again."

"Don't go thankin' me," the woman grumbled. "Manner's and gratitude are misplaced on someone like me."

Despite her rough words, the woman proved to be a gentle and devoted nurse. For days Mariah hadn't the strength to do anything but swallow down whatever nourishment was spooned into her, and then she would invariably fall back into a deep sleep. It was nearly a week before she was able to open her eyes, think, and focus once again. The afternoon sun was streaming through the window and she managed to sit up. She was just catching her breath, for even that bit of effort was tiresome, when two women entered her room. Although she didn't recognize her by sight, the heavy perfume was as familiar as the low-twangy voice of the woman who had been tending to her so faithfully.

"Well now, look who's sittin' up, pretty as ya please." Setting a tray down beside the bed, she added. "Sure is good t' see them beautiful eyes of yours open fer a change."

Mariah tried to hide her shock as she watched her faithful caregiver pouring out the tea. She was a tall, shapely woman wearing an exceedingly short red dress; it was as short on top as it was on the bottom. For some reason she had envisioned her nurse as a no nonsense rancher's wife. Now, she realized that all this time a saloon girl had cared for her. Not really a girl—but a woman who was a bit past her prime. Her eyes were lined with coal, her lips and cheeks painted with rouge and her face reflected the pain and sorrow that came with a harsh life. However, Mariah thought she was still pretty, and that she must have been quite striking in her youth. Her hair was black with streaks of silver running through it. Her red dress, what there was of it, was frilly and trimmed with shiny black ruffles. Mariah couldn't help but blush, her most revealing under-garments were more modest than this woman's dress. Suddenly, she was ashamed of her judgmental thoughts. After all, not a soul in this town had wanted to help her. However, this dear woman had spoon-fed and bathed her day and night and more than anything, she wanted to express her sincere gratitude!

While Mariah struggled to sort all this out, the woman sighed and sat down on the side of the bed. "I bet yer plum full o' questions. I'm Shotsy, by the way." Waving her hand at the curly brown-haired girl standing in the doorway, she added, "Now that there's Velvet; she's been helping me take care of you but ya may not a known it, 'cause she's the quiet type. We figured up until now, you didn't know who you was, so there weren't much need in us telling you who we was! So, tell me hon, how do ya really feel now that ya've got yer wits about ya?"

Confused was how she felt, but Mariah stuttered out the first thing she wanted to say, "I'm—I'm very grateful! I was in a pretty bad way, and now thanks to you, I'm all right." Frowning slightly, she added, "But—I suppose I do have a few questions. First—where exactly am I? How did I get here—and what happens now?"

Shotsy bit her lip as she smoothed the blankets self-consciously, "Ya passed out in the street a few days ago. Yer in the Long Shot Saloon, hon. It's a cryin' shame that things have worked out this way!" Shaking her head she shrugged, "'Course things usually do get rough for us women when we're all alone." Glancing over at the girl by the door she added, "Now me and Velvet can't change a thing, but we've made a vow to help ya—just as much as we can! Right Vel?"

When the younger woman stepped closer and nodded her head, Shotsy added, "We both want ya to know that—no matter what—yer not alone—for what it's worth—ya've got us—we're yer friends!"

Sleepily, Mariah sighed, "Friends, you have no idea how much that means to me." You both have already been so very kind, thank you." Yawning she added, "I'm sorry but I'm having a hard time understanding all you've just told me. I don't mean to be rude but I think what I need right now is just to go back to sleep!"

Shotsy and Velvet exchanged sorrowful glances but then Shotsy stood and yanked the covers off Mariah. "Hon, we're the ones that are sorry, but what ya need right now is to do what I tell ya. A bath has been ordered and I'm sure ya'll feel better for having it."

"Oh no, please—" Mariah begged, "It's almost night time, isn't it? Can't we wait until mornin'?"

Her protests fell on deaf ears as Velvet opened the door and began carrying in bucket after bucket of steaming water. Mariah hadn't even noticed the tub in the corner of her room. Though she moaned and whimpered, the next thing she knew, the two women had helped her undress and she was up to her shoulders in warm soapy bubbles. She hadn't had an all over, soaking bath since she'd left Texas and she had to admit, it felt wonderful!

"Now, we're just gonna wash yer hair, hon." Shotsy said, sounding oddly sad. "Just lean you head back. We're supposed to make you look like an angel—but darlin'—ya already do—even after being so sick."

"Look like an angel—why?" Mariah asked, "I don't understand?" These women had just promised to be her friends but they weren't making any sense.

Velvet pulled Mariah from her confused thoughts when she held out a dark purple garment. "We've got this satin robe for you to wear. This color will look beautiful on ya. Have ya ever seen the columbines that grow wild up here in the mountains? Some are as purple as this robe and others are the same shade of violet as your eyes. Absolutely beautiful!"

Mariah patted the girl's hand, "You're very sweet, and that fabric is lovely but I'm still shiverin'. I see you've brought my satchel. I have a nice flannel gown inside, and it would feel so much warmer than your pretty satin robe. I think that would be a better choice, don't you?"

Shotsy placed her hand on Mariah's shoulder, and shook her head miserably. "Indeed it would, hon. But yer flannel days are over. Yer life is about to change. Velvet and I are tryin' to do what we can to—well make things easier for ya. In fact—I have some medicine for ya to take."

"Oh, no thank you." Mariah said as she gently pushed the glass of green liquid away. "I feel all together, too muddle headed as it is.

Shotsy's expression became stern and her voice gruff, "Now you listen to me, hon. I know what is best for ya right now. And…ya need to take this—please—don't fight me!"

"No, of course not, Shotsy—I'm sorry." Mariah couldn't bear the idea of upsetting her new friends. She couldn't imagine what she'd done to displease the woman, but she could only assume that it must be very important for her take the medicine.

"Of course I'll take it, if you say I need it! You and Velvet have been such wonderful nurses—you know best—I'm sure." That said, Mariah took the small glass from Shotsy's hand and put it to her lips. The women wrapped her in the beautiful purple robe and it wasn't long before the bed seemed to float towards the ceiling.

Velvet's youthful voice sounded farther and farther away as she spoke words of comfort while she brushed her hair dry.

Soon Mariah was dreaming of kind smiling people and warm sunny days. A short time later, while her mind was still floating in a cloudy haze, she awoke to the sound of her door opening and then clicking shut. Her eyes fluttered open just enough to see that the room was dark but for a thin sliver of pale moonlight that shone through the window. Just beyond the door, she could hear the muffled sounds of raucous piano playing and people talking and laughing. Struggling to focus her eyes, she saw a dark figure stepping towards her. It was a man, dressed in dark clothes, and although her mind was still fuzzy, her heart quickened when she realized that it was Jimmy Todd. He was smiling, but it was a cold smile; the kind that didn't reach his eyes as he slowly made his way across the room.

Although her brain seemed to be filled with cotton wool and her body felt weighed down she struggled to sit up, "This is a lady's room, Sheriff. It is not proper for you to be here. I will not be your mistress—not ever! And if you don't leave right now—I'll scream!"

Todd simply shook his head; he even chuckled as he unfastened his gun belt, tossed it on a chair then slowly unbuttoned his shirt. "Yer in a saloon, Mariah. Nobody will hear ya and if they do, they won't care!" When Todd lit the lantern beside the bed Mariah scooted as far away from him as she could. When she pulled the sheet up to her neck, he yanked the covers from the bed and glared down at her. "Don't deprive me of the view, darlin'. I've paid good money for this! While you were eatin' garbage, I rode all the way to Denver to buy that pretty purple robe." When Mariah glared up at him with hatred in her eyes, he laughed, "What? Ya don't like it? That's all right; you won't have to wear if for long. You do look like an angel. Of course when the men of Otter Run are finished with ya, you'll be a—fallen angel!"

Todd gazed down at her as if she were something to be devoured. Mariah could no longer bear the reality of what was about to happen and she squeezed her eyes shut. The medicine Shotsy had given her wasn't nearly strong enough. It dulled her senses, yes, but that was all. Sadly, she was keenly aware of the evil that had come into her room and was now hovering over her. He pulled his boots off, and she flinched when she heard the spurs jangling as they hit the floor.

"Please, Jimmy, I'm begging you. Leave me alone—don't do this!"

Ignoring her words, Todd sighed, "Hey, you're the one that's been beggin' for a job, a roof over your head, and decent food. Now you've got all three! I've even heard ya made friends with Shotsy and Velvet. That's good! Soon, you'll be able to go shoppin' at the mercantile. 'Course ya'll have to remember that the workin' girls from the Long Shot are only allowed in there on Monday mornings. The few decent women that live in these mountains know not to come to town that day. They don't want to associate with *harlots like you!"*

Mariah's head was swimming, "No—I don't want to be a harlot—please go away." Todd only laughed and as he drew closer, her stomach rebelled at the smell of whiskey and tobacco.

He grabbed her arm and pulled her close; she tried with every ounce of her strength to get away but Todd easily pushed her down. "Now, Shotsy gave ya that medicine so ya wouldn't fight us! Her first night in a saloon, Shotsy fought and got a broken jaw for her efforts. Velvet got three broken ribs! You are here to stay now and ya have no one to blame but yerself. I told ya how it was gonna be." He taunted, "You belong to me alone or I share ya with everyone. You answered me with a slap across the face—as I recall." Rubbing his cheek, his eyes were hard and cold as he leered down at her. He grabbed her by the arm and slapped her just as he had in the sheriff's office. "Go ahead and fight us if ya want, but we'll win. You've been a stupid woman, Mariah. I gave ya the chance to be my mistress and ya turned me down. So now, I reckon that makes me yer first customer instead." Then Todd added mockingly, "But I won't be your last! Theo's paid a lot to be next and then good old

Cyril. Don't know who you'll be entertaining after him. I've heard Ox is gonna hold a raffle every night! There are twenty men downstairs that have all put money down just to get their name in the hat for tomorrow." His eyes burned lustfully as he came closer. "Maybe after a week or so, you might just rethink movin' in with me!"

Mariah's heart hammered in her chest and she felt like a wild animal caught in a trap. How had she ever thought of this man a friend? The same way Victor had made her believe that he was her friend, no doubt. She had seen what she wanted to see. Her mother had warned her time and again to be cautious around men but foolishly, she hadn't listened.

As Todd pulled her close a scream sprung from Mariah's dry throat, but she was so weak, the sound didn't even pass through the paper-thin walls. Her eyes darted to his gun belt that lay in the chair across the room. Oh how she wanted to fight him off and escape, but her face was still throbbing, and then she remembered his words: 'Shotsy fought and got a broken jaw for her efforts.' It was no use; she was powerless to stop what was happening. Yet in her mind at least, she could still run away. Shutting everything out, Mariah was suddenly back at the Candlestick ranch, riding her favorite horse. Nothing bad was happening. No—no—no—she wasn't in this evil place—she was running her horse flat out across a green meadow. Tears were streaming down her face because of the bright sun and the wind in her face. She was not crying it was just the sun and the wind. She was running away—free from every one—and everything—far, far away!

The following morning, Mariah awoke to a day that was warm, clear, and sunny. The effects of the strange green liquid had worn completely off and her mind was sadly, all too clear. Gone were the cloudy thoughts, the fever and the racking chills from her illness. Gone, along with everything else—was her honor and virtue. Oh yes—those were gone as well. She tried to convince herself that her illness and the medicine had given her nightmares—but—no. She knew that what she'd experienced had been all too real. She not only knew where she was—worse yet—she knew what she had become—just another harlot. Yes, the despicable men of Otter Run had planned this all out very carefully. They had waged this war against her and it seemed that they had finally won.

Chapter 15
Long Shot Rescue

"O Lord, rescue me from evil people. Protect me from those who are violent." Psalm 140:1

As Preacher trotted Flint into the town of Otter Run, he struggled with mixed feelings. There was so much he *needed to do*. However, all he *wanted to do* was check on the beautiful young widow he'd met the last time he was there. He hadn't been able to forget her hauntingly sad violet eyes, sunlit hair, or her honey sweet southern drawl. Daily, he reminded himself that his heart belonged to God and to his mountain ministry. Still, it seemed that allowing his thoughts to turn to Mariah Kent had become a powerful temptation.

After Preacher had escorted Clem Talbott home to his family, he spent a few days hunting meat and chopping firewood for Slim and Jozy Warner. Once the elderly couple were back on their feet, he'd paid a visit to Black-Eyed Jack. There were other's he could have, and probably should have checked on. Still, he just couldn't seem to rest until he got back to Otter Run. He wanted to see how the young widow was doing. Was she still in town or had she returned to Texas? Even though he reminded himself that, he had given the bank instructions to provide for her every need—he still worried about her. Perhaps he shouldn't have encouraged the sheriff to court her. Then again, it might have work out just fine. The couple might even be asking for a wedding today. That thought, however, made Preacher feel worse rather than better. It stirred up strange feelings—feelings he'd just as soon not contemplate. Whenever he thought of the fragile young woman with the sheriff, or any man for that matter, his stomach suddenly felt like it was buzzing with angry hornets. Usually weddings were his favorite duty, but the thought of performing that particular ceremony—gave him no joy.

Preacher was just reining Flint to a stop in front of the sheriff's office when the man himself stepped out the door. "Good day, Sheriff Todd."

Preacher greeted, "I returned as soon as I could. I've been concerned about the widow woman, Missus Kent. You seemed to have courting on your mind the last time I saw you. Do you have any news you'd like to share with me?"

Jimmy Todd looked up in surprise. At first, he seemed at a loss for words, but then he chuckled, "Well—I'll tell ya Pastor Long. I know a man in yer line of business has to be fussy about morals and rules and such. But we're livin' in the wild and free Rocky Mountains, amigo. This ain't Boston—ya know! Mariah Kent is one beautiful woman but she was a lousy housewife. Victor Kent used to complain that his wife's cookin' was so bad it'd poison a rattlesnake. So—the men of Otter Run agreed that it was a pure waste for a beauty like her to get married and make one man miserable when she could make all the rest of us happy!"

Todd lost his haughty grin when Preacher quickly stepped down from his saddle, "What have you done?" He demanded. "Where is she?"

Stepping back Todd held up his hand nervously, then he reminded himself that Long was a religious man; he wasn't going to do anything. Still, just in case he slowly rested his right hand on the butt of his gun and said smoothly, "No need to get riled, I know you're a civilized man, but this country ain't civilized. Sure—I wanted the woman—but not as a wife. I offered for her to move in with me and she refused. She ran out of money for room and board not long after she moved to town. Took to living out in the forest and picking through the garbage for food. Then she got real sick. Ox was the only one that would take her in, Shotsy and Velvet took real good care of her and they're all-good friends now. Leave her be Preacher, she's doin' just fine where she is!"

Preacher didn't want to believe what he was hearing, "I don't understand? I told Hank to make sure that they took funds from my account. She was to have whatever she needed, whether she stayed in town or returned to her home in Texas. I made sure he knew to pay for room and board! Why would she live in the forest and eat garbage? I tell you, I made sure she was provided for before I left!"

Todd just shook his head, "Pardon me for sayin' it but you're a fool, Preacher. Like I said…this ain't Boston. You may have told Hank to do all that, but he works for Theo Krane. You know what kind of man Krane really is. You know what kind Ox Hennessey is too! Did you really think they would pass up a chance to have a woman like her working at the Long

Shot? They both made sure that no one in town gave her a penny—nor a way to earn one. Heck they wouldn't even allow anyone to let her sleep on their porches or barter with her for a crust o' bread." Seeing the anger rising in Preacher's face, the sheriff quickly added, "I was out of town, but I heard she was in a real bad way!"

Naturally, Todd didn't admit that, all the Highlanders had agreed to this plan. The Association included himself, Krane, Hennessey, Cyril Castle and a few others. They had all agreed to keep everyone from helping the young widow, for the benefit of the Highlanders of course.

When Preacher ran his large hand over his face and shook his head miserably, Todd added softly, "Don't take it so hard, friend. Lots of widow woman earn their livin' in such a way. At least at the Long Shot, she'll get three meals a day and a roof over her head. Besides, having a beauty like her in town was just too good a thing to pass up. She was a lousy wife, but with a face and figure like she's got—I think she may have finally found her callin'!"

Preacher moved so quickly that Jimmy Todd didn't have time to pull his gun or even step away. Instantly, the big man had him by the shirt collar.

"Let go o' me, Preacher." Todd choked. "I could arrest you for assaultin' an officer of the law!" Then he delivered the final blow to preacher's conscience. "You could have told her, that you had provided for her. You could have taken her down to Colorado City, Denver, or Canyon City. You could have put her on a train home. So, why didn't you do more for her when you had the chance?" When Preacher winced at his words and loosened his hold, Todd continued, "We both know why, 'cause she got under yer skin like she did the rest of us. You didn't trust yourself to get that close to such a pretty woman—did ya?"

Preacher released his hold on Todd and stepped back. "Missus Kent is a proud woman, I did talk to her but—she wouldn't take my help when I offered it. I am a fool though. I thought this town had better men in it! And I really thought you might be ready to settle down. I'm guilty of misjudging everything and everyone!"

"Now why would you think I wanted to settle down, Preacher?" Todd sneered. "Think back, you saw me coming down the stairs that morning after spending all night with a saloon girl. If you'd given it some thought, you'd known I wasn't the marryin' kind. No sir, you thought what you wanted to—and that's your fault—not mine."

Preacher's eyes flashed and his right hand tightened into a fist at his side. Quincy Long hadn't been in a fight since a drunken sailor decided to challenge the ship owner's son. He hadn't wanted to fight that sailor, but he had. They had fought until neither of them could stand or throw another punch. At this moment, however, he hungered for a fight. In fact, he wanted nothing more than to plant his fist in Jimmy Todd's smug face.

"Go ahead, preacher man—throw that punch!" The Sheriff taunted. "'Course I'll have to toss ya in jail. If ya really wanted to help her, you should have done it before leavin' town. Now, you're just too late! What was done—can't be undone. Still and all, she is one beautiful woman—and I guarantee you that the men of this town won't let her get lonely."

Though the sheriff's words made him seethe with anger, Preacher realized that he was as mad at himself for what had happened to the poor woman, as he was at every other man in town.

"I won't skin my knuckles on you, Jimmy Todd, but you'd do well to remember that even if I don't lay a hand on you, my Boss deals harshly with men who prey on the innocent. And there's something else you should know. This may not be civilized Boston, but I have powerful friends in civilized places from New York to Washington D.C.. I regularly correspond with and can request at any time the support of Governors, Senators and Judges in the Territories as well as the States. So don't you ever think of hurting anyone else like this again, because you have no idea what kind of earthly hellfire I can and will bring down on you!"

Preacher walked away leaving Todd standing in the street. Glad that he hadn't dropped Flint off at the livery, he grabbed the reins and headed for the saloon. With every anguished step, he confessed his sin of failing Mariah Kent. In times past, The Boss had always told him when and where he needed to act. So why hadn't God told him to come back sooner, or had he just not been listening? Todd's jeering words seemed to echo in Preacher's head, '*So, why didn't you help her when you had the chance? We both know why, 'cause she got under yer skin like she did the rest of us. You didn't trust yourself to get that close to such a pretty woman—did ya?'*"

As he tied Flint to the hitching post outside the saloon, he felt the subtle counsel from The Boss. *Wisdom is better than strength. Be as gentle as a dove and wise as a serpent.*

Gazing up and down the street, Preacher pulled his scattergun from its sheath on his saddle and checked the load. Then he reached into his saddlebag and put a few extra shells in his pocket. This gun was the kind used to bring down a bear. He was counting on the fact that no mortal man wanted to face the business end of a weapon like this—especially at close range. The moment he pushed through the saloon's swinging doors, he calmly leveled the barrel on Ox Hennessey's chest, as the man stood behind the bar.

At that moment, Quincy Long was more warrior—than preacher. He was an exceedingly big man and had to duck slightly to get through the doorway. At six feet six inches tall, blonde hair, wide shoulders, powerful build and fierce expression, he was every bit as intimidating as his Viking ancestors.

Ox wasn't pleased to see Quincy Long. He had hoped it'd be a few more weeks before that man came back to town. When he saw him riding in, he knew he'd be getting' preached at, once the man of God heard the gossip about the young widow. He had not—however—expected this! Rolling the large chaw of tobacco deeper into his cheek, Ox called out, "Well now, top o' the mornin' to ya, Preacher!" even as he stealthily reached for the shotgun he kept under the bar.

"Bad idea, Ox." Preacher warned as he cocked the scattergun. "Best to keep your hands pressed down on the bar where I can see them. Then tell me where she is!"

Ox grunted as he splayed his meaty hands across the bar then asked innocently, "Now, who would ya be lookin' for in a place like this? Ain't no one on the premises but a few drunks from last night and three doves—asleep upstairs—where they belong!"

"Hennessey—you will tell me where Missus Kent is—or—"

"Or what? I seem to recall there's a place in the Bible that says Thou shall not. You're bluffing and I know it!"

Keeping his gun trained on Ox, Preacher nodded towards the crude painting hanging over the bar, "You've always been fond of that painting—haven't you? I've never liked it, always thought that poor woman looked cold. Thought she should be wearing more than a smile. How about I dress her up in some double-00 buckshot?" Stepping back, he raised his gun towards the painting, "I'd move aside if I were you, Ox. This gun has a wide pattern."

"Hold on there, Preacher, yer not a violent man. Don't be acting in a way you'll only regret. Now, that little widow woman would o' died—but for me. I was the one to have her carried in here, after she passed out in the street. 'Twas me and only me t' give her food and shelter. It's all for the best, I tell ya. She ain't got no money and she ain't got nowhere to go. Now, at least she'll have a decent roof over her head and three meals a day. That's more 'n her own husband ever did for her. So I say, be off with ya, and leave well enough alone!"

Ox's glib look quickly turned to one of fear when Preacher's eyes flared with anger and he once again leveled the barrel of the scattergun on him. The Irishman's normally ruddy face grew pale, but Mariah Kent was as good as a gold mine and he wasn't about to lose her. As soon as word spread that a young beauty with flaxen hair and violent eyes was working in his saloon, men would come from all over the mountains, might even come up from the lowlands. The prospects of more money in the till outweighed Hennessey's fear of anything a peaceable man of God might do.

"Listen to me lad, ya've come too late," he reasoned. "Yer wantin' to do a good thing, but the truth is, she's one of me doves now and there ain't no goin' back for her—she is what she is!"

Preacher's jaw clenched as he quickly took two long strides and shoved the scattergun right into Ox's soft belly. The man was so startled that he swallowed his plug of tobacco. His face turned a dark reddish-blue and he doubled over, choking and sputtering. Taking advantage of the moment, Preacher reached around and grabbed Ox's shotgun and swung it under his arm.

Though it was early, there were still a few men there, nursing hang-overs. However, when Preacher's stern gaze fell on them they found them-selves staggering to their feet, anxious to be on their way. While Ox coughed and retched into the nearest spittoon, Preacher grabbed the last man before he could get through the swinging doors, and demanded, "What room is she in?"

Mariah stared out the window—her mind was numb one minute and recalling strange memories the next. It had been exactly two years ago that her family had hosted the annual Harvester's Ball at the Candlestick Ranch. She'd worn a dress of silvery satin trimmed in dark purple with earrings and matching necklace made of silver and amethyst. When the gala was over, she stood with her parents at the door bidding their guests goodbye. In the procession was an elderly senator's wife, who had gently touched her cheek and whispered, 'My dear girl, you are so like an angel! So lovely, sweet and innocent. I hope you never lose those qualities!' The memory made Mariah feel empty, for she had indeed lost those qualities. She had lost everything! That sweet woman had compared her to an angel. Ironically, Jimmy Todd had told Shotsy and Velvet to make her look like an angel.

"He said the men of Otter Run would turn me into a fallen angel—and I suppose that's what they did." She whispered to her reflection in the window. "My life began to unravel when I married Victor Kent. And the men last night—those evil men—they just finished the job. Why—oh—why," she moaned. "Why couldn't I have just died in the forest?"

Shotsy and Velvet had come into her room that morning carrying buckets of hot water for a bath and a tray of hot tea and biscuits. They had acted as if what had happened to her in the night had been her decision, as if she had agreed to become another of Hennessey's doves, working at the Long Shot Saloon.

At first Shotsy, the older and wiser of the two, had sat down beside her and listened to her cry. She had stroked her hair, like a mother would her child. When she finally spoke to Mariah, her voice was stern. "You listen to me, hon! Me and Velvet we know how yer feeling this mornin'. We were both down on our luck just like you. We had t' swallow our pride...just like you! A body has to keep a roof over their head and eat—don't they? Ya don't want to go back out to them woods again—you don't want to search for food in the towns' garbage again—do ya?"

Mariah tried to turn away but Shotsy cupped her face in her hands and spoke harshly, "There are worse things than, doin' what we're doin'! Now, me and Velvet promise to help ya whenever and however we can."

The woman's words were unbearable to Mariah; she could not accept that this was now her life. Pulling away from Shotsy, she asked through gritted teeth, "How can you two act as if what happened to me, or either of you last night was acceptable? We are slaves to those evil men and it will never be all right! Please—I do appreciate all you've done for me and what you're trying to do now—but I need to be alone." Mariah rebelled at the thought that she was expected to tolerate this way of life, just as Shotsy and Velvet had done. She knew that if she didn't get out of this wicked place—she'd go mad!

After the two women returned to their rooms, Mariah felt as if her body and soul were empty and hollow. Sliding to the floor beside the bed she picked up the purple robe they had dressed her in the night before. For the next hour, she ripped and tore at the dark fabric until it was little more than a pile of threads. She made sure that every scrap was too small to be used, ever again. It came to her then, there was only one-way to escape. Holding that idea in her mind she straightened the room, washed and dressed as a proper lady should, including hat, gloves and reticule. Then she stood by the window with her neatly packed satchel beside her—and waited. Eventually a man would knock on her door and this time she could only hope it would be a man who understood mercy. If not, then she would find a way—she had to find a way! When the knock finally came, Mariah was shocked when she found out who was on the other side.

"Missus Kent, this is Pastor Long, ma'am. I just want to talk with you."

He spoke with his back to the door, his gun aimed towards the top of the stairway. Ox had finally recovered from his choking fit and was now standing at the bottom of the stairs, his face red with rage and his eyes shooting daggers. Preacher had taken Ox's shotgun and was holding it under his left arm while keeping his own gun trained on the bartender. Still, Preacher knew that it would take a miracle for the two of them to get out of this place, let alone out of town, without someone getting shot.

When Mariah opened the door, she didn't even look at the man; instead, she returned to the window. Keeping her back to him she said in her soft Texan drawl, "You are too late, sir." Her voice was void of emotion and her words filled Preacher with shame. "But—I beg you. Please—do me just one favor, it's the only thing I can accept."

Preacher feared what she might mean by that, for he could feel her shame and defeat the moment he entered the room. He took his eyes from Hennessey for only a moment and saw her silhouetted against the window. He had prepared himself to find her looking disheveled and wan, but he had not expected to find her as prim and proper, as the day he had first seen her. Mariah stood there with sunshine slanting through the window wearing a dark green traveling dress. The small matching bonnet she wore did not cover the tight bun at the nap of her neck, revealing her shining pale blonde hair. Her fully packed satchel sat beside the neatly made bed. Then he heard her sad and broken voice, and his own feelings of failure washed over him.

"Sir..." she began stoically, keeping her voice low and her face turned away, "All my life I've heard that a decent woman would rather die than become a harlot. I tried! But dyin' was a more difficult task than I had imagined. So now sir, I have but one request from you—I beg you not to question me—just—lay your pistol on the bed—and walk away."

Preacher shook his head and clenched his jaw. Making sure that he could see the top of Hennessey's baldhead, he spoke softly, "No ma'am, I won't do that! Believe me; death will not free you from your pain. And—for many reasons—you are not ready to die!"

"I am more ready than you know, Pastor! I cannot bear the shame and disgrace that has befallen me. Please allow me this last dignity and know that I take what I do upon my own soul, if there is such a thing. This is my doin' and no one else's!"

The woman's strength and composure touched Preacher deeply. "Missus Kent," he said gently, "I am here to help you escape from what has befallen you. I take responsibility for this. I gave the bank instructions for you to have all the funds you needed and I foolishly trusted them to do as I asked. I will never forgive myself for how I've failed you. All I ask is that you trust me to take you away from this evil place and allow me to protect you. You have nothing to fear from me—you can trust me ma'am—I promise!"

Turning away from the window, Mariah gasped, "Really? You'll take me away from this awful place—now?"

"Yes, ma'am—" Glancing down the stairs he added, "and if you don't mind—the sooner the better!"

Victor had told her he would protect her. Mariah didn't think she'd ever believe those words again. She didn't know what to expect if she went with this man but she knew what to expect if she stayed! Instantly, she wiped the tears from her face and picked up her satchel, but when she made to brush past the big man, he stopped her.

"No ma'am—you follow me, and please don't question anything I tell you. Do exactly as I say—and as quickly as you can!"

When Hennessey saw Mariah following Preacher down the stairs, he clamped both of his paw-like hands on the railings, effectively blocking their way. Once again, Preacher cocked the scattergun and this time he aimed it right in Ox's face, "Move aside Hennessey."

"I know yer bluffin'. Men of God don't go around shootin' people." Hennessey jeered, and then he gazed up at Mariah, "Gal, I've given ya room and board. Ya paid off a bit o' what ya owe me last night but you still haven't paid it all. After that, like I told ya, I'll let ya keep half o' what ya earn. Now, go on back to yer room and I won't be holdin' this against ya."

Preacher could feel Mariah's panic as she huddled as closely to him as she dared without actually touching him, "Please, sir," she begged. "Don't let him keep me here. Truly—I would rather die."

Taking another step down the staircase, Preacher said calmly, "Ox, you told me once that your mother read you Bible stories. Remember the one about David and Goliath? Goliath was a bully who shouted his disrespect of God and his people. God gave David the ability to kill Goliath! David didn't regret killing a bully who was determined to do evil and neither will I. If you force me…I will shoot you!"

Ox looked a bit worried but then he smiled again, "Nah. You've tried too hard to win me soul. Ya wouldn't send me to hell over a little thing like this."

"What you've done is not small in God's eyes, Ox. Of course, I'd rather not have to kill you. However, I wouldn't mind…" Preacher swung the scattergun back at the nude painting over the bar while he aimed Ox's own shotgun straight at the big man's belly, "I've sworn to protect this woman, so don't doubt for a second that I'll pull both these triggers if I have to! If you don't move right now, I'm gonna fill that expensive painting full of holes. If that doesn't convince you to move aside—then you better prepare yourself for an eternity in hell—because you're next!"

Hennessey's face was a picture of hatred as it grew red with rage, but he dropped his meaty hands from the railing and slowly stepped back allowing Preacher and Mariah to walk past him and out the saloon doors.

"Missus Kent," Preacher commanded. "Untie that big gelding there, then I hope you can climb up into that saddle. I'm afraid I can't assist you just now."

Thankfully, Mariah was comfortable with horses and she was quick to climb aboard. Preacher was surprised and relieved when without a word she instantly took Hennessey's shotgun from his left hand and pointed it at the gathering crowd, while he swung up behind her.

Just then, the sheriff stepped from the café across the street and headed towards them. He was just a few feet away when Mariah immediately turned the shotgun on him. Todd skidded to a stop and everyone behind him dove for cover.

Cocking both barrels, Mariah hissed, "Well now, Jimmy Todd! I'm gonna give you two easy choices, just like you gave me! Would you rather be gut shot—or gelded?" There was pure steel in her voice and hatred in her eyes. "I shot a rabid dog once, Sheriff and it bothered me for days. But shooting you—that won't bother me at all!

Fortunately, for Jimmy Todd, Preacher knocked the gun up and away just as fire leapt from the barrel. If his action triggered the gun or Mariah had truly meant to shoot the man, Preacher didn't know.

The sheriff assumed the latter, however, and a savage rage covered the man's dark face as he shouted: "Mariah Kent, yer under arrest—for attempted murder!"

Since the shotgun that Mariah held was now empty and harmless, Preacher quickly turned his scattergun on Jimmy Todd. "Listen Sheriff," he explained, "it was my fault that the shotgun was discharged. It was an accident and no one got hurt."

Staring into the scattergun seemed to help the Sheriff regain his composure. "Look here, Preacher, this has nothin' to do with you," he said smoothly. "I'll call it an accident and I won't charge her for threatening me, if she goes quietly back to her room—where she belongs. She owes Hennessey for room and board ya know."

Preacher shook his head, "Missus Kent has no room in that saloon. As for what she owes Ox, tell Theo Krane to pay the man for a week's room and board from my account." Gazing around at the on-lookers, he raised his voice enough for all to hear, "I gave the bank permission to draw from my account and to pay Castle for this woman's room and board—indefinitely! But the President of the Bank chose to allow her to nearly starve to death, so she'd end up at the mercy of the men in this town." Preacher gazed up then and saw both Shotsy and Velvet as they peered out an upstairs window. "I say no woman should have to sell themselves in a saloon or anywhere else. I promise to pay for schooling and provide a new life to any woman who wants my help!"

Shotsy and Velvet stared at each other for a moment, and then they looked down and saw Hennessey glaring up at them. Instantly, they both stepped back and closed the window.

When Preacher noticed a group of grumbling men heading that way from the livery, he tugged on Flint's reins, and slowly began backing the horse away from the crowd, not daring to turn his back on any of them.

The growing assembly of men followed, cursing and complaining. Jimmy Todd shoved some of the men aside and sneered, "What do ya think yer gonna do with that fallen angel ya got there, Reverend Long?" He mocked. Then he directed his words at Mariah. "Come on darlin', don't burden that man with your troubles. Think this through. You're better off here and so are Shotsy and Velvet. None of ya are capable of anything better, and that's not gonna change. You know what they say...once a harlot...always a harlot!"

Disgusted by Jimmy Todd's words, Preacher clenched his jaw as he looked down at the man. Then slowly shifted his gaze to include the other men as well. They were muttering to themselves and he'd heard a few remarks about rushing them.

"Listen to me—all you men. Hear me, now!" Preacher demanded. "I've worked or hunted alongside most of you, and you know that I'm a fair hand with an ax, a knife, a gun or my fists if it comes to that. Now, I'd hate to send any of you men to hell. I'd rather introduce you to my Boss so you can go to heaven one day. But I promised to protect this woman and now I'll make all of you a promise. If ANY of you follow us," Preacher's dark gaze quickly turned to the sheriff as he added, "or try to bring this woman back here. I'll use all the strength and power God has given me to protect her! And if that means sending you to your judgment a little early—then so be it!"

The men that knew this big man knew that he wasn't boasting nor was he making an idle threat. They believed his warning right down to the soles of their boots. Mariah was a rare beauty—yes—and they had all lusted after her. On the other hand, most of them had benefited from Preacher's kindness as well as his unusual strength, at one time or another. He had tended them when they were sick, dug them out of their shacks when they were snowed in. They had been nourished with game he had hunted and lived in cabins he had helped to build. Although many of them had come west to get away from God and civilization, the God that this man worked for seemed to be one they might one day like to know better. After all, until now, the man they called Preacher had done nothing but give of himself and offer his help and friendship and the help and friendship, of the God he served.

Preacher continued to back his gelding away while some men lowered their heads in shame and others grumbled even as they let them go. The moment he felt it was safe, Preacher spun Flint around and the powerful gelding carried them up the mountain path, away from Otter Run and the Long Shot Saloon.

Chapter 16
Place of Rest

"He said to them, 'Come aside by yourselves to a deserted place and rest a while." Mark 6:31

As they rode higher and higher up the mountain path, Mariah wavered between feeling nothing at all and feeling too much. Her mind kept whispering that it was all just a nightmare—nothing really happened. Then the truth would break in and she'd become so filled with rage that all she wanted was to return to Otter Run and set that evil town on fire!

She was still weak and exhausted, but all she could think of was that she wished she hadn't made so many mistakes.

You're such a fool Mariah. Will you never learn? How could you have been so blinded by that lustful devil, Jimmy Todd? Now, you're trusting another man, and you don't even know where he's taking you.

Preacher could see that the woman was drawing deeper and deeper inside herself. The only time she reacted to anything was if he accidentally brushed her arm with his while reining Flint. Each time she felt even the slightest touch, the poor woman flinched and let out a tiny cry as if it brought her pain.

They had ridden for hours before Mariah gathered enough presence of mind to speak, "Pastor, I don't have the words to thank you for taking me away from that awful place. It was a brave thing to do, you could have been killed!"

"Please, Missus Kent, don't thank me. I can't even begin to tell you how sorry I am. I foolishly entrusted Theo and Hank to pay for your room and board. You suffered because I misjudged them. I can't even ask you to forgive me, for I know I'll never forgive myself for what has happened to you."

"No," she moaned, "I should have accepted your help when it was offered. I made the choices that put me in that dreadful place. There's nothing to forgive you for, so please put your mind at ease. It seems though that you and I share one frailty, we both hoped to find good in our neighbors. I shall not make that mistake ever again. In fact, I need to harden myself and I'll begin now by walking for a bit—if you'll let me down. I don't like riding double anyway. My father was always against horses carrying two riders."

Preacher's lips lifted in a sad smile at her words. He knew her concern for his horse might be genuine but he also knew that his nearness was un-nerving her. The nearness of any man would be frightening after what she had suffered. Still, he knew even if she did not—that she was not strong enough to walk or even to ride alone. What she needed was distraction and since she was interested in horses, he'd tell her about his.

"Ma'am you don't need to worry about Flint. I came West with one of my family's best Thoroughbred mares. Of course, it didn't take long to see that I needed a mountain horse. The biggest and strongest one I could find." As they zigzagged their way up a steep hill, Preacher chuckled lightly, "You can feel the spring in his step-can't you! I've ridden this character all over these mountains and I've yet to really wear him down. I promise you; that he could carry us both over Pike's Peak—and just as soon as we got to the other side—he'd be pleased as punch to carry us both right back again."

Leaning forward she slowly ran her hand down the horse's muscular neck. "He's a handsome animal. I grew up with horses but I've never seen one this color before. The dorsal stripe and banded legs tell me he's a buckskin or a lined back dun, but his coat's the wrong color—it's almost a gun-metal gray."

"Yes ma'am, that's why I named him Flint." Mariah could hear the pride and affection in the man's voice as he explained, "The color is rare, it's called grulla, *(grew-ya).*" A good friend of mine from Boston, Timothy Grainger, told me that he and his twin brother Tytus owned a ranch just north of Colorado City called, The Bar 61. Tim wasn't a braggart but he told me that if I needed an exceptional horse, I'd find it at The Bar 61. The man in charge of selling the horses was an old black man by the name of Joseph. He had once been a slave on the Grainger plantation, but I knew my friend Tim and his brother loved and respected that man, like a father. I had hoped to meet him! Sure enough, Joseph was the kind of man that you know you should listen to and trust, the moment you look into his eyes. Anyway, when he and Tytus heard that I was a friend of Timothy's they welcomed me like family! Naturally, they wanted to know all about Tim. Then I told them about my ministry to the mountain folk. They agreed with me that I needed a very special horse, one with uncommon good sense and a great deal of stamina. Instead of taking me out to look over the herd, they invited me up to their big Mexican style hacienda. They fed me well and we talked for hours, but before sending me off to a luxurious room for a good night's sleep, Joseph took me aside. He told me that he would talk it over with the Lord, and in the morning, he'd introduce me to the horse God wanted me to have. Sure enough, the following morning, as I was stepping outside, I saw him leading Flint out of the barn—already wearing my saddle! Joseph was grinning to beat the band and he said, 'Son, God has put a fire in this gelding's belly. He's always wantin' to see what's over that next hill!' Then he pointed to me and winked. 'I'm thinking God put that same fire in your belly! The good Lord thinks you two will travel real well together."

Preacher was silent for a while then he added, "I've had Flint for almost five years now and the only time I've seen him breathe hard was when we were making our way over the great divide. That was one ride that challenged us both! Flint's perfect for me and for the kind of work I do. Sometimes he has to carry someone who's sick or wounded. That's when Flint truly amazes me. Normally he has so much vitality, but if I put a child or someone who is hurt on his back, he instantly calms down and walks as if he were stepping on eggshells. Of course, when I get back on him, he's full of vinegar again. Joseph was right, Flint has been a good partner, and we have traveled very well together."

It wasn't long before they rode into a small mountain clearing. It provided both excellent cover and a breathtaking view of their back trail. This was where Preacher always left his pack mule to graze and where he always made camp after leaving Otter Run. He especially liked this camp for its vantage point. It would be next to impossible for anyone to sneak up on them, while he could see for miles!

He slid off the back of the big gelding then looked up at Mariah, giving her a moment before he tried to help her down from the saddle. Though she was trying to hide it, she was exhausted—and now that he could see her violet eyes, he realized that she was not over her illness. Still, she hadn't breathed a word of complaint. He knew without asking that she was miserable, in both body and spirit. He wanted to help her deal with all she'd been through, but he knew it would be a slow process. Understanding that even though she was weak she would not want to be touched he asked gently, “May I have your permission to help you down?”

Mariah hesitated for a moment, then she gave a slight nod, “Yes, thank you, I am feeling a little dizzy.”

When he carefully lowered her to the ground, she swayed as if she might not be able to stand. Touching the back of his hand to her cheek, Preacher was alarmed, “You’re burning up with fever! Come now; let me help you get comfortable while I set up our camp.” He guided her to a fallen log to rest upon. An instant later, he returned and placed a warm blanket around her shoulders. The sun was just creeping behind the tallest peaks when tremor after tremor began slicing through her. Her teeth were chattering by the time Preacher had a brisk fire going. While he boiled aspen bark tea to bring down her fever, he also brewed up enough coffee for them both. When he sat her satchel at her feet, it tipped over and a soft melodious sound came from inside.

“A violin?” he asked.

“No, nothing so grand sir, just my little heart-shaped zither. I never go anywhere without it. My brother gave it to me before he left home.” Mariah’s expression was wistful as she closed her eyes and rubbed her temples with her fingertips.

Since her eyes were closed, Preacher took the opportunity to study this pale young woman for a few moments while he swirled her tea in the tin cup to cool. Mariah suddenly looked up and caught him staring at her. Their eyes locked for one long moment. Both what she saw and did not see in this man’s eyes told her what she needed to know. In his piercing blue gaze, she saw neither lust nor pity. Instead, she saw only concern and compassion. Greatly relieved, Mariah sighed knowing it was safe to close her eyes again.

Preacher’s heart broke for this woman. In spite of all she’d been through; she seemed so genteel and innocent. The emotional wounds she bore so silently were raw and deep and he knew they would not heal easily. Kneeling beside her, he placed the cup of bitter tea in her hand, “I hate to ask you to drink this but we need to bring your fever down.” His voice was as warm and comforting as the fire that burned beside her as he added, “When you’ve got that down I’ll give you sweetened coffee to rid yourself of the taste. The tea will lower your fever and the coffee will sooth your headache.” When Mariah took the cup and dutifully began to drink, he said gently, "And…not tonight of course, but soon, you should play something on your zither. I've always found music soothing when my soul is troubled. It might help you; in fact I think it might help us both!"

Mariah swallowed the last of the tea, grimacing as she handed back the empty cup, "I'll take that sweetened coffee now." When Preacher exchanged her cup for one with heavily sugared coffee, she took a few sips then shook her head. "Your soul may be *troubled* as you put it, Pastor. My soul isn't troubled—it's *damned forever!* There is not a melody in the world that could sooth me."

"Forgive me, Misses Kent, I didn't mean to…"

Mariah put hand to her forehead and moaned, "No—please—forgive me! I sound so un-grateful. I'll be forever indebted to you for getting me out of that dreadful place. You risked your life to do so. If it weren't for you, I would be reliving last night's events all over again! Even so, life holds nothing but regret for me now. I would long for death but—I've been thinking about what you said, I'm not ready to die. In fact, I'm afraid now more than ever of the punishment that awaits me!"

Preacher poured more coffee into her cup, seeing that she was still shivering; he took his coat off and wrapped it around her shoulders. "You've been through so much and you're still not over your illness. Right now, both your mind and body need rest. Try not to dwell on anything. Put your mind on some pleasant thought or memory. Later, when you're stronger and up to listening, I do have words of hope and encouragement to give you. For now, however, the best medicine for you—is sleep!"

Not knowing what to think on just then, Mariah watched this big man as he went about the business of preparing their dinner. First, he pulled a sharp knife from a scabbard on his belt. Then he walked a few paces away and dug up some wild onions. With quick efficient movements, he peeled off the dirty outer skin, sliced them up and dropped them into a pot of boiling water to which he added small pieces of jerked beef.

It seemed to Mariah that she had only blinked but she must have dozed off because when she looked up, the man was handing her a steaming cup of beef and onion broth. It was exactly what she needed. From the very first sip, it seemed to soothe her scratchy throat and her trembling stomach. Holding the cup with both hands Mariah soaked up its warmth. Though she didn't exactly smile she did mumble sleepily, "Your tea was horrid—your coffee was better—but this—this is good—thank you!"

"I'm glad you like it. And while you're sipping your broth I'm going to make you—your own private wilderness bed."

When Mariah suddenly looked frightened, Preacher reminded himself that she was understandable wary. Hoping to calm and reassure her, he decided to talk while he worked. Ax in hand he began chopping boughs from a nearby tree. "The nights get cold this time of year, especially this high. I'm building us ***each our own shelter***. I often just roll myself in a buffalo robe and sleep under the stars. Of course, I often wake up covered in snow. So tonight I thought I'd build one for myself as well. If a storm should blow in, I wouldn't want you to worry about my being out in the cold or having to share your own shelter with me. No matter the weather tonight, I promise that you will have your very own private place—and I'll have mine! I hope that will be a comfort to you and help you feel safe."

Mariah ducked her head, "You are very thoughtful, sir. I've heard you're from Boston and yet you seem quite at home in this wild-country."

"I suppose I am; although I've only lived here in these mountains for about five years. I traveled the world with my parents and survival became kind of a game in our family."

"A game—what do you mean?"

"Father always liked the challenge of making a home wherever he found himself. Our family's residence and business was in Boston but we were a seafaring lot. My parents and I sailed everywhere. Whenever we dropped anchor, be it near a deserted island or desolate coast, my father and I would go ashore and make a shelter with whatever was available and hunt and eat whatever was there. I've had numerous occasions to be thankful for his wisdom in teaching me how to survive with nothing but my wits and a sharp knife!"

Mariah found the man's deep voice and calm manner soothing. She swallowed down another sip of broth and watched him work. He stepped a few paces from their campfire, then pushed his way through the lower branches of a nearby spruce tree. Using a small hatchet he cut a handful of the lowest branches smoothly against the edge of the trunk. He left the branches above and on either sides to form the walls and roof of the shelter. The cut branches he carefully arranged on the hard ground to form a nice bouncy mattress, which he covered with a buffalo hide. When he was satisfied with the soft and furry bed, he tied the overhead branches together using rope made of sinew. Over the connected branches, he draped a waterproof oilcloth and then tied it down to the ground with tent stakes. When he had finished his task, Mariah saw that he had indeed made for her a very private bedchamber. It would be warm and dry—and it was just for her!

When Preacher looked back, he saw Mariah watching him. Wanting to comfort her, he began hesitantly, "I know how you must—no—I have no idea how you're feeling. I can't even begin to imagine. Nor can I tell you why this has happened. All I can do is promise that I will do everything in my power to help you and that you have nothing to fear from me. All you need do now—is rest!" Looking uncertain, he held out his arms, "You and I both know that you are not strong enough to walk. May I have permission to carry you to your shelter?"

Mariah hesitated, but she knew he was right; shyly she nodded, giving him her permission. Preacher frowned when he lifted her into his arms for she weighed next to nothing. Suddenly he thought of this delicate woman rummaging through the town's garbage and he fought down an overwhelming anger at the people of Otter Run.

Although, he was terribly gentle and respectful as he laid her down and covered her with another blanket, Mariah was rigid in her arms and he could tell that she held her breath until he moved away.

Kneeling beside her shelter, Preacher grimaced as he ran a hand over his reddish-blonde whiskers. "I didn't have time to shave or clean up when I got to town today. Even my sweet mother used to tell me that when I don't shave I look way too much like my Viking ancestors." When Mariah just blinked up at him, he shrugged his shoulders, "And I uh—I have other blankets so don't worry about me. I want you to keep my coat tonight, too. Your fever is making you feel like it's colder than it really is!"

Mariah hadn't realized until just then that she was still bundled in his coat. It smelled of mountain winds, pine trees, campfires and—of the man himself. Somehow though, that fact didn't disturb her, instead she found it strangely comforting. Although the horrors of the previous night reared up to taunt and shame her, she knew she was too weak to deal with them just then. Mariah searched her mind for something pleasant to think on. The only thing that came to mind was the nursery pasture her father had fenced in for the pregnant mares at the ranch. It was a lush green meadow, with grass as tall as the brood-mare's wide bellies. In the springtime, she practically lived in that pasture, frolicking with the new colts. Unfortunately, along with the good memories came the bad, as the angry face of her father suddenly flashed before her. A truly pleasant memory—might be very difficult to find.

At least the nasty aspen bark tea combined with the sweet coffee had begun to do their work. Her head was no longer throbbing and she wasn't shivering as much. Turning on her side, she decided to watch the big man while he continued to work. He was unusually tall, powerfully built, blonde hair and blue eyes. Now that she thought on it, he did resemble a schoolbook drawing of a Viking warrior as he moved easily about in the light of the campfire. She marveled at how safe she felt, even though she was all alone with an obviously powerful man who could do with her as he wished. Perhaps it was because from the beginning, this man seemed to be made of a finer mettle than all the others she had known. It was as if Ruxton Hunter, Victor Kent and especially Jimmy Todd—weren't men at all—just poor counterfeits, and now perhaps, she had finally met a man who truly understood what being a man was supposed to be. He seemed to exemplify the ideal of chivalry, honor and integrity. She almost laughed; she was such a poor judge of men. Was she seeing only what she wanted to see? Perhaps her feverish mind was telling her lies again.

Mariah tried to sleep, but instead she found herself watching the big man, studying him. Was there really such a thing as a good man? Could a man that was handsome and strong, still be trusted? He had a straight nose, firm jaw, and it wasn't just that his eyes were the deepest shade of blue she'd ever seen; more importantly, they were the kindest eyes she'd ever seen. His skin was bronzed and leathery, probably because he spent his life in the sun and wind. As he arranged the branches for his bed, his well-knit muscles flexed and bunched beneath his deerskin shirt. Quincy Long was a man of God. Her father had told her men like him were weaklings and inferior. Perhaps that's just one more thing her father had gotten wrong. This man of God was a tower of strength, and completely at home in this wild country. Just then, the fanciful notion came to her that he was the perfect combination of spirit and earth. His every move was graceful and fitted to the purpose at hand, as he wielded his wickedly sharp hatchet. He made his shelter like the one he had made for her, but she noticed that he didn't take the same care with it as he had with hers. A strange thought entered her fevered mind; perhaps this man wasn't human at all. Perhaps he was nothing more than a hopeful dream—and when she awoke—he would be gone. And if he were gone—where would she be? On the cold hard ground outside of town or in an upstairs room at the Long Shot Saloon?

Mariah fought back the fear those memories aroused until the man who was spirit and earth stepped towards her shelter. He bent down, balancing on the balls of his feet as his deep voice rumbled, "Missus Kent, I'll be turning in now. But I'm a very light sleeper; if you become afraid, you need only whisper my name." Mariah nodded while Preacher once again made sure her blankets were covering her properly, then added softly, "Sleep well ma'am."

Just then her small white hand reached out to him, "I've forgotten—what is your name?"

"Well, most folks up here just call me Preacher, ma'am.

"No—I don't want to call you that, and I don't want you to call me Misses Kent. I'm not a Kent or a Hunter anymore. I'm just—Mariah, and I want to call you by your name!" she insisted.

"All right, Mariah, my name is Quin. If you need anything at all or even if you just feel a little scared—just call for Quin."

Mariah sighed and settled back on her soft bed. For some reason, knowing his name soothed her fevered mind and soon, she was breathing softly—then she drifted into a deep sleep.

Preacher couldn't remember the last time he'd thought of himself as just, Quin. He smiled as he pondered this; he put more wood on the fire, then sat down beside it. There was too much on his mind to sleep although he was certainly weary enough. Gazing up into the night sky he whispered, *"Lord, this is one of those times when the ways of the world are too harsh to understand. Help us not struggle with questions that have no answers—this side of heaven. Please guide me in helping this special young woman. To show her that in spite of all that's happened You do have a hope and future for her. I ask you to take away her fever and heal both her body and her wounded soul. And—please God help her to know that You and I are both watching over her, that she is safe in our care!"*

Mariah slept—not only through the night but until evening of the next day. Quin checked on his patient and prayed over her constantly. When she awoke, he sat beside her and fed her broth and biscuits, a bite and a sip at a time. Then, as if she were a child, he gently washed her face and hands. Feeling nourished and soothed, Mariah once again fell into a deep, healing sleep.

When she awoke the following day, her fever was gone and she felt almost like her old self. In her mind, she could almost believe that the terrible events at the Long Shot Saloon were the disconnected pieces from a horrendous nightmare. Sadly, it hadn't been a nightmare—it was real. What tormented her most was that she alone suffered. She regretted living through the ordeal, while those awful men regretted only that they could no longer take advantage of her night after night. It was all so unfair, so very wrong!

When Quin came back from the creek after washing their breakfast dishes, he could almost read her thoughts. Her hands were fisted at her sides and she was pacing in circles around their campfire.

"Mariah, you have every right to be angry and upset. Maybe right now would be a good time to talk about it. I thought I was wise to the evil ways of this world but I was a naïve fool. Never have I misread a situation so completely—or failed anyone as I have failed you!"

"Please—don't blame yourself, Quin. Missus Castle at the mercantile told me that I was reaping what I had sewn. I married against my parent's wishes and they turned their backs on me. I've never had much to do with God. I suppose it's no wonder that He would turn his back on me as well."

Quin shook his head, "I know it feels like God doesn't care…but He does! When people do bad things we must remember that God gives everyone free will. We all have been given the 'freedom' to do right or wrong. Sadly, many people use that freedom to do their worst."

"But—if God is God, and He cares for me," she muttered angrily. "Then why did HE allow it?"

Quin motioned to a log that wasn't far from the fire and said gently, "Please, let's sit here for a while; you still haven't completely regained your strength." When they both were seated, he turned to her; his blue eyes were both sad and intense. "Everyone who has ever suffered has asked why bad things happen to innocent people? Most of the time there just aren't any answers, but other times, perhaps years later, we can see why certain calamities came into our lives. Although we wouldn't want to relive those times, we can look back and see that we became stronger, better, kinder, and wiser than we would have been, had we not suffered through the catastrophes of our life. And God does promise that He will see us through these hardships and that he will work these difficult times out for our good if we love Him and are fitting into His plans."

"That sounds like you have to be a Christian first. I know very little about God or how I might fit into His plans." She said dejectedly. "Doesn't sound like there's much hope for me, does it?"

"On the contrary, you can have all the hope in the world. The other day, you said your soul was damned. You were right!" When he saw anger and hurt flash in Mariah's eyes he quickly added, "Because ALL our souls are bound for hell. No one can earn their way to heaven! It's only through the sacrifice of Jesus Christ that we can be made right with God and be allowed through the gates of heavens."

Mariah blew out a long sigh. "I've heard my father, the great Ruxton Hunter refer to himself as Christian, but only when he was in public. Mostly he just used God's name followed by a curse word. I don't know what my mother believes. She was so afraid of Father that she rarely spoke of anything or to anyone. I had a brother, but Father refused to claim his step-son, so he decided to teach me how to run his beloved Candlestick Ranch."

Quin was surprised when Mariah brightened a bit as she added proudly, "You might not believe it to look at me, but my father taught me how to ride and shoot, and select good quality stock—be it cattle or horses. To know the best time to cut hay and when to stack it and how to balance the books. Once I helped our foreman deliver a calf and a colt on the same day. I've helped arrange formal dinner parties for governors and generals. I can select the perfect menu and instruct the servants to set the table with the proper china, cutlery and crystal."

Shaking her head, Mariah let out a soft contemptuous laugh and her countenance fell as she reached down and picked up a small branch and threw it into the fire. "Unfortunately, none of those things made me of any use to Victor Kent. After all, what does a poor man want with a wife who can entertain dignitaries but can't cook a decent meal or mend a torn garment or sew on a button? The people of Otter Run weren't any more impressed by me than Victor was. I have only my brother now…and..." Mariah huffed sarcastically, "His life is probably even worse than mine. I've heard rumors that make me fear that he's in prison or maybe even dead!"

"Tell me about him. Were you close?"

A sweet expression filled Mariah's face, "Ladd was a loner but, he was always good to me. Yes, we were close. He was my half-brother; Mother was a widow and Ladd, or Laddy as she called him, was just a tiny newborn when she married Ruxton Hunter. Mother had a number of miscarries and Ladd was nine by the time I was finally born. Father was terribly cruel to that poor boy. He told Ladd that he was nothing but a cull. Had he been a calf he would have taken him out and shot him. My little heart-shaped zither was a gift from my brother. When he decided to leave home for good, I begged him to take me with him. But he said he was goin' to become an outlaw, and that was no life for his little sister." Mariah's face grew sad. "I never heard from him again. Mother was always afraid to mention him, and Father was openly relieved to have him gone. Unfortunately, he was also my only protector. Victor Kent never would have gotten close enough to seduce me, if Ladd had still been there. Of course, after Father told me that he had arranged a marriage between me and my cousin, Ralph, I made it easy for Vic to win me over. When he heard about my father's plans, he laughed, "We'll fool him!" He said. "So we ran away and got married. The moment we returned, my parents informed me that they no longer had a daughter."

Quin gave her a puzzled look, "I've heard of the Candlestick Ranch. It's one of the biggest in all of Texas. As their only child and heir—surely your parents must miss you! If they knew that you were a widow now and that you're all alone and in trouble—surely +they would..."

"Welcome me back?" Mariah scoffed. "My father truly is a tyrant and after living with Vic, I understand how my mother suffered under his rule. Mother probably would take me back, but no one defies Ruxton Hunter. I'm dead to him. I wrote to them, remember? I didn't lie when I saw you in the bank that day. I was truly desperate, and I did send them a telegram. Since Victor was gone, I hoped they would change their minds. Then too, I hoped my only friend Sally would urge them to take me back. I received my answer." Mariah's eyes clouded as she recited the words: "Missus Kent—stop—sorry for your loss—stop—Sally and husband Ralph are well—stop—do not contact us again—stop.'"

Swiping away a tear Mariah shrugged, "I have no other family, and Victor was an orphan—at least that's what he told me. I hate to admit it but Jimmy Todd was most likely right. He said that Shotsy and Velvet and I weren't capable of anything better, and no matter where I go, that isn't goin' to change. Every town will be the same. I have no place to go—and nothing' to offer!"

Quin started to say something but Mariah held her hand up to stop him. "Please, I know I've slept for days, but I don't think I can keep my eyes open another minute." At that, she rose gracefully from her place by the fire. Knowing he must be patient, Quin nodded his understanding and silently watched her as she disappeared inside her sanctuary of evergreen boughs.

That night their high mountain camp was bathed in silvery moonlight. Quin poured himself another cup of coffee as he kept watch. Although, it seemed the men of Otter Run had taken his threats seriously, he would continue to watch and pray just the same. He stepped away from the fire while he listened to a chorus of wolves sing their ancient song, a horned owl hooted and a mountain lion screamed. His ears, however, were listening for the sounds made by two legged animals. It wasn't until the morning sun chased the last star from the sky that he allowed himself to relax.

The following morning when Mariah stepped from her shelter, Quin greeted her with a warm smile and a hot cup of coffee. Then he returned to the fire to finish making their breakfast. Glancing about appreciatively he filled his lungs on the sweet aromas of mountain air, coffee and bacon.

"Beautiful morning isn't it? You know this mild weather is a blessing. I've lived in these mountains for quite a few years now but this is my first Indian summer. It's hard to believe that exactly one year ago this spot was under two feet of snow!"

Nodding quietly Mariah sipped her coffee and sighed, "It's not hard for me to believe; we barely survived! I doubted that we'd live to see another winter—and—Victor didn't."

Quin listened to the emptiness in her voice as he balanced on the balls of his feet and dropped biscuit dough into the pan of hot bacon grease. He knew her emotions were still raw and he hadn't expected Mariah to appreciate the scenery or the weather. Still, he believed it was a gift from God. When the heavy snows came it would trap this hurting woman behind four walls, and that was not what she needed. A plan had begun to take shape in his mind. What Mariah needed was to spend some time with another woman who could understand her and help her. Quin had to wonder if God hadn't brought Copper McKenna to these mountains, not only for Shad's sake but for Mariah's as well. Of course, he felt badly about intruding on the couple so early in their marriage, but the McKenna's would be good for Mariah. He was sure they would agree to take her in—at least until spring.

Just now, however, Preacher felt that Mariah was too vulnerable to face strangers. He truly believed that being out of doors in these pleasant and warm days was good medicine. The solitude and peaceful surroundings seemed to comfort and calm Mariah. Physically, at least, she was becoming stronger. Quin led her on short walks and encouraged her to go just a little farther every day. The exercise increased Mariah's appetite and it seemed to help her sleep with fewer nightmares.

Mariah followed Quin along the shadowy mountain path; as usual, he was humming softly in his deep baritone when suddenly she took hold of his arm. "Please," she huffed, as she caught her breath, "I know these walks are to strengthen me, but your stride is probably three feet longer than mine. I can't keep up!"

The big man was instantly contrite. "I am sorry. I should have realized. Why don't we rest here for a while? And tell me…do you still have that headache?"

Mariah fanned herself with her hand then rubbed her temples. "It's not as bad but—yes I do. Actually, that reminds me of a favor I need. I hate to ask; you've already done so much."

"What is it? You know I won't mind."

"Could you teach me some of the things that your father taught you? I need to learn how to feed myself and doctor myself when necessary!" Gazing off into the distance, Mariah frowned and shook her head, adding, "I was starving even before Vic died. If I could have come up here and built a shelter. If I could have fed myself and known how to make some of that nasty aspen bark tea—things might have turned out quite differently! The only things I can recognize are wild onions or berries, of course."

A thoughtful expression spread across Quin's face as he stepped over to an aspen tree. Taking the large knife from the sheath on his belt, he began cutting away strips of bark. "This is your first lesson. I have a smaller knife back in camp and I'll make it a gift to you. Now you watch me and then tomorrow I'll watch you do this." He shaved off the outer bark, allowing it to fall to the ground. The inner bark he caught with his hand as he explained. "Now what we want is this inner bark. When we get back to camp we'll boil these strips in some water." Giving her a crooked smile he added, "It may not win any prizes for taste but it is good for fever, swelling and pain."

Relief and gratitude shown in Mariah's deep violet eyes, "Yes, thank you Quin." She murmured. "This is exactly what I had in mind. If I don't want to end up like before, then I have so much to learn!"

Dropping the bark into his pocket, they walked down the path a little farther. Quin stopped and pointed to another plant with long thin stems. "What's this, Mariah?"

"Oh, that's just wild onions. I told you I could spot those. Might as well take them back to camp for dinner." Bending down she pulled the onions from the soft, rich dirt.

"Are you sure those are onions?" He asked. "What do they smell like?"

Mariah sniffed and made a face as her eyes immediately burned and watered, "Why did you make me do that? You know very well what they smell like…very strong onions!"

"Now, I wasn't being mean, I was teaching you something important. There's another plant that looks like a wild onion. Although it usually isn't found this high up, it's called death camas and it's poisonous! If you don't die from it, it can make you sick enough to wish you would."

"But how can you tell the difference if they look alike?"

"That's why I wanted you to smell it. Wild onions, especially this time of the year, as you just learned, have a very powerful scent. If it looks like an onion but doesn't smell like one…it's not safe to eat! That's why it's important for you to recognize plants by their scent as well as sight and how their appearance changes from season to season."

"Yes, I understand. This is just the kind of thing I'd hoped to learn. Now, please…teach me something else!" Mariah was suddenly more alive than Quin had ever seen her. Her lovely eyes danced as she examined each plant. As they continued their walk, he taught Mariah the various uses for mountain sorrel. How to recognize sage, wild celery and asparagus, as well as where to look for wild strawberries. That evening Mariah sipped the aspen bark tea and it soothed her headache while they discussed poultices for congestion. He even explained how to use cobwebs to stop bleeding and if that didn't work how to cauterize a wound.

The following morning when Quin began packing up the camp, Mariah panicked, "No Quin—I am not leaving this place!" Looking both fearful and defiant she added, "I am not ready to go to another town. I don't want to see other people—not yet! I know you must have work to do. I won't stop you—but I'm stayin'—I'm stayin' right here!"

Ashamed that he hadn't handled this better, Quin ran his hand over his jaw and groaned, "Mariah, I'm so sorry. I should have talked this over with you last night and explained that we needed to move our camp to another spot. We've hunted the game and gathered up pretty much all of the vegetation we can eat. Now, it's very understandable why you're afraid to be around other people." Quin studied his large hands for a moment then he looked into her eyes willing her to see his sincerity. "And yet, we both know it's not proper for us to stay up here together. Even so, I do not intend to take you anywhere until you're ready. I hope that you can learn to trust me and then you can trust others as well. Right now I just need to move our camp. The place I have in mind is a wonderful place and it has advantages that this camp doesn't. I promise you'll like it. Please trust me."

Embarrassed by her earlier outburst Mariah blushed, but she looked him in the eye and said sincerely, "Quin, I have learned many things from you, but trusting you was the easiest of all. I'm sure the new campsite will be lovely."

Although they were still enjoying an unusually warm autumn, a cool breeze skipped over the tops of the pine trees, causing them to sway and send their whispering hush throughout the forest. When Mariah shivered, Quin wrapped a blanket around her shoulders. Then with a silent question in his eyes, he held his arms out. When she shyly nodded her permission, he lifted her into the saddle. This time he didn't mount behind her but led Flint up a narrow mountain path until they came to their new campsite.

This was the mountain preacher's favorite retreat. He saved this spot for times when his body and soul needed to be refreshed and restored. Until today, he had not shared it with anyone and had intentionally waited to bring Mariah here until he believed she might actually see and possibly even benefit from the beauty all around her.

Quin walked backwards as he led Flint into the new campsite. He wanted to see Mariah's reaction, and was pleased when he heard her soft gasp of wonder and saw a spark of joy in her lovely face the moment she saw the waterfall and the enchanting little clearing surrounding it.

Snow white water cascaded from the high jagged rocks, then quickly thinned into a silvery veil as it splashed into the pool below. Encircling the area were a dozen gold leafed, white barked aspen trees. It was as if the clearing we surrounded with flaming torches.

He smiled, allowing himself the pleasure of just looking at her. Yes, she was still pale and thin, and yet more and more he was coming to appreciate what a lovely, intelligent and noble woman she was. He saw too how fragile and vulnerable she was! He understood why she didn't want to be with strangers. Still, he warred with himself as to whether or not he should have already taken her to stay with Shad and Copper, rather than bringing her to the falls. This responsibility laid heavily upon him. Hadn't he left her in the care of strangers before and the results had been tragic. Although he knew it wasn't proper to stay with her, he just couldn't leave her in anyone else's care. Not even a special couple like the McKenna's—not just yet anyway.

Quin suddenly frowned and turned away from the sight of his favorite place reflected in Mariah's expressive eyes. He feared he was walking on dangerous ground. He was enjoying being with this precious woman far too much! The quiet moments of walking together under the lacy shadows of the evergreen boughs, were becoming dear to him. He knew his presence was a comfort to her, and it was always good to be needed. Yet he sometimes wondered if he wasn't beginning to need her even more?

"What an enchanting place!" Mariah sighed, but then she reined Flint over to some greenery and quickly dismounted. Quin grinned proudly when she dropped to her knees and immediately began pulling up the wild onion. Sniffing the round bulb, she made a face then choked out. "Oh yes, this is definitely an onion!"

Quin could only laugh. It seemed that his lessons about food, herbs and medicine here had given Mariah a purpose and although he was sure she didn't recognize it, this pursuit was helping her heal.

Gazing around, happy to be back at his favorite place, Quin patted his flat stomach, "I'm hungry. How about you fry up those smelly onions, while I catch us some nice big trout for dinner?"

Giving the man a dubious look, Mariah glanced down into the beautiful pool that was nestled at the bottom of the waterfall, "I think it will just be fried onions for dinner. This water is as clear as glass, and there aren't any fish, not trout or any other kind."

"You're right. Go ahead and put your hand in that water and tell me what you think?"

Touching the water, she looked back at him and smiled. "It's warm! How could that be? That waterfall has to be as cold as ice!"

"Right again! The water coming off those rocks would give you frost-bite. However, there are hot springs all over these mountains, and one of them just happens to be feeding that pool. And since you're so smart…what luxury comes from the perfect combination of hot and cold water?"

"Bath water!" Suddenly, violet eyes that had been habitually dull turned bright.

"Thought you'd be quick to pick up on that," he laughed. "There's a nice river that flows about two hundred yards down the mountain from here. That's where I'll find the trout—I hope! Should take me about an hour or so to catch enough for our dinner. Should give you plenty of time to enjoy a nice warm bath." Coloring a bit, he scratched his chin then stammered, "I—uh—I know how we can manage this. When you are ready for me to come back into camp, just start frying the onions. The river is downwind from here. I won't come back until I get a good whiff of fried onions!"

Before he left, Quin unsaddled and hobbled Flint then took his Henry Rifle from his second scabbard, checked the load then placed it near the pool for Mariah. "Keep this where you can reach it at all times. All right?"

Mariah assured him she'd be watchful, then waited a few extra minutes, to make sure Quin didn't forget something and come back. Like a mouse scurrying around while the cat's away she hurried to her satchel and yanked out a change of clothes. After draping them over the bushes that grew beside the pool, she quickly undressed. A moment later, with soap in hand she dove in. The water felt like warm satin against her skin. The moment she rose to the surface of the pool, she began soaping up her hair and body, and then dove back down to the bottom to rinse away the bubbles. The feeling of freedom was nearly intoxicating, and she swam the length of the pool again and again. When she noticed her fingers were beginning to wrinkle, it dawned on her that Quin couldn't come back until she fried the onions. Getting out proved harder than getting in, but she finally managed it. Fearful that someone might be watching, she quickly blotted herself dry. Goosebumps were spreading over her body as she hurriedly slipped into the clean camisole, pantalets, and petticoat—then pulled a blue and white gingham dress over her head. Her pale hair was still ringing wet and the mountain air seemed quite chilly after the luxury of the warm pool, but it didn't matter. She'd been longing for a bath and now she felt refreshed. In no time at all she'd built the fire and had sliced up the onions. After dropping them into the pan, she turned aside and quickly combed her hair. Quin had never burned anything when he was doing the cooking, so Mariah watched them carefully, and took them from the fire just as they were turning a golden brown.

The fish must have been as hungry as Quin, because he caught a nice fat trout every time he dropped his line. In twenty minutes, he had six of them tied together on a string. Assuming that Mariah was still enjoying her bath and since his work was done he decided he might as well take a bath as well. Though he would have preferred jumping into the warm pool he feared that might make Mariah uncomfortable. Therefore, he stripped down and washed in the cold river instead. As he stepped from the water, his teeth were chattering and he had to shake his head like a dog to dry his hair. That was the best he could do under the circumstances. After giving Mariah more than enough time to bathe, he slowly headed back towards camp, smiling when he breathed in the wonderful scent of frying onions. He stopped mid-stride when he heard the sweet melodious sound of Mariah's zither. The lovely music floated towards him like a mist through the pine boughs.

"Thanks Boss," he whispered, "This is a good sign. There's such a sweet soul inside that woman. Still, when I look into her eyes—I can see her pain. Please Lord—help her—she needs you so badly."

Believing that this was an important moment for Mariah, Quin decided to honor her privacy and stay out of camp for a while longer as he listened and prayed. Just then, she began to sing in a low sweet alto.

Can you count the stars of evening
That are shining in the sky?
Can you count the clouds that daily
Over all the world go by?
God the Lord, who doth not slumber,
Keepeth all the boundless number;
But He careth more for thee,
Yes, He careth more for thee.

Quin's heart seemed to swell in his chest as he listened. The simple melody of the zither blended so sweetly with Mariah's voice. It pleased him that she was finding solace in her music. How strange for her to sing this of all songs, for it was his mother's favorite lullaby. He closed his eyes and imagined Mariah's shimmering blonde hair falling over her shoulder as she played. He had known many beautiful women from wealthy and refined homes, but somehow this woman-defied description. The way she looked, the way she spoke and moved—it all seemed so special to him. These feelings for this young widow continued to confuse him. All that Mariah had experienced made her bitter; nevertheless, she was still so sweet and innocent. Now as he listened to this simple lullaby, he whispered, "Lord, she is such a dear little thing. I know it's not important that we understand your ways—because—I know you always have a plan and a purpose. Please help us both to know your will and to walk in harmony with your plan. Guide me Lord, for how am I to minister to her, as I should, when my own heart is so powerfully drawn to her? Please keep my desires and thoughts pure—as I try to help her. Oh, help us Lord—help us both!"

Mariah's lilting voice continued to float on the wind.

Can you count the many children
In their little beds at night?
Who without a thought of sorrow
Rise again at morning light?
God the Lord, who dwells in heaven,
Loving care to each has given;
He has not forgotten thee,
No—he has not—forgotten thee.

Suddenly the music stopped and there was a long silence as if all the forest had been listening. And then he heard Mariah's tormented voice crying out, "But you have forgotten me! If you were ever there at all God—you surely have forgotten me!"

Quin's legs were running before his mind even registered that he must go to her. He jumped over logs and trampled bushes as he raced back to their camp. He was almost there when he heard the violent sound of the zither crashing against the side of a tree. And then he heard the keening lament of her heartbroken sobs. He found Mariah in a crumpled heap on the ground, clutching the broken pieces of the instrument to her breast as if it were a dying friend.

As Quin stepped closer she looked up at him; her lovely eyes awash with tears, "Oh—just look what I've done." she sobbed, "I've always thought my little zither was so sweet, but I'm not worthy of it anymore. Now—it's ruined—all broken to pieces—just like me."

Quin felt as if his own heart were tearing apart as he dropped to his knees beside her, "No Mariah—*not ruined!* Yes, it is broken, just as you *feel* like you are broken. But I promise you—things that are broken—can be mended. And when a master craftsman makes the repair, those things that are broken are often better for the mending."

With tender care, he took the shattered instrument from her hands and set it aside. Then, although it was sweet torture to do so, he opened his arms, allowing her to make the decision to receive or decline the comfort he offered. She hesitated only for a moment before she flung herself into his arms. For a long while, she wept against his strong chest while he held her close and stroked her long hair that fell in waves down her back. When Mariah's tears were spent, she shyly drew away from him and he was surprised at how empty his arms suddenly felt.

Needing something to do, he turned aside and began picking up all the broken pieces of the little zither. Gazing tenderly at Mariah he asked, "Will you trust me to take care of this? I know you treasure it!"

Believing that it was beyond repair, she simply sighed and shrugged. Quin however, believed that nothing was beyond repair and he carefully picked up each piece and fragment and placed them back inside the leather instrument case.

He took Mariah's hand and led her back to sit beside the fire then poured them each a cup of coffee. He spoke softly to her as he cooked the trout and they ate their dinner in silence. Later as the sun disappear behind the high mountain ridges, it seemed to comfort them both as they watched the muted shades of moonlight settle all about them. Feeling that he had given Mariah enough quiet time, he poured them both another cup of coffee then sat down beside her. "In spite of your hardships, you are mistaken in what you said, God does care for you, Mariah. He loves you and—He has not forgotten you."

Mariah shook her head, and allowed the bitterness she felt to surface once again. "I don't believe in your God…***Preacher!***"

Quin was startled by the rancor he heard in her voice. She had never called him Preacher before. It had always been Pastor or Quin. And when she said the word, she'd said it as if it were a curse.

"As I've told you," she muttered softly. "I'll always be grateful that you got me out of that evil place. But this is a man's world. God may have given man free will—as you call it. But we women have little freedom." She added in disgust. "I didn't choose for my parents to toss me aside like an old saddle. I didn't choose to have my husband beat me after he gambled away everything we owned, then kill himself. And I didn't choose what happened to me in that saloon! Shotsy and Velvet are perfect examples, they hate their lives but Ox would kill them if they tried to leave. They are looked down upon by the very men who force them to do—what they do! There is no freedom in that. They don't have a choice."

"You heard me offer to help them both. I've been determined to get them out of that place for a long while but I guess I hadn't really realized that they were afraid to accept my help. Getting you out of there opened my eyes. I promise you I *will* help them!"

"Maybe you will—I hope you do. In the meantime, Jimmy Todd, Cyril Castle and Theodore Krane, are still the leading citizens of Otter Run regardless of their immoral ways. Everyone in town knows that those men make regular visits to Shotsy and Velvet, and no one cares. But if I ever show my face in that town again, I won't be remembered as the widow of Victor Kent. No—now and forever more I'll be that 'soiled dove' that *Preacher* rescued. What was done *to me*—has ruined me! Did you know that Sephora only allows Shotsy and Velvet to step into her fine store on Monday mornings? Apparently, the few decent women all stay away that day for fear of being corrupted I suppose. Did you know that Shotsy tried to run away once and Ox brought her back and nearly beat her to death? How is it that these wicked men's reputations remain untarnished while the women who are forced to work there or die are considered the scourge of society?"

Quin shook his head sadly…he had no answers, and right now Mariah needed to talk and so—he listened.

"I have no hope or future, ***Preacher***." She sneered. "A saloon girl is the only life I'll be allowed, from now on. No matter where I go, this kind of thing tends to follow a person. My reputation is ruined but despite how I've fallen, I could never lie about it. If a decent man were to ask me to marry him—the first thing I'd do would be to tell him what a lousy cook and housekeeper I was—and for one awful night—I was a harlot. It's easy to believe that a decent woman would rather die. As it happens, dyin' isn't as easy to accomplish as one might think. I was carried into that saloon and drugged…but…I honestly don't know how much longer I could have held out. When you're starvin' and freezin'…the temptation of a warm place to stay and decent meal have a siren call like no other. All that dreadful night those men kept remindin' me…once a harlot, always a harlot. And maybe they're right!"

Quin's jaw clenched when she spoke of herself that way. To him she was the picture of wounded innocence. "They are not right!" He nearly shouted the words, then he sucked in a breath to calm himself before he continued. "What you are is the victim of evil men. I don't know yet what God's plan is for you, but rest assured He has one. When you're feeling up to it, I plan to take you to some very good friends of mine." When he saw the look of panic filling Mariah's eyes, he quickly added. "But not until you're ready. I promise you will like them, Shad might even be able to fix your zither and Copper can…well…"

"Fix me?" Mariah asked cynically.

Frowning, Quin shook his head, "That is not what I was going to say—but you could use a good friend, couldn't you? Copper's a little wonder—she snares rabbits for food and uses their hides for clothing. She could teach you how to cook and sew. I've seen how you love learning, and she could teach you things that could really make a difference in your life! Besides that, she's been through some pretty rough times herself. I think she'd be someone you could talk to, and Shad's a good man and a good friend of mine—you'll like them both!"

Mariah wasn't so sure, "Like I've told you before, I may be a fallen woman, but I'm not a liar. The first thing I'll do is tell this paragon of yours the truth. She doesn't sound like the type that will want to make friends with a whore like me." When she saw the shock and hurt on Quin's face, she was instantly ashamed, "I'm sorry, Quin. I'm taking my anger out on the man who risked his life to rescue me. You are so noble and kind, I don't think you can even imagine how worthless I feel now."

Seeing her shiver, Quin put a blanket around her shoulders and added another log to the fire then he said gently, “Mariah, I don’t have to imagine the cruelty of people. If you don’t mind, I’d like to tell you about a woman I knew who was in a similar situation. I think what you’ve endured was worse perhaps, but you remind me of her. Sophie was a sweet, dear woman with fair hair and soft blue eyes. Her parents were tailors to the rich men of Boston. Sophie tried, but she just didn’t have the talent for sewing. On the other hand, she had a naturally keen mind for business and by the time she was fourteen she was doing the bookkeeping as well as purchasing all the fabrics and supplies for her parents shop. When she was sixteen, an influenza epidemic swept through Boston. Her mother and father became ill and then on one horrific day, she lost them both. Dutifully, Sophie arranged for their burial and paid off all the medical, business and personal debts. By the time all the accounts were settled—she was penniless. There was no other family and in spite of her bookkeeping experience, she was so young, no one would hire her!”

Mariah leaned forward, “Poor Sophie and she was only sixteen. What happened to her?”

“Well, after the funeral, a bachelor, one of her parent’s best clients told her that he felt sorry for her and offered to marry her. Poor Sophie—indeed. All she knew of the man was that he had expensive taste and had always paid on time. He was rich and handsome and she truly was a damsel in distress. To an innocent like her, his proposal seemed chivalrous and romantic. Unfortunately, the marriage did not rescue her. Instead it quickly became a form of torture and enslavement.”

“Enslavement?” Mariah winced, “What did he do to her?”

Quin wasn’t surprised by her sympathetic reaction, but he was touched by her genuine concern for a woman she didn’t know. “Well, it all began on Sophie’s wedding night.” He said sadly, “Her husband arrogantly explained that she did not fit in with his social circle, but not to worry, for he would teach her. He called his teaching method—*instructive punishment*. If she didn’t pour his tea properly, he would scald her hand with the boiling liquid. If the ruffles on her dress were uneven or a hair out of place, then he would pinch her so hard that it would leave huge black and blue bruises on her arms and legs. There were other punishments but she told me they were too indelicate to share.” Quin grimaced as Mariah nodded her head and rubbed her arms as if she were remembering her own bruises. Then he continued, adding sternly, "That scoundrel took a lovely young woman who had been confident of her own intelligence and capabilities and berated her to the point that she began to think of herself as ugly and stupid and worthless!"

It was easy for Mariah to commiserate with Sophie's pain. Quin's expression was tender when he saw her eyes cloud as she wrapped the blanket around her shoulders more tightly as he continued his story.

"One morning, after they had been married for almost a year, he found her retching into a wash basin. He was so repulsed by her unseemly behavior that he told her that his punishment was going to have to be much more severe. She had just begun to suspect that she was with child." Quin paused for a moment then said, "Mariah, I have a heartfelt understanding for all of this because—I was the child, and Sophie was my mother! The scoundrel, whom I can only refer to as my sire, for I cannot think of him as my father, had taken his belt to her before but she feared that if this beating was to be more severe, then quite possibly it could cause her to miscarry. She tried to tell him that she was carrying his baby! However, to her horror—he said that he never wanted children, and that he would soon see her rid of the affliction."

Mariah couldn't help but shutter as she whispered, "Oh, Quin—that's dreadful!"

"Yes, it was, but Mother was determined to keep us both alive. So, while he was removing his belt, she snuck past him and ran. He caught up with her right at the very top of a long stairway. Up until then she had meekly submitted to his punishments but that time she said she had someone worth fighting for and that day she fought like a wildcat! They struggled so violently that they both fell all the way down the staircase. When the housekeeper found them, he was dead from a broken neck and my mother was unconscious and bleeding. An old doctor lived next door and the cook ran to fetch him. He was quite old and almost never saw any patients but God provided the right man for the job. You see he specialized in difficult pregnancies and more importantly, he was a sincere man of a prayer. As it happened, he had been concerned for my mother and he came immediately. The dear man remained by her side, day and night for so long that his son came to check on him. The doctor's son was Caleb Long. He was a struggling business man at the time, but like his father, he was a true Christian and believed mightily in the power of prayer."

"Caleb—Long?" Mariah asked.

Quin shook his finger in the air, "Wait—don't get a head of my story. My Mother was restricted to her bed until I was born. Sadly, the old doctor took sick and died. Even though another one took his place, Caleb remained constant. He visited every day, and before he left, he always prayed for mother and for me. My mother said that she lived for those visits, and as it happened, so did Caleb! He had been trying to start up a shipping company and he and mother talked over his plans during the long months of her confinement. Actually, it was she who came up with the strategy that made Long Orient & Asia Company a success! Still, what he gave my mother was so much more. Her first husband had robbed a beautiful and intelligent woman of her worth. Each time Caleb came to visit her with his kindness, and his true and heartfelt respect, my mother said it was as if he were giving water and sunshine to a dying plant. She couldn't help but blossom once again. They were married a week before I was born."

Mariah pondered his story as she gazed at the fire, "Why didn't God just make your real father into a good and decent man?"

"Because God doesn't want to make us do the right thing." Quin sighed. "He gives us each the freedom to choose good or evil. My sire took that freedom and lived a cruel and self-indulgent life and now he's paying for his choices in hell. While the man I proudly called Father chose to follow God and His ways. Mother and Caleb died seven years ago but now they're enjoying the rewards of heaven. If mother hadn't married the first man she might never have met Caleb Long, and they both needed each other's strengths. People all over the world have benefited from their union." Quin suddenly gave her a crooked smile adding, "And there would be no Quincy Long sitting here with you now. Horrible things happen all the time, but it's hard to say what God should and should not allow. We have no foresight at all—while God sees around every corner throughout eternity. Sometimes He must allow hardships and difficulties because He knows that these exact experiences will ultimately bring about glorious results. Father used to say that the worst storms often leave behind the most beautiful rainbows."

Over the following days, Mariah pondered Quin's words, but they didn't speak again of such complicated matters. Each day she grew stronger as they shared a congenial camaraderie. Mariah helped Quin fix the meals and gather the firewood and they took long walks down to the river and along its winding path. Quin continued to teach her about living on only what you could find. Occasionally, Mariah spoke of her heartaches, her parents and her lost brother. Other times they walked in amiable silence. Then one night as they finished another dinner of trout with onions, Quin took the empty plate from Mariah's hand then cleared his throat before he asked, "From what you've told me, your parents seemed indifferent or at least confused about God. May I ask what you believe?"

Mariah sighed. She wasn't in the mood to talk about God. Sounding a bit flippant, she said, "According to Daisy. God made everything—and loves everybody!"

"Daisy?" he asked, ignoring her sarcasm. "Who was Daisy?"

The look on Mariah's face suddenly became soft and wistful, memories of the woman always made her smile. "I guess I don't mind telling you about her. She was the wife of the ranch foreman we had when I was little. Daisy was also our housekeeper and while she worked, she would tell me stories—Bible stories. I loved her—she even looked like a Daisy. She had golden hair, not pale like mine," Mariah added with a wrinkled nose, "but real yellow gold! She had big brown eyes and a beautiful smile. She was the one that taught me the song I was singing the other night—" Mariah stopped and pushed away thoughts of her broken zither, then with a sigh, she continued, "Well—anyway one day I said, 'Daisy, I wish there really was a God and that the Bible wasn't just a bunch of stories.' At first she frowned and put her hands on her hips, then she smiled at me and said. 'Oh my sweet chick-a-pee, God is as REAL as you and me!'" Mariah smiled, "Daisy was a happy soul. The only time I saw her cry was when she saw me cryin'. Then she sat down and cried with me. Every day, after her work was done, she'd take me on nature walks. A little like what you've been doing with me, Quin. Daisy was always sayin' that God made the ground I stood on and the air I breathed. She told me, God breathed life into all living things and had a purpose in everything he created; from bees to weeds—right on up to where mankind lives at the top of God's special design."

"She sounds like quite a woman. Did she tell you about Jesus?"

Mariah shrugged sadly, "She tried to. One day she was telling me somethin' about Jesus being God's son. When Mother heard us talkin' she sent Daisy on an errand. That same evening while we were having dinner, I told my parents all the things that Daisy was teaching me. Mother's face went pale and Father jumped up from the table and stormed out of the house.

The next day Daisy and her husband were gone! He didn't even let them say good-bye. I finally got up the courage to ask Father if it was my fault that he sent them away. He said, yes it was because of me that he sent them away! Then he explained that it was acceptable to say you believed in God when speaking to townsfolk. He said that simple people like them needed to pretend there was a God, because they were poor and weak and scared. Then he said arrogantly that the Hunter family was wealthy and strong and brave! We had no need to pretend there was a God."

"That explains a lot." Quin sighed, "Sounds like your home life was a difficult one. I'm glad that you had a friend like Daisy, even for a short while. Would—would you allow me to tell you what she would have if she'd had the chance?"

Mariah's eyes lit up. "Yes, of course I would!"

Quin smiled at her open eagerness. He suspected that the bright, sweet expressive woman was the real Mariah. All that she had been through had naturally made her angry and bitter even a bit belligerent at times. However, he believed that those traits ran contrary to her nature. Being open and sweet was who she really was.

"Well," he began with a gentle smile, "just as Daisy told you—God made every creature with a purpose, from the tiniest bug on a rosebush, to the fish in the sea, to the buffalo that roam across the prairies."

"Yes, Daisy was always trying to explain to me how God created life in sort of a circle. All living creatures, both plants and animals are all dependent on one another. All of nature is so simple and yet it's profoundly perfect, isn't it?"

"That's a good way of saying it, God's creation and plan is '*profoundly perfect*'. When we humans meddle with it, that's when the imperfections arise. God loves His creation and He gave every human an eternal soul, so that we might live with him forever. Yet, God gives each of us the freedom to choose. He doesn't force Himself on us. We can choose to spend eternity with Him or without Him!"

Mariah's expression grew thoughtful. "That's the 'free will' you're always talking about. The Sheriff and the other men in town—they could have just as easily helped me—but they chose to hurt me instead. They chose evil!"

"That's right." Quin agreed. "We live in a fallen world full of evil. No one is perfect; no one has ever earned their way into heaven. Not one person in the world has ever lived a sinless life, except for Christ! Of course, sin can be anything from shooting someone in cold blood to simply thinking an unkind thought. Regardless of what the sin is—it separates us from God. Since Christ was able to live a sinless life, He was able to become the bridge between us and God!"

A sudden awareness filled Mariah's mind as she remembered holding the gun on the Sheriff, she truly *had* wanted to kill him—she still did! She had certainly harbored unkind thoughts towards every person in that awful town. Not just the men that hurt her but those that refused to help her in any way. Sephora's words continued to haunt her as well, 'You must pay for your own sins—just as I must pay for mine!'

The accusing words of the older woman whirled through her mind as Quin continued to speak, "God wants us all to choose Christ as our Lord and Savior. But He will not force us. God says, 'What I am commanding you today is not too difficult for you or beyond your reach…I have set before you, life and death, blessings and curses. Now choose to love the Lord your God with all your heart, so that you may live a better life on earth as well as spend eternity with Christ.'"

Mariah's violet eyes glistened in the firelight, then she shook her head sadly. "But—isn't it too late for *me*? You know, because of what happened, because now that I'm a…a..."

"No Mariah," he said sternly. "Don't you dare say it or think it! You are a woman who was used by evil men for evil purposes. God does not hold you responsible for their sins. But—He does hold you responsible for you own. God's offer of salvation is as freely given to you as it is to me, Shotsy, Velvet or even to a cur like Jimmy Todd. Right now, we are talking about you. You have every reason to be angry and bitter, and you can allow this experience to taint the rest of your life. Or you can choose to turn your life over to God and allow Him to heal you and to direct your path from this day forward."

Mariah felt the resentment surging through her. "How can I go forward? Don't you see that what has happened to me *has* changed me *forever?* I can't be rid of it or forget it!"

"No…you can't. Even so, God promises to heal the brokenhearted and bind up their wounds. This experience will always be a part of you—that's true. And God doesn't give us explanations, as to why bad things happen.

Instead, He gives us His love and strength to help us get through them—and become better people because of them. God is giving you the opportunity to make a choice that will change your life—from this day forward. Will you ask Jesus into your heart to be your Savior and Lord?"

Nothing in Mariah's life had been good or had even made sense in such a long time. Yet here before her sat the finest man she'd ever known. A warrior-angel come to earth, who used his strength to serve rather than dominate. He had risked his life and probably compromised his ministry just for her! All he asked was that she believe in his God.

"Yes…" Mariah whispered as her heart pounded in her chest. "I want to be like you Quin. I want to have the peace and faith that you have. Will you tell me what to do?"

More than anything, he wanted this woman to share his faith. "Of course I will," he said, feeling greatly relieved. "God makes it very easy. First, you simply acknowledge that God's perfection is incompatible with our imperfections. Then confess your sins and ask Him to forgive you and to come into your heart as the Lord of your life." When Mariah nodded in understanding he continued, "Now, I'll pray and—if you sincerely mean them—just repeat the words as your own prayer."

Mariah faltered at the word sincere. She was confused about God but she sincerely believed in this good man. For now, she would place her trust in him, while he placed his trust in God. Together they knelt on the ground, her small hand in his larger one.

"Father in heaven," He began and Mariah repeated each word. Although Mariah spoke the words, in truth it was more like she was asking Quincy Long into her heart. After all, she believed that he was the one that had saved her!

Chapter 17
Friends

"Love one another with brotherly affection. Outdo one another in showing honor." Romans 12:10

Even though it was a beautiful day and the scenery along the winding mountain trail was breathtaking, all Mariah could think of was that every step carried her closer to the McKenna cabin. The knowledge that she was about to be abandoned to the mercy of strangers again made her stomach tighten into a dozen knots as her mind tormented her with past regrets and fears for her future.

Quin is just too good and kind to realize how judgmental people are. He's so sure that, Copper, that young paragon, will 'fix me'! She'll think I've reaped what I sowed just like Sephora Castle did. She'll see me as a threat. After all, what virtuous young bride would want a fallen woman to move in with her and her brand new husband? So what is Quin to do with you, Mariah? For once in your life, you want things to stay just as they are—don't you? You want to hide away in these mountains with the only truly decent man you've ever known. You can't do that though—being alone with him is improper. Of course, if we married it would be all right. No—it would not be all right—it would ruin him! Preachers don't marry women they rescue from brothels. When, Mariah June, will you stop dreamin' o' things that can never be?

Although Mariah would never have guessed it, Quin's thoughts were just as confused. They hadn't even reached the McKenna's and he was already missing her. Despite her understandable bouts of melancholy, she was for the most part an extremely pleasant companion. There was just something about her that he found soothing. He had always made it clear, to everyone he met, that he believed he was never to marry. Yet each time he attempted to explain this to Mariah, he couldn't seem to find the right words. He feared she might misunderstand—at least that's what he kept telling himself. This special rapport he shared with her troubled him, for she was becoming too much a part of his life. The mere sight of her was a comfort and a joy. It seemed that the day just couldn't begin until he saw her lovely face emerging from her little shelter. He tended to loiter about the camp whenever she was combing out her long blonde hair. In the evenings while he cleaned his gun or sharpened his knife, he would tell Mariah his favorite Bible stories. He extolled the bravery of the boy David as he fought the giant Goliath, and the faithfulness of Daniel as he entered the lions' den. Whenever he got to the most exciting parts, he made a point of looking into Mariah's face so that he might catch a glimpse of her smile or enjoy the way her eyes sparkled like amethysts in the firelight. However, when her sweet face began to haunt his sleep, he realized that he must put some distance between them. He needed to get Mariah settled at the McKenna's, because anything more than friendship was just not meant to be.

Much of that day's journey was traveled in silence and even though Mariah was careful not to touch him as they rode, she still feared she'd done something wrong when Quin suddenly drew rein, threw his leg over Flint's neck, and slid to the ground.

Lord, help me! He begged inwardly, I'm in real trouble with this woman. I know what she needs is a good husband, and once Copper teaches her how to cook and sew and run a house, she'll have the makings of a perfect wife. In fact, with her sweet ways, education, lovely singing voice and ability to play an instrument, she'd make a fine Pastor's wife!

When that last thought flashed in his mind like a bolt of lightning, his heart seemed to plummet to his feet. The thought of another man, especially another preacher like him, having Mariah as his helpmate, waking up to her sweet face each morning. It was just too much to bear.

What's the matter with me? I'm green-eyed jealous…that's what...and… "It's got to stop!"

"What's got to stop?" Mariah asked.

When he realized that he had shouted his last thoughts out loud, Quin froze in the middle of the path. Flint, however, kept going and nearly knocked him over! Embarrassed, he spun around and frowned up at Mariah, "I uh—suddenly realized how thirsty I was—need to stop and get some water." he said gruffly. "How about you?"

Feeling the warmth climbing up his neck, he jerked the canteen from the saddle, tilted it back and chugged down half the contents. Then he grimaced as he wiped the rim with his handkerchief and lifted the canteen to Mariah. "I'm sorry; a gentleman would have offered this to you first."

"That's all right." Smiling hesitantly, she lifted the canteen to her lips, took a dainty sip, then handed it back. Quin couldn't make himself look away as he watched her. It took every bit of his will to turn around and continue leading Flint down the trail.

So many things were swirling around in his heart, things he had never felt before. He cherished the fact that God had called him to a life of service, even though it was often a lonely life. Still the idea of having a wife was a pleasant one and he had always loved children. Until now, God's direction for him had always been crystal-clear. Indeed, he had never once question or wavered from his calling. For almost six years, he had joyfully ministered to anyone that needed him. It had always felt good when he left people better off than when he found them and then moved on in search of someone else in need. As Joseph of the Bar 61 had said, he and Flint had a fire in their bellies to see who and what was on the other side of the hill. It was time now to leave Mariah, but the thought of moving on made him feel—empty. No, he had never felt anything like this before.

As he led Flint into the yard, Quin snapped impatiently, "Hello in the cabin." They had arrived much too soon, and his mind was still crowded with questions but there didn't seem to be any answers. When he realized how gruff he must sound, he softened his voice and called again. "Hello friends—McKenna's you have company!"

The couple strolled from the barn just as he lifted Mariah from the saddle. Instinctively, she moved to place Flint at her back and Quin in front of her as the strangers came forward with happy smiles.

Shad grinned broadly, "Preacher! You sure are a welcome sight—and an answer to prayer ta boot. I just killed the biggest elk I've ever seen. Just come to fetch Copper to help me, but now that yer here…oh?" Shad was surprised to see that Preacher wasn't alone. There was a beautiful woman, pretty much hiding behind him, using the man as a shield. "Hello ma'am." he said gently, seeing her discomfort. Then he refocused his gaze back on Preacher, "I see you've brought along a friend."

"Yes indeed, that's exactly what I've done, brought you and Copper a new friend!" Putting his arm protectively around her shoulder, he said gently, "This is Mariah Kent." Pointing to the couple that now stood side by side he said, "Mariah, this is Shadrack and Copper McKenna. They are two of the nicest people I know." With his eyes telling them as much as his words, he added, "Missus Kent is a recent widow and she's also a brand new Christian. Otter Run can be a terribly rough place and it's certainly not suited for a young widow alone in the world. I'd be beholden to you both if she could stay here for a while. Just until the Lord tells her what direction she's to take next."

Copper's expression was tender as she stepped forward and offered her hand. "I'm sorry for your loss Missus Kent and—I know all too well what it's like to be alone in these mountain; you are most welcome to stay here." Shad was quick to add his agreement, and even though they both were gracious in their welcome, Mariah purposely made no reply. She believed that their kindness would soon be withdrawn—just as soon as they learned the truth about her.

The silence was awkward until Copper spoke up again. "Well, you men better go butcher that elk. Missus Kent and I can get acquainted while we cook a nice supper that will go perfectly with elk steaks." Turning to Shad she smiled adding, "If you'll cook them out here—over an open fire, that way I can have the stove—you'll do that for me—won't you—please?" Copper accentuated her words with a loving expression that Shad had come to believe could easily melt a glacier.

Preacher smiled, pleased to see that these two had made such obvious progress since their wedding day. Then he found himself shoving down a twinge of envy as Shad pretended to frown at his little wife then gave her a wink.

"Oh, I reckon I can do that, but then yer gonna bake me a spice cake for dessert. Right?" He bargained.

While the newlyweds smiled playfully at each other, Mariah caught Preacher's eye and gave her head a slight shake, telling him that she was not ready for him to leave her. She dreaded being alone with the happy little redhead. This chipper little thing probably knew nothing of the hardships of this world. However, when Quin's blue eyes met hers, Mariah understood. He was telling her that she needed to start getting used to seeing less of him and more of other people. She must stay here until they could think of what she should do next.

As the women disappeared inside the cabin, Shad laid his large hand on Preacher's shoulder. "Ya see now, what you've done to me Preacher? I'm already henpecked and miserable!"

"Yes, friend, I see quite well. And I'd feel a whole lot sorrier for you—if you could wipe that crazy grin off your face." Slapping Shad on the back he added, "Come on—you can tell me how much you hate married life while we dress out that elk. We best get at it, before every other creature on the mountain helps themselves to our supper!"

Mariah followed Copper into the cabin with her head down. However, when she stepped through the door, it wasn't at all what she'd expected. She and Victor had spent last winter in a horrible little shack with dirt floors and holes in the walls. Of course, this cabin couldn't compare to the Candlestick mansion, but it was still beautiful! She marveled at the perfectly sized logs, fitted so tightly together that they needed only thin strips of clean white chinking between them. The plank floor beneath her feet shone like golden honey. Then she saw the carved mantle.

Copper smiled, "Not what you expected is it? Shad is a true craftsman. He built all this by himself, the carvings too." she added proudly. "This little bit of heaven was all boarded up when I found it. Shad had gone off to spend the summer in Canyon City. While he was away…I was wandering through these mountains, starving and hopelessly lost. I was in serious trouble—might have even died if God hadn't led me to this place. I thought it was abandoned and claimed it for my own. It's kind of a long story, but it ends well. When we have more time I'll tell ya all about it—if you like." Copper hurried across the room and pulled out one of the kitchen chairs. "You look worn out. Please, sit down and rest while I make you a cup of tea."

Mariah sat and watched mutely as Copper made the tea, then confidently began bustling about her kitchen. It was hard to believe what this slip of a girl was able to accomplish in such a short time. The redhead chatted amiably while she washed her hands then punched down the bread dough. Spinning around she put coffee on to boil. Then she returned to the dough, and after cutting it into four equal parts, she buttered her hands then smoothed each mound into evenly textured loaves. She covered the pans with a towel then turned back to the stove. Mariah studied the way Copper spread the coals out evenly before she turned back to the table. Using her hand as a measurement, she put flour, sugar and spices into a bowl added some eggs and milk, beat the batter smooth then poured it into a pan and slipped it into the oven. Somehow, it shamed Mariah to watch Copper.

Just look at her fly about this kitchen. Quin called her a little wonder! She surely puts me to shame. If I'd known a year ago what she knows right now, how different my life might be.

Mariah couldn't help herself, she suddenly felt so worthless. Covering her face with her hands, she began to sob.

"Oh, Missus Kent—won't you please talk to me!" Copper urged as she hurried around the table and sat down beside the woman who still hadn't spoken a single word. "I have no idea what all you've been through, and I know we're strangers, but if you just asked the Lord into your heart—that makes us sisters in Christ. I think we can be good friends."

Mariah stiffened and spoke through gritted teeth, "Believe me Missus McKenna, if you knew what I've been through, you wouldn't want to be my friend. Mine is a long story too, but it does not end well! You see, Quin rescued me from an upstairs room at the Long Shot Saloon. I know you don't want the likes of me staying here with you and your husband, and I don't blame you." Swiping away her tears she sucked in a deep breath, and waited for Copper to tell her what she thought of women who end up in a saloon!

To Mariah's surprise, the little redhead put her arm around her shoulders and hugged her. "Sounds like you really do have a long story! The men will be busy for quite a while. Since you've built up some steam, I think it might be a very good time for you to tell it."

At first, Mariah just frowned at Copper, then she took a sip of her tea, and squared her shoulders. "All right, I grew up on a ranch in Texas..." Copper listened patiently while this beautiful and fragile woman stoically told her story.

"I'd still be in that awful Long Shot Saloon if it weren't for Quin and his scattergun. He threatened every man in town. He risked his life just to rescue me! Now—Missus McKenna, be honest, you don't want a—fallen woman—stayin' here with you or your husband. Truly, I don't hold it against you. It's not proper for me to be staying with folks like you, and it wasn't proper for me to be alone with Quin, either. He didn't know what to do with me, so he brought me here. But you and I both know—this isn't the right place for me—no place is." That said, Mariah blew out a breath, and stood from her chair. "I'll just wait outside until the men come back."

Copper gently took hold of her arm. "Please—sit back down. You've told your story, now I'll tell you mine. You're wrong about Preacher not knowing what to do with you. If there was ever a man who knows the right thing to do, it's Quincy Long! He brought Shad and I together and he brought you here. He knew you would find friends who want only to help you."

"Weren't you listening?" Mariah scoffed at the young innocent sitting beside her. "Have you led such a perfectly sheltered life that you don't understand what's happened to me? Are you that naïve?"

"Oh, I understand perfectly well." Copper said sternly. "No woman should have to experience such a thing. And—I assure you I have not had a perfectly sheltered life! I've been a bondservant for most of it. My owners had one thing in common; they hit me whenever I displeased them. My last owner planned to sell me to brothel—and yes—I know what that is. We were crossing a river just south of Denver when the wagon tipped over, and the man who owned me drowned. I would have drowned too, but for an outlaw by the name of Vernon Riley. The trouble was that he wanted me to be his woman and so did his partner, an albino by the name of Dirk Culley. A few hours later Vernon forced me to marry him." Copper let out a long sigh, "I'll admit I have been more fortunate than you. After the Reverend pronounced us husband and wife, Vernon was dragging me back to his bedroom, when the sheriff broke through the door and arrested both, Vernon and Dirk. They were sentenced to four years in prison. After that, Vernon's mother, let me stay with her. She told me that God loved me." Copper smiled, "She also taught me how to snare rabbits and garden. Even though her loyalty was to her son, I think she cared for me in her own way. Still, I always felt like her servant, a beloved servant at times, but a servant nevertheless!"

Copper gazed into Mariah's eyes, trying to show her sincerity, "Ma Riley was very wise. She always said, no one passes through this life without hardships. Some are worse than others, but it's what we allow ourselves to learn from our hardships that makes the difference. You said earlier that you couldn't cook. I saw the way you watched me—as if I was performing magic! I wasn't born knowing how to do these things—no one is. The only reason I learned to sew and cook at an early age—was so the people who owned me—wouldn't have to. What you've been through is horrible, but you are here now. Let me be your friend and teach you what I can. It will be fun for both of us!"

Mariah shook her head. "But don't you, don't you think that I'm a—a—"

"Hurt and confused? Yes I do!" Copper spoke the words quickly before Mariah could call herself something unkind. "Yes, you're discouraged and scared! Just like I was when Vernon pulled me from the river and forced me to marry him. Just like I was when I got lost in these mountains and was terrified and slowly starving to death. But I was given a helping hand and that's what I am offering you, along with my friendship!" Bright green eyes sparkled when Mariah only stared at her, so she added, "In case you haven't noticed…I'm offering you a gift. I've always heard southerners were very polite. Of course, it would be terribly impolite to turn down a gift!"

Fresh tears slid down Mariah's cheeks even as her lips lifted in a tentative smile, "Well, I'm guilty of a lot of things but—I surely wouldn't want to be called impolite!"

Although Mariah tried to concentrate on Copper's promise of help and hope, her ears wouldn't stop ringing with the words, outlaw and albino. The name Dirk Culley meant nothing to her and yet...what if? Suddenly she felt dizzy, and she gripped the table with one hand and covered her face with the other.

"Mariah, are you all right?" Copper quickly made sure her new friend wasn't about to fall from the chair then she hurried to fetch her a cool cloth.

Patting her face and neck with it, Mariah muttered, "I don't know what came over me. I suppose I just got a little too warm—I'm all right now. While we work on dinner, why don't you finish your story. You married Vernon and then he was sent to prison. How did he die? And—what became of his—unusual albino partner? Is he still in jail?"

Copper was distracted for a moment as she sniffed the air to see if her cake was close to getting done, knowing that if she opened the oven door too soon it would fall like a pancake. Deciding that it wasn't ready to come out, she sat down beside Mariah.

"Well, about seven months ago, the Sheriff came to Ma's place and told us that both Vernon and Dirk escaped from prison! Vernon and his cellmate were both found dead. It was assumed that Dirk killed them although they didn't know for sure. Even though a posse chased Dirk to the Wyoming border, the sheriff believed he would come looking for me. Shortly after that we received a letter from Vernon and it had a…well that's another long story. Anyway, my mule Remy and I came up to these mountains and we promptly got ourselves lost! One night, God led Remy to this cabin and I tracked her here." Copper shook her head and her voice became reverent. "Mariah, I know God meant for me to be here. Now He has brought you here too! Your wounds are invisible, and I know for a fact that unseen wounds are the slowest to mend—but they do mend—and I am going to do everything I can to help you!"

Shad and Preacher washed the blood off their hands in the river. Since Remy and Flint were loaded down with meat, they led them back to the cabin. They had intentionally left the carcass, as well as the strong scent of a fresh kill, far from the homestead. No sense in tempting scavengers to come near the cabin when they could just as easily find this place to satisfy their hunger, and nothing was wasted.

As the men walked across the meadow, Shad decided that this was a good time to share his concerns. "Preacher, that sure is a pretty widow woman ya brung with ya today. I'm wonderin' though, have ya noticed the way she looks at ya?" When the big man shrugged, Shad smiled, "Well—I'll tell ya—she looks at ya the same way my first hound dog used to look at me when I was a boy in Tennessee."

Preacher laughed, "Shadrack McKenna, what does a hound dog have to do with Mariah? I mean…with Missus Kent."

"Mariah is it? Uh—huh, yep, that's just what I thought," Shad mumbled. "Pard, I think it's time I preached ya a little sermon." When Preacher stiffened, Shad pretended he didn't notice, "Remember me tellin' ya stories about Buella? I was sitting on the porch one summer day eating a bowl of cornbread floatin' in buttermilk. I looked down and there was the scrawniest little long eared pup I ever saw. So—I just sat the bowl down and let her have her fill. Maudy McKenna came out that back door like a shot. Thought Ma was gonna tan my hide for sure, 'cause food wasn't plentiful at our house. 'Course all she did was put her hands on her hips and say to me, 'Boy, you've gone and done it now! Why that silly pup ain't got no sense. She'll follow you across a dry desert from now on, and don't you go tellin' me she won't!' 'Course I thought that it'd be just dandy to have that pup followin' me everywhere. So, up I jumped and sure enough, Buella was my shadow from that day on. Ma tried to act all mad, but I could tell it tickled her almost as much as it did me. She always felt bad that I had to take on a man's role when Pa died. Buella and me had us a lot of good times. We turned into the best huntin' team in the county."

Preacher smiled indulgently, "I suppose you're about to come to the other side of that bush you're beating about—but I fail to understand what you're trying to say."

Shad stopped and put his hand on Preacher's shoulder, "I'm sayin' that pretty woman looks at ya like Buella used to look at me. Like you was her very own guardian angel. She may be a recent widow but—she's already in love with you! This summer, while I was tryin' to court every woman in Canyon City, they were all making eyes at you. The first thing ya did though was to set 'em all straight. You were polite but they all knew real quick that ya weren't in the market fer a wife—and that ya planned never to marry!"

The muscle in Preacher's jaw twitched as Shad continued, "Pardner, I don't think ya realize it but you look at her—pretty much the same way she looks at you. Like she's—yer woman! Ya may not see it Preacher—maybe she doesn't either...but it would be clear to a blind man that ya've both staked yer claim. Could it be that ya've changed your mind? If ya have, I'm truly happy for ya. But—if yer still sure God don't want ya to marry—well I'm worried that yer both gonna end up with wounds that'll take an awful long time to heal—if they ever do!"

Preacher frowned and gazed up at the path leading towards the cabin. Finally, he blew out a breath he hadn't know he was holding. "You're right of course. Didn't realize it was so obvious! Shad, from the day I surrendered to preach, I've felt God's direction just as plain and clear as a mountain stream. But from the moment I met this woman—and I mean from the very first moment—it seems I just don't know what God would have me do next. I could have saved her from ruination, but I was so drawn to her—that to my shame I gave the task to someone else. Because of that mistake, she's been horribly abused. I won't disobey God but I can't bear to hurt her either. I know this is a great imposition on you and Copper, but you're the only people I could trust to take care of her! To tell you the truth, I haven't been this troubled since my parents died. She's such a dear little thing. Besides giving Mariah room and board, I really need you and Copper to pray—for both of us. I need God's direction now more than I ever have in my life!"

"Now is as good a time as any, Preacher." With that said, both men dropped to their knees.

Later, as they neared the cabin they were both a bit uneasy, wondering how the two women might be getting along. Quin especially was concerned, remembering the pleading look Mariah had given him earlier. However, when he walked through the cabin door and saw her face aglow with pride, he couldn't help but laugh out loud.

"Quin." she beamed, "It may taste like an old shoe…but Copper just taught me how to bake a pie. It's the first one I've ever made!"

Chapter 18
A Sincere Heart

"Perfume and incense bring joy to the heart, and the pleasantness of a friend springs from their heartfelt advice." Proverbs 27:9

Moonlight spread a soft pewter glow through the window. It wasn't quite morning yet, but Mariah couldn't sleep. Instead, she gazed about in wonder at the snug little cabin. It had been such a relief to know that she was not expected to sleep in the same room as the newlyweds. There were two cabins connected by a dog run. Shad built the larger one for himself and the family he had hoped to have one day. The smaller one was built for his mother, at her request. The 'granny cabin' was what Maudy McKenna had called it. Sadly, the dear woman had died before it was finished. Over the years, it had become a storage place for traps, hides, snowshoes, carving tools and the like. After Copper married Shad, she had the idea of turning it into a private room for Preacher. The couple had enjoyed working together, as they emptied, cleaned, polished, furnished, and transformed the storage room into a welcoming haven for the man who had no real place to call his own.

Although Preacher was very pleased when he saw it, he believed that God had Mariah in mind for it all along. The cozy room boasted a pot-bellied stove in one corner, a bed with a sweet, grass-filled mattress, a wooden trunk, a washstand with bowl and pitcher, and a bent wood rocking chair by a curtained window. Though the smaller cabin was not as lovely as the larger one, it was built just as well. Mariah had known both luxury and want, but to her, this little cabin was paradise. The roof didn't leak, the wind didn't whistle through the walls, the floor was made of smooth planks rather than dirt—and best of all—she had it all to herself!

Dressing and fixing her hair by lantern light, Mariah decided to read until it was time to help Copper with breakfast. Mindful of the McKenna's privacy she never entered their cabin until she saw Shad heading for the barn to do his morning chores. And because she had promised Quin, she sat down in the rocker and reached for the Bible he had given her. When it opened to the book of Hebrews, she began to read.

"Let us go right into the presence of God with ***sincere hearts*** *fully trusting him. For our* ***guilty consciences*** *have been sprinkled with Christ's blood to make us clean, and our bodies have been washed with pure water."*

Grimacing, Mariah slapped the Bible shut. Preacher had promised her that if she read her Bible every day, it would be an encouragement to her—it would strengthen her and help her heal. Instead, the words always seemed to accuse her. The words stung. It was like pouring alcohol on an open wound.

"Sincere heart, guilty conscience." Mariah repeated the words and frowned, "You're an imposter Mariah June and you know it! You were not sincere when you prayed with Quin. You might not have truly understood that it was wrong at the time—but you do now! You put your trust in the goodness of Pastor Quincy Long—not the God of the universe."

Mariah bit her lip as she rocked nervously, wishing she could undo a lifetime of mistakes. Not just this one but all of them. It was a great relief when she finally saw the first whisper of sunlight slipping through her window. Of course, Remy began her braying, followed closely by the unmistakable crow of a disgruntled rooster. Mariah couldn't help but smile. Although she was still struggling mightily with so many things, she constantly reminded herself that had it not been for Quin, she would still be a captive saloon girl in Otter Run. Instead, she was here in this wonderful little cabin. Outside she heard the familiar whistle and saw Shad's broad back as he made his way towards the barn. She waited a few moments then smoothed her dress, pinched her cheeks, and went to help Copper with breakfast.

Carrying a basket full of eggs, Copper stepped into the cabin, only to have her nose inform her that all was not well, "I think the biscuits are burning."

Startled, Mariah's hands flew to her face, "Oh, no—not again!" Flinging back the heavy oven door, she reached for the hot pan.

"No—use the towel or you'll...."

The warning came too late as Mariah cried out in pain. Remembering the harsh reprimands she had received when making similar mistakes—Copper said nothing. Instead, she guided Mariah to the sink, instructing her to pump cold water over her burned fingers while she carried the charred biscuits out the back door and flung them into the yard.

"I am so sorry! How will I ever repay you for all the supplies I've ruined? Honestly, I kept thinkin' the bacon was burnin', and then when I took up the bacon I thought it was just the grease. How could I forget that I had biscuits in the oven?" Mariah stared down at her scorched fingers and mumbled. "Victor and Jimmy Todd both called me worthless. And all I'm doing here every day is proving them right!"

Copper put one arm around Mariah, then leaned over, snagged a piece of bacon from the plate and took a bite, "Mmmm, just—perfect." Smiling playfully, she added, "Yesterday you burned the biscuits *and* the bacon. I'd say you're improving—don't you?"

"How come all this is so—dad-blasted—easy for you?" Mariah huffed then scowled at her blistered fingers. She knew she sounded petty and jealous, but she couldn't help herself. It was just so embarrassing! Copper was five years younger and ten times better at everything! Sometimes the little redhead's perfection was like a stone in Mariah's shoe; it wasn't just a bother… it hurt!

"My dear friend, it only looks like it's easier for me because I've done these things most of my life. Believe me; I've been called worthless more times than I care to remember. You are the only one that has ever called me perfect. You told me that first day that this is the closest you've ever been to a real cook stove. You were never taught any of this. While I on the other hand was painstakingly taught these things from an early age, but only so that my father and my *owners* wouldn't have to do them."

Sniffing back tears, Mariah glanced over at Copper, "It's just so frustratin' and shameful. You're eighteen and I'm twenty-three. You've been married for two months while I was married for fifteen. I feel like such a failure…"

"You're much too hard on yourself. Learning is always a process of finding out what to do as well as what not to do. It just takes time. On top of which, we both know that you're still trying to heal and to cope with what has happened to you. I think sometimes, you are just distracted—and there is no shame in that! All I can tell you is that when you feel discouraged just remember that God loves you and wants to comfort you. I can't tell you how much reading, praying, and daily putting my trust in Christ helped and encouraged me—when I first became a Christian. I know it's hard to create new habits like study and prayer, but I know that when I'm troubled the more I read God's word the stronger I feel and the more peace and contentment He gives me."

Again, the words from that morning's reading seemed to be pounding in Mariah's head in time with the throbbing of her heart. *Guilty conscience—sincere heart.* "I—I don't know," she stammered. "I do try, but the Bible doesn't come easily for me—not like it does for you and Shad. I have to force myself to open it and it's hard to understand. Plus, the verses I read always seem to accuse me rather than comfort me!"

Mariah's words worried Copper, but they didn't surprise her. The Bible had been totally new to her as well. However, when she had accepted Christ, it seemed that she was instantly filled with an unquenchable hunger for God's word. It had been the same for Shad. They both had been drawn to it—as if it were water and they were dying of thirst. Sometimes it was difficult to understand, yet the more they meditated on it the clearer it became. According to Preacher, Mariah was a new Christian. However, neither Shad nor Copper saw any growth in her as a child of God or any interest in knowing more.

After dinner that night, as was their habit, Shad read a chapter from the Bible while the women washed the dishes. Later they discussed what he had read. As always, Mariah listened patiently to Shad and Copper's comments, but she never added or questioned anything. At six o'clock, each night Mariah would excuse herself and hurry to her own cabin, declaring that the couple should have some evening time together and that she needed her rest.

The newlyweds happily made good use of their private moments together. Cradled in rays of moonlight shining through the window, they explored the delights of marriage. They snuggled under the buffalo hide, making love and talking into the night. Somehow, their happiness made them both keenly aware of all that Mariah had lost or more likely—never had!

Shad was just nodding off to sleep when he heard Copper's loud sigh. "Ain't getting' tired of me already are ya sweet girl?"

"Mmmm, not quite yet," she teased. "I am fairly certain that when the Rocky Mountains have all worn down to dust—I'll probably be awfully tired of you!" Smiling, Copper turned in his arms. Laying her head on his chest, she hugged him tightly. “Until then, you don’t have anything to worry about.” Feeling Shad’s smile she added, “I won’t ever be able to tell you how much I love you. I sighed just now because sometimes I miss having you all to myself and then I think about, how we *have so much* and how Mariah has lost *so much!* You don’t mind terribly that we’re sharing our little bit of heaven with her…do you?”

The big man kissed the top of Copper’s silky head. “Well, to be honest, I reckon I do mind a little. You do spend a lot of time with her and I don’t always cotton to sharin’ ya. But I know we’re doin’ the right thing.”

“I think so too. Oh Shad, have you ever stopped to think that—what happened to Mariah could have easily happened to me. Instead, here I am—so happy and so in love. God blessed us and now I think He wants us to share our blessings with her.”

“I’ve thought the same thing.” he grunted. “It surely was God’s doin’ when that watch dog, rooster and moose you call a mule wondered onto this place. You know I think she’s finally startin’ to like me a little.”

“I think she is, Shad, but I also think she’s secretly in love with Boone and wants your approval. Come to think of it, you took longer than usual checking on the animals tonight. Was there a problem? Remy hadn’t tried to open the grain bin again—had she?”

“Nope! I know to lock it up tight, but that dang mule wouldn’t let me out of the barn ‘til I read her two bedtime stories!”

Copper giggled then pinched Shad’s ticklish side. He grabbed her hand to stop her, and a gentle tug of war ensued. “Admit it, McKenna,” she huffed trying to pull her hand free, “you love Remy almost as much as I do.” When Shad made a face, Copper snuggled closer, “Well, maybe you don’t love her—but you like her—I can tell. I just bet you were out there scratching her ears. I know from experience that once you start on that acreage, she won’t let you out of the barn until you’ve done a thorough job of it.”

Shad sighed contentedly and brought Copper’s hand to his lips, kissed it, then laid it back on his chest and held it there, “I’m not admittin’ anything, except that I’m grateful that she led ya here to me! Speaking o’ Remy—I’d swear that silly mule was trying to get Mariah to perk up today. She was wiggling her ears, and nipping at her apron. Seems even that crazy beast senses the pain that woman carries around with her. Mariah pretends that she’s doing fine—but she’s not! Actually, she was the reason I was late coming back from checking the stock tonight. The lantern was still lit in her cabin and I saw the shadow of her pacing back and forth. I know—I heard her cryin'. I stood outside her door, wondering if I should say something or come and get you. Finally, I just stood there and prayed. That's why darlin', even though there are times that I wish it were just you and me here. I surely don't begrudge yer spending time with her or us doing anything we can to help her."

Copper reached up and kissed Shad's cheek, "You are a good man Shadrach McKenna. The trouble is, we ***are*** doing all *we* can—but *what she needs is God!* It's not our business to judge whether she's a Christian or not, but despite her praying with Preacher, I don't think she is. If she had truly asked Christ to come into her life, I know it wouldn't just make all her pain disappear but we would see—some improvement! She never wants to read the Bible, talk about God, or pray. She tries not to show it but sometimes she's downright resentful of me. I don't really blame her; I have a wonderful life now...thanks to the Lord and to you. Most of my life I've been miserable and alone. Things were still far from perfect after I gave my heart to Christ, but despite everything, I had an inner peace and even a courage that I had never possessed before. She doesn't have that. Shad, I think God is nudging me towards having a sincere talk with her. Please pray that I say the right things. It's not going to be easy. I'm afraid she'll think I'm judging her! The last thing I want to do, is make her feel worse or drive her away! I need God to tell me when the time is right and to guide every single word I say."

While the couple prayed for their friend, Mariah paced within the four walls of her tiny cabin. She hadn't even realized that she was weeping until she saw the reflection of herself in the windowpane. There was a vast emptiness inside her, which she could not describe. Quin had brought her here and then left the very next day to return to his mountain ministry. Mariah felt his absence so keenly; it was as if she were missing an arm or a leg. She knew this was probably another of her many sins, for she was grieving far more over the departure of Quincy Long from her life than she had over her parents' rejection or the death of her husband. She also was mourning the fact that she could no longer consider herself a '*decent woman*'. No, now she was a '*fallen woman*'. Oh, how she hated the men of Otter Run, and Sheriff Jimmy Todd was at the top of the list of those she would never forgive!

Just a few miles away, as an eagle flies, Quin had returned to his high mountain camp by the waterfall to fast and pray. He had tried to continue his service to others, but he found that he was too confused by his own troubled heart to minister to anyone. So—while the wolves sang their nightly serenade to the moon, the big man kneeled beside a glowing fire and begged God to heal Mariah, body and soul, and to restore the zeal he had once enjoyed for his humble and lonely mountain ministry.

On that same moonlit night, it seemed many hearts were crying out to God…and of course…***He was listening***!

The following day was the kind that inspired sonnets and poems extolling the shining mountains for their majestic beauty. The sky was a pure, robin's egg blue while the sun tossed bright rays of golden warmth across the valley. However, early winter in the high-country could be fickle at best. Any day now this entire territory might be blanketed in a deep snow or a white-out blizzard. Copper and Mariah decided to take advantage of this fine day as they gathered all their washing and headed down the hill to the hot spring.

"Can you imagine?" Copper said over her shoulder with Mariah following close behind. "I was here all last summer and never knew this hot spring existed. When it gets colder we can wash our things in the bathing cave behind the pantry—but things don't dry as quickly in there; it too humid." Copper's voice was a bit out of breath as she added, "There are so many reasons why I love this place!"

"I can't argue with that." Mariah huffed under her own heavy load. "It's a wonderful place all right. When I think of how hard my last winter was, just to find food let alone stay clean. Victor didn't even think I washed his clothes right. I suppose you'll do this better than me—like everything else!"

Copper spun around and frowned at Mariah, "You silly goose, the only things I do better than you are the things I've been trained to do—because I was a servant! You, my friend, are smart and well educated. My schooling ended when I was twelve. You are outrageously beautiful, while I have to be content with orange hair and freckles. We are not competing against each other—but if we were—I would lose!" As they reached the pool, Copper sighed then added, "Now, let's just enjoy every second of this warmth and sunshine. We may be snowed in any day now—and who knows for how long!"

Shrugging, Mariah set her basket down beside Copper's. The spring fed pool was small, about five feet in diameter, the water was held back by large waist-high rocks, worn smooth by centuries of dancing water. Steam rose from the surface and between bubbles you could see that the water was as clear and clean as a freshly polished window.

"It is perfect here," Mariah admitted. "I always hated kneeling beside an ice-cold stream or leaning over a boiling pot to wash our clothes. It was always a constant worry to keep my skirts from catching on fire. I don't suppose doing laundry will ever be fun but—" Giving Copper a slight smile she added, "This just might be the closest thing to it."

Copper gave Mariah a mischievous grin, "We'll make it fun, my friend! When we're done, we'll take a nice long bath. Let's wash our change of clothes first, so they'll be dry to change into after we've washed ourselves. This pool is like our bathing cave—the water is always emptying and refilling itself so the dirty soapy water is pushed out as the new clean water comes in."

"Of course!" Mariah muttered, trying, but not succeeding in tamping down her bitterness. "This is Copper's very own little bit of heaven—isn't it? All perfect and clean!"

"It's yours too Mariah—here for you to enjoy. Shad and I are happy to share this with you, especially me! You know how lonely it gets for a woman in these mountains. Black-Eyed Jack or Preacher or some other miner or rancher might stop by for a rare visit, but that's not the same. There are precious few of us women around. I value your friendship, and Shad and I have no doubt that God brought you here just as surely as he did me. Our home can be a place of healing and renewal for you—or at least it can be if you let it!"

Mariah gave Copper one of her almost smiles while her lavender eyes remained dark and solemn. She believed it was Quin that brought her here—not God!

Choosing to ignore Mariah's mood, Copper hummed as she dumped the first batch of clothes into the bubbling spring. The two women fell into a comfortable silence as they scrubbed the garments with bars of lye soap, then rhythmically beat their dirty laundry against the smooth rocks. As planned, they washed a change of clothes first and laid them over some nearby bushes to dry. Next, they began washing Shad's things. Mariah flung his blue muslin shirt down against the rocks with an air crackling slap. Copper was surprised, then she laughed and whacked the shirt she was scrubbing against the rocks just as hard. It was only a game to Copper but it was a challenge to Mariah, and they smacked the garments down again and again, harder and harder until soon both women were out of breath. Finally, Copper stopped, "Oh my, this is a good way to let off some steam. We should think of all the people that have hurt us and then—just take it out on our wash. Our clothes will be cleaner than ever." Dabbing the droplets of water from her face with her sleeve she sighed, "The truth is…I think I've pretty much forgiven most of them. Well, I'm working on it anyway."

"Well—I don't believe it!" Mariah huffed, "Am I finally gonna outdo the paragon, Copper McKenna at somethin'? Because, I haven't forgiven anyone—and I don't intend too! I hate one man especially. So I guess my wash will come out cleaner than yours—won't it?"

Copper didn't know what to say. She had hoped her words might lead them into a peaceful discussion about forgiveness. Suddenly, it was as if a shadow had passed over Mariah's beautiful face. Tears of hurt and rage clouded her eyes as she reared back and slapped the shirt against the rocks with all her might. When it caught between two rocks, she yanked it away with such force that it ripped the fabric!

At first she stopped, horrified at what she'd done. Then a wild, blind fury seemed to overtake her, and she shouted, "What's the matter with me? Must everything I touch get ruined—just like me?" Then assuming the shirt was already destroyed, she reared back and beat the torn garment against the rocks, over and over and over, until she was so exhausted that her knees buckled, and she collapsed to the ground. Doubling over, she buried her face in her hands, rocking back and forth, as she wept.

Instantly, Copper fell to the ground beside her and gathered Mariah into her arms, "Oh my sweet, sweet friend, you've been through so much and you've tried so hard to be brave. You can't just pretend that you're not hurting—you must deal with it! Letting your anger out is at least a beginning."

Hours passed as the two women sat beside the hot spring. They wept together and consoled each other as they shared the deepest hurts of their lives. Finally, when Mariah seemed calmer, Copper decided that now was the time to share what was on her heart. "Mariah, I love you like a sister, but I think that if Christ was really in your heart, you wouldn't be this miserable. I beg you not to be angry with me—but were you *sincere—truly sincere* when you prayed with Preacher?"

A flash of indignation sparked in Mariah' eyes, even as words of anger perched on her lips. Then she saw the love and understanding in Copper's face. "No—I wasn't sincere at all," she groaned. "I'm so ashamed. I wish I could believe like you and Shad and Quin. But—God doesn't love me and it wasn't God who rescued me—it was Quin! He risked his life to get me out of that awful place. Don't you see—I owed him so much. So when he asked me to pray—I prayed! I didn't think it was wrong at the time, but now—I know it was. I'm scared of what God might do to me. I keep expectin' Him to rain lightnin' down on me or squash me like a bug."

"No Mariah, God just wants to love you! He understands how hurt and confused you've been. And He wants to bring peace and joy into your life…not misery!"

Sighing loudly, Mariah's expression became hard and her lips quivered as she asked, "Why did God help you and not me, Copper? Why did He let those men hurt me? Why didn't he send Quin sooner—just a day sooner? Quin thought the bank was providin' for me and…that lowlife sheriff was courtin' me. But instead—he—they all—" Mariah hid her face in her hands.

"I know—and I'm so sorry they hurt you." Copper whispered, as she gently pulled Mariah's hands down so she could look into her eyes. "None of it was your fault—and you most certainly are not ruined. I'll admit though, I've had similar questions. Why was I sold? Why was I beaten so many times? I wish I had answers—for both of us! All I can do is tell you what Ma Riley told me. She said, 'When something horrible happens to you—you can do one of two things. You can turn your pain over to God and allow Him to do something productive with it; or you can hold that pain close to you and allow it to fester inside, until you can't see or feel anything but pain and hate and anger! Then she reminded me that sometimes we have to swallow down bitter medicine before we can get well. And that many are the blessings that are fashioned from wounded hearts that have born their pain with grace. Perhaps God has a special plan for you and this horrible experience will give you the insight and tenderness of heart that you'll need someday. Oh, Mariah, faith is trusting God, even when we don't understand Him."

"It's so unfair!" Mariah sighed. "Does havin' faith mean I can't even ask where was God when I was sufferin'?"

"I know where He was, Mariah! He was in the exact same place when His very own son Jesus was dying on the cross, for your sins and for mine. God could have intervened when they were driving nails into His son's hands and feet, but He looked away—for the good of the world! God allowed His own son, Jesus, to take on our punishment. Mariah, do you remember what we read in Isaiah yesterday? 'He was pierced for our transgressions, he was crushed for our iniquities; the punishment that brought us peace was on Him, and by his wounds we are healed.' Christ suffered terribly. And God allowed it—for our sake!"

Mariah felt as if a tug of war was raging inside her. "Maybe He does love me, but every time I try to focus on God, the faces of those men seem to block the way. The only sleep I get is filled with nightmares of what they did. I can't get peace about it—I can't get free! I feel too dirty, too broken!"

"Oh Mariah, we all come to Christ dirty and broken. That's why we ask Him to come into our lives, and create in us a new clean heart. When we confess our sins and invite Him into our lives, it's like He comes into our hearts when its winter and He turns it into spring!"

"I think I'd do just about anythin' to be made new—livin' like this—it isn't livin' at all!"

A spark of hope glimmered in Copper's green eyes, "First, you need to *sincerely* ask Christ into your heart. God can't be fooled. Then you need to ask Christ to forgive your sins AND help you forgive all those who have hurt you. I know how difficult it must sound but that means your parents, Victor—and—yes—even Jimmy Todd and all those other no accounts, too!"

"Forgive them? Not a one of them deserves my forgiveness!" Mariah spat out the words and her face grew hard. "That's asking too much! It's impossible."

"Impossible for you alone, yes! But Christ tells us that—with Him all things are possible. Mariah, forgiving others isn't a request, it's a command! Jesus told his disciples, 'Your Heavenly Father will forgive you IF you forgive those who sin against you, but if you refuse to forgive them, He will not forgive you.' Believe me, God knows those men are dirty rotten polecats and He will deal severely with them in His own time. However, if you want to be a child of God you must obey Him. You said it yourself; living with this anger is torturing *you*, not them! Refusing to forgive an enemy is like stabbing yourself and expecting them to feel the pain!"

"I hate the idea..." Mariah whimpered. Then she nodded in understanding, "Even so, I know you're right."

Copper squeezed her hand and asked, "Would you like to start over and invite God in....and this time with your whole heart. God promised that when you receive Him, He will make you a brand new creature—behold all things are new!"

There beside the hot spring, with heartbreaking sobs Mariah asked Christ to forgive her, come into her life and make her new. This time her prayer was unquestionably sincere as she asked God to help her take her first genuine albeit faltering steps towards forgiving all those that had misused and abused her.

Afterwards, the women cried, hugged, and laughed as they gathered up their wash. As they hurried toward the cabin, eager to tell Shad, Mariah's news, they had no idea that he had a special surprise waiting for them as well!

Sound travels easily in the high-country and even before they arrived at the cabin, the distinctive notes of a zither being tuned and strummed floated towards them.

"Oh Copper," Mariah cried. "Do you hear it?" Without waiting for an answer, she moved her basket to her hip, picked up her skirts and ran to the cabin. Her heart was beating wildly as she threw open the door and found Shad sitting at the kitchen table.

"Well, it's about time you two were back." Shad muttered only just glancing up, then he pressed a small harmonica back to his lips. He blew a note, plucked a string, turned a knob, and then started over again until the delicate little instrument was finally in tune. Not knowing the emotional afternoon the women had spent or that both of them had tears streaming down their faces, he looked up and said happily, "Thought we all might enjoy a singing tonight and..." Shad's face fell sharply as he watched both women sink into the chairs on either side of him, their mouths open and their red-rimmed eyes wide as they stared down at the zither.

Mariah's hand trembled as she reached out to touch it. The words she wanted to speak were held captive in her throat. Lavender tears clouded her eyes and she frowned and shook her head. It was—and yet—it was not—her old zither. The instrument before her was the same—except for now—it was a work of art! Wiping her eyes with her apron, she sniffed and studied it more closely. It was her zither, small and heart-shaped, with two swirling teardrop sound holes that had been carefully cut into either side of the rounded fret board. The difference was that the instrument that Shad had re-built was skillfully carved with amazingly delicate scrollwork, and the wood was polished to a high luster.

Shad cursed himself for not showing the thing to Copper first. He wasn't sure what he'd done wrong, Mariah's chin began to quiver and then she covered her face with her hands and wept!

"Oh ma'am—Mariah—I," he groaned and ran his hand over his face, "I'm awful sorry! Truly, I never meant to upset ya—I had hoped this would cheer ya up some." Bowing his head, he spoke mournfully, "When Preacher gave me the pieces, I tried to use as much of the old one as I could. Honest I did, but I reckon I should have asked yer permission first before I just took it on myself to rebuild it. I don't know what to say..."

Shad rubbed the back of neck, feeling lower than a tick on a dead dog. When he looked into Copper's green eyes and found that she was weeping too, he swallowed hard, fearing *he* might be next! Then she completely mystified him by throwing herself into his arms—laughing and sobbing at the same time.

"Oh, you dear thing!" she cried, as she held his face in her hands and planted kisses all over it. "If you aren't just the most wonderful man in the whole world. It's perfect Shad—and—so are you!"

At that moment, Mariah looked up and sniffed as she wiped the tears from her eyes, and once again, she reached out her hand. Instead of touching the zither she laid it over Shad's and gave it an appreciative squeeze. "Shadrack McKenna," she whispered tenderly. There was so much more she wanted to say, but the words wouldn't come. Finally, she managed to smile, "She's right, this is wonderful and—and so are you! You thought to do me a simple kindness—but it's so much more!" Exchanging knowing glances with Copper she said: "Only God knew what this would mean to me—and even the day and the hour it would mean the most—God knew—didn't He Copper!"

Lightly running her fingers over the strings, Mariah explained. "My half-brother gave me this—this—silly little instrument for my birthday before he left home for good. It was old when he gave it to me and it was cheaply made at that—but I loved it. It may sound strange but, for many years, this little bit of wood and string and the music it made was my only friend. When those men—when I thought that my life had been ruined—in a fit of self-pity and anger, I broke it into pieces—because—I felt as if I had been broken into pieces."

Giving Shad and Copper the first joyful smile they had ever seen, Mariah said softly, "I'm just now understandin' something Quin tried to tell me that day. He said that the touch of the master—can not only restore what was broken—but can make all things new! Shad, that's what you did for my little zither—and I can tell—God is beginnin' to do the same thing with me. I just asked him into my heart—and He's already changin' me!" Stroking the carved and polished wood, she added reverently, "God is goin' to take all that's been wounded and broken in my life and make me better than I was before." Lavender eyes suddenly filled with happy tears as she looked over at Copper, "Behold, all things are new!"

Chapter 19
Truth in Love

"Speak up for those who cannot speak for themselves, for the rights of all who are destitute. Speak up and judge fairly." Proverbs 30:8

Quin knelt beside the beautiful waterfall. He had prayed and fasted for a week now and yet his emotions were still in turmoil. "Please Boss—help me," he groaned. "You've called me to be a shepherd to these mountain people. Yet when I think of how they treated Mariah, I want to storm into the town of Otter Run like Samson and wreak vengeance on all of them. And if I can't do that, then I just want to shake the dust from that filthy town off my feet and never return. Of course I know what you expect of me, but I sure am going to need your guidance and strength to do it."

The big man started to rise, but then he fell back to his knees for the second petition he had to bring before God weighed even more heavily on his heart. "And what Lord, is Reverend Quincy Long to do about Mariah?"

Just then a breeze blew down from the mountains and he felt it swirling about him as he admitted the feelings he had tried so hard to deny. "Shad said that I treat her as if she was my woman. It would have been a lie to deny it. I'm just a man, Boss, just flesh and blood. You've helped me overcome temptation before, so, why is this time so difficult? You know I love You and the work You've called me to do. I don't ever want to give it up. That's why I am so confused because I also have this great love for Mariah! Are you testing me? If so, help me learn, whatever it is You're trying to teach me. Despite how this hurts, I know You must mean it for my good. So, please guide me and I beg You—restore peace to my heart once again!"

Rising from his knees there was no peace and there was no "amen" for his prayers continued, even as he put out the campfire, grabbed his rifle and set out to walk the forest. His thoughts and prayers were as tangled as the thickets he was forced to walk around. He told himself that, perhaps resisting this powerful love he felt for Mariah was a sacrifice God was asking him to make. Surely if God was asking this of him, there was a purpose, perhaps it would make him a better and more understanding pastor.

"Whatever Your plan is Boss, Mariah must never know how I feel. And please, lead her to a good man, a better man than me to be her husband."

Saying the words out loud made his stomach clench into a twisted knot, and before he could stop himself, he slammed his hand against the thick trunk of a tree. The pain that raced up his arm was nothing compared to thinking of Mariah with another man. "Lord," he sighed, "if it's not Your will for me to make vows to her, then I'll make them to You. I will honor this love I have for Mariah until the day I die. All I ask is that You heal, provide and protect her. Please let her to know of Your abundant love for her—because she can never know of mine."

As Preacher trotted Flint down the Main Street of Otter Run, he struggled to keep from scowling. Not only had the peace and comfort he sought continue to elude him, but he was expected to preach his monthly sermon the next day. All he could think about was what these people had done to the woman who was now the secret love of his life. His jaw worked as he reminded himself that God commanded believers to forgive others even as Christ loved and forgave them. If anyone needed to practice what he preached...it was Pastor Quincy Long. However, never in his life had it been more difficult!

As he passed the mercantile, he worked to keep his voice pleasant as he tipped his hat, "Good morning, Cyril, Sephora." The couple were washing the storefront windows, and Cyril's face turned a deep shade of red, while Sephora pressed her thin lips together as she gave a curt nod of her head. With grim satisfaction, Preacher noticed that neither of them were able to look him in the eye.

As always, he headed straight for the livery. His first priority was to see to Flint. Then he usually remembered that he too was tired and hungry. Typically, everyone was pleased to see the big man ride into town. Today however, he couldn't help but wonder what kind of reception his sermon would be receiving the following day. Assuming there was anyone in town who wanted to hear it.

A few years back, when gold was first discovered, Otter Run showed signs of becoming a boom town. Unfortunately, those first veins had turned out to be shallow. Two mines were still operating but they were finding little ore, and even it was of poor quality. Now there were just enough miners, trappers and ranchers occupying the surrounding land to keep Otter Run from becoming a ghost town. The Long Shot was the only saloon remaining, and it did well enough, for there would always be men who wished to spend their coin on liquor, gambling and loose women. Small town gossip and bar room brawls gave the otherwise quiet settlement its main source of entertainment.

The only other form of amusement for the inhabitants of Otter Run, regardless of what they believed, tended to be Preacher's monthly sermons. As a rule, they were well attended, not only by the leading citizens, but also by the rougher sorts like Ox Hennessey and his two saloon girls, Velvet and Shotsy. At first Sephora Castle and Nelly Krane, the banker's wife, had complained loudly about, 'those girls being unfit for church', but Preacher had insisted that he would only preach if everyone was welcome. Since no one wanted him to stop, everyone came and he preached on. The man had a way of keeping folks on the edge of their seats, with his seemingly endless supply of amusing and wild mountain stories, as well as his tales of hair-raising experiences he had known while sailing to far away ports. Then without anyone knowing exactly when the tide turned—they'd find themselves listening intently to scriptures read straight from God's word, and lessons shared that kept them thinking until his next visit the following month.

Now as Preacher led Flint into his usual stall, he felt a war being waged within himself, for his thoughts naturally went to Mariah. Her pale blonde hair, lavender eyes, as well as her honey sweet southern drawl seemed burned into his memory. The past few nights he had been plagued by nightmares that forced him to watch as all the town's people passed Mariah by, ignoring her plight. He looked on helplessly as she walked the dusty street, begging for food and shelter. When he saw her being carried into the saloon, a group of cold-hearted men surrounded her like a pack of hungry wolves. In the nightmare, Quin fought to reach her, but it was as if an invisible chain held him back. Every time Preacher awoke from the nightmare, he was in a sweat, trembling with rage. Shaking the memory away, he clenched his jaw and told himself that it was not his job to judge these people, no matter what they had done!

Deliberately taking this time to get his feelings under control, he pulled Flint's saddle and slowly began grooming him while he silently prayed. *Boss, I need Your help. You wanted me to return to this sorry little town—so here I am. You know I'm not ready to face these people. And I know my attitude is wrong. You want me to be a good shepherd to this flock, while I'd like to bust their heads together. I have no idea what You want me to say to them. For now, help me to forgive and love these people the way You do. I'm your servant Boss; help me to serve them in a way that pleases You.*

A short time later, Preacher stepped out of the livery, then had to skirt around a dozen men that were waiting for their horses or pack mules to be shod by the blacksmith. It was the usual gathering of tradesmen, miners, trappers and ranchers. When they noticed who he was, a sudden tension filled the air and they grew silent. There had been a great deal of gossip about how the mountain preacher had ridden into town and carried off the beautiful young dove. They all believed that, had it not been for his meddlesome ways, she would be where she belonged, pouring their drinks and a great deal more. The fact that he had rescued the beautiful young widow from degradation didn't make him a hero—not to these men. Instead, they all wished the big man had minded his own business.

Tick Hobbs, a short and cantankerous miner, known for his loud mouth and quick temper, suddenly stepped in front of Preacher, blocking his way. "Well now looky here fellers." Her jeered. "Iffen it ain't the Rocky Mountain's very own know-it-all preacher man. He's one o' them highfalutin' nabobs from back east." Wrapping one dirty hand around the rope that replaced a broken suspender, he laughed, showing yellow, tobacco stained teeth. With his free hand, he encouraged all the men to gather around.

"Just in case any of you fellers don't know this oversized galoot…his name be Reverend Quincy Long," he crowed, as he strutted like a rooster before the big man. "Long on wind and short on brains—at least that's how I've heard it told." When some of the men chuckled, that was all the encouragement Tick needed. "Yep, he's one of them men that think, what he's got to say is so important, he's got to call a crowd together and take up the hotel dining room and the lobby too, just so everybody can hear him blow hot air."

Preacher gave a self-deprecating smile and nodded his head, “I suppose there are some that might say, even that is too high a compliment for some of my sermons.”

A couple of the men that had been helped greatly by Preacher over the years came to stand beside him while the other men laughed and added some off color jests of their own.

Ignoring the rude comments, Preacher tipped his hat, “Thank you, Mister Hobbs for helping me spread the word. As you’ve just mentioned, we’ll be having church services in the hotel lobby and dining room as usual. You can judge for yourselves if my sermon has substance or if, as Mister Hobb’s says—it’s just hot air. We’ll begin at ten o’clock tomorrow morning, and—you’re all welcome!

When Preacher turned to walk away, Tick called out to him. “Hey preacher-man, a couple of these men here vow that yer more ‘n jes’ a no account—Bible thumper. They say yer a fair hand—some even swear that ya’ll get yer hands dirty—when the mood strikes ya. ‘Course I find that powerful hard to swaller—I dare ya to prove it.” When Preacher raised his eyebrows, Tick stepped forward, “Tell ya what, I’ll come ‘n hear yer talk—fact is—I’ll even sit right down in the front row. All ya gotta do is jes’ humble yerself a mite and maybe get yer hands dirty. Jes’ bend down and pick up that thar rope that’s a lying in the mud—‘n pitch it to me.”

Preacher saw the coiled rope in the mud, all right. He also saw that it was just behind Tick’s notoriously ornery pack mule. He knew that there were a lot of even-tempered mules, just like Copper McKenna’s, Remy. Then again, he knew there were others that could easily kick a man—right into next week! And even a mild mannered mule didn’t necessary take kindly to a stranger walking up behind him.

All the men grew quiet as they watched Preacher and then they glanced over at Tick. The little man’s eyes were dark and challenging as his lips curved into a mocking smile. And yet, he lost his smile when Preacher’s eyes flashed and he grinned broadly.

“You know—Tick, that seems like a fine bargain to me. Front row—right?” He asked, loudly enough for all the bystanders to hear.

Tick narrowed his eyes, but he nodded in agreement, as Preacher stepped towards the mule. The beast did just what every man there expected him to do. He laid his ears flat against his neck and struck out with his back leg with the speed of a rattlesnake! However, what came next—no one expected. For though the mule was quick—Preacher—was quicker still!

Grinning from ear to ear, the man caught the mule's hoof in his massive hand. What was even more surprising—was that no matter how hard the mule tried to free himself, Preacher held on. Murmurs, curses, and exclamations abounded because none of the men had ever seen such a thing. They watched in awe as the powerful mule struggled and loudly brayed out his complaint. It seemed the louder he was and the harder he kicked—the more Preacher laughed.

Tick's pinched face turned a dozen shades of crimson, and he couldn't believe his eyes as he ran a dirty hand over his somber face. He was the only man there that wasn't seeing this as a great joke.

"Hey Tick." the other men called out, "whose gonna quit first—the minister or the mule?" Soon the men were wagering as to who was stronger. The animal wasn't hurt by this tug of war but he was humbled; so much so, that he suddenly stopped, then he turned to look at the man holding his leg and shook his head, his long ears flapping side to side. Soon it seemed as if the whole town was laughing, for they all had heard the ruckus and had come to watch the show. Finally, still holding the mule's hoof with one hand, Preacher bent down and retrieved the muddy rope with the other. He pitched it to Tick, who was the only one there with a solemn face.

Now that the mule had quit his fighting, Preacher did something that continued to surprise the crowd. He loosened his hold on the hoof but didn't let go. Instead, he slowly began to rub the mule's hind leg, all the while speaking in a kind and soothing voice. Finally, Preacher stepped to the animal's side and lowered the hoof to the ground. He didn't stop there, but ran his hand down the mule's leg and hip, gave his ears a good rub, then fed him a bit of peppermint candy he had in his pocket.

While the mule enjoyed the treat, Preacher turned to Tick Hobbs who had taken off his hat and was scratching his head, "Tick," he began, all humor forgotten. "I work for God, He's my Boss, and the job He has given me to do is minister to the mountain folk—any way I can. We all are in need of a helping hand, from time to time, so that's what I do. I never mind cutting fire wood or moving stock or hunting meat—but that help is temporary at best. It pleases God for me to do those things, but mostly He wants me to give the kind of help that lasts forever. So, after I've given earthly help I also give a heavenly message. God wants me to tell folks about Him, and about His son Jesus, and to teach from His Word—the Bible. Today, I hope I've helped you by teaching your mule not to be so quick to kick. Tomorrow, I'll tell you and anyone who wants to hear, about the kind of help and healing that only God can give." Preacher's blue eyes were unflinching as he stared at the little man, adding, "And Tick, I'll be sure to save you that front row seat."

While everyone watched Preacher walk away, they realized that the tension that had prevailed earlier was suddenly gone, and they weren't quite sure how that happened. Anger and gossip had buzzed around town like a tree full of honeybees. Now they all had something new to buzz about. The dramatic tale of how the preacher had stolen the prostitute was old news. The new story was now…how the minister had tamed the mule. Of course, there were additional jests as to who learned the greater lesson—the mule or Tick Hobbs?

Sunday morning came a bit too early for Quincy Long. It had always been his favorite day of the week, even more so when he became a preacher. However, on this particular Sunday, he wasn't ready—he still didn't know what The Boss wanted him to say. Nevertheless, all too soon, he found himself standing in the hotel lobby greeting the townsfolk as they arrived. Despite the entertainment he'd provided with the mule the day before, the greetings ranged from curiously friendly to silently disdainful as they took their seats in the dining room and lobby. Preacher was genuinely pleased when he saw Tick Hobbs strolling through the door. The little man slipped his hat from his head, revealing that his hair had been slicked down and combed away from a ruddy face that was quite nearly…clean. As promised, he took his seat on the front row.

Although these sermons were usually well attended, today the crowd was impressive. Every seat as well as every step on the wide staircase was occupied. There was even a rough looking group of men standing in the back. As Preacher maneuvered his way to a spot where everyone could see him, he silently sent up one last fervent plea: *Boss! I'm getting pretty worried here. What am I supposed to say? A little help right now sure would be appreciated!*

When he finally looked up, he noticed the black board with the dining room's menu for that day. Written in chalk it said simply GROUSE or RABBIT DINNER—2 BITS. A relieved smile spread across his face.

"Thanks Boss!" he muttered, then spoke loud enough for all to hear. "It's good to see you all today. As you know, I like to share adventures that come from my earthly father as well as my Heavenly Father. Just now I noticed that today's menu offers either grouse or rabbit, and that reminds me of one of the times when my father and I went hunting on one of the many English Moors."

There was a noticeable sigh from nearly every person in the room. They had expected this mighty man of God to storm into town, filled with righteous indignation and call down fire and brimstone. Some thought they deserved it, for what had been done to the young widow, while others had boasted that if that preacher started in on them—they were going to get up and walk out. Or—if the man wanted a fight, they'd be happy to give him one. However, when he calmly began one of his boyhood stories, they had been more than a little surprised and the truth be told—relieved! Preacher almost laughed when he noticed the sudden change in his congregation. Those who had been leaning back with their arms folded across their chest suddenly dropped them and sat forward to listen. Whether they believed in his God or not, Preacher was a man that could tell a good story, and if that's what he was about to do—no one wanted to miss a word!

"As most of you know, Caleb Long was the man that I was fortunate enough to call Father. He was a man of almost infinite energy, always had to be doing something. Whenever possible he included me in his never-ending activities and somehow he always managed to sneak in a lesson about life. He was an avid hunter and fisherman and he never went anywhere without wire for snares, a slingshot, hooks and line for fishing, and of course, a good rifle or shotgun. I'd ask, 'what's our quarry for today, Father?' His reply was always—'For whatever the good Lord provides, son.'"

"Whenever we sailed the North Sea, we almost always weighed anchor near one of the inland rivers between Whitby and Saltburn-by-the-Sea and from there we'd take a dory inland to one of the many Moors that lie in that region. The moors are a strange and beautiful kind of wilderness. On one such journey, Father and I happened upon a huge covey of grouse. Of course, we both were carrying our shotguns. In no time at all we had more that we could eat, and with me having the appetite of a growing young boy, that was saying a lot! My mouth was just watering at what a fine meal we were going to make of those fat grouse, when we came across two rabbits all tangled up in a dense and thorny thicket. Most of the time rabbits can get free of a natural snare and how they got in there and then couldn't get out was a puzzle, but they were in a mighty bad way when we found them. When we got closer to them, they fought and cried out something fierce. I asked Father if we were going to kill them and take them back to camp, along with the grouse."

Just then a nostalgic look came across Preacher's face and he paused for a moment, as if he were hearing his father's voice once again. "He just smiled that gentle smile, I remember so well and said, 'No, not today, son. As I've always told you, we hunt what God provides. Now, if God hadn't already given us plenty of grouse I'd say yes, we'll take those rabbits, and we'll thank God for providing them. However, today I don't think God provided the rabbits for us. On the contrary, today, I believe that God has provided us for the rabbits!'"

Pausing, Preacher smiled at the people seated around the hotel dining room, along the wall and sitting on the staircase. "I can still see that dear man tying his knife securely onto a long stick, then he handed it to me and said, "You be careful not to injure the rabbits while you cut through all those thorny branches to set them free." He wanted me to be the one to free them. After we watched those rabbits run away he turned to me and I can almost feel his hand squeezing my shoulder. 'Quin,' he asked, 'can you imagine yourself crying out for help and having folks just pass you by or take advantage of your misery?'" Preacher looked around the room and then said, "To tell you the truth, I had to think on that for a while. My parents had always been there for me. I had an awfully good life and I knew it. And yet, I had seen enough of the world to know that cruelty and betrayal were all too common. Then my father said, 'God tells us in His word that we should treat others as we want them to treat us. So, if you intend to be a man of honor and integrity, then whenever it's within your power to help someone, that's just what God would have you do!'"

Preacher's expression was thoughtful as he chewed on his lower lip and gazed out at the rugged mountain people that were spread around the room, "Many of you know that my father and mother drowned at sea, nearly seven years ago. It wasn't until a year later that I finally got around to asking God what he wanted me to do. And The God of the Universe, whom I now call The Boss, answered me. Not in a voice I could hear, but I heard his challenge in my heart. He was asking me, 'Quincy Long, since I've given you a heart for people in need, will you go up into the Mountains and when you come across someone who needs a friend—will you be that friend—for both of us? And wherever you go and whenever you can, I want you to take a moment and tell our new friends that I loved them so much that I let my Son die for them, that they might have everlasting life! Will you do that?'"

Feeling uncomfortable with the way this sermon was heading, one of the young miners that stood in the back called loudly, "I'm in need, Preacher. Iffen ya want to help me, then bring that pretty young blonde back to the saloon!" The man laughed and there were chuckles and a few coarse jeers came from some of his friends.

Before anyone could respond, including Preacher, Tick Hobbs got to his feet and glared at the man. "That'll be enough out of you, Gunner Davis. Preacher's givin' us a fine sermon today. A lot better than we deserved I reckon, so iffen ya don't cotton to it then find the door!" When Davis frowned but didn't leave, Tick nodded curtly then sat back down, "Go ahead on—Preacher, yer a doin' just fine!"

Quin was dumbfounded for a moment. He had been expecting Tick to be the one to do the heckling, so having this little man stand up for him was quite a shock. Still, he nodded his thanks then continued, "You know, we are like those rabbits from time to time. We get all tangled up in the sins of the world. We tell ourselves not to worry, that we can break free if we try hard enough, but the truth is, we can't get free! Not without God's help!"

Lifting his Bible, he gazed around the room, "This book is a letter from God to mankind. It explains how sin is a snare that leads to an eternal death, and how only Jesus dying on the cross made it possible for us to be forgiven and freed! There isn't a person in this room, including me, that has not sinned against God and who doesn't need Jesus to save them."

Preacher looked at the all the people gathered around him. "I stand before you, an imperfect man but Jesus took the punishment for my sins when He allowed Himself to be nailed to the cross. Are any of you ready to receive the gift God has provided for you? To admit that you're a sinner! To receive Christ as your Savior and begin a new and better life?"

"I am Preacher—I don't doubt that I'm a sinner!"

Everyone in the room seemed to hold their breath. Surely, it hadn't been Tick Hobbs who spoke! The man that had taunted Preacher the day before for being a 'know-it-all Bible thumper. Had it not been for Tick speaking out for him earlier, Preacher might have thought that possibly the man was baiting him. But Tick's sincerity was obvious for he was fighting tears.

Silvery rays of moonlight shone through the window, but that's not what kept Preacher from sleeping. He was amazed at the sermon that God Himself had preached and blessed that morning. He had longed to vent his anger at these people, put them in their place. But God just wanted to love them. Lives had been changed all day. Tick Hobbs had asked Christ into his heart and even more surprising, if that was possible, Sephora Castle had asked that Preacher pray for her. She hated her husband, but like Mariah, she had no family and had no other recourse but to accept the things her husband did. She would not and, more to the point could not leave her husband, even though she knew his behavior was deplorable. Others had also come to him throughout the day to ask for prayer. It had been one of the most moving days of Preacher's life as a minister.

Still exhilarated, sleep would not come. He rose from his bed and began pacing the floor as he prayed for God to give him wisdom as to what he could do for women like Sephora and Mariah—for Shotsy and Velvet—and a world full of others who suffered silently, for they were allowed no voice. Just then, as he gazed down from the second story window he saw two men talking behind the hotel. Preacher took his pocket watch from the bedside table. Three o'clock in the morning was an unlikely hour for a chance meeting.

Keeping to the shadows of his room, Preacher couldn't quite see the men's faces, even in the moonlight. The first man's muscular build was telling, but it was the star on his chest, confirming that it was Sheriff Jimmy Todd. It wouldn't be a surprise if this man was up to no good—but it was the other man that caused Preacher's blood to run cold. He wore dark clothing, and the long braid trailing down his back shone with the same white luster as the moon overhead. Instantly, he remembered Copper's description of the albino she feared. As he stood there hidden in the dark, a third man joined the first two, and Preacher thanked God for leading him to the window to see this gathering. The last man was none other than young Hank Wyatt, the teller at the bank. Seeing him with the others was a disappointment. Preacher had known Hank for five years—known him and had trusted him. Hank being included in this clandestine meeting suggested an obvious connection with the bank. Preacher could only guess at what this might mean, but he was determined to find out. And more importantly he had to warn Copper and Shad!

The three-hour ride to the McKenna cabin was usually a pleasant one, but Flint seemed to sense Preacher's growing anxiety. He pranced and crow hopped the whole way. Quin looked on Shad and Copper as his closest friends. It was seeing Mariah again that troubled him. The closer he got, the harder his heart pounded in his chest. It was a strange kind of blissful agony; he desperately wanted to see Mariah—and yet he dreaded it—almost as much.

"Lord, I've vowed to love her until the day I die, but will it always hurt this much? I want to watch over her—be near her, at least until she's settled and—married." Again, Preacher felt the familiar stab of pain whenever he thought of her with another man. "I'm sorry, Boss. This possessiveness and jealousy is inappropriate and sinful. You and I both know that it would be better for me to stay away but—I have to warn Copper and Shad. Help me please! I can't let her know how much I care. Can't let her think there might be a future for us. I'm not sure she'd even want that, but if she did, it would make things even more painful for both of us."

As he and Flint rode into the yard, the McKenna homestead looked quiet and deserted. When Remy didn't rush from the barn braying out her call of alarm and he saw no one else around, he heaved a long sigh of relief as he swung down from his saddle.

Even as he called out, "Hello in the cabin!" He silently prayed that they were all down at the river or off hunting herbs or snaring rabbits. Now he could simply leave a note. He'd warn them to be on guard and to stay away from Otter Run. He would apologize for leaving so quickly, but explain that there were others needing his help. As he mentally wrote the note and thanked God for this reprieve—he heard her voice. The effect her soft hon-eyed drawl had on him was so powerful—it nearly buckled his knees.

"Oh Quin, it's so good to see you!" Mariah hurried from the chicken pen, not even attempting to hide the joy she felt. So much had changed and she had so much to tell him.

The big man spun around and watched her hurrying towards him. She wore a simple dress of purple and white gingham. Her pale blonde hair was done up in a thick braid that fell over her shoulder and was tied with a matching ribbon. He didn't think it was possible, but somehow the woman had become even lovelier. There was something in her eyes, her face, a brightness and a serenity that he had never seen before. Silently, he begged God once again to help him mask his feelings and not allow her to suspect how much her nearness affected him.

As she approached him, he somehow managed to school his features. Tipping his hat and mumbled, "Good day—Missus Kent. I—uh—I've some important news for Copper and Shad. Where are they?" He flinched when he realized how distant and gruff he sounded, but what else was he to do?

Mariah's happy expression fell away; something was terribly wrong. He had gone back to calling her Missus Kent. He didn't smile or seem at all happy to see her. Immediately, she chided herself—the news must be very serious for him to act this way.

"Shad and Copper just went for a ride, but they'll be back soon." She assured him, as she studied his face, "You look so weary. I'll go put some coffee on while you put Flint in the barn. You can rest and keep me company while I start dinner."

Quin glanced about impatiently, searching the surrounding hills and valleys, hoping he would see the couple riding back. His forehead creased into a deep frown when he saw no sign of them. The very last thing he needed right now was to be alone with Mariah. Just then, she ducked her head and said shyly, "And—I have something important to tell you—before they return—it's about me and the Lord."

Although the man in love might have declined her invitation, the man of God could not do so. "All right, you go put on that pot of coffee—I'll be in as soon as I tend to Flint."

When Quin headed towards the barn, his horse refused to follow. Flint hadn't been allowed to greet Mariah, and it seemed the big horse was determined to do just that. He pulled against the reins as he stepped towards her. Then he bowed his neck and pressed his forehead against Mariah's arm.

"Oh, Flint, you dear old boy, have ya missed me?"

Watching the affectionate exchange between Mariah and Flint just added another layer of pain to this visit. His horse had always seemed a bit skittish around women. However, from the first time Mariah had climbed into the saddle, Flint had responded to her with an uncommon affection.

Suddenly, Quin grew impatient, and grunted, "Come on Flint." He gave the reins an insistent yank, then led him away.

Tears threatened as Mariah watched them walk towards the barn and she shook her head. *How should he act around you, Mariah? He's the finest man you've ever known but you're certainly not the finest woman he's ever known. You are just some poor woman he rescued from a saloon. He's always helpin' someone, and you shouldn't try to make more of his kindness than it was.*

When Quin finally entered the cabin and settled his tall frame onto a kitchen chair, he felt a hundred years old. It seemed that wrestling with yourself was exhausting. How could he look into Mariah's face, without her seeing what was in his heart?

Her first words were, "You seem very upset. Is the news you have for Shad and Copper that bad?"

Her observation didn't surprise him. Mariah always seemed to understand him. Giving her a half smile he said, "There is some cause for concern. Beyond that—I guess I'm just a bit tired, that's all."

Setting a cup of steaming coffee before him, Mariah backed away and wrung her hands. "You certainly have a right to be tired, you're a busy man. You—you also have a right to be upset—with me! That's what I wanted to talk to you about."

When Quin frowned and just stared at his cup, Mariah wondered if she had just imagined that there had been a special friendship between them. The man acted as if anywhere else in the world would have been preferable to sitting there with her. He looked completely miserable.

Still, she owed him the truth. Gingerly, she sat down across from him, and keeping her eyes downcast she began, "I lied to you—you and God both! When I prayed with you, it was a lie. I truly didn't see it as a falsehood at the time but—after a while I knew it and so did Copper." Just then, Mariah couldn't help but glance up and when she did, she didn't see the stranger that rode in earlier. Now Quin was once again the man she remembered, his expression gentle, his blue eyes filled with kindness. Feeling better, she continued, "Copper talked to me and I realized that I needed to pray again, but with complete sincerity, so I did! She told me that I would know the difference. And when I prayed the second time...I meant every word. Oh, Quin—I felt such a joy, it was truly amazing! And then, instead of punishing me, God gave me a special gift—a miracle really." Mariah suddenly stood and hurried to the corner of the room and picked up her zither. "Remember when you told me that both the zither and I were not ruined—only broken—and that broken things are often better for the mendin'? Look—just look—isn't it wonderful!"

Mariah sat the zither down on the table, and the man couldn't believe it was the same instrument. The original had been poorly made. Perhaps breaking it might have been the best thing that could have happened to it. For in the hands of a skilled craftsman, like Shad, the simple zither had been transformed into something extraordinary. He looked up into Mariah's expressive violet eyes. Yes, he could still see a shadow of pain, but now the woman also glowed with an inner peace he surely had not seen in her before. The Greatest Master Craftsman of all was even now restoring and healing her wounded soul!

"Oh, Mariah!" he breathed, as he took her hands in his, "I do see God in your eyes now. I'm so glad Shad fixed your zither—and it's wonderful but not nearly as wonderful or as beautiful or as precious as you!"

His tender words were like a fragrance that enveloped the air between them and they gazed at each other for a long while. It was as if they both knew that this was but a stolen moment—meant to be cherished. When Quin realized he was doing the very thing he had warned himself not to do, his look of adoration turned to one of irritation. Then he released her hands, turned away, and frowned.

Feeling thoroughly confused, Mariah stammered, "Would—you like for me to play something for you?"

Not waiting for a reply, Mariah gracefully stepped across the room, her skirts billowing out as she dropped to the floor before the fireplace and opened a small book of music. "I'll just play over here where the light is better," she explained, for she didn't want to look into Quin's eyes again.

Taking the beautiful little zither onto her lap Mariah began to play and sing. At first, she sounded nervous, even slightly off key. However, as she concentrated on the words that swirled through her mind then rolled over her tongue—she began to relax.

Preacher spun his chair around, straddling the seat as he curled his arms around the back. He listened attentively and when Mariah finally calmed down, he found her voice enchanting; and it seemed to grow stronger and more perfect with each note.

'Twas then a voice I heard,
It came in winning tone,
Across my night, from far away,
To where I prayed alone;
It told me of a love,
That sought me long ago,
And of the Cross my burden bore,
Of sin and guilt and woe.
O blessed Cross of Christ.
Thou has my need supplied;
For, there upon thine outstretched arms,
I see the Crucified;
And He has sin to bear,
That none can call His own;
O, Christ, the sin and guilt Thou bearest,
Are mine, are mine alone.

Her lavender eyes sparkled in the firelight and her song drew him in, for he could see that each word touched her deeply. Preacher was touched as well, by her honesty, her confession, and her song. It took courage for her to admit that she had not been sincere before, but he was convinced she was now—he could hear it in her voice and see it in her eyes. The last time he had been with this precious woman, she was heartbroken and fearful. Now, it was so plain to see that God's spirit of love and grace had begun to work its healing.

When Shad and Copper quietly came through the door, they happened upon a strangely—bittersweet scene. Mariah was concentrating on her playing while Quin was concentrating on Mariah. The big man was completely enamored with the woman before him. Yet, his dark expression was that of hopelessness, and heartbreak. The moment he realized the McKenna's were there…he immediately gave them his slow easy grin, and though his eyes still betrayed his sadness, he jumped to his feet to greet them.

"Well now. How are my favorite newlyweds?"

Shad and Copper struggled to keep the conversation lively all through dinner. It was necessary, because the other two at the table seemed to be suddenly stricken with shyness. Quin did finally speak up to thank Copper for the excellent meal, only to be reminded that Mariah had been doing almost all of the cooking. Naturally, he praised her instead but it troubled him, for now she'd be able to get a job as a cook—or what was more likely, remarry.

Frowning, the big man cleared his throat, he had after all come up here for a very important reason. "Well friends, I didn't want to spoil our dinner, but I'm afraid I'm going to have to end our evening with some unpleasant news." When everyone became still he turned to Copper, "I'm sure that I've seen the man you came up here to escape. I preached in Otter Run yesterday and early this morning about three a.m., I looked out my hotel window and saw some men meeting in the alley. One of the men was definitely an albino. He was dressed in black and had a long white braid. He was meeting with..." Giving Mariah an apologetic look, he added, "Sheriff Todd and the young bank teller, Hank Wyatt. Something is very wrong! Why would the town sheriff, a known outlaw and bank teller meet in a dark alley, at that unlikely hour, unless they were planning some kind of mischief? Quin's expression grew pained once again as he looked to Mariah, "Before I learned what kind of man Sheriff Todd was, I told him that I'd heard of an albino that had escaped from prison. I gave him the description you gave me, Copper, without mentioning you. I also told him there was probably a reward. The sheriff has a reputation for collecting rewards. While I was riding up here today, I remembered there have been some cattle rustled and three stagecoach robberies the past few years. I have no proof but I can't help but wonder if Todd isn't connected to them himself! If so, he might be enlisting the aid of this albino so he would have someone to blame for their next robbery! In each of the previous hold-ups, only small portions of the stolen money was found because in each case, the sheriff was only able to bring in one of the robbers. He brought them in all right—but every one of them—was dead! As I recall all three of those men had prices on their heads. If this Dirk Culley is smart, he'll hear about the sheriff's reputation and decide that these mountains are not good for his health!"

Just then, everyone's eyes turned to Copper. She was frowning and shaking her head. No one noticed, however, that Mariah looked even more miserable than Copper. Her stomach twisted, as memories of long ago filled her mind. Her voice sounded almost desperate when she turned to Copper and asked. "This man—the one you've been running from—are you sure—absolutely sure he's—an albino? He's not just fair-haired like me?"

A shiver of revulsion ran through Copper and she didn't even notice when tears sprang to Mariah's eyes as she answered her question. "Dirk Culley is definitely an albino! He's actually quite handsome but the man has no color at all—even his eyes are glassy and pale. The last time I saw him he had a long white braid down his back and so does the man Preacher saw. It has to be him! If he followed me up here, why hasn't he come for me? And why involve the sheriff and a bank teller? Those three are probably up to some kind of thievery, but I'm thinking that there's a good chance he may not even know I'm here—at least not yet!"

"Those are my thoughts too!" Shad added. "Those reprobates are plannin' some kind of chicanery. Could be a bank hold up but it might be anything. Still, if that man knew ya was here, I think, we'd have seen him by now."

As the men discussed the possibilities, the women both seemed to grow quiet, filled with their own thoughts. However, Copper could not sit still. Soon she found herself standing behind Shad's chair, her hands on his strong shoulders. Shad doubted that she even realized what she was doing, but she had sought him out to comfort her fears and make her feel safe. Pleased with her actions and eager to give her what she needed, he gently pulled her around so she could sit on his lap. Then he turned to look into Copper's anxious eyes and said, "Now, listen here darlin'—I don't want ya worryin'. I ain't gonna let anything happen to *my sweet girl!*"

"That's right, Copper." Mariah added as she stood and took her friends hand. "We three love you, Copper Delaney-McKenna. We all want what's best for you and—I think right now we should stop and ask God to watch over you and keep you safe—and give us all wisdom!"

All eyes suddenly turned towards Mariah. She was the newest Christian in the group, and yet she was the first to suggest prayer.

"You're absolutely right, Missus Kent." Preacher agreed, and Mariah winced at his words, he sounded so formal. It was obvious that Quin the man was somehow at odds with Preacher the minister. Believing that he was telling her he wanted only a formal relationship with her she decided that from then on, she would call him 'Pastor'. Not Preacher, as everyone else did, but not Quin either.

Since Copper was still on Shad's lap with their arms wrapped tightly around each other, Preacher and Mariah ended up standing on either side of the couple. Then without thinking, they both instantly clasped their hands, encircling their friends. Neither Quin nor Mariah looked at each other, but they both cleared their throats as a strong current of awareness flowed between them.

Finally, Preacher sucked in a calming breath, "Lord, there are a great many things that we don't understand. It's exceedingly clear that you brought Copper here to be with Shad. You answered both of their prayers. This new danger though is confusing to us. We come together now, as your children and we ask for your guidance as well as your protection over Copper."

"Over all of us, Lord!" Copper added, as she placed her hand on top of Mariah and Preacher's joined hands and then Shad put his hand on top.

"Yes, Lord." Preacher corrected, 'Over all of us, as we seek to know and obey your will." He paused for a moment and was surprised when he heard Mariah's soft voice.

"And Father, this man whom Copper fears—this albino man—and the others he's in cahoots with. Speak to their hearts too, Lord. Help them to know that there is always another way! They may be on an evil path right now, but help them to know that they do not have to stay on it. They can choose a better way—Your way! Please, speak to these men—soften their hearts, Lord. Please help them to know that You always provide a way to escape from the temptation to do what's wrong."

Chapter 20
A Special Day

"A time to weep and a time to laugh. A time to mourn and a time to dance." Ecclesiastes 3:3-4

Overnight, a sudden blizzard descended on the Rockies. The biting wind felt as sharp as a wolverine's teeth, and the snow was coming down so hard and fast it was impossible to see. To keep from getting lost in this white-out, Shad strung ropes from the cabin to the outhouse and barn and from the barn to the chicken and goat pens. It would be foolish to travel in such weather, so Quin was trapped at the McKenna's until it cleared.

Neither man could remember a storm that was as fierce as this one. It continued to rage against the mountains for two days and three nights. Finally, on the morning of the third day, a bright, golden sun split the horizon. It was as if the tempest had worn itself out and now a drowsy hush settled over the valley. Remy brayed out her morning call, followed by the exaggerated crow of the rooster. The competition to see which one of them should announce the sunrise, continued. Shad, always the first one up, chuckled at the odd duet. He squatted in front of the fireplace, adding fresh kindling and wood to the fire, while Preacher snored loudly, rolled tightly in a buffalo robe just a few feet away. The blizzard was so cold and severe that they decided to be frugal with the firewood and heat only the main cabin. The women were given the bed to sleep in while the men had taken the floor.

As was her habit, Copper hurried to the kitchen when she heard Shad stoking the morning fire. Once again, she had woken with a sour stomach. While she put the coffee on to boil she nibbled on a dry biscuit. Preacher too began to stir but stayed where he was, giving the newlyweds a bit of privacy as Shad moved to join his wife in the kitchen.

"Mornin' sweet girl." He mumbled, his sleepy voice sounding deep and scratchy as he pulled his young wife into his arms. "Sure have missed ya these past few nights, darlin'."

"I've missed you too, and I—umfph…" Copper's words were stopped abruptly, for Shad refused to wait a moment longer for his first kiss of the day.

Preacher smiled to himself. He couldn't be more pleased. These two were indeed meant for a double harness. Then his rebellious thoughts instantly turned to Mariah. She had certainly changed from the quiet and sad woman he had left here such a short time ago. Now, she fairly glowed with an inner peace that exceeded his prayers and hopes. The change in her had been more dramatic and pronounced than any he had ever seen before. Her requesting that they pray together that first night had impressed him. Then, when he heard her praying for those who sought to do them evil—well—he knew that she truly was embracing a sincere walk with Christ. Mariah was becoming a devoted Christian woman. The kind his mother had always told him to look for—in a wife.

As the aroma of coffee brewing filled the cabin, Preacher decided he'd given the couple enough time to themselves. Laying there and thinking of Mariah was not good for his peace of mind. He stretched as he sat up and rubbed his face. Even as he ordered himself not to, he glanced towards the big bed in the corner. The soft pile of blankets moved and he heard her yawning. He knew in another minute, she'd sit up. Her glorious pale hair would be all tousled and it would fall in a mass of waves around her face and shoulders.

Standing abruptly, Preacher muttered as he headed for the door, "Well—the storms finally gone. Think I'll uh—I'll just head out and feed the stock."

Shad chuckled and shook his head, "Thanks Preacher, but ya might wanna pull yer boots and coat on first—might be a tad chilly out there!" When Preacher gave him a look that said, D*o you really want to tease me before I've had my coffee?* Shad laughed again, then added, "Tell ya what Pard, if you feed the stock I'll bring in more wood for the fire. Then tonight I'll feed and you take care of the firewood." When Preacher grunted his acceptance of the exchange of chores, Shad gave Copper another quick kiss then headed towards the door where both men shrugged into their boots and heavy coats. Winter had definitely settled in the high-country. Even though the sun was shining and the wind wasn't howling, it was still bitterly cold!

Later as the four were finishing their breakfast, Shad slurped down the last drop of coffee from his cup, then looked about the table with an infectious grin. Turning towards Copper he took her hand in his. "I've just had me an idea. Missus McKenna, we've been cooped up in this cabin for days—but the storm's finally gone. It's cold, but it's beautiful out there now. The sun is shining to beat the band, and it's makin' the snow look like a million diamonds have been spread out across the valley. They're all sparklin' just for you! In fact, it's a perfect day for sliding down Wolverine Hill. What do you say, sweet girl? I'm thinkin' that you probably haven't had much playtime. Bet you've never spent even one whole day just playin' in the snow—have ya?"

Copper gave her husband a sweet but skeptical look, "Play time? That was a dirty word to my father. I used to watch the other children sliding and skating but—well—don't we have work to do today?"

"Now—see that's what I'm talking about! There is a time fer work and there is a time fer—PLAY! Ain't that right, Preacher?"

When Quin suddenly found himself included in the conversation, he washed his last bite of biscuit down with the last of his coffee. "That's right—there's a time for every season." He added with a grin of his own. He knew Shad was right about Copper having a life filled with work. Then his gaze turned to Mariah. Her life had been easier but not much happier. He, on the other hand, had enjoyed a happy childhood, filled with glorious winter days sliding down hills and skating on the ice. Turning to Mariah, he asked, "What about you, Missus Kent? Growing up in Texas, I doubt you've had much opportunity to play in the snow. Is that right?"

Mariah's violet eyes suddenly sparkled at the idea of snow and fun. "No indeed! And my father was not one for frivolity either. We do sometimes have snow in central Texas, but not very much of it. One winter storm I remember brought a lot of snow. My brother, Ladd and I made a small snow castle, like a picture we'd seen in a book." Just then, her smile suddenly faded. "It didn't last long. When my father saw us he rode his horse over it—needless to say—we didn't try that again." She tried to make it sound amusing, but when everyone frowned, she quickly added, "But I've always thought snow was beautiful!"

It was obvious that Copper and Mariah hadn't had much joy in their lives, and suddenly it became very important for Shad and Quin to give these women some happy winter memories.

Preacher started to say something, but just then, Copper's handmade calendar caught his eye. "I don't believe it. Do any of you know what day this is? I can't imagine how I almost missed it, but with everything that's happened and then the storm—well—I don't know where my mind's been." Again, he asked, "Do you three realize that today is December twenty-fifth?"

Copper and Mariah shrugged at each other and then turned back to him with blank stares. It was just another day to both of them.

Then Shad began to smile, "Well I'll be. It's Christmas Day—ain't it! Ma and I always celebrated Christmas, but I'm ashamed to say I haven't given it a thought since she died."

Preacher's eyes grew bright as he looked at his three friends and boldly announced, "Well, it's Christ's Birthday and I'm for celebrating it—and I think we should start right now!"

"I'm for it Preacher!" Shad agreed then asked, "What should we do first?"

"Well, I guess we could start with a Christmas tree."

"I know just the one, Preacher!"

Quin turned to the women whose eyes were suddenly bright with anticipation, "Ladies, while we men cut down the tree, could you gather up some lengths of yarn or fabric? Anything we can tie on the tree to make it look festive and colorful. Maybe you could bake up some special treats for our celebration. Once we've got the tree up and decorated we'll all head to Wolverine Hill to play in the snow. This evening we'll share a nice meal, and then we can read the Christmas story from the Bible and sing carols. Would you like that?"

When everyone looked at him with eyes sparkling, Preacher laughed, "It's settled then…Happy Birthday Boss. And Merry Christmas everyone!"

That afternoon as they climbed Wolverine Hill, they breathed out plumes of white vapor into the air. Their words and laughter forming wreaths about their heads. When Shad pointed out the best spot for sliding, it was decided that he and Copper would go first. Copper couldn't help but giggle when her big mountain man plopped down on a shovel turned backwards with the handle between his legs, then he grinned up at her, looking exactly like a happy little boy.

"Come on sweet girl," he laughed. "Best way in the world to slide down a hill. Done it like this all m' life!"

Smiling at the comical picture her bear-like husband made, Copper sat down on her own shovel; her cheeks were sore from grinning so much, "Oh Shad, I just love today. You are the most adorable man!"

Shad's eyebrows swooped into a frown, even as he slipped his hand behind Copper's neck and pulled her close for a quick but thorough kiss, then he growled, "Reckon I'll let *you* get away with that kind o' talk, but I'll thank you not to call me 'adorable' in front of anyone else. Not Preacher and especially not Black-Eyed Jack! I'd never hear the end of it. Then he gave her a wink and said, "Now, lean back and hold onto that handle real tight and on the count of three, we'll both push off."

Copper nodded, but she didn't wait for him to count, instead she gave a good, hard push and…off she went. Then she squealed as she sailed down the hill. The shovel was a grand sled, and the world seemed to whoosh by as she heard everyone's laughter while she screamed and giggled the whole way down.

Shad was right behind her laughing and calling out. "Hold on tight—you little cheater—don't want ya fallen off that thing!"

Mariah frowned when she heard Shad's warning. The thought that sliding down a hill could possibly end with someone getting hurt hadn't crossed her mind—not until that moment.

When Copper reached the bottom of the hill, she jumped up and her shovel went sliding off into a stand of trees. Shad was right behind her and he bounded to his feet, laughing as he pulled Copper into a bear hug. He was so pleased that his hard working little wife was enjoying herself. When he left her to retrieve the runaway shovel, Mariah hurried over and whispered something into Copper's ear.

As Shad came walking back with both shovels, he handed them over to Quin then huffed, "All right now, you and Mariah are next."

The men wondered what the girls were up to when they found them staring oddly at each other. Deciding not to question them, Quin stepped towards Mariah and offered his arm. "Now, let's see if we can make it down that hill faster than they did—without falling off!" When the women once again exchanged glances, He thought Mariah might be afraid. "Just hang on tight—you'll be fine!"

Mariah clung to Quin's arm as they climbed the steep hill. He tried to hide his sudden intake of air as he felt her small hand resting on his arm. Even through the bear skin coat, somehow, he felt her touch. Her warmth went all the way down to his boots.

When they reached the top of the hill, the view was so magnificent, Mariah gasped, "I had no idea you could see so far from up here. The peaks and the valleys just go on and on—it's like an entirely different world. The sunlight reflecting off the snow makes everything glisten—like polished pearls in a thousand shades of white!"

"That's a beautiful description of it." Quin sighed, as he shared the view with the woman he loved, knowing that he could stand there and listen to her honeyed drawl and sweet words until he froze solid. Her cheeks were rosy and her eyes bright with—he didn't want to ponder what her eyes might be telling him. All he knew just then was that everything about this woman was enchanting and he couldn't help but wish for things that could never be. Sighing again he said, "Well, are you ready to slide?"

"No…not just yet. Let's wait a while longer." Though she still rested her fingers on his sleeve, she kept her eyes fixed on Copper and Shad. When Quin started to protest she added, "Something important is happening down there—let's not intrude."

Copper had taken Shad by the hand and was pulling him away from the bottom of the hill. "Why don't we let Preacher and Mariah slide, I think I'd rather build a snow man. Will you help me?"

"Hold on there, sweet girl. I saw how much you loved sliding down that hill. We can all take turns. And we can make a snowman too, if ya like."

Copper was suddenly feeling shy but her green eyes were shimmering. "I really don't feel like sliding. I probably never should have gone down that hill at all. But I didn't think about it being unwise until Mariah said something."

"What did she say?" Shad went from smiling to frowning in an instant. "Darlin—what's wrong? I have noticed ya've been a bit off your feed lately. Thought it was worry over Mariah."

"You noticed that? You do love me—don't you?" She threw her arms around Shad and hugged him tight. "I'm fine—or at least—I will be. It's just that Mariah's a little older than I am; she knows things that I don't. And the truth is I really haven't felt very well for a few weeks now, but…"

"Enough—I'm takin' you back to the cabin—right now! Why didn't ya say something? Ya shouldn't have let your feather brained husband drag you out here in the first place." Shad lifted her into his arms and headed for the cabin.

"Hey—put me down—I'm not sick." Copper scolded. Shad didn't put her down but he did stop when she cradled his face in her hands and kissed him. When she finally pulled away from him she insisted, "Now, will you please listen to me? It's just that Mariah and I figured some things out this morning. And just now she reminded me of—well—of what we discussed." Suddenly, a radiant smile covered Copper's face, "You are a handsome man Shadrach McKenna, and your eyes are as green as the forest—do you know that? I have green eyes too. I suppose you've noticed?"

"Yeah, I've noticed that we both have green eyes. So, what's that got to do with slidin' down the hill? Or you not feelin' well?"

"Actually, this playing in the snow got me thinking about children. I've always assumed that ours will have green eyes but we won't know if they'll have black hair or red. And this morning, Mariah helped me figure it out."

"Girl, you're worryin' me and you're talking crazy. How could Mariah figure out what our children will look like? That doesn't even make any sense."

Giving her husband another quick kiss, she explained, "Mariah told me that we'll know what our child will look like, come late summer. We'll know because by then our baby will be in our arms and we can just look at him…or her," she quickly added.

When Shad's eyes went wide, Copper nodded, "Late summer, Shad! That's when we'll be welcoming little baby McKenna into our home. If it's a girl, I'd like to call her Summer McKenna. What would you like to call our baby—if it's a boy?"

"If our baby is a boy?" Shad asked…then he laughed, "OUR BABY! Well ain't that somethin'!"

Preacher and Mariah watched from the hill above as the couple embraced. That was a common enough sight, for those two were always stealing kisses or at least holding hands. Quin glanced down at Mariah and noticed that her hands were clasped together, a joyful smile spreading across her face, while a tear slipped down her cheek. Then he returned his gaze to the couple below, just in time to see Shad toss his hat into the air. His grin spread from ear to ear as he hollered at the top of his lungs: "We're havin' a baby! I'm takin' this little Mama back to the cabin. You two take yer time and enjoy yourselves!"

For many reasons, none of them would ever forget this Christmas. Preacher's gift to everyone was a package of powdered chocolate and four peppermint sticks. The men had secretly cut candles into small lengths and after the sun set on Christmas Day, they insisted that the ladies both turn their backs and hide their eyes while they fixed the small candle stubs onto the boughs with melted wax, then lit each wick with care.

Once the lanterns were extinguished, the men called out in unison, "All right ladies, Merry Christmas!"

When Copper and Mariah saw the tree they exclaimed in delight. It was just a small tree—but it was lovely. Both men had been so pleased to do something special for these women. And when they saw their eyes filled with joyful tears, a quiet and holy reverence seemed to settle over the small cabin and upon everyone in it. Preacher stood near the tree and opened his Bible to the first chapter of Luke, and read of the events that prepared the way for the very first Christmas:

"The angel Gabriel was sent from God. And the angel said to her, 'Do not be afraid, Mary; for you have found favor with God. And behold, you will conceive in your womb and bear a son, and you shall name Him Jesus.'"

Although, both Copper and Mariah had read the story since becoming Christian's, the retelling of Mary's plight pricked their hearts. Copper thought of the young girl as she touched her own flat stomach. She marveled that now she too would be experiencing the miracle of life blooming within her. Mariah, on the other hand, felt an understanding for Mary's suffering. Surely, there were those who thought her a fallen woman. Most people would not have believed that the child she carried was a holy child. Mary had truly suffered, even from the first and then thirty-three years later to watch her perfect Son die such a cruel death. And yet it was for a greater good—as it happened, it was for the good of the whole world+!

Later that evening the four of them sat around the fire sipping hot chocolate and singing Christmas carols that Shad and Preacher had known from childhood. The Christmas tree had been a wondrous sight, but the gift they all shared was the knowledge that the Christ Child did not stay a baby in a manger but grew to be the Messiah, the giver of life, the eternal light of the world. A light that would never leave them!

Chapter 21
Water of Life

"For the Lamb on the throne will be their Shepherd. He will lead them to springs of life-giving water." Revelations 7:17

Preacher stepped through the cabin door holding a large pot filled with fresh meat. He instantly locked eyes with Mariah and shivered, "It is mighty cold out there. If you'll just take this off my hands for a moment, I'll pull my coat and boots off. Then I'll carry it to the kitchen for you."

Hurrying towards him, Mariah took the pan from his outstretched arms. "I'm so thankful you were able to shoot a porcupine. It seems unlikely, but we've tried just about everything else. According to Shad, his mama swore that was the only food she could keep down when she was with child. All we can do is hope and pray that Copper and baby McKenna like it too."

Quin sighed in agreement as he quickly pulled off his boots, then he stood and took the pot from Mariah and followed her to the kitchen. As they passed the big bed they both nodded to Shad as he sat beside his wife, his face pinched with worry. Copper hadn't been able to sit up without retching since the day after Christmas. The poor little thing seemed to be wasting away. Night and day, Shad sat in a chair beside her, trying to think of things that might soothe her, but nothing seemed to help!

Setting the pot down on the stove Quin whispered the question that had troubled them all for nearly a week. "Has there been any improvement at all, while I was out hunting?"

Glancing towards Copper, Mariah shook her head, "Three days ago she had a sip of tea and a tiny nibble of toast. Since then she hasn't kept anything down. I know she seems like such a hardy girl, but she's not taking in enough nourishment to keep her own body healthy, let alone a growing babe. I've tried mint tea, ginger tea, chicken broth…everything I can think of that might set easy on her stomach—but nothing will stay down." Tears of worry filled Mariah's eyes and she stared at her hands, "Pastor—early this morning when Copper and I were alone, she told me that she fears losing the baby. But—I'm afraid that if she stays like this much longer—we'll lose them both!"

The big man frowned and shook his head, "There's one more thing we can try. When I was out hunting, I remembered something I hadn't thought of for years, but it might help her. My first year here in the mountains, I stopped to help two miners that were traveling up Ute Pass. They'd come down with some sort of stomach ailment, they were both severely dehydrated and I feared the worst. One night a Ute brave just rode into camp. He said his name was Katori and that he was the son of a medicine man. He handed me a buffalo bladder, and told me it was filled with healing water from the spring of the Great Spirit and that I was to give them a drop at a time, then a spoonful and then a cup. I did as he said and they began improving almost immediately. Katori and I became friends, and eventually he told me that he had taken that water from the Manitou Spring. Later I remembered reading about these springs in one of my favorite books *Life in the Far West* written by George Fredrick Ruxton. The spring is at the base of Ute Pass. I have friends that live in a nearby settlement and they too believe this water has healing properties. I've never heard of it helping with morning sickness but it's worth a try! I'll head down the pass at daybreak. The snow is still too deep to ride so I'll have to go on foot."

"Oh Pastor, it's so cold and that's such a long way!" Then Mariah's glance fell on the small form in the big bed and sighed, "Still, that water may be Copper and the baby's only hope. You will be very careful—won't you?"

Although it warmed his heart to see her concern, he still didn't want her to worry. "I'm always careful, but you must remember, helping folks is what The Boss has called me to do. I'll be all right! Downhill will be the easy part, coming back up will be more challenging but," he grinned, "I'm not nearly as fragile as I look you know."

The big man looked anything but fragile and his smile only grew when Mariah rolled her eyes. "I should be able to make it there and back in two days. Of course, I would appreciate your praying for me and pray especially that this water has what both of them need."

Mariah turned her sweet face up to his, "You know very well that I'll be praying over every step you take!"

At that moment, the current of awareness that bound them together was impossible to deny. It was almost as if they shared an unspoken dialogue, flowing between them, from one heart to the other. Had things been different they could have shared all the joys that come from finding your kindred spirit. There could have been a loving marriage—children—a lifetime of sharing the challenges of life and the pleasures and passions of lovers. They each held separate reasons, however, why a union between them was not meant to be. Preacher knew that he would always be in love with Mariah, but believed that the success of his ministry depended on his remaining single. Mariah loved Quin with all her heart, but believed that the wife of a man of God must be pure and untainted. After what happened to her, she couldn't see herself being anyone's wife—but especially not—Missus Quincy Long.

In the midst of Mariah's prayers for Quin as he journeyed down the mountain, she once again relived Christmas day. They had laughed and played in the snow like two happy children. They reveled in each other's company. It was almost as if they were a courting couple, with a world of possibilities ahead of them. Shad and Copper had been so happy and so in love that joy-filled day. It had felt as if romance sparkled all around them just like the snow that sparkled in the sun. It had been the most wonderful day of Mariah's life. Just one treasured day spent with Quin. Seeing his kind smile, hearing his deep voice, holding his hand as they walked up Wolverine Hill. It had been a magical day, and for a precious few hours, it was just Quin and Mariah—not Pastor Long and Missus Kent. They forgot about who and what they were while they basked in the warmth of each other's company. For that one perfect day, they put aside all the reasons why their being together—could never be.

Preacher stopped and stared up at the night sky. "Thanks Boss! That full moon tonight sure has been a blessing," he sighed, as he wearily made his way through the shadowy forest. Strips of moonlight shone brightly between the trees as he stepped from darkness into light, then back into darkness again.

He began his journey early that morning—even before Remy had brayed out her morning call, and downhill or not, it had been a long, hard day! His snowshoes and long legs gave him an advantage, but he was wise enough not to hurry to the point of sweating. Damp clothing could easily freeze to your skin, even under a heavy coat. Such carelessness had caused many a tenderfoot to freeze to death. Still, it was always the last few miles of any journey that seemed the hardest, and the big man had to encourage his weary body to keep moving. "Come on you lazy dog—" he grunted. "You must be getting old, Quincy Long. Walking down a mountain in snowshoes didn't used to bother you this much!"

When he finally saw the first lights shining from the humble settlement, Quin let out a long sigh of relief, "Well, now if that isn't a welcome sight." His warm breath formed a white plume that billowed about his face as he continued to walk, and he promised his tired body that the next time he had to travel this far, he'd let his energetic horse do the walking. The combination of moonlight forming dark and light shadows in the snow, the constant rhythmic swoosh—crunch, swoosh—crunch of his snowshoes, along with the whispering hush of the pine forest, all seemed to be doing their best to lull him to sleep. Of course, he knew that could easily prove fatal.

He knew the first leg of his journey was nearly over when he was able to fill his lungs with the friendly aroma of wood smoke that curled upwards from a dozen chimneys. The first thing he needed to do was locate the spring. After that, he promised himself that he would build a fire, make a shelter and brew up some hot coffee. Mariah had filled his pack with a number of porcupine sandwiches. Copper had not been able to tolerate Maudy McKenna's favorite meat any better than anything else they'd tried. It seemed that this special water might very well be her last hope. His plan was to get a few hours rest. Then even before dawn had time to chase all the stars from the sky, he would fill his water bags and head back up that mountain. He fully intended for this to be the quickest trip he'd ever made!

The well he would draw from was filled with water from the Manitou Spring. Manitou being the Algonquin name for The Great Spirit. Katori had explained that many tribes believed that The Great Spirit had given these waters healing power! Medicine water they called it. When he found the well, Preacher leaned over it and sniffed, his nostrils filled with a slightly metallic bite. *This has to be it,* he thought, as he turned the handle that brought up a full bucket of water. Dipping his hand in, he put it to his lips and it was so cold it burned, and he frowned at the strange taste. After Katori told him of this mineral spring, he had also met a geologist. He too had sworn that the water had saved his life! The man had explained that these mineral springs rise up from aquifers fed by rainwater and snowmelt that rush down from the mountains, like the mighty Pikes Peak. While passing through deep underground rock caverns, the water absorbs high concentrations of minerals, like limestone and dolomite. The flavor is often different each year depending on the intensity of the iron, sulphur or soda in the water.

"Brother Long—Quin—wake up son—wake up!" Preacher heard the familiar voice as if it were coming from a great distance and then someone was shaking him by the shoulder and slapping his face.

"What?" Preacher struggled to open his eyes, and when he did, he looked up into the concerned face of his old friend, Reverend John Haze. Embarrassed by his own foolishness, he groaned, "John? Oh, don't tell me I allowed myself to fall asleep! Of all the greenhorn things I've ever done. Friend, I think you might have just saved my life!"

Instantly, Preacher tried to get to his feet but the cold had seeped into his bones and he struggled to stand up straight. He had all but raced down the mountain, forcing his long legs to cover the miles down the pass in record time. Once he had located the well, he remembered sitting down, intending only to rest for a brief moment while he scanned his surroundings for a likely spot to build a fire and shelter. He knew he was awfully tired, but he hadn't realized the toll his hurried pace and the cold had taken on his normally strong body.

"Son, what in the world are ya doing out here on a freezing cold night like this?"

Quin stopped for a moment to clear his thoughts, "Well…I couldn't wait for better weather, John. There's a sick woman up there. She and the baby she carries aren't going to make it if she doesn't start keeping her food down. I'm praying this special mineral water will help her." Preacher ran his hand over his face and grimaced, "I still can't get over my foolishness. I know better than to sit and rest before I build a fire and shelter. Guess I just didn't realize how tired I was." Preacher suddenly stopped and asked the older man, "Now you know why I'm out here. But—I can't imagine what you're doing out walking this late on such a cold night!"

John chuckled, and clouds of white floated in the air around him as he laid his weathered hand on Quin's strong shoulder. "Need you ask? 'Our Boss' sent me, of course! Willy and I always pray before turning in for the night and we both sensed that someone was out here, needing our help! She's back at the house heatin' up some squirrel stew while I came to find out who was supposed to eat it—and—here you are!" The older man's wrinkled face lifted in a gentle smile, "Son, yer the care-giver for a lot of people, but tonight, I reckon the good Lord's given me and Willy the privilege of takin' care of you! That woman will be tickled pink when she sees who I've brought home! She'll go to fussin' over ya and she'll love every minute. Tonight boy, yer gonna fill yer belly and sleep in a feather bed. We promise to wake ya up long before daybreak, fill ya up on flapjacks, bacon and prayer—then we'll send ya on yer way!"

Preacher gazed down at the older man while he rubbed his bewhiskered jaw, then he gave his friend a wide grin, "Willy's stew and a featherbed you say? I'd be a fool to turn that down—thank you friend!"

Wilhelmina Haze was as good as her husband's word. Her sweet godly spirit always reminded Quin of his own mother and he grinned indulgently as the little woman pushed him into a kitchen chair and placed a steaming bowl of stew before him. As he breathed in its warmth and rich aroma, then closed his eyes to pray, Willy placed her small wrinkled hand over his and prayed for him.

"Sweet Heavenly Father," she began, her kind voice, both confident and gentle. "You know this good man and we ask that you bless his errand of mercy. We thank you so much for lighting his way with the full moon tonight and for giving him the strength to make it all the way down that snow packed trail in one day! John and I give you our special thanks for telling us that Quin needed our help tonight. He's always taking care of folks and we feel blessed that You called on us to take care of him. You never cease to amaze and delight us with your goodness, Lord! And we know that at this moment you have that precious young woman, Copper McKenna and her child, safe in your mighty hands. Please, wrap Your loving arms around and about them, and around those who are caring for them, too!"

Preacher found it hard to swallow as Wilhelmina finished her prayer, and then placed a motherly kiss on his forehead, exactly as his own mother would have done.

Nodding his thanks to the sweet little woman, he picked up his glass of milk to wash down the lump in his throat. If ever there was a woman after God's own heart, it had to be Wilhelmina Haze! She was the perfect Pastor's wife, with an almost profound trust and faith in God. Preacher was always ministering to others but his Heavenly Father knew that just then, he was the one in need—and God in His great wisdom had provided John and Willy! At that moment, Preacher began to relax—truly relax. Of course, it was confirmation of something he already knew. That God had been watching over him, and even as he sat here in this warm kitchen, He was watching over them all!

Quin hadn't realized just how hungry he was until he had finished off three bowls of the dark flavorful stew. Afterwards he was ushered to the spare room where, as promised, a lush featherbed awaited him. From the day he had rescued Mariah Kent from the Long Shot Saloon, he hadn't slept well, but that night—he slept! And, just as promised John woke him even before the first hint of light shone in the east. When he made his way to the kitchen, Willy greeted him warmly and set two plates before him: one stacked high with golden flapjacks all drizzled with melted butter and hot syrup and the other was covered with thick strips of crisp bacon.

After another sweet prayer time with all three of them praying, the big man pressed a sonly kiss to Willy's forehead, just as she had done for him the night before. The tender gesture touched the little woman. A bit flustered, she turned towards the kitchen muttering, "Well, you get back up that mountain and I best be getting back to my own work. If I don't get to those sticky dishes soon, I'll have to use a hammer and a chisel on them!"

Before his wife could hurry to the kitchen, John stopped her and kissed her on the cheek then quickly shrugged into his own coat, muttering, "I need some air, Willy dear. Besides I want to make sure Quin finds his way back to the mineral spring."

The two men walked in silence for a short while until finally, John stopped and turned to Quin, "Son, Willy and I have known ya since ya first came to these mountains. Ya do a good job of covering it, but we've never seen ya so troubled." John drew an envelope from his coat and tucked it into Quin's pocket, "Just a few words I hoped might be helpful. For some time later when ya have a moment to think and…" John's words trailed off as they walked along together, then he suddenly added, "We know yer concerned for the McKenna woman—but she's not what has you weighed down. Willy and I prayed half the night for ya, boy! We asked that if God had some wisdom for us to share…that he'd give us both the same message by morning." John handed Quin two scraps of paper. "When we woke up this morning we both wrote down what God had placed on our hearts. When we saw that we'd both written the same scripture we felt sure God meant for us to share it with ya!"

Quin glanced down, and though it was dark, there was just enough moonlight to make out the words. The slips of paper had different writing but they both said, "*Go and learn what this means: I desire mercy and not sacrifice." Matthew 9:13*

A muscle jerked in Quin's jaw and he frowned down at the two scraps of paper, then nodded as he slipped them into his pocket. "You and that Willy of yours—you're quite a pair. Of course, you're right! I am weighed down as you call it. I think I'm going through a time of testing. John, I've come to a fork in the road and I don't know which way The Boss wants me to go. Don't have time to tell you much, but I've fallen deeply in love with the most amazing woman! But my ministry up in those mountains is rough and often very dangerous. My only choices are to give her up or give up the work I know God has called me to do! If The Boss doesn't want sacrifice, I afraid I still don't know what He wants of me. Either way requires the biggest sacrifices I've ever made in my life!"

John clamped his hand on Quin's shoulder, "God does present us with some pretty big challenges. Kind o' makes me wonder—have ya considered that there might just be a third fork in in that road? One ya haven't thought of yet. We'll pray that God gives ya clear direction. I think—when the snow melts off the pass and the stage makes its next run, Willy and I will come for a visit. We'll bring along more water and we can have us a good long talk. It so happens that we've both been feeling that our church here needs a younger man at the helm. More and more we've been feeling that we're supposed to come and help you with your ministry in the mountains." John grinned when the younger man raised his eyebrows, "The Bible never talks about us old folks retiring son, He might adjust our workload a bit, but He never tells us to stop serving Him!"

Quin laughed, "No sir, I can't imagine you or Willy retiring from God's work, and there's certainly a need for you two in the high-country. You both are very dear to me. I look forward to seeing you again, soon!"

When they reached the spring, Quin filled a buffalo bladder and two canteens with water. John continued to walk with him until they reached the edge of the forest, where they embraced as if they were father and son.

Quin headed up the path at a quick pace his snowshoes kicking up the white powdery snow as John called after him, "God's speed son! Know that we'll be praying for you—all of you!"

Copper was so weak she could barely open her mouth when Shad placed the first droplets of mineral water on her parched tongue. "Now, we're gonna start slow, sweet girl," he crooned. "Just one drop at a time, and then Lord willing one spoonful and then one cup." Once again, the mountain man was showing his young wife the gentle touch of a gentle man.

It was such a tender scene that Quin and Mariah couldn't help but be transfixed by it as they watched from the front door. Actually, Quin was still a bit stunned by the way Shad had welcomed him into the cabin. The burly, mountain man had rushed to the door, pounded Preacher on the back at least a half a dozen times then grabbed the man's big hand and pumped it vigorously. "Thank the good Lord above that you're back and thank ya fer doin' this!" he sighed, as he wrestled the water from Preacher's shoulder and hurried back to Copper!

Mariah's greeting also left Quin a bit off-balance and it warmed him from head to toe. For when Shad hurried away, Mariah took his place. She looked as if she was about to throw herself into his arms, when she suddenly stopped in mid-stride. Turning a lovely shade of pink, she smiled up at him with such a look of adoration and relief in her violet eyes that he almost felt as if she had embraced him. For a long moment, they simply stared at each other. The familiar spark of awareness was there as always, as if their hearts were communing, because words were not allowed. Even so, they could not hold back their smiles, for being together was a pleasure they found nowhere else.

Mariah was the first to turn away on the pretense of fetching the returning hero a cup of hot coffee. Quin watched her feeling more confused than ever. The two pieces of paper along with John's letter lay heavily in his pocket. He had prayed for direction and now he wondered if God had indeed answered him—by way of these two dear saints! Was the Boss saying that He would bless a union with Mariah? If so, did it mean his ministry was over? Could it possibly be that Mariah was being called to minister with him? After what had happened to her, would a congregation accept her or reject her? Was there a third fork in the road, as John had mentioned? It still felt as if he had more questions than answers.

While she fussed with the coffee, Mariah closed her eyes and silently thanked God that Pastor Long, as she must now and forevermore think of him, was back safe and well. She harbored no illusions of hope and a future. It was blessing enough just to watch this dear man shed his heavy pack and frozen boots, then hand him a steaming cup of coffee.

"I'm so glad you're back, Pastor! I prayed hard, just as I promised I would. It sounds silly but I even asked that God would give you wings!" She smiled shyly, her eyes downcast, "I think He must have for you got back so quickly."

Sipping the hot brew the big man sighed with pleasure, "Mmmm, you make the best coffee—it even tasted good to me cold in my canteen." He grinned when Mariah flushed at his compliment. "I sure thank you for your prayers. It was quite a trek, but never have I felt that I was being prayed for more than I have in the past two days. The Boss certainly heard you! I probably shouldn't tell you this and I'm ashamed of it myself but I fell asleep at the well." Quin couldn't help but smile when Mariah gasped, but he quickly went on, "Like I said, God heard your prayers. I awoke with one of my dearest friends giving me a hard-shake. He said that God sent him out to help me. He and his wife treated me like the prodigal son and even gave me a featherbed to sleep in. I felt so good when I woke up this morning, that climbing back up this mountain seemed easy—just as if—I had those wings you requested!" Suddenly Preacher looked into Mariah's lovely eyes as he whispered, "I—I really could feel your prayers—just like you promised: every minute—every step!"

As if an invisible cord was pulling them together, he lowered his head even as she rose up on tiptoe. Abruptly, he blinked and pulled away so unexpectedly that Mariah nearly lost her balance.

"Forgive me—Mari—I mean Missus Kent. I—I really should go now and speak to Copper and Shad!"

Chapter 22
Finding God's Will

"In the same way the Holy Spirit helps us in our weakness. We do not know what we ought to pray for, but the Spirit himself intercedes for us with groans that words cannot express." Romans 8:26

Copper smiled as she carried the coffee pot to the table. "Ready for that second cup, Preacher?"

"Yes ma'am." he grunted appreciatively as he watched the young redhead moving about the kitchen as if she hadn't been at death's door a few days ago. "You know you're still a little pale, but I just can't get over how quickly you're regaining your strength!"

"I know—God surely blessed that water—it's a miracle! I'm still a little shaky in the morning, but I can't thank you enough for making that long treacherous walk. I really was in trouble, wasn't I? But from that first drop of water, I knew it was going to be just what I needed!"

"Well, it's warmed up considerably and the pass should be open soon. My friends said they'd bring you more water the next time the stage makes a run up here. If for some reason they can't come—then I'll be happy to go fetch you some more."

"Thank you, but I think what you brought should last for quite a while. Shad brings me half a cup and a dry biscuit every morning before I get out of bed. That seems to do the trick 'cause if I do that, then I'm fine for the rest of the day. Of course, the sight and smell of raw food still bothers me. I don't know what I'd do without Mariah—she's been such a blessing. I know your plan was for us to help her, and I hope we have, but she's helped us too—especially now. In fact, she's out milking the goat and gathering the eggs. She was already doing a lot of the cooking, so she could learn. But when she realized that cooking turned my stomach, she insisted on doing it all!" Copper's expression grew thoughtful, "Still, I don't want you to think we love her because she works so hard—I know what that feels like. Mariah isn't just a houseguest. She's dear to us. It's been amazing to see how much her faith has grown. When she first came here she was angry and bitter, and rightly so! I've come to know her very well and I don't think I've ever met anyone with a sweeter spirit. There's just something so very exceptional about her, don't you think?"

When the man's expression grew distant and he merely nodded, Copper continued, "I marvel at the wisdom and peace she has now. I've even wondered if God might be preparing her for some special service. Kind of like you, Preacher!"

Quin's heart hammered in his chest. He certainly agreed with Copper's words. Everything she said rang true—for he had seen it too. Mariah was born with outward beauty. Now, there was also an inner beauty, which defied description. Hearing Copper praise the woman he loved only made him want to find Mariah and declare himself. And yet he was still uncertain of God's exact will in this matter.

Suddenly, the big man stood to his feet; he couldn't abide the confines of the cabin any longer. "When Shad gets back from checking his trap lines," he said as he headed for the door and shrugged into his heavy coat. "Tell him—just tell him that I—had some things I needed to do. He won't mind if I leave Flint here." When Copper nodded in agreement but still looked troubled, he quickly added, "Now, don't worry about me—I'll be back in about a week." Preacher knew his behavior might seem mysterious, even rude, but he couldn't explain something he didn't understand himself, and he didn't want to speak to Shad face to face. His friend saw too much as it was. More specifically, he didn't want to see Mariah, for he didn't know what to say to her—not yet. Before Copper could talk him out of leaving, or Shad and Mariah returned, the big man had pulled on his walking pack and grabbed his rifle. With a solemn nod to Copper, he left the cabin.

Quin breathed in the crisp mountain air as he gazed out across the expanse of saw tooth ranges. Despite the terrible blizzard that had trapped him at the McKenna's through Christmas, and his snow covered trek down the mountain., the past few days had been unseasonably warm. Drifts of snow were still deep in the shade while everywhere the sun touched was melting fast. It was much too warm for his heavy coat. So he carried it over his shoulder until he reached his favorite camp site. When he came to the waterfall, he stood there for a long while and enjoyed the sight. The water was frozen on top, as it rolled over the rocks above like an old man's white beard. Then it split apart in icy sheets above the hot spring of water that lay clear and warm just below. Of all the magnificent places in these mountains, this was his favorite sanctuary. Here he would stay until God spoke. He would breathe in the splendor all around him, free his mind and listen!

The trout filled river that meandered just a few hundred yards away called to his empty belly, but once again he felt the need to fast and pray until God gave him direction. What he was most hungry for right now, were answers. He allowed himself a cup of warm water from the pool, and then he sat down on a nearby rock ledge and opened his worn Bible. He pulled the two slips of paper from his pocket, still amazed that John and Willy had both given him the exact same verse. *"Go and learn what this means: 'I desire mercy and not sacrifice."* Quin turned to Matthew 9:13. Then he went on to look up every verse he could find regarding mercy and sacrifice.

Each morning, just as the sun rose from the flatlands in the east, the big man would hike up to the top of a high ridge. He would read and pray, and listen for God to impress upon his heart—what he must do! Then late one evening, Quin sat by the tranquil little pool as the moon spilled a silvery light over his special haven. The air around him had a sharp bite to it and it felt good to just breathe it in. He tossed another log onto the fire and decided it was finally the right time to read John's letter. He wanted to seek God's direction first, before listening to anyone else. Even someone as wise as John Haze.

Slowly unfolding the pages, he took special note of the older man's distinctively fine hand, for it reminded Quin of his father's. An unexpected stab of melancholy went through him, but he pushed the sadness away then began to read.

Dear Quin,

Willy and I love you like a son, and every night we pray for you and your ministry. In these past few months we've felt especially burdened to increase our prayers for you. Seeing you tonight, confirmed that need. There just wasn't time for a long talk, still I felt the need to share with you how I began in this ministry and how the God we both serve became Willy's and my...Boss!

I was a happy young lad when I first felt God calling me to preach. The very idea horrified me. Preachers endure a dreary life of sacrifice and solemnity—and that was not for me! So it was with herculean determination I avoided God's call. Instead, I threw myself into becoming a skilled fisherman and an expert squirrel hunter. My only other ambition was to find a way to sweep Wilhelmina Tuttle off her feet. I wanted her to become as fond of me as I was of her!

Quin stopped reading as he tried to imagine this very special, now white-headed couple in their youth. Then he found his place again, and read on;

God kept whispering what he wanted me to do and I kept telling him—NO! I feared serving God would make me miserable. Ironically, the more I ran from Him the more miserable I became.

Then one day as I sat on a river bank—fishing for my supper, the prettiest girl in town…Miss Wilhelmina Tuttle herself, was suddenly standing over me. I was chewin' a piece of sour grass, trying to look as if I hadn't a care in the world. Truth be told, I was feelin' lower than the worm that dangled from my hook!

That pretty little thing put her hands on her hips and says to me: "John Albert Haze. Are you planning on both of us staying miserable forever? Or are you going to quit being a scallywag and do what God's tellin' ya to do? So that I can do what God's tellin' me to do!"

Course, I tried to think of somethin' clever to say but I was dumb-fuzzled. And I says, 'Miss Tuttle, I won't argue that I'm a miserable scallywag. But what does my misery have to do with yours?'

"Mister Haze," she said. "Have you forgotten that you kissed me when we were five years old? And did you or did you not promise to marry me someday?" Before I could answer she said, "We've been sweet on each other ever since—as you well know. Now, God has called us both to serve Him and do it gladly. I know it and you know it! So just how long are you going to be stubborn about it?"

Well, you know Willy. She was right of course. I thought serving God was a sacrifice and a punishment. I forgot that He had already proven His love for me. At that moment I realized that God wanted what was best for me—and if His will for me turned out to be a challenge—then He would give me whatever I needed to stand up to it. I feared I'd never win Willy if I was to become a Preacher but the truth was I would have lost her for sure—if I hadn't! God in His all-seeing wisdom had called us both to serve Him. What took me so long to grasp, was that He had also given Willy and me the great and abiding love we had for each other! We were always meant to share a double harness. Always meant to serve God—and always meant to do it—together!

Quin, I don't know what has been troubling you. I'm not sure if sharing this helps you at all. But remember that God wants what's best for you. Remember too that our Boss is as generous as He is powerful. If he asks you to give something up, then it's because it's wrong for you and because He has something better for you. So if you are trying to figure out what God wants you to have and what He does not want you to have...ask yourself a few questions.

Does having it go against God's written word? Does this bring harmony or disharmony into your life? Are you being selfish? Can you honor God with this in your life? Is God perhaps bringing about changes in your life so that He might enhance or perhaps even expand your ministry?

Seek God son and remember that He loves ya and so do Willy and John Haze. We're praying with you! If The Boss is willing, we'll see you soon!

Your friend and fellow servant,

John A. Haze

Preacher gripped the letter as he stared into the night sky. If ever there was a perfect woman to be a Pastor's wife...it was Mariah! What had Copper said before he left? 'I've even wondered if God might be preparing her for some special service. Kind of like you, Preacher!'

Mariah's horrible experience did not make her unfit to be a minister's wife. On the contrary, her terrible experience made her the perfect person to speak with and console used and abused women with true empathy. More and more he had been drawn to minister to the abandoned, abused and forgotten. Mariah's specific hardships made her uniquely qualified to help him minister to wounded women. Her life was a portrait of how God can take a broken vessel and mend it—making it better than new. Mariah was the perfect partner for the special work that God had been leading him to do, for many years now. Why he hadn't thought of this before, he didn't know, but right now it was as if his eyes had been opened!

Quin laughed out loud, and the joyous sound seemed to echo all around him. It was probably a bit too soon to propose...but he didn't think he'd have to wait much longer! In that instant, the water, the breeze, the hoot owl and the cry of the wolf—all became one melody. A song of answered prayer, played on a heart-shaped zither, by the woman The Boss had given him to love. He didn't have to give Mariah up, nor did he have to give up loving and serving his God. Reverend and Missus Quincy Long would minister together—as loving partners in God's service. Another smile spread across his face, and he pulled out the two scraps of paper and read them once again:

"Go and learn what this means: 'I desire mercy and not sacrifice."

Chapter 23
Deception

"A good man brings good things out of the good stored up in him, and an evil man brings evil things out of the evil stored up in him." Matthew 12:35

Black-Eyed Jack had always considered himself a brave man, but just now, he felt the sweat trickling down his back and was forced to dry his clammy hands on his leggings. It was a beautiful, early spring day, but not even that could bolster his spirits. He'd faced grizzly bears and attacking Indians with less trepidation than what he was facing now. This had him in a near panic! Still, he reckoned he'd do just about anything for little Copper and he'd tend to this dad-blasted chore even if it killed him. His mouth went dry as he stepped inside—the Castle Mercantile. He felt like a rabbit in a den of hungry wolves as he turned right and began walking towards—the Ladies Area! Being surrounded by dainty unmentionables trimmed with ruffles and lace made the confirmed bachelor shake in his boots, and he felt like his face might just burst into flames at any minute. Never once in his life had he ventured a stroll down this mysterious part of any store. Frowning, he took off his skunk cap and scratched his head in wonderment over how truly complicated the female of the species must be—to need all these things! He was just about to rethink his promise to Shad, when Sephora Castle stepped up to him with her arms folded and one dark eye-brow raised skeptically.

"Now—Mizz Castle, yer a lookin' at me as if I was intruding where I don't belong or was lost—and—for sure and certain—I'm both!"

Sephora pressed her lips tightly together while the mountain man nervously fingered his skunk cap, and tried to explain his presence in the Ladies Area. Even as he scowled at the bolts of fabric, as if they were Indian braves preparing to take scalps.

"Ya see—I agreed to do a friend a favor." He explained in his low and gravelly voice, "And—I am sorely ill prepared fer the task. Ya know, Shadrack McKenna, well he's got his self a new bride. He asked me to buy her a pack-mule full of female foofaraw. But now that I'm here—I see it plain—that sorry rascal—he knew full well that I weren't up to this kind o' chore—no how! 'Jes' get her some o' whatever they got, says he. And I says—like the old fool I am—why shore—be glad t'. I tell ya ma'am, he tricked me—plain and simple—that's what he done! Bet he's up at his cabin just a laughin' hisself silly thinkin' o' me—sinkin' in this here quicksand o' *ladylike—frippery*. Mizz Castle—I surely do need yer help—I feel as off kilter as hog on ice!"

Though Sephora Castle was not known for her sense of humor, the odd little man's dilemma struck her as amusing and she found herself enjoying a rare smile. As a business woman, she also knew that Black-Eyed Jack was known to carry a hefty purse. How he came by it no one knew, but she wasn't about to let him leave without doing his friend that favor, and reducing the weight of his purse—in the process!

"You may put your mind at ease, sir, I would be most pleased to help you." Sephora cooed, "Sounds like McKenna has an excellent friend in you!" she added as she moved her hands from where they rested on her ample hips and raised them to indicate the vast variety of choices all around her. "All this looks daunting I know, but rest assured, the man who brings the gifts is a hero indeed. I wouldn't be surprised if the young bride didn't thank you with a kiss on the cheek!"

When the old man stared at the floor and grinned, Sephora knew the man would need to purchase an extra pack mule before this day was done. "Now, why don't you tell me all about her?" She beamed, "What's her name? Is she large or small, serious or cheerful, dark or fair?"

Jack grinned, showing a few missing teeth. He'd been in love with a redhead once. And he'd come to love Copper like the daughter they might have had. So it was no wonder that when he described her, he sounded just like a proud papa. "Ma'am, her name is Copper, and Mizz Castle, I took to that little darlin' right off. She's a young thing, but smart as a whip! Can't hardly describe to ya jes' how pretty she is. Her hair's like her name—the color of a bright new penny or autumn leaves. Her eyes are the same shade as the first green up o' spring. Big and bright and just a sparklin' and plum full of life. And sweet—why she's just as good natured as she can be!"

A tall, pale man in the next isle quietly tried on a pair of leather gloves his thin lips lifting in a sly smile. So, Copper Delaney had come to these mountains after all. She had gone to a lot of trouble making it look like she'd headed for Texas. He hadn't followed her down there for he was a wanted man in Texas. Now it seemed her efforts had all been a waste of time. Soon, she would finally be his! Dirk couldn't believe his luck. He had stepped into the mercantile at just the right time. Or perhaps it was fate, just as the gypsy had foretold. The little red head was meant to be his, as was the treasure she would lead him to!

Riding into Otter Run two months ago had been pure destiny. After all, the first person he met had been his old cattle rustlin' partner, Jimmy Todd. They were both wanted for killing a rancher back in Texas. It was a shock to find that Todd had become the town Sheriff, but it wasn't a surprise that his old chum had not gone straight. Quite the opposite in fact. Todd had joined forces with the other not so law abiding town leaders. Together they were all making a good living off the unsuspecting citizenry. They called themselves the Highlander's Association, consisting of: the bank president, Theodore Krane, one of the teller's, Hank Wyatt, Cyril Castle, the owner of the mercantile and hotel, Ox Hennessey, the owner of the saloon and naturally, Jimmy Todd, the town Sheriff. These men knew things they could all benefit from, like when a rancher was taking out a loan to purchase more stock or when he was sick and a few strays could be herded away without him noticing. They shared information regarding when funds for the local bank would be coming in on the next stage, or when someone had won big at the gambling tables. The Highlanders would meet and exchange these bits of information and plan accordingly. Todd had been quick to employ Dirk's assistance in some of these activities. And though Dirk knew he wouldn't get rich doing these small jobs, he knew that Tar O'Leary had been a trapper up here in these mountains and he had hoped that his little redhead would eventually find her way here.

Dirk kept his back turned while he listened to the snooty sales lady and the old codger discussing what to purchase for *his woman*...even while memories of the gypsy's predictions flooded his mind. He would never forget the old woman's warnings or her description of the two women who would lead him to salvation or ruination. She had said one would have hair the color of sunset and eyes as green as clover, and would lead him to something of great value. That woman, had to Copper, he was sure of it. Although finding his little red-head pleased him, he couldn't help but remember the old gypsy's words about the other woman, and it troubled him.

"She stands in the light, but so close to you that I can see only that she wears a band of gold on her left hand, and is covering a wound. Blood is bubbling up through her fingers. Your blood or her blood—I cannot tell. And yet, I know this wound will cause *you* great pain! It will also lead to great danger and it will mean death, to some whom you know well."

Dirk shoved down the old woman's words of warning. Instead he concentrated on Copper and all the pleasures and profit having her would bring him!

Seems destiny is finally smilin' on me. Vernon was right, little Red was sure enough penniless when he pulled her from the river. Maybe Vernon was supposed to steal her away from me. If he hadn't we never would have landed in prison, and he never would have met Tar O'Leary. Now, everything is lining up just right, and Red will to lead me to treasure! The gypsy said stay away from married women but she didn't say anything about—widows. And that's what Red's gonna be…just as soon as I can arrange it. Soon I'll have money and a woman of my own!

The hour was late and Hennessey grabbed up four glasses with the pudgy fingers of one hand and a bottle of whiskey with the other. His breathing was raspy and could be heard from every corner of the saloon as he headed for the back table. It was a rainy Tuesday night, and the saloon was quiet and empty, perfect for the meeting of the Highlanders.

"Well now, Hank me boy." Ox growled as he scattered the glasses about, then sloshed whiskey into each one. "Skeeter told me hisself that he delivered a letter addressed to Theodore Krane at the bank. Since Theo's been called out o' town I reckon ya helped yerself to that letter. So, what did it say? Has to be about money comin' in on the next stage—right?"

Hank Wyatt was a handsome young man with a boyish freckled face, chestnut-hair and bright blue eyes. His looks where an asset, for he could ask you the time of day with the innocence of a newborn lamb, and yet, when he turned away, your watch would be in his pocket. Though he wasn't a novice when it came to breaking the law, he was not yet as jaded as the other men who sat around the table. Of late, in fact, he'd been second guessing all the choices he had made that led him to this moment. His mind went to the young saloon girl, Velvet. He hadn't intended to fall in love with her—but he had. His greatest wish these days was to marry her and go someplace where they could both start over. But, like his mother had always said, "If wishes were horses, beggars would ride." He was here now, and quitting the

Highlanders was a death sentence. There was nothing to do but play out the hand fate had dealt him.

Hennessey slowly sat down in one of the chairs, his swollen red face a vivid contrast to the pale albino, Dirk Culley sitting beside him. The other two men at the table were Cyril Castle, a bald obnoxious little man, and to his right, the handsome and arrogant Sheriff Jimmy Todd.

Hank knew he couldn't trust any of these men, but he feared Todd the most. The man seemed to think a sheriff's badge gave him the freedom to do anything he wanted. Hank would never forget what happened to his friend Chub Doherty, the other teller at the bank. Todd said he'd caught Chub rustling cattle, and when he tried to stop him, the cattle stampeded and Chub was killed. Then there was the supposed suicide of Victor Kent. Todd told some people that Vic had killed himself but he told Ox that the man had drawn down on him and he had to shoot him. Why two different stories? Hank figured the truth lay somewhere in between. Because the fact remained that Jimmy Todd had wanted Chub's little house and Victor's wife. Todd now lived in the house and he'd almost gotten the woman too. Hank had other reasons for mistrusting the sheriff. Velvet had complained that Todd hit her for no reason and that he treated the older woman, Shotsy, even worse.

Staring into his half empty glass of whiskey, Hank fidgeted and glanced around the room. Attempting to calm his nerves he tossed back the contents of the glass and choked on the burning liquid.

Hennessey smirked in disgust as he slapped the younger man's back with his meaty paw, pounding harder than was necessary, and Hank was nearly knocked from his seat while Ox growled, "Quit ditherin' about, ya young whelp, ya better have read that letter. Now what did it say?"

Still sputtering Hank righted himself, then choked out his answer, "Yeah, I read it! The news ain't all that good, though. The letter said, old Reverend Haze and his wife are coming up on the stage. Seems they're friends with the bank president from Denver, and since they're friends with Preacher too and were coming up here anyway, it was decided that no one would suspect them of carrying Preacher's next deposit to the bank."

Hennessey poured another round for the men as he grunted, "That ain't bad news kid—that there be good news! Those meddlin' Haze's are planning on movin' up here and they want to build a real church and maybe a school.

Mostly they want to bring religion to Otter Run. We don't want or need folks of their ilk up here. We'll hit that stage and—sadly," Ox sighed in mock reverence, "there will be NO SURVIVORS!"

Todd grinned as he raised his glass in approval then downed his drink, "What about Long? I've been tolerant of that man, because he wasn't here but once a month or so. But he went too far when he waltzed in here and took my woman. I've had it with his meddling—I want him dead too!"

Hank turned pale as he rubbed the back of his neck. He didn't like the idea of killing in the first place, but killing preachers and an old woman—that didn't sit well. He had to talk these men out of doing something this evil. "Krane ain't gonna like us hitting the stage after he gets a letter like this. It points straight to him! And if he claims he was out of town, then it points to me and then to all of us. Why don't we just let this one go. The law down in the lowlands don't seem to care about rustled cattle up here or even if the stage is robbed a few times a year. But we're talkin' cold blooded murder! The Haze's are a nice old couple, and they're well liked in the lowlands and so is Preacher Long. If we try this—they'll send for the Territorial Marshal. We won't get away with it—not this time!"

"Ah, be quiet, ya tender footed flatlander!" Hennessey snorted, while his beady eyes narrowed in thought, "I say we're headin' off trouble. Them preacher types will ruin this town and they'd be sure to put an end to the Highlander's Association, and none of us would be wantin' that. Men come up here so they can live just as they please. Up here there ain't no God and that's just how we like it. So, listen up. You gents are gonna get that money and rid this country of that meddlesome old couple. And yer right, Sheriff. I'm thinkin' that there might even be a way—with a bit o' luck—we can be rid o' that uppity Preacher, Quincy Long—at the very same time!"

Ox managed to explain what he had in mind as he downed one glass of whiskey after another. He had barely finished telling Hank what he must do when his huge head finally dropped on the table with a loud thud. The young bank teller didn't hide his disgust or his relief. Instead, he simply nodded to the other men as he pushed away from the table. There wasn't any way out for him. He had joined the Highlanders for the extra money and for the excitement. However, more and more the jobs were becoming reckless and cruel! Still, as he glanced about the table, he knew there wasn't a man there that wouldn't kill him without regret if he went against them. The plan depended on whether or not he could convince Velvet to do her part. Tonight was the first time he had ever dreaded spending time with his girl.

Dirk sneered as he watched the freckled faced Hank Wyatt heading up the stairs. Then he reached over and lifted Ox's head by his gray-red hair then let it drop back onto the table. "Yep, I guess he's really out!" He leaned back, balancing his chair on two legs and sighed, "I've been doin' some thinkin'. You and me, we've got a bit more to gain than the others." His lips turned up in a rare smile. "Jimmy Todd, Sheriff of Otter Run," he mocked, knowing the man was more outlaw than lawman. "You still wantin' that gal the preacher carried off? I never laid eyes on her but I've heard she's somethin' to behold. I just found out that he took her way on up to McKenna's place. Seems the mountain man got married recently and that preacher thought he and his new wife could take good care of her."

Todd's jaw clenched, then he tossed back another shot of whiskey. "McKenna, huh? Didn't know where she was. Yeah—sure I still want her! I've only seen that mountain man a few times, 'cause he generally does his tradin' down in Colorado City or Canon City. He's not quite as tall as Quincy Long but—he's sure one big bear of a man. I've heard he's a crack shot and as tough as they come." Frowning, he ran his hand over a smooth jaw, "If my woman is up there, it won't be easy gettin' her out!"

The albino watched Todd sulking in his chair. Jimmy had always been the type to take the easy way. He took the job as sheriff—because he enjoyed violence and power—but only when he was sure to have the upper hand.

"I've never seen him, but I've heard stories about him." Dirk agreed. "The trouble is—ya see, he's not only got your woman up there; I just found out—he's got mine, too! And while Hennessey was spouting off how he wanted things to go—I came up with my own plan. Hank's up there with Velvet right now making sure she finds a way to get word to Long that the stage is gonna be hit and that Haze and his wife are supposed to be killed."

Todd frowned and cursed, "Yeah, I heard him, same as you...."

"We both heard him, but while he was tellin' us what he wanted, I was thinkin' of how we both can get what we want! So, while you and Hank are robbin' that stage I'll go fetch our women!"

"That's a coward's plan." Todd sneered. "I know yer white Culley, but are ya turning yellow, too?"

Dirk moved so fast that the next thing Todd knew the albino had grabbed him by the shirt collar with one hand and was pressing a razor sharp knife to his neck with the other. "Don't mock me—*friend*." He warned. "You best hold your tongue—*or lose it*."

"All right, all right—don't take on so." Todd winced as he tried to push the blade away, "Just wondered why don't I get the women while you hit the stage?"

Dirk released him, and then sat back in his chair, "Haven't you learned yet…that breakin' the law is part plan and part gamble? We've planned for Velvet to get word to the preacher that the stage is gonna be robbed. But he ain't fool enough to come alone. So, I'm *bettin'* that he'll ask McKenna to help him. Now, Danby the stage driver has standing orders to kill anyone who tries to keep the stage from being robbed. He's the best shot around so more than likely if Long and McKenna show up, he'll be the one to take 'em both down. That will just leave the killing of that old couple to you and Hank. Surely you two can handle that! Of course you could always call on Claw and Zeno to help. If ya don't think yer up to it!"

"Killing doesn't bother me, Dirk—and you know it! And none of us want to divvy up the money with those renegades—not if we don't have to. Still, it makes just as much sense for me to get the women while you hit the stage."

Dirk wiped his knife on his sleeve then slipped it back into the scabbard on his belt. With a glint in his glassy eyes, he said, "You said it yourself, McKenna's a bear of a man. Now, me—I like shooting bears! I'm still bettin' that he'll go with Long but the odds are fifty-fifty that he'll stay behind to protect the women. If he does…then whoever goes after the women will have to deal with McKenna—alone! If ya want to fight that man, fine, but just remember, that woman has told him all about ya. I even heard tell that she triggered both barrels of a shot gun at ya. She might not miss if she gets a second chance. Between her and McKenna, you might just have quite a fight on your hands." Seeing that Todd didn't appreciate his words, Dirk became more serious. "Face it Todd, no matter which direction we ride, you know we're both gambling that we'll be the ones still alive when the dust settles. All that matters is that we get the money and our women, and that we kill anyone that stands in our way. Naturally, if Long and McKenna manage to save the stage they'll take it on to Otter Run. If that happens then go get Claw and

Zeno and meet me at McKenna's cabin. One way or another, we'll kill the men and take the women!"

Velvet crept down the stairs, her mind racing with all that Hank had just told her. The man she loved was a thief and a swindler, but she was pleased to know that at least he drew the line at cold-blooded murder. The saloon was empty but for Ox who was snoring loudly slumped over the corner table. Careful not to wake the man, she scooted around the wobbly newel post and out the door. Knowing that she'd find Clem Talbott sleeping on the bench outside the saloon, she placed her small hand over his mouth and then, shook him awake. The man slept like the dead so she had to shake harder. Finally, he awoke with a start, his eyes looking terrified, "Shhhh, Clem, it's just me, Velvet."

The girl couldn't help but smile when the poor man jumped away from her, as if she were a rattler.

"Relax Clem. I know you're faithful to Celia—and I promise—I'm not here to have my way with ya." Seeing that he was now fully awake her face sobered, "But I need your help—lives are in danger! Do ya know where a man by the name of Shadrack McKenna lives? I've got a message for Preacher and he may be at McKenna's. I need ya to ride to his cabin as soon as you can and give him a message. If Preacher ain't there then go to Black-Eyed Jack's. If he ain't there neither, then ya've just got to keep ridin' 'til ya find him!"

Clem was still trying to clear the cobwebs from his mind. As he rubbed his face he asked, "So, what am I supposed to tell 'em?"

Velvet searched the street, it was too early for anyone to be up and about, or so she hoped. Finally, whether it was safe or not, she said, "Some men are gonna attack the stage coach—and they plan on killin' everyone on it! All I can tell ya is that there will be three men and one of them is an albino. Two of Preacher's good friends are coming up on that stage. I met them once; it's Reverend John Haze and his wife Wilhelmina." Nervously, Velvet searched the streets again, then added more vehemently, "Clem, these outlaws know that a Reverend and his wife are gonna be on that stage and that's why they plan to kill 'em! They don't want religion changin' things up here in these mountains. The Haze's are awful nice folks. Last summer they came up here on the stage and they walked around town." Velvet lowered her head sadly, "They knew what I was…what I am! But they stopped me as I walked down the street and said, 'We're here visiting the mountain saloons and we'd like to help ya—no questions asked. Ya can come home with us if ya like and we'll do all we can to give ya a new life.'" Her eyes filled with tears, "It took a lot o' gumption to offer to help me like that. Then Ox saw me talkin' to 'em and told me I better get back to work—or else. Then Sheriff Todd told 'em it wasn't safe in this town and that they had better leave."

"Miss Velvet," Clem groaned. "I don't want nothin' to happen to them folks, but our lives are in danger too if we cross Hennessey and the sheriff. You don't have to tell me—I know they're the ones behind this. They're behind everything that's evil in this town!"

Velvet shivered as she glanced nervously down the street again, "I know this is dangerous, but you listen to me, Clem Talbott. You'd have lost everything you ever had, if it weren't for Preacher. The Haze's are like Ma and Pa to him. I'd go myself but I don't know these mountains and I'd have to steal a horse. Besides, I tried to leave town once before—Ox caught me and nearly beat me to death!" Suddenly, Velvet remember Celia and the boys. "Oh, I'm sorry Clem, maybe I shouldn't ask this of ya. It's just that I know yer not one of the Highlanders. Yer the only one I could trust!"

"It's all right Miss Velvet." Clem was finally awake now and thinking more clearly, "You were right to ask me. And—I never realized. Just always thought you and Shotsy—well—that ya wanted to work at the Long Shot. Reckon I never thought how it was fer you girls." He pulled on the coat he had been using as a blanket, adding in a whisper. "I had planned to leave town this morning anyway. I'll head north towards my ranch then take a back trail to McKenna's place."

Clem stepped off the wooden sidewalk. He smiled slightly then tipped his hat, and speaking in an easy morning voice he said, "I'm a thankin' ya Miss Velvet for remembering to wake me this morning. Been trying real hard not to disappoint Celia, but when she sees me ridin' in early like this with no hang over, she'll know I weren't drinkin' nor doing nothin' else wrong. You have a good day now, ma'am." With another tip of his hat, Clem turned and, as if looking forward to a peaceful ride home, he slowly strolled towards the livery.

Chapter 24
Ladd

"Do not regard him as an enemy, but warn him as a brother." 2 Thessalonians 3:15

Copper handed Shad the bronze spyglass, "Please take this! It helped me when I was coming up here. It might help you scout out what kind of trouble you're riding into. I know you have to go." Suddenly, her emerald eyes filled with tears, "But I still hate it!"

While Shad pulled Copper into his arms and was giving her a long good-bye kiss, Preacher and Mariah turned to each other and their eyes locked as they made their own silent good-byes.

After the men had mounted Flint and Boone, Mariah looked up at them and said softly. "Now, you two take good care of each other—and may God watch over every step you take!"

Shad nodded, then his expression became grim as he gave one final order that he meant to encompass both women. "Now you two ladies listen—and listen good! I don't care if a hundred shingles blow off that roof while we're gone…you both stay off it! AND I don't care if Remy decides to run away from home and climb Pike's Peak, don't go chasin' after her! Please—no matter what—stay near the cabin. And every time ya step outside, fer a trip to the privy or to feed the chickens, be sure to take the Henry rifle with ya. The best thing ya can do fer us men—is keep yerselves safe! That and just keep on prayin'!"

Quin sighed as he lifted his hat, finger combed his dark blond hair, then replaced it. "That's exactly what I was going to say—keep yourselves safe! One more thing though, from what Clem Talbott told us, both Todd and that albino have murdered before and they're determined, one way or another, to kill John and Willy." A cloud seemed to pass over his face as he added, "It's likely that we'll have to do some killing ourselves, if we're to stop these men from carrying out their plans. Pray that God will not only protect us, but give us both wisdom!"

Copper and Mariah locked arms as they watched the men ride away, but the moment they were out of sight, it was Mariah who burst into tears. "I just can't see any way this can turn out all right," she sobbed. "I can't even imagine that God Himself could take what's happening here and make things right!"

Confused by her words, Copper put her arm around her friend's shoulder, "Mariah—this isn't like you. Your faith has become so strong! This is a bad situation yes, but nothing is too hard for God!"

When Mariah simply nodded sadly then headed for the cabin, Copper knew that she not only had to worry about the men, but Mariah too.

"I know what we should do." Copper said, trying to hold back her own worries and fears. "Remember the other day we were talking about when we did our best praying? I said when I was drawing and you said when you were playing your music." Before Mariah could reply, Copper handed her the delicate little zither and gently pushed her towards the fireplace. "Now, we both have a lot of praying to do so you sit by the fire and play your favorite song while I make a drawing of you." That said, she hurried towards the table and picked up her sketchpad.

Soon, the gentle tones of the zither filled the cabin while Copper studied the contours of Mariah's face. Her fingers held the bit of charcoal lightly, as the perfect likeness of her beautiful friend seemed to magically appear on the sketchpad. It was a tribute to Copper's skill that with only the white of the paper and a light or heavy hand with the charcoal she managed to capture the depth of her friend's unusual eyes and the way Mariah's pale blonde hair shone in the fire light. Copper balanced the sketchpad between her growing belly and the kitchen table. While Mariah, an artist's dream, sat before the fire, her skirts gathered about her in shadowy folds while she played the enchanting little zither.

"You know…" Copper mused as she added a bit of shading here and there, "I think I might be a better artist while you're playing. I don't know if it's your music bringing out the best in me or if you just become even prettier while you're playing because you love it so much!"

Despite Mariah's melancholy, she smiled self-consciously, and Copper hurried to capture that exact expression. She was sure that this was going to be the best portrait she'd ever done. Even though today Mariah was struggling greatly, Copper knew that her friend's new found faith was little by little healing her wounds. And with this healing came a peace and confidence that showed in everything that was Mariah. Copper smiled, for she had just decided that this portrait would be a gift to Preacher the moment he proposed to the woman he loved. Of course when that day might be...she had no idea. That man had certainly been pig-headed. Quincy Long was proving to be even more stubborn than Remy. She and Shad had lain awake many a night, talking and praying for their special friends. It was becoming painful to watch the two of them silently longing for each other. They both seemed to think that marriage was not an option, even though it was obvious that they were both deeply in love!

"Whew!" Copper sucked in a breath, and then blew it out slowly. When Mariah looked up with concern the little redhead sighed, "It's just the baby. I think that song you're playing makes him to want to dance a jig!"

"He, is it?" Mariah asked, "Shad always refers to that baby as *she*, while you always say *he!*"

"I know...Shad wants the baby to be like me, but I want it to be just like him!"

Mariah's expression grew tender, as her own longing for motherhood brought a sharp pain that she quickly pushed away. She truly was happy for this very special couple; she loved them both dearly, and yet her own pain was still there. Looking up from her zither, she asked, "Do you realize how very fortunate we've been, Copper? We've both been rescued from evil men. We both grew up so differently but I don't think that either one of us ever suspected that honorable men like Shadrack McKenna and Quincy Long even existed." A look of concern clouded her eyes as she added. "Oh, how I wish that those good men were back already. I wonder where they are right now—and—if they're safe?"

"I know..." Copper sighed. "It doesn't help to worry but I can't seem to stop myself. Of course, if what Mister Talbott said was true, they had to go! And you and I both know that there aren't two more capable men, in all the Rockies than our men."

When Mariah's lips lifted sadly at the reference to, 'our men' Copper said it again, "That's right, *our men* are both uncommonly smart and they won't take foolish chances! All we *can* do—we're doing! We're praying and having faith that God will help them succeed. If I've learned anything in the past few years, it's to trust in God's plan. I doubt that I'll ever understand it, but somehow He's used some of the worst experiences of my life and turned them around for my good. What I thought was the end of the world turned out to be a blessing. If all the bad things hadn't happened, I would never have run up here to these mountains and met my wonderful Shad or you, my dearest friend!+"

Although Mariah tried to smile, a shadow seemed to pass over her, "You are my dearest friend too, Copper. And I know you're right—about everything. Still, I want just one more blessing. I want to see Shad and Quin walk through that door. I want them to say, 'We are fine—we didn't have to kill anyone and—and all is well!'"

"Yes. I want the same thing." Then Copper added, "But also for your sake and mine, I also want to hear that Sheriff Jimmy Todd and Dirk Culley are safely behind bars with a one-hundred-year prison sentence!"

When Mariah's chin began to quiver, Copper added gently, "The only other things I want are for this baby to get here safely and for you, my friend, to be every bit as happy as I am!"

Hours later, as she put the final touches to her drawing, Copper rose from her seat at the kitchen table. She yawned and stretched and then groaned loudly. "My goodness, the day is slipping away from us and I don't think the baby likes my being so still." Glancing at Mariah, who had moved to the settee, she announced. "Now, I want you to listen to me and not argue. You have been doing all the cooking and all my chores while I've laid around like an old sow in a mud-wallow." With her hands on her hips she added, "I'm feeling ever so much better and the only thing I need now is a little fresh air and exercise. It won't hurt anything to do the chores a bit early and I'm getting hungry. So—I think I'll go tend to the animals and while I'm outside, you could start on an early supper. All right? I was thinking just a light vegetable soup since we don't have the men to cook for tonight. How does that sound?"

Pushing away her own muddled thoughts, Mariah took a moment to scrutinize her friend, "Yes, I suppose a bit of exercise and fresh air wouldn't hurt, you do seem to be getting stronger." Setting her zither beside her, Mariah rose to her feet and smoothed out her dress. "How about I make some corn muffins to go along with that soup?"

Copper smiled, "Sounds perfect! I won't be long." She promised as she left the cabin, humming the song Mariah had been playing while she walked across the yard heading for the barn.

After putting some water on to boil, Mariah went to the pantry and filled her arms with a variety of vegetables in glass jars. As she sat them down on the table, she stopped, it sounded like angry voices coming from the yard. One voice was distinctively male, and though it seemed familiar, it wasn't Shad or Quin, she was sure of it. Instantly, Mariah ran across the room, and by the time she heard Copper's scream she was already reaching for the rifle above the mantle. It was only then she remembered that Copper should have taken the gun with her. Shoving the thought aside, Mariah hurried to the front door. She didn't know what she expected to find—but what she saw was the culmination of all her nightmares and fears combined. Holding Copper in a fierce grip was a tall man, dressed in black with hair and skin as pale as moonlight—the albino. He held Copper by the arm, while he slapped her across the face and then back handed her again. As her small body slid to the man's feet, he reached down and grabbed a fist full of her bronze hair and twisted it around his hand.

"Are ya scared of me gal? Good, cause ya've got a lot of things I want and I won't take no for an answer this time—ya hear? The first time I saw ya, I told ya plain how it was supposed to be—that you belonged to me! Then ya married up with Vernon and now—just look at ya—carrying another man's whelp. Well, I won't have it!"

Instantly, Mariah pushed the cabin door wide, cocked the rifle and screamed, "LADDY NO!"

Dirk spun towards the sound with the quick instincts of a man who'd spent all his adult life on the run. He knew McKenna was gone, for he'd checked the barn and found only the girl's mule. And yet, when he saw his little redhead, he'd all but forgotten that another woman was to have been there too. When the cabin door was flung open, and he heard the rifle being cocked—nothing could stop him from reacting. Not even when he heard his own name spoken by a beloved voice from a long forgotten past. Almost on its own accord, Dirk's pistol leapt into his hand and fire exploded from the barrel. The shadowed figure silhouetted in the doorway jerked as the bullet sliced through cloth and skin.

Mariah clutched her bleeding side. "Oh, Laddy," she breathed as her legs gave way and she fell to her knees, "Is this what's become of you?"

LADDY—the name of an unfortunate and unwanted boy, rang in the man's ears. Hearing that name had not prevented him from instinctively drawing his gun and pulling the trigger. And yet, after all these years, it now shook him like nothing else could have. Instantly, he dropped his pistol and released his hold on Copper's long hair, as if he didn't know how either had gotten into his hands. Then he was assaulted by an unfamiliar feeling—*shame*.

"NO!" he roared as he ran to Mariah's side and fell to his knees before her, "Dear God—**SIS!** Dear God—what have I done?"

"Oh Laddy…" Mariah moaned, "God has never been *dear to you*—it's blasphemy for you to even speak His name." Then, she softened her reprimand as she gently touched his cheek. "But, He could be dear to you Laddy, just as He's become dear to me!"

Copper was still dazed, as she lay in the dirt with her arms protectively encircled about her unborn baby. Her heart was hammering in her chest at the shock of stepping into the barn only to find Dirk Culley waiting for her. She had tried to run, but he had quickly caught up with her. Her face was still burning and her ears ringing from the hard slaps he'd given her. As she gazed towards the cabin, she realized that Mariah had been shot! As she struggled to her feet, the world seemed to spin and her thoughts were all in a tangle. Everything had happened so fast and none of it made any sense. This was the man she feared more than any other, and just now he was sitting on the porch, gently cradling Mariah in his arms. This was her enemy—the albino who had just threatened her and the life of her unborn child! Cautiously, she stepped around the man, and knelt beside her friend to examine her wound. Then her gaze went up to the splintered door frame. Though the bullet had cut a bloody trail along Mariah's trim waist, miraculously, it had lodged in the wood. Gathering all her courage, Copper forced herself to look into the pale eyes of her enemy, "I—I can't tend to her here—can you carry her to the bed?"

When Dirk glared at Copper, as if he might still mean her harm, Mariah surprised them both when she reached out her bloody hand and grabbed Dirk by the shirt collar. "You are my brother, Ladd—you know I have always loved you and I forgive you for shooting me. But you listen! I will never forgive you if you hurt Copper! So if you're thinkin' of hurting her again, then you can consider us both as your enemies. She is dear to me—as is her husband Shadrack McKenna and the circuit preacher Quincy Long. They cared for me when—when I was in the greatest despair of my life. They are the best people I have ever known. So, if you have any love left for me, then you promise that no matter what happens—you will not harm them—and that you will protect them with your life if need be!"

Dirk gritted his teeth, but when his sister's eyes clouded with tears he blew out a breath and placed his hand over hers, "All right, Sis. I promise." With infinite care he lifted Mariah into his arms. His own face wincing in sympathy when she let out a cry of pain. While he carried her to the bed he spoke softly; "How in the world did ya wind up living here? Guess it doesn't really matter. Don't you worry, from now on I'm gonna take good care of ya just like you always took care of me. Do you remember? Every time Pa beat me, you were always there to patch me up!" Awkwardly, Dirk lowered his sister onto the bed and then knelt beside her. "I never forgot that Sis! You're the only truly good person I've ever known."

While brother and sister continued to speak in hushed tones, Copper hurried to the kitchen and splashed water on her face. Then she washed her hands thoroughly, just as Ma Riley had taught her. Thankfully water was already boiling on the stove, and she poured some into a basin and dropped a clean rag into it. Closing her eyes, she drew in a deep breath. It took all her gumption to carry it towards the bed, where Dirk Culley, of all people, was kneeling beside his sister. Brother and sister—of all things—Copper couldn't imagine anything that could have surprised her more. Biting her lip, she nervously sat the basin down then gingerly stepped over Dirk's sprawled legs so she could open Maudy McKenna's trunk. Quickly searching through the contents she retrieved a clean apron for herself, two clean sheets to put under and over Mariah, and bandages she had rolled for just such an emergency. Of course she had never expected anything like this!

Dirk suddenly jumped to his feet and paced the floor. After a year if waiting in prison and months of searching, he finally had control of the little redhead. He knew she was married, and should have been careful, but when he saw she was pregnant with another man's child, he'd gone into a rage. Now of all things she was tending to his sister's wound—a wound he had inflicted. Why was Sis here, of all places? He hadn't felt this confused and helpless since he was a boy—and now—it was as if an army of unfamiliar feelings were waging war against him.

Copper pressed hard against the bloody wound then lifted the cloth away. Sighing, she gave Mariah a hint of a smile, "Well now, we can thank the Lord for this! I'm sure it hurts, but it's not nearly as bad as it could have been. That bullet snatched a good bit of flesh from your side, but it buried itself in the wall and not you. That's the good news. The bad is that I'm still going to have to make sure that no bits of material from your dress are left inside. Even a tiny thread could cause infection." Biting her lip Copper added, "Then I'll have to douse it with whiskey. That will be the worst of it. After that I'll bind it up, then I'll leave you alone and let you rest. Still, we have a lot to thank God for!"

Beads of perspiration glistened on Mariah's forehead as she let out a long sigh. "I am thankful Copper. God was surely watchin' over me. If that bullet had been just a few inches to the left, I could be dead!"

Dirk ran his hand over his face and felt dampness on his cheek. Shocked and embarrassed that he had actually shed a tear, he scowled down at them both, "What's the matter with you two? Are ya actually thankful that she got shot—are ya both crazy?" Giving Copper a look of contempt, he sneered, "You were supposed to lead me to treasure not bring me bad luck! As far as I'm concerned this is all your fault."

The man was no longer the remorse stricken brother, but once again the villain Copper remembered, and she backed away from him as he continued his rant, "If you hadn't married Vernon, if you hadn't run away when I got out of prison, if ya hadn't screamed just now, she wouldn't have come out of that cabin. My sister is lying there with a hole in her side 'cause a you!"

Copper and Dirk just stared at each other but then strangely enough the next voice that filled the room was that of Mariah's. Her voice was slightly weak but she was furious. "You stop it, right this minute!" she fumed. "I had a brother I was proud of once; his name was Ladd O'Culla. He wasn't the kind of coward that would strike a woman—let alone a pregnant woman. And—he wouldn't blame someone else for *his* mistakes. Copper didn't shoot me! A scoundrel by the name of Dirk Culley shot me! My brother was a good man. But—this Dirk Culley—whom I don't ever care to know, is not only an outlaw; he's a coward and a bully! I'll say it again brother, what has become of you?"

Eyes wide with trepidation, Copper feared that Mariah might be pushing the man too far. Her brother had obviously changed. He was dangerous and his sister was refusing to see it. Even when Copper touched her friend's arm to calm her, Mariah persisted with her tongue lashing.

"You asked me if I remembered? Well, I most certainly do! I remember the day you left home for good. And you were right to do so, because Ruxton Hunter was a monster." Mariah's voice cracked with emotion then it softened, "I missed you so much—but I was glad that you'd run away. Now, I'm wondering—do you remember what a hateful man Father was? You used to be proud that you were only his step-son. Ladd—you of all people know how dreadful it is to be treated with cruelty. When I opened that door and saw my own dear brother striking my dearest friend." Mariah grabbed Copper by the hand, "It was just as if I were seeing father beating you again. I can't believe you were abused by a monster only to become one yourself!"

Dirk's eyes blazed with a glassy fire, then they clouded with shame as he stared at his sister's bloody wound. Cursing he yanked the hat from his head and flung it across the room, "You're right—I have become a monster! I've turned into the kind of man—you and I both always hated. And that's just the way it is, Sis. Like him or not, I am Dirk Culley now, through and through. That decent boy you knew as Ladd died a long time ago. No one—not even you as dear as you will always be to me, can bring him back."

Gritting her teeth, Copper scowled up at the man, "That's enough, your sister is already in enough pain. If she stays upset and tense, this will just hurt her all the more." Turning to Mariah she added softly, "Now, you have to relax. I want you to take a sip of laudanum. It will calm you and ease the pain while I clean and bandage your wound."

Just then, Dirk blew out a breath and noticeably tried to calm himself, "She's right, Sis." Nodding his approval to Copper as she gave his sister a spoonful of the medicine. "You take that and rest," he said. Then glancing down at the settee he saw the little heart-shaped zither that he'd given her so long ago. Shaking his head, he said, "I can't believe you still have that little thing. It was the last present I ever gave ya." Bending over Mariah he whispered, "Close yer eyes and dream about that day—it was one of our few happy ones." When Mariah nodded, he added sadly, "Reckon I've hurt lots of people Sis. But—I never thought I'd hurt you!"

The next hour passed in silence. Dirk knew that both women feared what he was going to do. The trouble was, he didn't know himself. It was good to be reunited with his sister again, but now really wasn't the best time or place. He was also glad to finally have this little redhead in his grasp. Her sunset colored hair and bright green eyes had fascinated him from the moment he'd seen Vernon pull her from the river. It was beyond strange that these two women had become friends—but now as he thought on it, he decided it was just meant to be. Maybe everything wasn't so complicated after all; Red was going to be his woman and Mariah would come with them. The three of them would be together from here on out.

Every time Copper glanced across the room, Dirk was staring at her. And each time she felt like making a run for it. Of course that wasn't an option—she couldn't leave Mariah. The only thing that gave her courage was seeing the gentle way this man treated his sister. Still, she couldn't forget how he had treated her when he had first seen her. A sudden feeling of fear and confusion surged through her and she slid to her knees beside the bed and silently began to pray.

Lord, Shad and Quin, Mariah and I...we're all in trouble and we need Your help. I don't understand why all this is happening...but I do thank you that Mariah wasn't more seriously hurt. And her being here—Lord if she wasn't Dirk's sister, I don't know what would have happened. Please speak to Dirk's heart. Help him to become again that better person he once was. It seems as if evil is all around us and is trying to overtake us. Please protect us and give us wisdom and direction. I ask this in Jesus name. Amen.

When Copper glanced up, Dirk was watching her with a puzzled expression. Finally, he leaned over her, keeping his voice low so as not to wake his sister, he grunted, "Come into the kitchen, Red. We need to talk."

"My name was never Red." Copper whispered, while she slowly got to her feet and followed after him, "And you should call me, Missus McKenna."

Dirk snorted at her words as he pulled out a kitchen chair, swung it around and straddled it. He would call her Red until she answered to it. He needed her to forget that she was Missus McKenna. Even as he hoped, that 'bear of a man,' Shadrach McKenna was dead by now.

"Red." he repeated again, with an arrogant sneer as he cradled his arms over the top of the chair. "I think it's time you told me what ya've done with Tar O'Leary's gold." The man looked almost friendly as he pulled another chair beside him and patted it. "Come and sit down and tell me everything ya know. Vernon was my partner, and now that he and Tar are dead, that plunder belongs to me! I'll use it to take care of Mariah, and since you two are such good friends, I'm guessing you won't mind handing it over."

All Copper wanted was for this man to leave as soon as possible. Shrugging, she slowly walked towards the kitchen, still keeping her distance. "I did come up here looking for it but actually, I forgot about it when I found this place. I never even told Shad. I ran to these mountains before I thought it through. I never could have gotten it anyway. I'm terrified of dark places, and the directions say you have to walk in a dark cavern until you get to the treasure. After I married Shad, I felt like I had all the treasure I ever wanted. I'll gladly give you Vernon's letter. It contains a code that tells you where it is. You're welcome to any gold or plunder it leads you to!"

That said, she hurried towards the shelf in the corner and took down a small sewing box. Opening it, she retrieved a folded sheet of paper and handed it to Dirk. He snatched it from her hand and skimmed over the words. Then his eyes noticed the scripture verses penned at the bottom of the page. "The Riley's and their Bible code," he sneered. "You and Ma Riley must have figured this out." He grabbed Copper by the arm and twisted it, causing her to wince. "What's the message? Vernon and that old man didn't get religion. I was in the next cell, and I cut a small hole through the adjoining wall. I could hear *almost* every word. One-day Tar was talking about a stagecoach that had been caught in a mudslide, his voice got lower then, but I know I heard the word **gold!** After that, their talk was more guarded, but I heard Petrified Forest and then they started looking up Bible verses. I bribed the guard to tell me if either of them sent out any letters. Vernon sent one and this has to be it! I want to know what the message says."

Copper stiffened, "I'll tell you anything you want to know, if you'll just leave Mariah and me here when you go!"

When Dirk released her Copper quickly stepped away from the man and rubbed her arm, "Ma figured it out but I didn't bring the paper with the directions in case it fell into the wrong hands. I'll look up all the verses for you. But that money is most likely stolen and your sister won't want anything to do with it. If you'll just leave us, I will gladly write down these directions for you. I'll even fill your saddlebags with food to speed you on your way.

You needn't worry about Mariah—Shad and I will always make sure she has a home here for as long as she wants or needs one. Being with you will only put her in more danger!"

Dirk only sneered, "I'll do as I please. For now, explain this code. Vernon never would tell me how it worked and I want to make sure yer not tryin' to trick me."

"It's very simple, first you just look up each book, chapter and verse. The colon here, see these two dots, that's what separates the chapter number from the verse or verses. The second colon here doesn't make any sense, but if you aren't in the habit of looking up Bible verses you wouldn't know that. The number that's behind the second colon tells you which word or words within the verse that are to be used as part of the message."

As Dirk looked on, Copper quickly flipped through the pages of her Bible and patiently showed Dirk how she found each book, chapter, and verse and then using the number after the second colon she counted the words until she came to the exact word or phrase that Vernon meant to include in his message. When she finished the page looked like this:

Job 21:6:7	petrified
1 Kings 7:2:12	forest
Genesis 1:16:3	two
Matthew 23:17:3	fools
Job 28:1:4	mine
Hosea 12:1:6-10	chase after the east wind
Lamentations 3:2	he has led me, brought me into darkness, not into light
Jeremiah 48:28:21-26	by the mouth of a cave
Proverbs 2:4:12-13	hidden treasure

"Still looks like gibberish to me," he grumbled. "Those are pretty poor directions."

Copper shrugged, "Yes, I thought so too. At least you know where to begin. I don't think the Petrified Forest is very far from here. Your biggest challenge will be to find the Two Fools Mine."

Dirk cursed, then glanced apologetically towards his sister. Seeing that she was still asleep he kept his voice low, "This place is only about a day's ride from the edge of the Petrified Forest, but I've never heard of the Two Fools Mine—it could be anywhere!"

Rubbing the back of his neck Dirk shook his head. "Nothin' has turned out like I wanted it too. I'd hoped you already had the gold and you and I could be well on our way by now. Hoped to get clean away before Todd showed up. Now, I don't know what to do!"

"Do you mean Jimmy Todd, Sheriff Jimmy Todd?" Copper sounded frantic, "He's not coming here, is he?"

"Yeah..." Dirk shrugged, "I had figured on you and me lighting out before he got here." He gave Copper another one of those looks that made her want to run, "I came for my woman and he wanted his...so..." Suddenly he turned towards Mariah, her pale blond hair fanned out across her pillow. She looked like the angel he had always thought her to be. As realization struck, he grabbed Copper roughly by the arm, "Tell me that you've had another woman up here! A saloon girl—a prostitute! I heard the Preacher took Todd's woman away and that she was here at the McKenna's." Dirk's eyes filled with a mixture of rage and horror. "It couldn't have been Sis. No—it couldn't have been her that Todd and those other men—tell me it wasn't Mariah!"

Copper shook free of Dirk's grasp and spat out her reply, "Of course it was her! She told you how Preacher and Shad and I helped her through a time of despair! We've even heard rumors that Victor didn't kill himself, that Todd killed him—just so he could have Mariah. Her husband had gambled everything away and she had to move to town from their ranch. Not a sole would hire or even befriend her. It was all Todd's doing and some of the other men in town too. They threatened all the townsfolk, told them not help her in any way. Every night she had to search through the town's garbage for food and then sneak into the livery at night for a warm place to sleep."

Dirk listened with his jaw clenching, while his hand curled into a fist. He didn't want to hear any of it but Copper kept telling him more!

"Finally, Mariah's only desire was to end her misery, as honorably as she could. She went up into the hills in hopes that she would fall asleep and die from the cold. But she awoke the next morning with a high fever. She stumbled into town simply for a drink of water. That's when Hennessey found her unconscious beside the well. That's when he had her carried into the saloon! The very day her fever broke, Todd and the other men in town..."

"Enough! I know what they did!" Dirk spoke the words through gritted teeth. "I know—they all bragged about it. I heard about what they did but—I didn't know who the woman was—it was just—I mean it didn't..."

"It was just some widow woman, right? That's why it didn't matter—did it, Dirk?" Copper challenged, "When a woman is down on her luck—it's just too bad for her. She's fair game for any man who wants to take advantage of her, isn't that right? After all, women are meant to be used—aren't they? Isn't that what you and Vernon wanted when you found me? Isn't that just how you saw me then—and how you saw me today? Suddenly, you see what those men did was...*evil!* Because this time it was your beloved sister that was shamefully abused. You know as well as I do that there is no sweeter woman in the world than Mariah. She didn't deserve to be treated that way. But I contend that—no one does! People who abuse someone for entertainment are cowards and the lowest of all creatures. And Jimmy Todd is..."

"I said that's enough, Red! I know more than anyone does about Sheriff Jimmy Todd!" Dirk spoke the name like a curse, then added. "And for the first time, in a very long time, I'm ashamed to admit that I'm pretty much—his equal." Suddenly Dirk jumped up and ran a shaky hand over his white hair, his braid trailing down his back. He had just remembered the bargain he'd made. Todd could have his woman and Dirk could have the redhead. Only now, everything had changed. He spun around and stared at Copper. "Jimmy Todd is on his way here—now. I've got to get you both out of here—and quick!"

When Copper shook her head, Dirk grabbed her and gave her a hard-shake. "Listen to me," he shouted. "I love my sister and I'm gonna take care of her but I'm only one man. Todd might come here alone but if the stage holdup didn't go as planned then he'll be comin' here with more men. Some of the toughest men I know. If I try to tell them that—Mariah is my sister—they won't just walk away—they'll kill me and keep you both for themselves. We've got to leave! Now I'll go see if that mule of yours will let me put a saddle on her. Meanwhile you get Mariah ready to travel, make a bedroll and pack up some food."

Copper didn't want to leave, "I'm a good shot and we can hold them off long enough for Shad and Preacher to get back! They'll fight against the Sheriff and those other men. You don't know my husband, he's..."

"A bear of a man. Yeah I've heard that already." Dirk grunted. He hated the adoration he heard in her voice. What surprised him was that he also suddenly hated everything about the trap they had set. Slowly he added, "The warning they got about the stage bein' hit—was all planned. We knew Preacher would go and we counted on McKenna ridin' with him. If things went like they were supposed to—both those men are dead by now. Along with that old couple, the Haze's."

"NO!" Copper cried.

Dirk grabbed her roughly again and shook her, "Listen to me! If that man's such a bear he can take care of himself. I can take care of Todd, if he comes up here alone. But if he brings Claw and Zeno, we're gonna be in a lot of trouble! They're both black-hearted renegades. I'm tellin' ya they're hard, rough men. I've never seen their equal in a fight and if they decide they want you and Mariah for themselves—I won't be able to stop them—not both of them together!" When Copper's face grew pale he shook her again but more gently this time, "Red, you've got to keep your wits about ya. Help me get you and Mariah far away from here. The trouble is, I have no money—if we're gonna get very far we've got to find that gold Tar hid—and find it fast!"

They rode in silence long into the night, as they cautiously skirted the edges of the forest, avoiding any open valleys where they could be easily spotted in the moonlight. Both women struggled not to be lulled to sleep by the soft creaking of saddle leather and the rhythmic scuffing of the horse's hooves, for they seemed to harmonize with the distant serenade of a wolf pack. They continued on in the shadowed light until the trail looked as if it disappeared into nothingness and they were forced to stop. So far, Dirk had been covering their tracks whenever possible, but he kept pushing them on. What with Copper's pregnancy and Mariah's wound, both women were exhausted long before Dirk found a safe place to make camp.

The weight of this journey fell hardest on Copper. At first Mariah rode in the arms of her brother, but Dirk needed the freedom to scout ahead then go back and brush out their tracks. It was decided that Mariah could ride more comfortably with Copper on Remy's strong back. The trouble was that Mariah was drowsy from the laudanum and yet still in pain. It was all Copper could do to keep her friend from slipping off the saddle! Finally, Dirk took a length of rope and tied Mariah to Copper's back.

It was a great relief to both women when the trail became too steep to travel in the dark. Mariah winced in pain as her brother lifted her from the saddle and gently set her down on a thick buffalo robe. Over his shoulder Dirk grunted, "I'll go feed and hobble our mounts. Red, dig a little hole in the ground with a stick then build the smallest fire you can make. We can at least have some hot coffee with the biscuits you packed."

When he returned to camp Copper handed the man a cup of steaming coffee and a cold biscuit, then answered his unspoken question: "Your sister is hurting, but so far at least, there's no fever!" Cradling her own hot cup between her hands, she sat down on a rock, "Mr. Culley," she asked. "From the day I nearly drowned in the river you've been telling me about things that had been foretold to you. Would you explain that to me?"

"That ain't none a yer business, Red."

Just then Mariah seemed to rouse a bit and said softly, "I'm hurting too much to sleep, please tell us Ladd. I'd like to hear about it too!"

Dirk grunted and scowled as he put the last of his biscuit into his mouth and washed it down with a slurp of hot coffee. He studied the dark brew as he swirled the remainder in his cup, "Now I remember why I've always steered clear of women—too meddlesome for their own good." He nearly smiled, then addressed his first words to Copper, "For obvious reasons, everyone has always thought me—odd. Everyone but Sis," he added as he locked eyes with Mariah. "You were the only person in this whole rotten world that thought I had any worth. You probably didn't even know when that gypsy wagon came around. But that's when all the townsfolk taunted me, said that I was a freak and that I belonged with them. So, I went to their camp one night." Dirk sneered mockingly, "and wouldn't ya know it—they said I was cursed and didn't want nothin' to do with me either! But the old grandmamma of the bunch called to me and said, 'You have no power over being different—but you do have power over what you do with that difference. You can do good or evil with it—it is your choice.' She talked to me for a long time and before I left she said, 'Young man, your future is laid out before me like a map. You will follow a dark path and along that path I see two women..."

"Go on." Mariah urged when her brother stopped talking and just stared at her and then at Copper, "What did she say about the two women?"

Dirk shook his head, when the day had begun he was certain he and Jimmy Todd had set the perfect plan into motion. But then he had heard Mariah scream the name Laddy, and that had changed everything. Worse yet, he learned that it wasn't just some faceless woman who was the ravished widow of Otter Run. It had been his own sweet sister. He was going to have to kill Jimmy Todd. It wouldn't be easy—but he had it to do!

"Ladd, please," Mariah whispered, pulling Dirk from his thoughts. "Tell us the rest of it."

"All right, Sis." He sighed. "That old gypsy told me that she saw two women in my future. 'Course it's plain to see that the first one was Copper." Her turned his gaze on her, and said, "The gypsy said that she would have hair the color of sunset and eyes as green as clover. And that she would lead me to somethin' important—somethin' of great value! Then he turned his eyes back to Mariah and continued reverently, "She said that the second woman stands in the light, and that she was always standin' too close to me—to see her clearly. That describes you Mariah. You've always been my light, and even when you were a little thing you always stood closer to me than was good for ya." Dirk fought down a sudden lump in his throat, then added, "The gypsy saw it all, Mariah. A woman wearing a band of gold on her left hand, blood seeping through her fingers as she covers a wound. She said, no wound would ever hurt me more and she was right! Nothing has ever been as painful to me as hurting you has been!"

There were other things the gypsy had told him but he didn't feel like sharing them although he remembered them well. The old woman's words haunted him. Instead he tamped down her warnings and allowed his eyes to roam over Copper possessively, "That's why I was so mad at Vernon when he took you away from me, Red. He said he married you to protect you. That was a lie, he knew about what the gypsy told me and he wanted to get that 'somethin' of value' for himself! It sure is strange, but the two women the gypsy told me about are the both of you." When Copper scowled at him, he asked, "How can you doubt it? How did my sister come to be your best friend? Mariah with a gold ring on her hand was covering her bloody wound and you're leading me to the Two Fools Mine, to hidden treasure! Face it, Red, you were meant to be my woman. We were all—meant to be together!"

Not allowing Copper time to reply, Dirk pulled the letter from his pocket and moved to sit on the ground beside her, "Here Red—let's look at this again!"

She became rigid when he moved closer, for she was still very much afraid of Dirk Culley! And yet, she knew from experience, that arguing with a violent man was never wise. There was Shad and the baby to think of and Mariah too! The best thing to do was to be respectful and within reason, to cooperate. Taking the letter from his hand, she began to read, "These directions aren't very helpful. But I suppose if we—well—sort of read between the lines. The first thing to do is find the *Petrified Forest*. Then, somewhere in the forest is the *Two Fools Mine*. Once you're inside the mine itself, is says to *chase after the east wind*. Possibly there's more than one tunnel, if so, then you must take the one that goes east. Or it could mean that there is a breeze coming from the east. This next line, *he has led me—brought me into darkness, not into light*. This sounds like you may have to walk for some distance in the dark. That line was enough to make me forget the whole idea!" When Dirk just frowned up at her she shrugged then continued, "All right—then you come to the last two lines. They speak for themselves—*By the mouth of a cave—Hidden Treasure*. I can only assume that the path through the mine becomes a cave at some point. When you get to the cave opening, you'll find whatever Tar O'Leary hid there."

"You're doin' a lot of guessin', Red!"

"O'Leary and Vernon wrote this. I'm just trying to help you figure it out, Mister Culley!" Copper huffed. "But until you can locate the *Two Fools Mine*, this message is worthless. Finding the mine and whatever is hidden inside it, might very well be impossible! That's another reason why I didn't pursue it myself. All the treasure I've ever wanted is back at that little cabin with Shadrack McKenna!"

"Forget about him and call me Dirk," he said as he tried to take Copper's hand. When she quickly moved away, he folded his arms and asked, "Ya got somethin' else of value, lady? The gypsy told me about you long before this was written," he added as he folded the letter and put it back in his pocket. "Maybe you have some other treasures for me. Ya have a rich uncle somewhere?" When Copper shook her head, he studied her with an appreciative eye, "Well, the fact is, you're a pretty woman. I don't like that you're carrying another man's baby but a pretty woman is a fine thing! I still think we'll find that money. When we do I'll take you and Mariah far away from here."

His words sent a shiver all through Copper's body, but she knew it would be useless to argue. Suddenly, a thought came to her and she said softly, "Come to think of it, I do have a treasure! It's the kind you don't have to search for or risk your life to find! But—it is not what you think. You don't dig it from the ground or steal it from a bank. It's a gift—a free gift from God himself!"

Dirk cursed as he flung his empty coffee cup to the ground. "I'll have none of that, Red—I don't want your religion and I don't need it."

"I used to feel the exact same way. You are a hard man, Mister Culley," she said ignoring the flash of anger that blazed in his glassy eyes. "And yet, from what your sister has told me, and what I've seen for myself, there is good in you! Like the old gypsy told you…being an albino makes you different—but that's all—it does not make you good or bad! You are—what you choose to be. I imagine that all your life people have misjudged you. I think you've come to believe that if everyone is going to treat you badly, then you might as well treat everyone you meet the same way. Isn't that right?"

Dirk glared at Copper. Her words were hitting a bit too close and he didn't like it. He glanced once again at Mariah and winced when she blinked up at him with that same caring she'd always had for him. Looking at her, his stomach rolled with feelings of guilt and regret. He had nearly killed the only person in the world that ever loved him. Getting to his feet he retrieved his discarded cup and sloshed more coffee into it. Instead of drinking it, he simply stared into the dark liquid and mumbled, "I can see my sister wants me to listen. So go ahead Red, say whatever ya want."

Surprised by his response, Copper silently prayed for the right words, then turned to him, "Do you remember the man that drowned while Vernon was pulling me out of the river? I think you knew I was his bondservant." When Dirk simply shrugged Copper continued, "I've been a servant pretty much all my life. I was set free that day. Free from Percy Barr and free of Vernon Riley, my husband of two minutes. I thought my life would be perfect from then on—but it wasn't. Instead I felt lost and angry!"

Dirk just sat there scowling at the ground but he also seemed to be listening, so Copper continued, "Ma Riley told me that I felt that way because I was trying to find my way through life without the proper directions. That's why God sent his son to show us the way. Jesus lived his life as an example, and His teachings are written down in the Bible. God's word explains why and how Jesus died to pay the penalty for our sins. If we ask God to forgive our sins and accept what Christ did for us on the cross, then God can really show us the right way to go. When we follow Jesus Christ, he leads us straight to an eternal life with Him, and that's the greatest treasure of all!"

Dirk rubbed the back of his neck and threw a stick into the fire. "Not interested! Not in that kind of treasure, Red. Everything in my life has directed me towards the life I'm living now. That's the life I've chosen, and nothing can change that!" Dirk looked again at his sister, who was now sound asleep, and Copper could see worry creasing his brow. "I'll do right by her, and maybe even you, if you behave yourself." Standing, he tossed his untouched coffee into the bushes and gazed around their small encampment. "I'm used to sleepin' with one eye open so don't be scared to sleep. Lay down next to Sis, I'll bed down out there in the woods. If ya hear anything don't call out—or try anything clever—ya hear? Nothin' can sneak past me!"

Copper nodded her understanding but before Dirk disappeared into the dark she said softly, "I'll be praying for you, Ladd." When he spun around to correct her she held up her hand to stop him. "If you want to do right by Mariah, then you have to remember that you are, Ladd, her beloved brother. She will never accept Dirk Culley. Another thing you need to know is your sister is a child of God now. She and I both share the treasure I was just telling you about. Mariah will do her best to share it with you. She'll tell it and she'll sing it…but she won't let you forget it."

Dirk opened his mouth intending to let loose with a string of curses that would curl this little snippet's straight red hair. But strangely enough he found that the words would not form in his mouth. Feeling frustrated and confused he turned and disappeared into the forest.

Chapter 25
Ambush

"Let me describe for you a worthless and wicked man; first he is a constant liar. Next his heart is full of rebellion. But he will be destroyed suddenly, broken beyond hope of healing." Proverbs 6:12, 14, 15

Jimmy Todd smiled when he heard the stagecoach rumbling over the mountain road. It wasn't visible yet, but the swirling dust cloud rising into the air told him that Danby was probably trying to make up time. Mostly, this mountain trail was slow going, as it consisted of steep hills and valleys interspersed with mile long stretches of rolling hills. The road, if you could call it that, was constantly changing and sometimes wound around narrow mountain ledges that, if fallen from, meant a long scream and certain death.

Today he was not riding his flashy paint. Instead he rode a common bay gelding, who stamped impatiently. The saddle leather creaked as he stood up in his stirrups, "Yep, this is the perfect spot for an ambush. It's always the waiting that bothers me!"

Well hidden behind boulders and brush, he gazed across the narrow valley where a tiny creek provided a pleasant resting spot for passengers and horses alike. It was the only level ground after a long descent and before a steep climb. Todd couldn't help but smile, "This will be just like shooting fish in a barrel!"

While he waited, everything played out perfectly in his head. When the driver reached the hill overlooking the steep decline into the valley, he would stop the coach, jump down and slide a thick log through the back two wheels of the wagon. As he drove the team down the hill, the log would effectively lock the rear wheels, slowing the coach considerably and preventing it from overtaking the horses. Once the stage reached the valley below, Danby would rein in the team, set the brake and remove the log from the wheels. This was always a good place to rest and water the horses, and he'd probably invite the passengers to get out and stretch their legs. After such a bumpy and dusty ride, everyone, especially an elderly couple like the Haze's, would welcome this brief stop.

Todd gave a slight chuckle, "They just won't know how brief—or that this stop will be their last!" He liked this plan but he was beginning to have second thoughts about Long and McKenna. "We should have just sent Crow and Zeno after them," he hissed as his attention was drawn towards the rider coming up from Otter Run. It was the freckle faced bank teller, Hank Wyatt. The young man was obviously distressed as he came crashing through some brush at a full gallop!

"Sheriff!" he called, reining his horse to a sliding stop. "We got to call this off—Dirk never showed!"

Todd cursed and scowled at the younger man. He hadn't told Hank about the change in plan. "Don't call me sheriff out here ya idiot! And we don't need him for this—I've got him doin' another job today."

Hank was still breathing hard from the fast ride as he rubbed a shaking hand over his face. He had been relieved when the albino hadn't shown up, thinking that would be a good excuse to call this whole thing off. The idea of killing two preachers and an old woman—was surely the lowest job the Highlanders had ever pulled! Unfortunately, he was in too deep with this group of men to back out. And it seemed that Todd was still determined to go through with it.

"Listen," Hank implored, "let's not do this! I've got a real bad feeling and I think…"

"Think? Nobody cares what you—think!" Todd snorted, "Ya want to know what that albino thinks? He thinks you're a worthless fool! Of course I told him you're just a little wet behind the ears. So don't prove me wrong! This is the easiest job we've ever done. So, relax kid—breathe!"

Hank stiffened at the sheriff's patronizing remarks, "I'm breathin' Todd, and I'm not worthless and I'm not a fool! I'm smart enough to know that some jobs are worth the risk, and this one isn't!"

Todd reached over and grabbed the front of Hank's shirt. "Krane and Hennessey call the jobs," he sneered. "And—I make sure they get done. Furthermore, if you try to back out, I'll just pin this whole thing on you. And if Velvet didn't do her job and get McKenna and Long up here—I'll make her pay too!"

Hank quickly lost his boyish fears and shoved Todd's hands off his shirt, "I better never hear of you hurting, Velvet. If Long and McKenna don't show, it's not her fault. I trust her with my life!"

Todd shook his head, "Never trust a woman, kid. Every hussy wants two rings: one on her finger and the other through your nose. Now pay attention. That stage should be sliddin' down that hill soon and we've got to be ready!"

If he turned against Todd, Hank knew he probably wouldn't live out the day and then Velvet would suffer too. He was going to have to go through with this—all of it!

Todd scanned the surrounding hills for any sign of McKenna or Long. He was hoping that McKenna stayed with the women and then Danby would only have to kill the preacher. That would just leave the old couple for him to deal with, and yet, it might just take, him, Hank and Danby to kill off that preacher! Men that powerful didn't always die easy. But die he must, 'cause when Quincy Long was finally out of the way—Mariah no longer had a champion. Todd hadn't been able to stop thinking of her. Soon he would be running his hands through her pale blonde hair and looking into her violet eyes again. She would be his and that Bible thumper would never bother him again!

Twisting in his saddle Todd held up his hand, "Think I hear 'em!" When they heard horses nickering from the top of the hill, he and Hank both reached forward to slide their hands over their horse's muzzles to keep them from answering the greeting.

Jack's black eye squinted through the powerful scope of his .50 caliber Sharps as he scanned the area from his high mountain lookout. An obvious drama was unfolding right before him. From the east he spotted the twisting swirl of dust, kicked up by six horses pulling the coach over the sandy road. Just below him were two mounted men waiting behind the cover of boulders at the bottom of the hill. Swinging the Sharps to the west he saw two riders racing down a steep mustang trail that ended on the opposite side of the valley where the other men were waiting.

Jack frowned as he ran his hand down his braided beard, "My eyes sure ain't as good as they used to be, even using the scope, but there's no mistaken that buckskin appaloosa stud. That's gotta be Boone and the grulla—that's Flint for sure. Reckon it don't take a mastermind to see why Shad and Preacher are ridin' hell bent fer leather down that trail?" Jack shook his head and grumbled, "I know what's 'bout to happen here. That stage is gonna get hit by those two jayhawkers waitin' to ambush 'em when they stop to rest." Jack whistled through his teeth, "Lead's gonna be popping around here like water in hot grease!"

Just then the distant squeak of wagon wheels and the jangling of trace chains topped the high ridge above the valley. Danby, reigned in the horses, set the break, and jumped from his high coach seat. Just as Todd had envisioned it, he untied an eight-foot pole from the top of the coach and slid it between the spokes of the two back wheels. Once he was back in the driver's seat, Danby drove the team down the long, slow decent into the valley below. The stage skidded all the way, and even with the rear wheels locked, the six horses stiffened their legs, sliding most of the way down on their haunches.

"Okay kid, listen up," Todd ordered. "When that stage gets to level ground, down here in the valley, we're gonna come at 'em like a hailstorm! I'll call for the driver to throw down his gun. Of course Danby won't do it, because if Long and McKenna or both of 'em are out there, that's when they'll show themselves. Danby's fast, he'll most likely shoot 'em both the instant they show their faces. But remember this…those men have to go down before we kill the old folks. We might have to keep them alive for a while, just in case we need hostages."

Hank swallowed down his disgust as he ran a shaking hand over his face, "Okay Sheriff, I'll follow your lead."

"If you call me Sheriff one more time, I'm gonna bust your skull! And—I'll be the one to follow you, *boy*." Todd mocked, "Wanna make sure you don't turn coward on me."

Hank's jaw pulsed with anger, but finally he nodded his agreement and they both pulled the black bandanas up around their faces. The coach would soon be coming to a stop, less than ten yards from the boulders they were hiding behind.

Jack studied them from his high lookout and slid a bullet into the chamber of his rifle then turned his scope to the west. He watched as Shad and Preacher left their horses ground tied and began inching their way along the creek bed. He could only hope that they would spot the two outlaws that were waiting behind the boulders. Bandanas or not, Jack already knew who they were. He gritted his teeth as the coach slowly eased its way down into the valley.

"Them poor folks," Jack grumbled, "ain't got no idea they's about to be in the middle of a gun fight! Too bad I can't get any closer. Still, I reckon I can help Shad and Preacher iffen I worry them bandits a little!"

"Whoa now! Rest stop folks!" Danby called loudly as he tied off the reins and set the brake. A grim smile lit his face when he heard the crack of pistol shots and saw Hank and Todd riding out from behind the boulders. Firing wildly over their heads they called out, "This is a hold up! Driver, throw down your gun!"

Danby stood up in the driver's box, dangling his rife, as if he were preparing to drop it over the side. From the height of the driver's box he spotted Shad and Preacher trying to stay low as they made their way towards the stage, using the tall grass for cover. They were coming up on the right side while Hank and Todd were on the left. Instantly he swung his rifle up and turned it on the dark haired, bear like figure clad in buckskin.

Shocked that the driver didn't understand why they were there, Shad held up his hand, "Don't shoot—we're here to help!" he shouted, even as he rolled to the right just as fire blazed from the driver's gun and a searing pain burned through his left shoulder. Instantly, Danby cocked his gun, determined not to miss a second time, he aimed once again. Just as he was pulling the trigger, his own body jerked violently and he fell from the driver's box onto the ground.

Shad felt the second bullet whiz past his head, and his shoulder felt like it was on fire. Still, when he saw the driver fall, his first thought was that the team would bolt and run away with the Haze's still inside. Rolling to his feet he ran to get in front of the frightened horses as they reared and lunged against their harness. Even though the brake was set and the pole kept the back wheels from rolling, the powerful horses were still able to drag the coach yards away before Shad finally reached the two lead horses. His left arm was of little use, but he managed to block them with his body and hold the reins with his right hand. He used the horses as shields while gun fire was bursting all around him, but it took every ounce of his strength to keep them under control.

Todd cursed when he saw Danby fall. The man had only gotten off two shots. He saw McKenna, with a bloody shoulder, making a run for the horses. Since he hadn't seen Preacher he could only hope that Danby had killed him or that he'd stayed with the women. Todd wasn't sure of anything. Nothing was going the way it was supposed to. Gritting his teeth he suddenly realized that with Danby dead, everything fell to him!

Since McKenna was busy holding the team and there'd been no sign of Long, Todd spurred his horse towards the stage window. He'd kill the couple, then head for cover and wait to see how things played out from there. Pointing his pistol inside the coach, he grinned, "Yep, just like shootin' fish in a barrel!" He laughed when saw the white-headed John Haze throw himself in front of his wife. Out of the corner of his eye, he saw the flash of a pistol pointing at him from the opposite window and he turned his own gun and fired.

The two pistols were triggered at the same time. Todd's bullet ripped a hole in the coach door just above Preacher's head. While his bullet nicked Todd's gun with just enough force to knock it out of his hand.

Todd was furious! He reached for the second gun he carried on his left side, but before he could aim it, another bullet flipped his hat into the air! The shot had come from high up on the mountain. Then Preacher fired again and his bullet whizzed past Todd's cheek while another one grazed the flank of Hank's horse and it began to buck, then Todd's own horse began to buck as well. When they managed to get their mounts under control they ran for cover, all the while being peppered with sporadic gun fire.

Seeing that the Haze's were uninjured, and that the outlaws were heading for cover, Preacher yelled, "Stay down and hold on!" Working as quickly as possible, he reached down and yanked the pole out from the wheels and flung it aside. Fearing the horses would feel the wheels no longer locked, Preacher jumped onto the side of the stage and climbed into the driver's box. He grabbed the reins, released the brake then glanced towards the boulders. He needn't worry, the shooter that had been helping them from above was doing a good job of keeping the outlaws pinned down.

The moment Shad saw that Preacher was safely in the driver's box and had a good hold on the reins, he used his last bit of strength to swing onto the back of the lead pony that was the farthest away from the outlaws, then kicked the horse and bellowed, "HAAA. LET'S GO!"

Preacher echoed Shad's command and picked up the whip. He cracked it loudly over the heads of the six horses, who eagerly strained against their harness and hauled the stage up the steep hill.

When they reached the top of the hill, Preacher looked up, "Whew—thanks Boss—that was close!" he sighed, still trying to catch his breath. "And thanks for sending old Jack to help us get away!" He knew it had to be Jack, the report of his .50 caliber Sharps was as recognizable as the voice of an old friend. In fact, he could still hear shots. Jack was keeping those men from following, but there was no telling how soon Jack might run out of ammunition. The horses were breathing hard from the steep climb, but he didn't dare rest them any longer. They needed to get the stage and the Haze's into town. Just then, he saw Shad fall from the lead horse. There was a growing blossom of blood spreading across his upper left shirt sleeve, while another red stain spread over his right thigh. Preacher chided himself—how had he not noticed that his friend had been wounded, not only once but twice! Knowing the horses were still spooked, he kept a strong hold on the reins and called out, "John, Shad's been shot—he needs your help!" The old man jumped down from the coach with surprising agility for a man of his age and hurried towards Shad.

"Lord, have mercy!" The old Reverend prayed, as he half carried, half dragged Shad to the stagecoach door. It was all the big mountain man could do to stay conscious and try to help the elderly couple as they struggled to pull him inside.

Even before they'd closed the door, Preacher slapped the reins and headed the stage towards Otter Run. Willy was already tearing her petticoat for bandages, and John was applying pressure to Shad's wounds. The elderly couple worked over the big man as they sent up prayers that their rescuer wouldn't bleed to death before they got him to town.

The high lookout afforded Black-Eyed Jack the perfect view of everything. He could see when the stage reached the safety of the hill as well as what those two outlaws were doing below. He'd run out of ammunition for his Sharps. He had his Henry and his pistol but they lacked the range to do him any good. He didn't dare get any closer or he would become an easy target.

"Reckon I helped some but I sure wish I'd been close enough to finish them varmints off fer good. Still I know there's other's in that gang and I aim to get ever-one o' them ornery critters—once and for all!"

Using the scope on his rifle, Jack cursed when he saw that Shad had been wounded. He wasted no time in abandoning his high perch, and then let out an ear splitting whistle, which was Shad's special call for Boone. Immediately, the appaloosa stallion lifted his head and nickered, then he spun on his hocks and raced up the hill towards Jack, with Flint following close behind.

When the stage was out of sight and whoever was shooting at them stopped, Hank Wyatt grabbed his hat and threw it to the ground. "This whole thing has blown up on us. I told you this was a bad idea—I told ya!"

Todd sneered at Hank in disgust, "You coward! Did ya even fire yer gun? If you were any lower, I'd wrap you around a hook and use you for bait!" Stepping closer to the young man, his eyes looked wild as he asked, "So—you thought this was a bad idea did ya? Do ya want out?"

Hank knew he'd said too much. Todd was the kind of man who had a thirst for killing and since his thirst had not been quenched, Hank had no doubt that Todd would happily shoot him.

"No—I don't want out." Hank insisted, then half-heartedly asked, "Shouldn't we be going after that stage?"

Todd said nothing as he turned away from Hank and tightened the cinch on the bay gelding. He fought to cool the blood lust that surged through his veins. As he swung up on his horse, he finally calmed down enough to speak, "Forget the stage! This idea would have worked just fine, if that shooter up on that cliff hadn't butted in. But this day isn't over yet and what I wanted most from this day—I'm not gonna lose!"

Cautiously, Todd searched the rocks where the gunfire had come from earlier, "Mount up Hank, I'm done with playin' Sheriff and yer done with playin' the honest bank teller. We're gonna ride to the hideout and get Zeno and Claw. It was stupid and greedy of Hennessey not to bring them in on this. We're not takin' that drunken Irishman's orders anymore! We're ridin' to get my woman and then we're gonna go back to the hideout. And then boy, I'm gonna do whatever I want, 'cause from now on—I'm gonna be the boss!"

As they mounted their horses, Hank felt brave enough to speak. "Yeah, let's forget about those preachers. Then we can finally drive all the cows we've rustled down to Canyon City. We'll make a lot of money!"

"Shut up Hank!" Todd hissed. "We're not done with those Bible thumpers. Danby hit McKenna and I know I got another bullet in him. He probably won't last long. But I'm not gonna rest until that meddlesome Preacher is gone for good! First though, I'm gonna go get my woman! I should have gone to McKenna's and let the albino handle this. At least he should have both women by now, but I don't think I cotton to him being around anymore. Tell ya what...beginning tonight, Mariah will be my woman alone. But you, Claw and Zeno can toss a coin for Dirk's little redhead!"

Chapter 26
Facing Your Fears

"Be strong and courageous. Do not be afraid; do not be discouraged, for the Lord your God will be with you wherever you go." Joshua 1:9

When Preacher drove the stage into town, it was Tick Hobbs, who raced to open the coach's door, and it was he who helped carry Shad into the Long Shot. They took him straight to the saloon because it was common knowledge that Shotsy was the closest thing Otter Run had to a doctor. She was a woman of many talents. Along with her *upstairs work*, she sang and danced, but she also knew how to bring down a fever, remove a bullet or stitch up a knife wound. Ox grudgingly allowed her to use her healing skills, just so long as she didn't leave the saloon. Nothing seemed to ruffle Shotsy; it was all in a day's work for her. Nevertheless, she was a bit flabbergasted, when she saw the straitlaced, white-haired Wilhelmina Haze rolling up her sleeves as she followed the men through the saloon's swinging doors.

When the little woman stared up at her and said in her oh so sweet voice, "Hello dear, Quin says you have quite a healing touch! I've had a bit of nursing experience and sometimes an extra pair of willing hands can be a real help! So, feel free to order me about—I'll do whatever you say!"

Shotsy scoffed at her words. She knew exactly what prim and proper little women like this one thought of her. Lifting her chin defiantly, she sneered, "A real *lady* like you, I doubt ya'd have the stomach for what needs to be done here."

Just then the old woman truly did shock the hardened saloon girl when she put her arm around her corseted waist. "My name is Willy," she said softly. "Like it or not dear girl, I've come up here to be your friend. I'm a whole lot tougher than I look, and I've got the constitution of a sun dried brick—not much fazes an old gal like me. So, why don't we get to know each other while we patch up this poor man?"

Shotsy opened her mouth to say something that would surely burn the old lady's ears for a week, but just then Willy looked up with her guileless blue eyes, and the hate-filled words seem to dissolve in her mouth. Instead she muttered, "I—I'll take care of the leg wound. Looks like the bullet went all the way through his shoulder. Think you can clean and bandage it?" When Willy nodded, Shotsy took Shad's hunting knife from its scabbard and cut through his leather shirt around the shoulder wound and then slit an opening exposing the wound on his thigh.

"Hey, have a care," Shad groaned weakly, "these are my best buckskins!"

Instantly both women replied in unison, "Oh, HUSH!"

Willy and Shotsy locked eyes and smiled. Then Shotsy put her hands on her hips, "Mister, you've got a big o' hole goin' clean through yer shoulder and ya've got a bullet lodged in this ham sized thigh o' yers. So don't go fussin' over yer dag-gum buckskins. Now, I've gotta go fishin' for that bullet and it's gonna hurt!" She waved a small green bottle in the air and grabbed a shot glass from the bar. "I want ya to take some o' this." Pouring a small portion into the glass she held out to Shad, "It's laudanum; it will ease the pain."

Quin glared at the bottle and then at Shotsy. Mariah had told him how the two saloon girls had insisted she drink medicine from a green bottle. Probably from that same bottle. Finally, he shook off the thought and cleared his throat, "Listen to her Shad, it may take a while to find that bullet and remove it. It is going to hurt!"

"Put that stuff back in the bottle, ma'am." Shad grunted his jaw set in a firm line. "I need to keep my mind clear, gotta get home to Copper! Don't want her to worry." He looked up at Shotsy and said kindly, "I'd be obliged if ya'd just…get to work. I'm in a mighty big hurry to get home!"

The man stubbornly refused to take any laudanum nor would he take a glass of Ox's best whiskey. Finally, Shotsy shoved a thick piece of tanned leather into his mouth and told him to bite down. Beads of perspiration rolled down Shad's face while the women searched for the bullet lodged in his thigh. He managed not to pass out until Shotsy cauterized the wound. He didn't awake again for the next few hours, but it wasn't a restful sleep, instead his troubled mind relived the ambush. Over and over he saw the driver of the stage, the man had actually smiled when he shot him and then he'd try to shoot him again! Something else was tormenting him, some unseen danger was lurking in his thoughts—just beyond his reach. Finally, just as the sun was going down he awoke to his own voice shouting out, "The albino—he wasn't there!"

Shad sat straight up. His head was spinning and he hurt everywhere. Still, he fought to remember what he had just heard himself say. *The albino—he wasn't there!* The pale man with the long white braid was supposed to have been there—but he wasn't! Clem Talbott had warned them that three men would be robbing the stage. Clem didn't know the name of the albino, but he had reluctantly admitted that he believed the other two would be Sheriff Todd and Hank Wyatt. Shad buried his face in his hands and struggled to remember how the two outlaws had looked. He would have remembered a white braid and now that he thought on it, one was dark and the other had curly reddish-brown hair. The albino hadn't been there—he was sure! So, then where was he?

Surging to his feet, Shad roared, "He's got Copper—I know it!" Just then the room swirled around him and he fell back onto the bed. Sucking in deep breaths, he squeezed his eyes shut and willed the room to stand still and the nausea to go away. He had to get to Copper—but how? He couldn't even stand up!

"Think ya better take it easy there, mountain man." Shotsy's sultry warning came from the doorway as she glided into the room. Her short satin skirt rustling with each step. Sweet little Willy followed behind with his cleaned and mended buckskins draped over one arm. Preacher was the last to enter the room, carrying a tray with a bowl of stew, biscuits and a cup of steaming coffee.

Seeing that the old woman had his clothes, he glanced down and suddenly realized that he was wearing nothing but a wool blanket. Despite everything going through his mind, he turned a deep shade of crimson. Frowning his displeasure and embarrassment, he clasped the blanket tightly around him, then with his other hand he grabbed the pillow and covered himself with it as well. Naturally, all of his clothes had been bloodied and torn. It had been kind of these ladies to clean and mend them but doggone-it, he felt as helpless and naked as a new babe—and he hated it!

Even so, he owed these women his gratitude, "Listen…um…ladies. I surely do thank ya fer yer help," he muttered, "but—I need ya to hand over m' clothes and get on out o' here. I've got to get to my wife. She's in trouble!"

Shad leaned forward to take the clothes from Willy's hand, but even that made his head spin. His hand dropped and he pushed himself farther back on the bed so as not to humiliate himself by falling off of it entirely.

Shotsy put a firm hand on the big man's good shoulder. "You listen to me mountain man. We've got some news for ya and if yer gonna do anything about it, then ya got to stay calm and think straight. Understand?"

Shad blew out a breath and nodded his head, "You all know somethin' about Copper, don't ya?" He looked up at Preacher, "That albino's got her hasn't he?"

Preacher started to speak, but Shotsy answered instead. "She's in trouble all right, but there's a plan being hatched to help her, so you listen up. First of all, when Preacher Long carried you in here and told everyone that the stage got ambushed but nothin' got stolen, and nobody got killed but the driver—well—old Ox turned three shades o' ugly and lit out o' here like his tail feathers was on fire! Black–Eyed Jack was just ridin' in when Ox was ridin' out, so Jack followed him. He lost him in the dark so he went to check on yer women folk, thinkin' maybe he'd bring 'em back to town." Just then Shotsy stopped and bit her lip, some of this didn't make sense.

"So…tell me, what did he find?" Shad growled.

"Jack said he knew something was amiss right off…no smoke comin' from the chimney. No crazy mule actin' like a rooster—whatever that meant. When he finally made his way up to the cabin…no one was there…but there were a lot of horse tracks in the yard—three maybe four riders. The front door was wide open and it looked like there was blood on the front door and on the floor."

When Shad moaned and buried his face in his hands, Shotsy put her hands on her hips and frowned, "Now you just settle down—it ain't all bad news. Yer cabin was tore up a bit, and the women were taken but thanks to Jack and yer wife, we know what happened to 'em. You see Jack had a hunch and he searched until he found your wife's sketchbook. He thought she might have left you a message. But since he can't read, he just brought it here."

Preacher stepped forward and pulled a torn piece of paper from his pocket. "Jack saved us a good bit of time by goin' up there and bringing this back. If the men that tore up the cabin had found this they would have taken it or destroyed it, so we can assume they don't know as much as we do. This is what she wrote:

Dear Shad,

I pray that you and Quin are safe! Dirk Culley came for me and Mariah got shot! God is watching over us because, it was just a flesh wound in her side. The second miracle was that after Dirk shot her, he realized Mariah was his beloved step-sister!

Preacher still couldn't quite get over this and he had to clear his throat before he could continue.

Once Dirk realized that Mariah was the woman Jimmy Todd and his gang were coming after, he knew he had to take us away, to keep us safe! We are heading for the Two Fools Mine that's located somewhere in the Petrified Forest. As crazy as it seems, Dirk has promised to protect me, as well as Mariah. I believe he will.

I know you will come for me. Please, be careful! I love you, Copper

Shad grabbed his buckskin shirt Willy had laid on the bed and growled with pain as he tried to shrug into it. "Ladies." he grunted, "Get out o' here—please. I thank ya for yer care but I need ya to let me get dressed. Preacher, is Boone saddled? We've got to go now. Where's Jack?" When no one moved to do his bidding Shad wrapped the blanket tightly around his waist and tried again to stand. If he had to push them all out the door—he would!

Rolling her eyes, Shotsy placed one hand on his shoulder and pressed down. He hadn't the strength to resist and he fell back onto the bed.

"Please," he rasped out, exhausted from even that small effort. "I need you all to help me—not fight me! My woman's in trouble, I got to get to her. Don't ya understand?"

As if the man had said nothing, Shotsy took the cup of coffee from the tray Preacher was holding and gave it to Shad, "Drink this and listen up, Hon." she said with an amused smirk, "I just pushed ya right off those two logs ya call feet! If ya try to leave now yer just gonna pass out before ya reach that door. Yer banged up enough as it is, and I sure would hate to see ya fall flat on that handsome face o' yers. But yer in luck, 'cause you see, my new friend, Wilhelmina over there?" Shotsy tossed her head of silver and black curls towards the older woman and continued, "Well—we know a few tricks that will give ya some strength." Shotsy placed one long delicate finger beneath the cup in Shad's hand and nudged it to his lips, "First, ya drink every drop of this coffee. It's full of thick cream and sweet honey and a little somethin' special," she added putting the purr back in her voice. "After that yer gonna fill yer belly with some good food. Then yer gonna sleep! You're weak as a new born kitten and you've lost a lot of blood, but tonight Willy and I are gonna make up some special pemmican my Cherokee granny taught me to make. It'll keep ya goin'. 'Course yer still gonna feel like *h*___." Shotsy's coal lined eyes darted over at Willy, then she shrugged apologetically and said, "Yer still gonna feel, *lousy!* But we figure with all of us helpin', we can get ya ready to ride by daylight! Not one minute before though—ya hear?"

He hated what she was saying but he realized that Shotsy was just speaking the truth. Staring at the cup he groaned then drank it down. Copper was in terrible danger and here he sat drinking coffee. Preacher nodded his thanks to the women as they left the room. Then he sat the tray of food on Shad's lap. He prayed over it asking for healing and protection, then he looked up and said, "Eat friend! And while you work on getting your strength back I'll fill you in on the rest of it."

Feeling a bit more encouraged that there was more to know, Shad took the bowl of stew and began methodically shoveling it into his mouth.

"When Jack came back with Copper's note, I read it to him and he told me that he knew where Dirk was taking the girls and that he knew of a short cut. He gave me directions then went on ahead. I started to just go along with him but..."

"Why didn't ya?" Shad growled, "Todd and his gang against old Jack alone! Ya should have gone with him. I'd have caught up!" He bit into a flaky biscuit adding, "No tellin' what's happenin' out there!"

"We both knew that's how you'd feel, and believe me, it wasn't easy for me to stay behind either! But, Jack and I knew that if you rode after us alone—it'd be the last ride *you'd* ever make. And we knew there wasn't a man in this town that would help you. They're all afraid to go against Ox, and even more afraid of the Sheriff. Anyone that's ever crossed them has never been seen again, like Victor Kent, or if they do come back—they're dead—draped over the sheriff's saddle. So, we decided that I would stay here and ride with you when you were strong enough, while Jack kept going! No one knows these mountains as well as that man. Jack's short cut to the Petrified Forest is a rough trail, by tomorrow morning our horses will be fresh and you'll hopefully be a lot stronger than you are now. We will make it Shad!"

Willy and John stood beside Shotsy as they watched Shad and Quin ride away. Speaking into the crisp—early morning air, John spoke his prayer out loud, "Please Lord, guide, heal and protect Quin and Shad, Mariah and Copper. This is yet another struggle between good and evil, may good claim victory today! We ask that you take all this muddle of trouble, and work it all out in a way that brings honor and glory to your name!"

Shotsy listened to the prayer and was surprise when she felt herself nodding in agreement. Then she turned sad eyes on the sweet old couple. They had simply befriended her, and not once had they looked at her as if she were dirty or inferior or stupid. Giving them a wistful smile she said, "Listen…yer fine folks, but Ox could be back any time now and ya both need to go stay at the hotel until Preacher and Shad get back. And if I don't get back to work—I mean—at least mindin' the bar." She added, feeling embarrassed for the first time in a long while. "You see, it could go real bad for Velvet and me if Ox comes back and we're not watching the Long Shot for him. This is an awful place—and—it hurts me to see good folks like you even standing in front of it. Please—ya need to go!"

John just smiled his kind smile and Willy surprised Shotsy again, when she put her arms around her and gave her a motherly hug. Then she looked up at the tall, hardened saloon girl, "We feel the same as you, dear. This is an awful place and it hurts us to leave you here. We think you and Velvet should just come away with us—now! Just turn your back on this place and the life that goes with it—and God will give you a brand new way of life." Willy took Shotsy's hand, and John placed his hand over theirs. In her straight forward and candid way Willy said boldly, "You see, John and I have decided to adopt you!" When Shotsy gave her an incredulous look, the old couple just laughed as John added, "You and Velvet both of course! That is, if you'll have us?"

As it turned out, Black-Eyed Jack's short cut to the Petrified Forest seemed better suited for mountain goats, for the only time the trail wasn't leading straight up, was when the horses were sliding down it on their haunches! The ride was hardest on Shad of course and he gritted his teeth, as the wounds in his shoulder and leg went from throbbing to burning and he felt ashamed that they were even a slight distraction, when all he should or wanted to think about was Copper! He was at least pleased that they'd gotten an early start. The town was well behind them even before the sun had been a faint glow on the horizon. Still, the pain was getting worse, so he allowed

Quin to get ahead of him, and then he reached into one of the two pouches the women had prepared. The first contained the special pemmican that Shotsy claimed would build his strength. He'd eaten some for his breakfast and lunch, and felt better for it. Just now though, he reached into the second pouch and retrieved a three fingered pinch of shredded aspen bark. He slipped it into his jaw as if it were chewing tobacco and his eyes watered from the bitter taste. Shotsy had warned him about that, but promised that after he chewed it a while, the pain would ease but it wouldn't make him drowsy like laudanum.

The men had ridden hard all day but finally, just as the burnished light of dusk was coloring the western sky, Shad and Quin heard the distinctive cry of the Meadow Lark. That was Jack's call and they reined in their horses and waited. The old man made no noise as he stepped from the shadow of a spruce tree, suddenly appearing before them like a phantom. His rifle was in his right hand and with his left he motioned for them to follow. Silently he led them to his camp. There was no fire; they couldn't risk it. Still, Jack had chosen the spot carefully, and once he felt it safe to speak, he quickly shared what he knew.

"I ain't seen the women folk yet and that's a good sign. Looks like that albino is a savvy woodsman, he's bein' *real careful*. But I seen Hank and that low life, Sheriff Todd. What's worse, now they got two mean lookin' scallywags ridin' with 'em. Their mounts are hard and tough and so are they!" Jack started to tell the men where they could hobble their horses, but when he saw the perspiration building on Shad's forehead he said, "Hey pard, why don't ya rest yerself there on my bedroll while Preacher and I tend to these horses. Then I'll give ya a plate o' cold beans."

Shad was hurting too much to argue. Instead he nodded and nearly fell when he slid from his saddle. His friends pretty much had to drag him to Jack's bedroll, and he was asleep before they covered him with a blanket. Hours later when Shad finally awoke, Quin handed him the special tea Willy had poured into his canteen with the instructions that Shad drink it morning and night. It tasted like skunk breath and dirty socks, but Shad managed to get it down while he listened to Quin and Jack discussing what they knew.

Quin took Copper's note from his pocket and read it again. "She says Dirk promised to take care of both of them. I don't understand; if Dirk wants them both safe, then why isn't he taking them to Canyon City or heading for

Denver? Why is he riding deeper into the mountains? We've got to find those women before Todd and his men do!" Turning towards Jack, he said, "You know these mountains better than anyone. Have you ever heard of the Two Fools Mine?"

Jack seemed to ponder the question, his blackened eye squinted nearly shut while he cut a plug of tobacco then slid it from the edge of the knife into his mouth then chewed thoughtfully. Finally, he shook his head, "Reckon I know all there is to know about it—but that albino knowin' anything sure has me dumb-fuzzled! Why in tarnation would they be headin' to that hole in the ground? Didn't reckon anyone but me and Tar O'Leary ever knew about. I ain't seen him fer years, heard he went to prison!"

"Prison?" Quin mused, "That would make sense. Mariah told me once she thought that's where her brother might be. If those two met in prison, then that might be how Dirk found out about the Two Fools Mine?"

"But there ain't nothing there! Nothin' but a hole in the ground and a long walk." Jack frowned as he yanked on his beard and growled, "I ought t' know, 'cause me and O'Leary was the Two Fools that dug it and named it. That albino is takin' the women there fer a reason I reckon—but it makes no sense to me. Fer now at least, he seems to be keeping them gals safe, but it ain't good that the Highlanders are muddled up in this. They's nothin' but a bunch a cockalorum's, just a bunch o' little men with little ways, everyone of 'em worse than the next! Wyatt's just a kid, but that Sheriff, he's a rattler sure enough. But he's a gentlemen compared to them other two they met up with yesterday! One's a Comanchero, calls himself, Zeno. I've heard tale he hates everybody, animals as well as people. The other man is a renegade Indian, called Claw. Both those men are evil walking on two legs. So far that albino's doin' a good job of coverin' his tracks but Claw—he'll cut their trail tomorrow—I'm sure of it! At least we know where those scoundrels are. I seen 'em making their camp through Shad's glass, they's too far for us to get to before dark. There'll be no moon tonight, so they can't break camp 'til daybreak. Trouble is—neither can we!" Jack stood and squeezed Shad's shoulder, "Get some rest pard; we've got some mighty hard ridin' ahead of us!" Nodding to Quin he grunted, "You and me, we'll split the watch up between us. We still don't know where the rest o' them Highlanders are—so we best keep our eyes peeled."

Quin watched as Jack disappeared into the forest. He rolled himself in the buffalo hide and leaned back against his saddle. It would be his turn soon to take the next watch, but he couldn't sleep. He had put off speaking to Mariah, thinking he should give her more time to heal. Then Talbot came with his bad news and there wasn't time to tell her he loved her! He couldn't think about that now or give into his fears. At least Copper had managed to leave them a note, but it hadn't told them nearly enough. The albino was Mariah's brother and he shot her! Supposedly it was a flesh wound, but each time he looked at Shad, he imagined the pain Mariah must be suffering.

Looking up at the night sky, Quin whispered, "Boss, its times like this that I'm sure glad you're in charge here and not me. These are evil men we'll be facing and probably fighting tomorrow. We don't want to have to kill anyone but sometimes evil must be fought on its own terms. Please keep Mariah and Copper safe and protect and heal both Shad and Mariah of their wounds. Guide our every move, so that we may do whatever needs to be done! We ask that you keep us in the center of your will!"

Dirk didn't sleep, instead he kept watch all through the night. He was safely hidden above the camp where he could keep an eye on the women. He'd found a spot where there was a good wind-break and he could see and hear for miles. While he listened in the dark he contemplated the vast night sky. As a boy in school they had studied the constellations and now as he picked them out, one by one. It came to him that there was order in everything—even high in the heavens. Everywhere he looked, be it animals or plants and even in the stars that filled the night sky—there was order—there was a plan! What was it that Red had talked about? Something about God giving us His direction to show us the way. Dirk suddenly frowned. If all the outlaws he had ridden with could hear his thoughts just now, how they would laugh! But—here—all alone, the years of corruption, of going in the wrong direction, suddenly loomed large and shamefully before him. He could no more ignore his past than he could ignore the fathomless night sky that hovered above him.

Even before the eastern horizon could become a rosy shade of cobalt, Dirk quietly made his way across the camp on moccasin clad feet. "Wake up—Mariah—Red." Dirk whispered. We've got to be on our way."

Always an early riser, Copper was the first to stir, but when she started to re-build a small fire for morning coffee, Dirk stopped her. "Change in the wind," he whispered, "can't risk it."

He quickly sloshed the remnants of last night's coffee into their tin cups. He handed each woman a cup of cold coffee and a biscuit. "That's breakfast for now, but there's jerky in the saddlebags if you get hungry later." He turned to look at his horse and the mule picketed a few yards away. "I think that ornery mule finally trusts me. By the time I saddle our mounts I need you two to be ready to go. Red, I need you to pack everything up."

Copper sipped the cold and bitter coffee and longed for Shad. She couldn't tell Mariah what Dirk had told her about the ambush, but she had prayed constantly for God's protection over Shad and Quin. Of course Dirk might have been lying just to get her and Mariah away from the cabin. This strange albino had certainly become a different person after seeing his sister. Still, she wasn't ready to trust him. So for now she watched carefully as he approached Remy. Her mule's response was telling, for although she didn't nuzzle his hand, neither did she put her ears back or try to bite him. The beast surely hadn't liked Dirk one bit a year ago, but just now, she stood perfectly still while the man bridled and saddled her.

Mariah too was watching Remy's response to her brother, then she tugged on Copper's hand and whispered. "I thought Quin and Shad would have caught up to us by now. I'm worried about so many things. I want the men to come for us but I fear them running into Todd and his gang of outlaws. And then I fear what will happen when Quin and Shad meet up with my brother. Copper, my Laddy is not dead! Somehow we've got to help him see that Ladd O'Culla can have another chance at life!"

Copper took Mariah's empty cup then finished packing up their camp. "I'm trying, Mariah. When you fell asleep last night, your brother and I talked. He's a hard man, but seeing you again has shaken him. I don't think he knows who he is right now, or who he wants to be. I hate you being in pain and I hate what we're going through—but I do think God's hand is at work in this."

There was a sharp-edged wind coming down from the higher peaks, and it wasn't surprising when Mariah shivered and pulled her blanket closer. But when her teeth began to chatter, Copper frowned as she put the back of her hand against Mariah's cheek and then her forehead. Alarmed she turned to Dirk as he led the animals over for them to mount, "She has a fever! I checked her every few hours last night and she was fine—but now—she's burning up!"

Dirk cursed under his breath, "I'm sorry, Sis. The last thing I want to do is drag ya over a mountain—but—we've got to keep movin'! Come on, Red." He helped Copper awkwardly climb into the saddle and then got Mariah settled behind her. Although it seemed almost cruel to do it, as he had before, he took the length of rope and tied it snuggly around both women. It was actually the only way Copper could keep Mariah from falling.

Lifting his hat, he ran his hand over the top of his snow white hair, then resettled it. In a low even voice he said, "Listen you two, sound travels up here. I figure we've got four, maybe five men scoutin' all around, lookin' for us. I know Todd and Hank are out there for sure! Ox Hennessey might be with them and so might the two other outlaws I told you about. They hide up here in these mountains and ride with us whenever we need extra help." Dirk needed them to understand what he was trying to say. "These other men are—well—they make me and Todd and even Ox, look like—real gentle-men—ya understand?" As he looked at Mariah and Copper, he saw both fear and courage in their eyes. These women understood the danger they were facing—only too well!

It was a long silent ride as Dirk led the women along a path that ancient tribes had walked for centuries. The terrain was constantly changing. At times the trail was narrow and treacherous, then they would ride over rolling hills that passed through groves of white barked aspens and dark pine forests. And nearly every step they took, Dirk was constantly checking their back trail. Being followed or chased wasn't new to him, but the role of protector had not been part of his life since leaving his sister in Texas. Still, there was some-thing about it that felt good. The trouble was that a protector must also be a provider, and Dirk hadn't a penny to his name. He had to get whatever Tar O'Leary had hidden.

He wanted these women in his life, both of them. He had counted on Danby killing McKenna and Long. But now, being around Mariah and even little Red was muddling up his thoughts. Especially when he saw the love and concern that shown in these women's faces. Then he overheard their whispered words: "We mustn't lose hope. They've got to be all right. We just have to keep praying!"

McKenna and Long were lucky men he thought; they were genuinely loved. Dirk had only known sisterly love from Mariah, but a woman's love—never! Reining in, he checked the back trail again and for a long moment he stared at little Red. He might be able to steal her from her husband but he could never steal her love. Suddenly, Dirk desperately hoped that Long and McKenna were alive and well. Because if he was going to keep these women safe, he was going to need their help!

Dirk was pulled from his musings when the faint trail they'd been following seemed to just end in mid-air. Riding to the edge he saw that it continued—straight down! It was outrageously steep and once again, Dirk cursed his bad luck. He had no idea how he was going to get these two women safely down this hill. It was nearly a vertical plunge—a half mile at least to the valley below. He didn't know how Red had managed to keep herself and Mariah in the saddle as it was. She'd been riding Remy with a rolled blanket in front of her, to protect her rounded belly from the saddle horn. Making it worse, his wounded and feverish sister was draped over her like a shawl—and quite literally tied to her back. Neither of these women should be riding at all, let alone down rough terrain like this! Still, he had no choice but to force them to keep moving.

"Red," he ordered, "Ride into that stand of evergreens and stay there until I get back—and whatever you do, be quiet! I'm gonna scout on ahead and see if I can find an easier way down."

Copper just stared at him, as if she couldn't quite understand his words. Her head pounded, every bone and muscle in her body hurt and never in her life had she been this exhausted. When Dirk repeated his instructions a second time, her foggy brain finally grasped what he was trying to say. She frowned, nodded, then reined Remy towards the outcropping of trees.

When Dirk disappeared out of their sight, Copper slowly turned to Mariah and whispered, "Why are we following him like this? I know you love your brother but I can't help but wonder if we shouldn't be trying to hide from him instead. Hide from everyone—at least—until Shad and Quin can find us!"

Mariah breathed out a weak chuckle, "Copper, you're pregnant and I'm wounded and we're both so dog-tired we can't think let alone get on or off this mule without my brother's help. Do you honestly think that the two of us and Remy of all creatures, could hide from anyone? I understand why you're scared of Ladd, but I truly believe he is trying to protect us!"

"But what if the men that are following us aren't Todd and his ruthless gang? What if he's driving us so hard because he knows that Quin and Shad are closing in? He could be protecting us from harm or keeping us from being rescued—how do we know which it is?"

"Copper, if ya can't trust Ladd, then trust me! I know my brother has done a lot of bad things. But right now, he's actin' with my best interest at heart, and if I'm safe then so are you. You don't know Todd and those other men—they are more than ruthless! Ladd may not even know for sure who it is that's trackin' us. But someone is, and for now that means we have to keep runnin' and keep prayin' that God in His wisdom will keep us safe and sort all this out!"

When Dirk finally returned to fetch the women, he found them both asleep in the saddle. Then he saw that Copper had tied her hands around the saddle horn. He couldn't remember the last time he felt respect or compassion for anyone, but something akin to that twisted inside him just then. Neither of these women deserved what he was having to put them through. He was surprised to hear the gentleness in his own voice as he said softly, "Time to move on ladies. I'm sorry but we've got the devil's own trail ahead of us. I'll try to make it a little easier by zig-zagging back and forth, until we reach a level plateau that's about two hundred yards from the valley floor. Once we're there you two can rest, for a while at least. But…" Dirk studied them both, then groaned out the rest of what he had to say, "That last hundred yards or so are the worst of it. The trail is narrow and straight down. There's no way of makin' it easier 'cause there's shale on one side and boulders on the other. Our mounts will have to slide the whole way. I'm still trying to decide which way will be best for ya. Walkin' ya down on foot or ridin' each of ya down separately? Once we get to the valley though, we'll finally be in the Petrified Forest." Dirk took his hat off and wiped the sweat from his brow with his shirt sleeve. As he resettled it, he spoke to both women, "Now that mule is as sure-footed as they come. So, both of ya just lean back and towards the hill side of the trail. We'll all feel better once we're down in the valley."

Once again taking the lead, Dirk moved on while Remy followed slowly behind. They angled down the side of the mountain, going left then right, then left again. It seemed to Dirk that the women were doing well until they reached the small plateau where he'd promised they could rest. When he rode close to Remy he saw the beads of perspiration on Copper's brow. Unsheathing his knife, he quickly cut her hands free from the saddle horn and tried to hand her the canteen of water.

Refusing it, her voice sounding raspy and weak as she huffed, "Try to rouse Mariah, I think she's fainted. Even with her tied to me, it was all I could do to keep us both in this saddle."

Mariah's eyes were closed and she was draped over the younger woman's shoulder. Copper sighed and reached down and patted Mariah's leg. "Hey, honey—please wake up!"

Blowing out a frustrated breath, Dirk moaned, "Why does everything have to be so hard?" He doused his handkerchief with water then dabbed it against his sister's face and hands. "Come on Sis—I hate to do this to ya but—once we're in the valley I'll let ya rest—I promise!"

Although it seemed longer, it was actually only a few moments until violet eyes fluttered open and Mariah straightened, "Oh dear—I'm so sorry, Copper." Grimacing she put her hand to her throbbing side then asked, "Are we safe now?"

When her brother shook his head no…she sighed and peered up at the steep trail they had just come down. How Copper had managed she would never know. In fact, she couldn't even remember riding down the steep descent. Then she looked at the pathway below and was horrified. It looked even worse than Ladd had described. There was just the hint of path leading straight down with loose shale on the left and on the right, large boulders with twisted and misshaped pine and fir trees growing sporadically in between and around them.

Dirk frowned as he took in the exhausted state of both women. His sister had passed her limit of endurance early that morning. Then he focused on his little redhead, her pretty face was covered in dirt and perspiration and except for her freckles, she was nearly as pale as him. They were all sitting ducks if they stayed where they were but neither woman was strong enough to continue on her own.

"I've got to get you two off this last stretch of mountain!" Gazing back up to the trail they'd just come down, Dirk took his hat off and held it up to block the sun from his eyes. "I've got just one chance of stoppin' Todd and those other men that are trackin' us. Once I've got you both safely down in the valley, I'm gonna find me a good spot and then I'll wait. Just about the time the first man reaches the bottom, the last man will be slidin' down from the top. I'll pick 'em off, one at a time. Just like shootin' fool hens out of a spruce tree."

"Ladd, that's awful!"

"Does that shock ya, Sis? You know what Jimmy Todd's capable of, but those other men are worse. If they catch up with us, they won't think twice before they kill me and then you know what they'll do to you and Red!"

Just then a horse whinnied from the ridge above them and Copper and Dirk both stopped their animals from responding in kind. Instantly Dirk cut the rope that tethered the two women together then pulled Mariah onto his lap. "Red," he whispered, "you're too weak to stay in the saddle without help. I'll be back for you when I get Sis safely down."

Dirk was right. Copper didn't like being left behind but she was too weak to do anything about it. Her legs weren't strong enough to walk down that steep path on foot nor could she manage to stay in the saddle going down on Remy. All she could do now was close her eyes and pray!

Holding Mariah tightly in his arms, Dirk nudged his horse forward and gave him his head, allowing the animal to find his own way down the steep trail. Pushing his feet forward, he was pretty much standing straight up in the stirrups, and he leaned so far back in the saddle that his hat bumped against the horse's hip. Terrified, Mariah reached around both sides of her brother and grabbed hold of the horse's tail with her left hand and with her right she reached around the other side and held onto the back of the saddle. Her panic actually helped as it worked as a counter balance, but her side burned like fire. The pathway down was longer than Dirk had thought, but he didn't dare lean forward to see how much farther it would be before they reached level ground. His horse slid the whole way down on his haunches until they reached the valley floor, where gentle rolling hills, dotted with aspen and pine trees stretched out before them.

"Oh my, thank the Lord that's over!" Mariah breathed. "Quick Ladd, help me down then hurry back up there and get Copper!"

Swinging his leg over the gelding's neck, Dirk slid from the saddle with Mariah still in his arms. An instant later he settled her under a shade tree and handed her the reins. Without a word, he started back up the steep path on foot. His plan was to climb the hill then ride Remy back down, holding Red just as he had his sister. But before he'd taken a half a dozen steps, he heard shouting and two pistol shots. Then like a run-away steam engine, Remy came sliding down the steep path braying loudly as dust broiled up under her massive hooves. Dirk had to jump aside to keep from being trampled.

Remy was riderless, but a note was tied to the saddle horn. Dirk unfolded it as he ran towards Mariah. Reading had never come as easily for him as it had to his sister, so he handed her the note. "What does it say?"

Mariah began to tremble when she recognized Jimmy Todd's writing. "It says: '*Ghost man, ya got my woman and now I got yours! If you want this little redhead, put yer guns on the mule and send her back up. Then I'll come down and trade.*'"

Dirk cursed and ran his hand over his stubbly white beard. "Sis, I'll die before anyone hurts you again! All I can do now is hide you someplace safe, then I'll come back and see if I can help Red."

"Ladd O'Culla—shame on you! You think I want to be—someplace safe—while my dearest friend is in danger? I know we can't do what they're asking—that would be foolish. But I'm not about to let you take me to safety and leave Copper up there with those vile men!"

Mariah shocked him, she'd been so weak all day, but suddenly she seemed to be made of steel. She was indeed the finest person he'd ever known and she wanted him to be something he could never be. "I wish you'd get it through your head, Ladd O'Culla is dead," he hissed. Then he looked at his sister, she was—strong—honorable—sweet. He didn't even know how to be Ladd O'Culla anymore. Then again he didn't really want to be Dirk Culley either. Something else struck him. Perhaps for the first time in his life, instead of wanting to turn tail and run from his troubles, he thought about facing them! His glassy eyes quickly looked up the hill and studied the steep terrain. Then his gaze fell on the sure-footed Remy and he had a crazy idea.

"All right, Sis, lead my horse over to that stand of trees. No matter what, stay out of sight and stay quiet!"

Dirk swung up onto Remy's back and headed her towards a group of boulders that formed a natural stairway that led back up to the plateau. Multiple trees were growing between the boulders providing what Dirk hoped would be enough cover to get to his little redhead without being seen. This staircase of sorts was too steep for any horse to consider, but he thought he might just chance it on Red's big ugly mule. Of course he wouldn't know if

Remy would cooperate with his plan until they reached the first boulder and attempted to jump up onto the second. Then they would either sail easily from one boulder to the next or they'd end up at the bottom, probably both of them with a broken neck. Getting the mule to take the first jump was going to be the trick. However, just then the men must have told Red to call her mule. That was their first mistake, for it worked perfectly to Dirk's advantage. The moment Remy heard the familiar whistle, her flag like ears perked up and she jumped onto the first boulder and then the next and then the next after that. For the first time in years, Dirk wanted to laugh! This was something a skittish horse would never do, but then, Remy wasn't a horse. She wasn't an ordinary mule either. Dirk simply gave Remy her head and held on as she found her own way back up the hill.

When Remy had climbed about half way to the plateau, there came a terrible cacophony of caterwauling, loud shrieks and pistol shots. The horrific noise cut through the air sounding like Indian war cries, coming down the steep hill from three different points above them.

Hank's horse began bucking and rammed into Todd's black and white paint. Although Claw and Zeno's mounts reared and side-stepped nervously, their animals were better trained and the men held them in check for there was really no safe place to run. They knew Dirk would be waiting with his gun loaded at the bottom of the hill and they had no idea who was attacking from above. Nevertheless, Zeno decided to take a chance on his nimble mustang and spurred him straight up the steepest part of the hill. Unfortunately for him, he chose the same path that Black-Eyed Jack was sliding down. The two men were less than ten feet apart when they spotted each other. Instantly, they both drew their guns and fired. The bullet from Zeno's gun sent splinters exploding from the tree trunk a hair's width from Jack's head. But the older man had taken a split-second longer to aim and Zeno cried out in pain when Jack's bullet struck him in the chest and he tumbled backwards off his mustang. Terrified by the noise and the smell of gun powder and blood, the wiry mustang bolted towards the treacherous pathway leading down into the valley. He squealed as he bucked then tumbled all the way down the path. Todd and Hank jumped from their mounts, and stood back to back, using their horses for cover, while they threw wild shots up the hill.

Claw, the renegade Indian, quickly decided that this was not a good day to die. He too rode a mule that was sure footed and game. He too believed that Dirk would be waiting at the bottom of the steep pathway, so he spurred his mule towards the boulders. His dark leathery face contorted in rage when he saw Dirk coming up, the same way he had planned to go down. Both men spurred their mounts and charged into each other—their mules grunting as they collided. Remy was bigger and more powerful than Claw's mule and the smaller beast was knocked back and spun around. The animal desperately tried to keep his legs under him, then finally made a jump for the nearest boulder. The effort had been ill-timed and off balance, and his hooves skidded off the slippery rock and over the side of the boulder. Claw tried to jump free but his moccasin clad foot slipped through the stirrup. The mule somersaulted over one boulder and then onto another; rolling over his rider again and again. By the time they reached the valley floor—they were both dead.

In the midst of the mayhem, Todd and Hank were still standing back to back, circling their horses and shooting over their saddles, but neither man had been able to get a clear shot at anyone. Meanwhile, Copper could do nothing but try to stay out of the way. The area was too small for her to find any cover.

Suddenly, Todd locked eyes with Copper. A look of pure evil covered his features, but his words were for Hank, "We're done for kid—we're gonna die here or hang! All our plans went sour." He hissed, "Just 'cause that greedy albino wanted that little redheaded she devil and my woman too! But I'm gonna even things up. If I don't get my woman—then—neither will he!"

Grinning, Todd gave Copper an arrogant wink as he pointed his pistol at her heart. Her hands went protectively around her unborn baby. There wasn't any use to scream or run, she could do nothing but stare at the man and the gun in his hand. Still, she jumped when she heard the shot. Her gaze went down over her own body, but then she saw the sheriff stagger forward, as a trickle of blood bubbled from lips that had lost their smile. He looked confused and he stared down at his hand only to find that the gun was slipping from his fingers. Then he turned and looked knowingly at Hank and saw his smoking gun. "Huh? So ya finally got the guts to kill a man—why did ya have to start with me?"

Hank frowned at his gun, and then at Todd. "Couldn't allow ya to kill a woman! I still don't hold with shootin' people though—not even you."

At that instant all the chaos and violence turned to silence, and once again the hush of the mountains prevailed. The hair raising noise and turmoil that had ricocheted all around them moments earlier—was simply gone—as if nothing out of the ordinary had ever happened. And yet now, three very evil men were dead and the only sound that remained was the constant hush and whisper that is always present in a forest, even when there isn't a hint of a breeze. It was a melody as old as time, like life and death itself. After all the action and noise, this sudden stillness somehow seemed almost as unnerving.

The once proud and arrogant Sheriff Jimmy Todd was dead; his body slumped on the ground as if all his bones had turned to sand. Copper and Hank stared at each other as Quin, Shad and Jack slid their horses down to the last few yards to the small area of level ground. Shad raced to Copper while Quin and Jack kept their guns trained on Hank.

"Don't hurt that man." Copper called out. "He just saved my life!"

She spoke the words just as Shad was sliding awkwardly from his saddle. Bursting into tears she stumbled towards him with her bound hands stretched out. But when she saw the blood seeping through her husband's buckskins and sweat covering is face, she cried out, "Oh, Shad you're hurt!"

The man surprised her when he grinned broadly and shook his head. Taking the knife from its scabbard he cut through the rope that bound her hands and sighed, "As long as yer all right, sweet girl, then I am fine and dandy!"

At first Copper held her husband at arms-length so she could look at his wounds, but he would have none of that and pulled her close, "Nah, these are old news, darlin'. They just opened up a bit. We did ride mighty hard gettin' down here!"

Copper hugged him tightly, but seeing that her big man had used up his last ounce of strength, she quickly pulled him down to sit beside her on the ground. There was much to talk about, but just then all they wanted to do was drink each other in.

Holding his hands high, Hank stood before Quin and Jack. The old man was the first to speak, and in his scratchy voice he warned, "Don't cotton to the idea o' shootin' ya son—so just go ahead on and take yer gun belt off—but do it real easy-like. Ya understand?"

As his holster fell to his feet, Hank's voice broke, "Never w-wanted—any of this! Jimmy Todd and I rustled some cattle back in Texas. I got away from him and went straight. Thought he went straight too when he took the job as Sheriff. But then he and Hennessey and Theo Krane came up with the Highlander's Association. They did a lot of bad things and I'm ashamed to say, I helped 'em. Todd said if I didn't, he'd make sure I was sent back to Texas face down over my saddle and he'd collect the reward." Mournfully he looked down at the sheriff's dead body, "He liked killin' folks. He did it too often and he liked it too much! He was gonna kill that little woman. He said he wanted to get even with Dirk but I think it was just so he could kill one last time. Someone had to stop him—and it ended up that it was for me to do."

Quin gazed all about him, "We thank you for saving her life, Hank." Then he turned towards Copper, "Where's Mariah? Please tell me she's all right too!"

Pointing down the steep path, Copper explained, "Dirk carried her down first, he planned on coming back up to get me when Todd and those other men captured me. Then you all came down that hill like some kind of storm and...I don't know what's happened to them exactly. They can't be far and they should both be all right!"

It was pure agony for Mariah to listen to the war cries and gunfire and not know what was happening on the hill just above her. Leaning against an aspen tree, she closed her eyes and prayed that God would somehow get them all through this. Just then, the bitter odor of unwashed body and stale whiskey assaulted her senses. Even before his meaty hand wrapped around her arm and spun her around, she already knew it was Ox Hennessey. When she tried to screamed, he shook her and hissed, "None o' that now! Ya best stay quiet or I'll be teachin' ya a few lessons ya'll never forget!"

Too weak to fight, Mariah said nothing as Ox bound her hands, then lifted her onto Dirk's horse. "That albino that took ya and that other little gal—well now—he works fer me. I heard him and Todd makin' plans to get you two. Seems he decided to double cross Todd and keep ya both fer him-self. He'll not be double crossin' me though. He knows where Tar O'Leary stashed his loot. I don't know what it is or where, but that's where he's taken ya, isn't it?"

Certain that Ox didn't know that she and '*that albino*' were brother and sister, Mariah shrugged, "That awful man just made me and Copper go with him! He asked us about Tar O'Leary. We didn't know the man, do you?"

"Aye, I've known that little man all me life. Didn't know he'd found his very own pot of gold though. Not until about a year ago, for that's when a stranger came into me bar. A crying drunk he was—boastin' that he would o' had a string of saloons that would o' put mine to shame—if things had been different. Seems a few years back he had two well-to-do partners that were to meet him in Otter Run. They planned to build a bunch of gambling houses and bordellos in every mining town in the west. When he heard the stage, they were to be on, was carried away in a mudslide, he went down there and searched through the rubble. He found nary a thing, neither bodies nor baggage. He reckoned those men got waylaid somewhere else or never came at all. But I knew those men had been on that stage. 'Cause Tar and me—we heard their screams! Whatever loot those men were carryin', Tar found it and hid it someplace safe." Ox pounded his chest with his fist adding, "'Twas me that paid the way fer Tar to escape from prison. Then I found out a few days ago that Tar asked special to have an albino escape with him. I know Culley's here lookin' fer what Tar hid—and I want it!"

Ox paused for a moment, listening to the shouts and gunfire coming from the hill above, then he leaned closer to Mariah. "Well now pretty girl, I reckon yer scared o' that ghost man and rightly so. But ya better hope and pray he makes it back down that hill. 'Cause me plan is to let him keep yer little redheaded friend he's so keen on. But only if he tells me where Tar hid his stash. Once we find it, you and me will go to San Francisco. It'll be just the two of us. O' course now, if that man should die up there or we can't find the gold...well then...ya'll go back to workin' fer me at the Long Shot."

The idea of Mariah going anywhere with Ox was revolting, but the image of her going back to that room at the saloon—terrified her. The valley and the trees around her seemed to swim before her eyes and she sucked in a deep breath to keep from fainting. Then again maybe she should allow herself to fall from the saddle. Her mind was too muddled with fever and she was in too much pain to think clearly, even enough to pray. The only words that came to her troubled mind where...*Lord...we need you—oh how we need you!*

Still holding the reins to Mariah's horse, Ox clumsily mounted his own stout gelding. "Reckon we'll put a bit o' distance between us and whoever comes sliding down that hill. Ya don't have to worry about me sharin' ya with any o' those men up there. I plan to shoot every one of 'em that comes down that hill, except for the albino o' course. I need him, at least for a while yet."

Just as Ox was riding past a tall boulder, Mariah's attention was drawn to a slight scuffling sound and she noticed pebbles bouncing on the path before her. To her utter amazement, she glanced up and saw her brother and Remy perched on the boulder just above Ox. The big mule's quivering muscles bunched as she prepared to jump. Mariah clutched the saddle horn tightly with her bound hands, just as her horse spooked and yanked the reins from Ox's hand. He turned to glare at Mariah, but cried out when he saw the mule and rider sailing towards him. Remy slammed into Ox's big gelding with the force of a cannon ball. It was quite a jolt and Dirk was catapulted over Remy's head. Somehow he managed to grab hold of Ox and they both rolled over the saddle and hit the ground hard.

At first, the wind was knocked out of both of them and they were too stunned to move. Dirk, being younger and more agile was the first to get to his feet, and he slammed his fist into Ox's belly and then his jaw. That last punch was hard enough to knock most men out, but unfortunately Ox was as tough as his namesake. He was also just as awkward, clumsy and powerful! Soon the two men were circling each other in the deep meadow grass. Again and again, Dirk managed to duck and slip away from Ox's huge fists, while he pummeled the bigger man with jab after jab. Finally, Ox resorted to the only thing left for him to do. He simply grabbed hold of Dirk and fell on top of him, pinning him to the ground. Utilizing his greater weight, he straddled the younger man and soon the albino's face was turning blue from lack of air.

Mariah's horse only trotted a few feet away from the brawling men, then dropped his head and began cropping grass. The moment the horse stopped she half slid, half fell from the saddle. By the time she reached the men, Hennessey had his meaty hands around Dirk's throat but he was careful not to kill him. He needed him too much!

"I know ya was in prison with Tar O'Leary—so tell me or die. What did he find in that stage coach and where did he hide it?"

Dirk was barely able to breathe but managed a raspy, "D-d-don't know!"

"Yer lying!" Ox bellowed, "I paid dear to arrange that prison break. Me own nephew was nearly killed. I just got a letter from him; he finally got clear headed enough to tell me what happened. Said that the only man that got clean away that day—was an albino—whose name was—Dirk Culley. He said you was partners with Tar's cellmate. And that they asked special that you be let in on that break. Ya owe me Ghost Man. Ya owe me fer yer freedom. So, tell me what ya know and tell me quick and I'll let ya live!"

Mariah trembled as she crept up behind Ox. She had to help Ladd but with her hands tied, what could she do? It was then she noticed the small derringer Ox had tucked between his backbone and his belt. The brute seemed to have forgotten all about her—that is until she grabbed the small gun with her bound hands, cocked it and then shoved the barrel in Ox's ear.

"Let my brother go or I promise you…I *will* pull this trigger!"

Hennessey immediately released Dirk and holding his hands high he shifted his weight. Coughing and sputtering, Dirk managed to crawl out from under the big Irishman. Ox tried to stand but couldn't seem to find his feet, his great weight made him ungainly and he fell back. It was a trick—for he instantly rolled to his left side as he drew his gun. He had only just cleared it from the holster when two shots rang out. The man pitched to the side then fell face down in the dirt.

Mariah dropped the derringer and covered her face. In an instant Quin was pulling her into his arms. "I didn't really think I'd have to shoot—but I did Quin—and I've just killed a man!" She sobbed. "I should have thought to take his gun from his holster, but it just happened so fast. I saw him lifting his gun and I—I pulled the trigger!"

"Shhhh, sweetheart, I'm just grateful that you're all right!" Quin soothed as he cradled Mariah in his arms, thanking God with every breath that the woman he loved was alive and safe. When Dirk approached them and reached for her, Quin shook his head and tightened his hold. He was not about to release the woman he might have just lost. The two men eyed each other and without a word spoken, the message was clear. *She may be your sister—but she's my woman!*

Seeing that his sister was more than content to be in this man's embrace, Dirk slowly nodded his acceptance and stepped away.

Finally, Quin leaned back and gently lifted Mariah's chin with one finger. "You mustn't feel guilty about this. I'm certain it was my bullet that killed that scoundrel. I was sliding down that hill when I heard the commotion. I saw Ox roll away from you and I knew that big brute would go for his pistol. He chose his own path Mariah, and hell is where it led him."

Mariah nodded, but when she shivered, he took his coat off and draped it around her shoulders. Quin's coat—it was familiar and comforting. It felt like heaven to Mariah, it was filled with his own special warmth and the clean scent of pine forests and wood smoke. Despite all that she had been through she was surprised at how his simple gesture was already calming and strengthening her. Just to be near him again was a blessing too great to comprehend. What she didn't know was that this dear man needed the reassurance of her presence just as much. He cupped her cheek with his broad hand, and his heart thrilled when she nuzzled his palm. He could no longer deny himself. Taking Mariah's hand in his, he pulled her away from the gruesome scene and from her brother's skeptical gaze. When he found a secluded spot he instantly spun around and lowered his lips to hers. At first the kiss was like the touch of a butterfly—it was just that gentle and sweet. But they had both hungered so long for this kiss that it quickly deepened. It was a charmed moment, the unlocking of two hearts that had, for far too long, been kept apart.

Reluctantly, Quin ended the kiss. He took Mariah's hand and gently sat her down on a fallen log. "Now you precious woman, you just rest right here! Shad and Jack are helping Copper down the hill. And in the meantime I'm going to build a fire and set up camp." When Mariah refused to let go of his hand he smiled in understanding, "Hey now, I promise to stay close. But you're shivering. You've been wounded, you've got a fever and you're probably in shock." Giving her that gentle smile she loved so well he added, "Right now I'm going to brew up some of your favorite aspen bark tea. And I think all of us could use some hot coffee!" Quin kept up a soothing dialogue as he quickly gathered wood and built a fire. When he whistled for Flint and the gelding trotted to Mariah first, and nuzzled her outstretched hand, Quin smiled and shook his head. "That horse has always been skittish around women—until he met you!" Giving her a roguish wink, which she had never see him do before, he added, "Guess he and I have that in common!"

Mariah just stared at him, what had come over him? Had he actually kissed her? And now was he flirting with her? She wondered for a moment if she weren't dreaming and was only imagining this new Quin. Then he spread his bedroll down on the ground, took her hand, kissed it, then helped her get settled onto it so she'd be more comfortable. Her mind continued to reel while she watched him brew up aspen bark tea and coffee.

As she had so many months before, Mariah watched this big man moving about the camp—comforting her, calming her. Still, her mind was muddled by everything that had happened in the past few days, let alone the past few moments.

"I need to tell you about my brother, Quin. I'm sorry, I mean Pastor." Remembering their passionate kiss, she shook her head, "No, I guess I mean…"

The big man grinned as he stopped what he was doing. Dropping to one knee beside her, he said tenderly, "Of course—I'm Quin to you. Unless you'd rather call me darling. That would be fine, too!" When she just blinked up at him he became more serious, "I know we have a lot to talk about—you and I. I had planned to tell you gently how I felt. But when I saw Ox pointing that gun at you and then I saw you crying. I couldn't stop myself from pulling you into my arms. Guess my kiss told you what my feelings are for you. And—" he added with a smile, "you certainly did kiss me back, you know! Can I assume that with that kiss you told me how you're feeling—about me?"

When she glanced down looking confused and embarrassed, Quin's voice became stern, "Mariah, you know as well as I do that our hearts connected the first time we met. And that connection grows stronger every time we see each other. Quin gently pulled his coat more tightly around Mariah and sighed. "I know I'm getting ahead of myself and like I said, we've got a lot to talk about, but…" Seeing that they were still alone he whispered, "Know this—Mariah June—as far as my heart is concerned, it's you and me…forever!"

"Forever?" she whispered. Her violet eyes filled with tears as she looked up at the man she adored and nodded as if in a trance, "All right."

The couple shared another long kiss, then Quin left her, only to return with a cup of the nasty tasting tea. Mariah made a face and he laughed. It was so good to be together again.

Up on the hill, Jack was helping Hank tie the dead bodies of the outlaws onto the backs of their horses. It was Jack's idea to allow young Hank Wyatt to prove his desire to go straight, by taking these outlaws all the way down to Colorado City. They would deal with the bank president Theo Krane when they all returned to Otter Run in a few days.

Blissfully unaware of all the sorted and gruesome details, Mariah snuggled deeper into Quin's heavy coat and rested, savoring the knowledge that she was once again surrounded by all the people she loved. And thankfully they were all safe!

Chapter 27
Two Fools Mine

"There are those who rebel against the light, who do not know its ways or stay in its paths." Job 24:13

"Store up for yourselves treasures in heaven, where moth and rust do not destroy, and where thieves do not break in and steal." Matthew 6:20

It was a pleasant campsite and a beautiful evening. The stars were bright and there was a soothing breeze sliding across the mountains. So much had happened and there was so much to say that for a long while no one knew how to begin. They ate the biscuits and bacon Copper and Quin had prepared in silence. The only sound was the crackling fire and an occasional hoot of a night owl. Laying on their bedrolls, they gazed lazily up at the pearl-like moon that was centered in a canopy of stars and thanked God that they had all survived.

Everyone seemed content, except for the wily old mountain man, Black-Eyed Jack. He'd had enough of the silence—he wanted answers! In fact, as he leveled his gaze at the five people sharing the fire, he felt more confused than ever as to how they'd all come to be together. Suddenly he blew out a disgruntled breath and slapped his knee. "I jes' got to own up that I am purely dumb-fuzzled by all these goings on! I've been ridin' hell bent fer leather up and down these mountains. Been doin' my best to keep you-young'uns alive but I got t' tell ya—I got me no idea—what this is all about! And I ain't a waitin' no more for somebody t' explain it. First of all, I want to know why in tarnation was ya all headin' fer the Two Fools Mine? It ain't nothin' but dirt and rock no how." Jack scowled as he rubbed the back of his neck, "I swan, if I ain't as confused as a two headed calf!"

Copper smiled at Jack. Somehow the two had become kindred spirits and since she had brought at least some of this mayhem upon them, she knew it was her place to explain. Rising from her place next to Shad, she went to sit beside the old man.

"Siah, I don't blame you a bit. It is all terribly confusing. You've done so much for us and I hope that you know how very grateful we all are! I'm certain Shad wouldn't be alive if it weren't for you!" Glancing back at her husband, she added, "And I couldn't have borne losing him."

Shad couldn't speak for the lump in his throat, so Preacher spoke for them both, "She's right Jack, God sure put you in the right place! Shad and I and John and Willy Haze probably all would have been killed. And I can't bear to think about what would have happened to Mariah and Copper, had it not been for you! We are all very grateful."

Both embarrassed and pleased by all this attention, Jack ran a hand over his face and mumbled, "Had to be someplace might as well been helpin' out some."

"Oh you dear thing!" Copper whispered in his ear, then kissed his cheek.

"Hey now." Shad barked. Only half jesting, he grunted, "Missus McKenna, what have I told you about givin' *my* kisses away?"

Rolling her eyes Copper got up and hurried as quickly as her body would allow, back to Shad's side. Kneeling down beside him she began covering his face with kisses. "Now do you feel better?" she asked. While everyone laughed she added sternly, "But you listen to me tall man, anyone who saves your life gets a kiss from me—and there'll be no arguments from you!"

Old Jack gazed around the campfire, he cared more for these people than he had for anyone in a very long while. But if he was going to keep on helping them, he needed to understand what was going on and they still hadn't told him a thing. Narrowing his eyes, he tugged on his steal gray beard and growled, "Now, I ain't needin' no thanks from you-young'uns." When he caught Copper's eye, he winked, "'Course a little o' kiss on the cheek now and again is all right by me. But what I do need is fer ya to tell me what this is all about? Copper girl, will ya tell this old man what ya know?"

"Yes, Siah, I'll try." she said eagerly, then she glanced at the others. "If anyone else can add to it—then please do. Actually, I suppose this mess begins with me in a way. I think you all know that for about two minutes I was married to a man by the name of Vernon Riley. Vernon was in prison with Dirk Culley who is Mariah's brother." Copper motioned to Dirk and Jack nodded to the albino. The others seemed to trust this man, but Jack wasn't ready to do that—not yet. Instead he studied him for a while through narrowed eyes as he listened to Copper.

"You see," she continued, "Vernon shared a cell with a man by the name of Tar O'Leary. In the last letter we received from Vernon, he included a message written in sort of a code with clues as to where O'Leary hid some kind of treasure! We really aren't even sure what it is. When the message was deciphered it said that a treasure of some kind had been hidden inside the Two Fools Mine, which was located in the Petrified Forest."

Dirk was the next to speak up, "I was in the cell next to Tar and Vernon. I dug a hole between our cells but I couldn't always hear everything. What I did hear was..." Dirk continued to tell Jack the story of how Tar had seen the stage go down in a mudslide. Finally, he ended with: "They got real quiet after that. I know Tar found something of value; I thought I heard the word—gold—but I'm not really sure! I couldn't make out exactly what it was or where Tar hid it. But I knew they wrote a letter that included the directions and that they sent it to Vernon's mother, Ma Riley and to little Red."

Just then Mariah shuddered, adding, "When Ox grabbed me, just before—just before he was killed, he told me that about a year ago he learned that there were two men on that stage and they had a great deal of money! That's when Ox realized that Tar must have it and that's why he arranged for the prison break. Somehow things went wrong and Tar and Vernon were killed, but my brother escaped."

Staring into the fire, Dirk sighed, "Ox's nephew was one of the prison guards. He must have told Ox that O'Leary was dying. He didn't want Tar to take this secret to his grave so that's when he planned the prison break. There was a big fire that day. We smashed the box that held the guard's guns and Vernon and I both took one. Tar was in bad shape that day. The smoke from the fire made it nearly impossible for any of us to breathe, but it was hardest on the old man. When we got outside the gate there were two horses waiting for us." Dirk stopped and looked directly at Mariah, "I'm telling the truth, Sis. "I set my gun down while Vernon and I helped Tar onto the first horse. I was about to jump on behind him when Vernon turned his gun on me! I knocked the gun up and away just as he pulled the trigger and...it accidentally hit Tar. Then Vernon and I fought over the gun. I'll admit that I did kill Vernon but it was him or me—he didn't give me a choice! I tried to help Tar, but he was already dead. I did the only thing I could do then…I jumped on the horse and headed for Wyoming."

When he saw Mariah's eyes filling with tears, he said, "Sis, I swear, Tar was shot by accident! I was angry at Vernon, and I wouldn't have minded giving him a black eye, but I didn't want to kill him." Shaking his head, he mumbled, "I'm sorry Sis." Then he looked at Copper, "You too, Red. For the first time in my life…I truly am sorry!"

"Her name is not Red," Shad growled. "She's Missus Shadrach McKenna!"

Shad and Dirk glared at each other until Jack let out a long low whistle. Then he slapped both hands on his knees and threw his head back and laughed. "I knew it! I knew if my sweet Copper would just start talkin' then things would start makin' sense. And then—old Jack would be able to unravel the tangle you-young'uns has got yourselves all mixed up in!"

Shad rolled his eyes, "Jack, ya wooly rogue, will ya stop flirtin' with my woman and tell us what in the world yer talking about? You really think that from what ya've just heard, ya can make sense of all this?"

"Hah—I should hope to shout—I can! Josiah Jackson and Tar O'Leary was partners back in the early days when the Injuns hardly knew what a white man was. And sure as shootin' I reckon I'm the onliest man in all the Rockies that can lead ya to that there Two Fools Mine!" Jack gave his audience an impish grin then added, "'Cause I'm one o' the fools that dug it. That place has secrets—and I know 'em all!" The old man grinned broadly, enjoying the fact that he had everyone's full attention. "Well, now as I recall…" Frowning, he bent over and slowly poured coffee into his cup. With eyes twinkling at the eagerness of his young friends, he tortured them by taking his time to settle back while he enjoyed a long, loud slurp. Finally, he set the cup on his knee and began, "Reckon 'twas 'bout thirty-five years ago when me and Tar O'Leary headed west to trap beaver in the Rockies. We was as green as a couple of river toads and not afeared o' the devil himself. Yep—two young fools to be sure. And then one day we spotted something a shining up on the hill and…."

Sleep didn't come easy for any of them after Jack's tale of the old mine and its secrets. At first light Remy woke everyone up with her loud braying. Dirk grumbled and threw his boot at her but nothing could dampen their spirits—an adventure was awaiting them! The day was crowned with a sky of sapphire blue and warmed by a lemon yellow sun. Floating on the high mountain currents were row after row of delicate clouds that resembled tufts of soft cotton wool. Jack was in especially high spirits when he laughed and stopped Preacher from breaking camp.

"No need to pack up son." he insisted. "I told ya last night—we was only a skip-and-a-holler from the mine. Now that I see things in daylight… we ain't even that far." Glancing down at Shad and Mariah he added, "Won't need to move our wounded; they can just keep on a restin' while we take a little stroll."

The news was a relief to everyone, especially Shad and Mariah. Neither of them were up to a long ride. While they rested, Preacher and Dirk followed along eagerly as Jack studied the terrain then paced over to some wild shrubs that grew along a nearby rise.

Jack grinned at the two younger men, "Fetch yer axes boys—this is it!"

It didn't take long for the men to clear away the vegetation that had grown up in the years since Tar O'Leary had been there. The men were surprised, although Jack wasn't, to find of all things, a rough looking door stuck into the hillside. On the door, were peeling black letters that said, *Two Fools Mine.*

"We set that door in the hillside and Tar did that writin'. We worked awful hard and fer nothin', but we wanted to make it look like it were somethin'." Jack laughed, "Like I said we was just two young fools." Jack gave the door a yank but the thing wouldn't budge. When Dirk and Quin added their strength, the door didn't open so much as it just crumbled into pieces. At any rate the entrance was cleared. But Jack was quick to warn them that this was merely the opening to a deep shaft. Quin began fashioning torches and Shad, not being able to stay away from all the excitement, sat by the opening and tied all their lariats together.

Dirk was the only one who seemed content to be idle. He simply watched, and if possible, he looked even paler as the sun rolled higher into the sky. Though no one had discussed it out loud, he knew this task was for him to do. He was not a small man, but he was smaller than Shad or Quin. And—it was he who was most desperate for the gold! As he peered down into the musty smelling shaft, his throat went dry. He saw only a splintered ladder that disappeared into the darkness. Since the day he had left Texas and his sister behind, he had done nothing of which he could be proud. His gaze roamed from Jack to Shad and then to Preacher Quincy Long. He had heard of these three men before and everyone spoke so highly of them. He'd spent only a few hours in their presence but he couldn't help but wonder if he had fallen in with men like these years ago, might he have become a different kind of man? At least once in his life he was suddenly determined to do something honorable. He would not allow any of these men to risk their lives. There were two reasons why he didn't want Quin to go down. First of all, he was the biggest. Dirk nearly smiled. What if he got stuck down there—how would they ever get him out? But the most compelling reason—was Mariah. All he had to do was look into his sister's eyes and see that she was deeply in love with Quincy Long and it seemed that the big man felt the same way about her. As he thought about those two, it came to him that he needed to be assured of Mariah's future before he risked his life. And this moment, was possibly his only chance to get that done.

He gazed once more into the dark interior of the mine, then Dirk turned to the other men and said stiffly, "Don't need to discuss this. I'm the one for this job." Still, he surprised the men when he grabbed Quin's arm with one hand and shook his thumb towards his sister with the other. "Mister, that's my baby sister over there." Mariah was sitting beside Copper and she turned to listen. "I should have been watchin' over her all along, but I let her down. I'm here with her now though, and I'm not going down there until I get a few things straight with you!"

Quin met Dirk's serious gaze with his own, pleased that this man was taking his role as brother seriously. He knew this would embarrass Mariah, but he hoped it would please her as well. "All right," he mused. "What do we need to get straight?"

"Mariah has been treated poorly her whole life." He groaned then added sadly, "I haven't done so well by her myself. But—I won't stand for you or anyone else hurting her. We all know what she's been through but I've seen the way you two look at each other. So, what I want to know is—do you love my sister enough to marry her? Or are you just gonna give her false hope and then when you get around a bunch of judgmental church folk, tell her that you sure are sorry but it just wasn't meant to be?"

Quin's gaze was tender as it swept towards Mariah, but Dirk shook him by the arm, "Are you going to marry my sister? I've got witnesses here and I just want to hear an honest, yes or no!"

"Stop it Laddy." Horrified and embarrassed, Mariah held her side and gingerly made her way to her brother. "Pastor Long is the most honorable man I've ever met. He deserves your respect and as for what his future plans are? Well—that is none of your business—nor is it mine!"

Dirk spun around and frowned at his sister, "I'm about to go down into that hole in the ground, Sis. I may not make it out and I'm not leaving you again, not until I know you're gonna be all right! Now I saw him kiss you but that doesn't mean a thing. Still, it gives me the right as your brother to find out what his intentions are."

"Well, of course I'm going to marry your sister!" Quin growled, even as he grinned and winked at Mariah. "You think I'm the kind of man that goes around giving passionate kisses to a woman I'm not going to marry? I just haven't had time to ask her yet."

Dirk actually grinned as he folded his arms across his chest. "That won't be necessary—she says yes!"

Quin laughed and took Mariah's hand, "You know, I think my brother-in-law and I are going to get along just fine." Staring into her eyes, and willing her to see the love he felt he said sincerely. "Mariah, I tried to distance myself from you because I thought God was asking me to give you up. I thought I had to sacrifice either you or my ministry. But after a lot of prayer and some godly counsel, I realized that God wanted me to have both. He brought us together because He knew we needed each other. We'll serve God together—you and me!"

Mariah marveled at the glow of happiness on Quin's face, she was amazed by his words and yet she had to ask, "You're truly serious? I mean about me—about us—a marriage and a ministry together? Even though I'm…"

"Perfect—yes you are—perfect for me!" He said, before she could say otherwise. "And I've never been more serious about anything. I need you, Mariah—we need each other." His face revealed his vulnerability as he added softly, "For quite some time I've been feeling God leading me into a ministry to help women who have been hurt like you. I could never make it work because it wasn't a ministry that a bachelor could do properly. It needed a husband and wife working together. I look at you, my beauty, and I see God's perfect choice for me—a perfect partner for my life and a perfect helpmate for my ministry. Maybe we'll build a special retreat, right here in these mountains. What do you say Mariah? Will you marry me? You and me—forever?"

She answered him by stepping into his arms and in the next instant his lips were covering hers. They were sharing a long and very thorough kiss when the sound of laughter and applause from their friends surrounded them. Aware that they were making a spectacle of themselves, they reluctantly drew apart.

Jack sniffed and wiped his eyes with the back of his hand, then tugged on his beard. "Well, things sure are looking up in these here mountains. Say now Preacher, when ya build that thar special place fer ladies, reckon ya'll need a good man ya kin trust—ya know—to kind o' help take care o' things?"

Keeping Mariah tucked close to his side, Quin laughed. "Jack, we surely do need a good man like you to help. In fact, both you and Ladd could make a big difference. Of course it could be a dangerous place for bachelors. You both might find sweethearts of your own!"

Jack grunted but the idea brought a sparkle to his eyes. "Just imagine, me—Siah Jackson—with a sweetheart! Now I'd call that a mighty tall order. 'Course, iffen I've learned anything of late, it's that bad men get buried and the good ones get married. I surely do prefer the latter! Why Preacher, I might even think on takin' a bath."

Everyone laughed but Dirk. Jack's words were ringing in his mind—bad men get buried. Women had always been afraid of him. Of course he didn't know for sure if it was his pale skin as much as it was his abrasive manners. He couldn't see himself married—but buried—that he could see! His thoughts immediately went to the four dead men who had so recently been his partners. If he hadn't run into Mariah, his own dead body would most likely be slung over his saddle and headed down the mountain, just like the others.

Attempting to act as if this conversation had no effect on him, he stepped towards Mariah. "Well, time's a wastin'. Better give me a hug, Sis. According to old-long-tooth here, I'll be walkin' for a couple of days before I find that gold! Then I've got to turn around and do it all over again. So, don't go worryin' if I'm gone for a while."

Mariah stepped from Quin's arms into her brother's, "None of us care about that gold, Ladd. Just leave it where it is. It will be a terribly long time spent in the darkness. We both know it will bring back memories of days and nights spent down in that cellar—at least—I know it would me. You don't have to do this!"

Placing his large hand on Dirk's shoulder Quin nodded his agreement. "That's right, you've got family and friends now. I've got some sway with the territorial Governor, I might be able to have you put into my custody until your sentence is worked out. Then you'll be a free man and won't have to be looking over your shoulder anymore. And I wasn't jesting about needing your help. You'll always have a home with us, Ladd."

Strange emotions twisted in Dirk's chest, then he shook his head sadly, "Thanks, but I don't know who Ladd O'Culla is anymore. Trouble is—I don't think I know who Dirk Culley is either. Reckon I've got an awful lot to figure out." Turning to Mariah he forced an air of confidence, "I'm a grown man now, Sis. I'm not a boy who's scared of the dark anymore." His lie sounded convincing—at least he hoped it did. He didn't want Mariah to worry, even though his heart felt like a snare drum, pounding double time in his chest.

Mariah shook her head. He couldn't fool her, for she knew he had to be fighting the deep horror they both shared. And yet, her next words surprised him, they even surprised her. "All right, it could even be that God's hand is in this. Perhaps walking in darkness—will help you finally see the light! Do something for me, Ladd. Listen carefully while you're down there, brother. God doesn't shout when He has something to say, He whispers. All I'm asking, is that you listen. And I promise to pray for you—every moment—every step of the way." Mariah kissed him on the cheek then whispered in his ear, "I've always loved you and nothing will ever change that."

Dirk looked embarrassed by his sister's words, but he gave her a stiff hug then hurried past the men that waited at the entrance to the shaft. Without a word he began tying the end of the long rope Shad had put together around his waist. He shrugged into the pack they had prepared for him, that looped around both shoulders. It held a couple torches fashioned from sticks wrapped with strips of material torn from the women's petticoats, then covered in pine pitch to keep them burning longer. There was also a lantern filled with coal oil, a small coffee pot with a pouch of ground coffee, biscuits and jerked beef. Then he slung a canteen of water over each shoulder.

Nodding towards Quin he muttered under his breath, "I'm glad yer gonna marry my sister. I'm not lookin' for any handouts, though. I'm gonna get this gold or die tryin'."

Quin nodded his understanding then placed his hand on Dirk's shoulder. "It could be dangerous down there. I'd like to ask for God's protection over you, if you don't mind."

Dirk sighed over all the religious falderal he was having to put up with, and yet as he glanced down, the musty shaft smelled like death. The darkness reminded him of pain and fear and he rubbed his sweaty palms against his pants before he put on his gloves. As he fought down the familiar feeling of panic he nodded impatiently, "Pray on, if that's what you want to do."

"Dear Lord," Preacher began, "we ask that you keep Ladd safe, and Father while he's down there, let him know that you are with him and that you care for him."

Dirk had expected some long winded sermon-prayer. But Quincy Long, the preacher that was soon to be his brother-in-law, was already tugging on his own pair of heavy leather gloves. Then he picked up the rope and began setting things in motion. "Shad," he called, "light that torch and hand it to him when he's ready. All right, ease down on that first rung of the ladder. Go down slow, one rung at a time. We'll keep the rope tight until you're all the way to the bottom of the shaft. And Ladd, if you should get into any trouble—just holler—we'll bring you up here in a hurry!"

"The name's Dirk," he groaned. Then his lips lifted in a scant smile. "Then again, if I holler and you bring me up in a hurry—I might just let ya call me anything you like!"

When the men around him chuckled in response it seemed to drain some of the dread from Dirk's heart as he stepped onto the first rung of the ladder. He let out a sigh of relief when it held his weight. "Guess I'm ready for that torch now."

Just as Preacher began lowering him into the shaft he asked, "Hey, Reverend, reckon you know more about prayer than I do, but I always thought you were supposed to say, *'Amen'* when you stop praying?"

Preacher locked eyes with Dirk and grinned, "That's because I haven't stopped. And I'll keep on praying—till you are out of there, safe and sound and back with all of us!"

His words stunned Dirk. Not knowing what to say, he simply frowned down at the shaft, swallowed hard then continued on. The ladder seemed to be solid enough and he took the next several steps into the darkness. The farther down he went the harder it was to breathe, and then he began hearing strange noises. Surely it was just his imagination, but the shaft seemed to growl a warning as he stepped from one rung onto the next.

Quin kept his legs braced apart and secured the rope with his left hand guiding the rope while his right hand anchored it firmly against his hip. Inches at a time Quin let the rope slip through his gloved hands. Shad and Jack stood behind, slowly feeding him more. The ladder was old and it proved to be a wise precaution, because when Dirk was about half way down the shaft, one of the rungs broke and his boot smashed through the next three rungs. Dirk cried out in terror, but the men above stopped his fall after only three or four feet. Of course it seemed much farther for Dirk, and he felt sure that his heart was permanently lodged in his throat!

Jack leaned out over the shaft and called down with a relieved chuckle, "Hey there boy, ya all right? Didn't lose any a yer innards' in that *'little fall'*—did ya?"

It took Dirk a few moments before he was able to respond. When Jack wiggled the rope and called again he answered: "My innards' are fine old man. But if I don't find gold down here…yours are gonna be spread out all over the place!" Jack just laughed and wiggled the rope again, while Dirk fought down the familiar panic and tried to hide the fact that—that *'little fall'* had taken a decade off his life. It was even more sobering to realize that this journey hadn't even begun yet.

He feared few things, but dark, tight spaces terrified him. It was a fear that he shared with his sister although she hadn't been punished nearly as often as he had. Still, they had both suffered the childhood terror of being locked in dark moldy cellars as punishment for infractions as small as spilled milk or uncombed hair.

When Dirk finally reached the bottom of the shaft, he looked up and nearly choked when he saw only a tiny speck of daylight above him. "I—I've reached the bottom!" he shouted, then with trembling hands, he untied himself from the rope. Even though Jack assured him that the shaft had been dug into a granite cavern, and that he need not fear a cave in, the rope was a lifeline he hated to sever.

That old goat better be right about this black hole in the ground or I'll feed his sorry carcass to the buzzards!

Holding the torch high, Dirk cursed and grumbled while he struggled to remember what the old skunk domed mountain man had instructed him to do: *"Now boy, you be real careful once you take your first steps into that darkness. I recollect three separate caverns that spur off from the mine shaft. Two of 'em are as treacherous as a rattlesnake, both of 'em droppin' off sudden like. Tar threw a stone down into one of 'em and we never did hear it land. Now the third cavern that's the one ya want. You'll know it's the one, 'cause yer torch flame will dance like a willow tree in a gale!"*

The old man's words seemed to echo in Dirk's mind and he cautiously took his first step away from the ladder. A cold sweat rose across his brow and he wiped his forehead on his sleeve and reminded himself to breathe. His mouth was dry and he was trembling all over when he found the first opening that led off into the darkness. It was a black so thick it felt like he would need a knife to cut through it. His arm shook as he held the torch towards the first opening and took a few cautious steps inside—the flame remained steady. He moved back and then went farther into the darkness in another direction. He found the opening to the second cavern, again his torch simply burned steadily on. Suddenly starved for air, he realized that once again he was holding his breath, so he filled his lungs and slowly stepped a little farther away from the main shaft, the ladder and the rope that could have taken him back to safety and light. The third spur of the cavern was farther away than he had expected but when he finally reached it, just as the old mountain man had predicted, the fire leapt up and began to dance, and he felt the faintest hint of a breeze blowing against his skin. Stepping back a few paces he cupped his hand around his mouth and called up the shaft. "I found the right cavern—I'm going in."

"God's speed!" Quin called down to him. "We'll be waiting right here for your return."

Then he heard Mariah's gentle voice calling down to him, "Please Laddy, be careful!"

Dirk was surprised how much hearing their words of concern affected him. How long had it been since anyone had cared if he were alive or dead… let alone safe? Certainly not since he had said goodbye to his sister years ago. Now she was once again part of his life, or at least she could be. And Quin would be his brother-in-law. Dirk couldn't stop hearing the man's words: "You'll always have a home with us, Ladd." "Ladd…" Dirk repeated the name, wondering again if it were possible to be Ladd O'Culla again?

He sucked in a long breath, then lifting his torch high he stepped into the darkness. As he walked he yanked the bandana from his neck and wiped the sweat from his face. With every step he searched for a satchel or strong-box or saddlebags, anything that might hold or conceal whatever it was that Tar had brought down here. Hoping that he'd trip over it any minute so he could return to sunshine and fresh air. Dirk stopped, he suddenly couldn't remember any of the clues. Where the treasure was supposed to be? He withdrew the paper from his pocket on which Copper had written Vernon's code, then struggled with each word as he slowly read the meager message:

Petrified—Forest—Two—Fools—Mine—Chase after the east wind—He has led me—brought me into darkness, not into light —At the mouth of the cave—Hidden Treasure.

His hand shook as he wiped his face with the bandana again. *Old long tooth told me plain that I'd have to walk in darkness for two days before I got to the mouth of the cave. I haven't been down here for five minutes and I'm already desperate for this to be over. I've got to get a hold of myself. I need what's down here and if that means I have to walk clean to the other side of this dang mountain—I'll do it—I have to!*

As Dirk continued on, there seemed to be plenty of air, and yet he kept sucking in more. As if each lung full might be his last. The faces of the four men that had died the day before seemed to be lurking in the dark shadows, floating just beyond the light of his flame. They had all been birds of a feather, all having lived the same kind of debauched life. And just as sure as rain fell and steam rose, someday he was going to die too—probably in the same way they did. Dirk jerked to a stop. The way was becoming more narrow, and it curved sharply to the left and then to the right. Jack had warned him to expect this, but it was still unsettling. He tried not to think about how much he hated being down here alone! The damp air, the musty smell, it was so like the potato cellar at Candlestick. The old scars on his back seemed to burn anew as if his step-father might be waiting around the next bend with his whip. First came the lashing, followed by a day and night of being locked in the cellar. A cold shudder rumbled through him as he thought of his past. Back then he'd just been a boy. He hadn't been an angel but he hadn't deserved that kind of punishment either. Of course now—Dirk figured he'd committed just about every sin there was and he deserved any kind of punishment that was handed down to him.

As the darkness closed in around him, he found himself talking out loud. He didn't even realize at first that he was talking to God, "I don't even think you exist. Or that you can hear me." He groaned. "I don't think I'm ready to die though. 'Cause I reckon if ever a man was bound for hell—it's me. I've never believed in God—but I've always believed in hell!"

Just then he remembered how he used to boast of being evil. "I'm as low down as any man that's ever lived!" He used to say and he would laugh when he said it. But now the laughter rang hollow. Dirk kept walking as his voice grew louder, angrier, "Why did Ya have to make me the way You did, anyway? My pale skin and white hair has always been an excuse for people to fear and ridicule me. I've always hated You and blamed You, for the way my mother and step-father treated me." Just then he stopped and took a swig of water from his canteens. Then he walked on putting one foot in front of the other with nothing but darkness beyond the torch light. "Only Mariah ever saw me as having any worth. She and Red seem to think Your making me an albino wasn't You punishin' me, any more than You givin' Red, red hair was to punish her! They both seemed to think You love me. Hah! If that's not hard to believe I don't know what is." Dirk stopped again and gazed all around him, seeing only the blackness, then he called out defiantly, "Okay God…I'll just test the water so to speak while I'm down here. If there is any worth in me—then show me—show me if ya can!"

Dirk was breathing hard after his rant, but he waited and listened for a long while, not knowing what to expect. Maybe that he would hear God whisper, as Mariah had said, or that the cavern would be filled with light so he wouldn't have to walk in the darkness. The only sound he heard was his own breathing and felt his heart pounding in his chest. Finally, he gave up on waiting and feeling justified for his disbelief, he continued on with his journey. Hoping with every step that Tar O'Leary and Black-Eyed Jack weren't just two crazy old men, and this whole thing wasn't just a bad joke!

Since there was no sunlight it was impossible to tell when he had walked a full day? Finally, Dirk grew tired and decided it was time to sit down and rest. He drank some water from his canteen and ate a few biscuits that were still soft and fresh and some jerked beef.

He hadn't meant to fall asleep in that horrible place, but the next thing he knew, he awoke in complete darkness for his torch had gone out. It felt like he was trapped in the nightmare of being buried alive! He cried out as the terror of it threatened to overwhelm him. Then suddenly his hand touched the second torch he had unpacked, along with the box of matches. He fumbled wildly at first! The first three matches broke when he scraped them across the rock wall, but thankfully the forth match sparked into a flame. When glorious light finally washed over him, his knees buckled under him and he sucked in a lung full of calming air, then gave himself a sharp rebuke.

"Settle down you fool—panic will do ya no good. Remember ya've got to do this all over again when ya come back." He had no way of knowing how long he'd slept but he was thirsty and hungry and when he had satisfied himself, he got up and walked again. It was not only the idea that he was walking deep in the bowels of the mountain but there were strange noises in the cavern. He told himself that he was just hearing bats or the natural movement of the earth but he hated these sounds, even more than he hated the darkness. Still, he kept walking. Finally, he groaned with relief when he rounded yet another curve in the long tunnel and felt a stronger breeze stirring the air all around him. It was much sweeter and cleaner and he quickened his pace.

"It can't be much farther." He promised, keeping his eyes peeled for even a pin prick of light that might give him hope. Though he fought it with every step, the gut wrenching fear was always there. It was like strolling in a tomb with death itself stalking him. The oppressive darkness weighed him down with memories of a life filled with loneliness, pain and depravity. "If hell is reliving your worst fears and mistakes, then this is the kind of hell that awaits me!" Dirk groaned then wiped the sweat from his brow and kept walking. "Stop remembering," he shouted, "stop thinking. STOP!"

Stop—Stop—Stop. The single word echoed over and over throughout the long stony cavern. Dirk tried to laugh off the sound of his own words taunting him. Wiping away the sweat that was running into his eyes, he focused his thoughts on Black-Eyed Jack smiling into the campfire as he shared his story of The Two Fools Mine.

"As I recollect…" the old man began, his voice sounding like gravel on a dry road, "'Twas 'bout thirty years ago when me and Tar O'Leary come to these here mountains to trap beaver. Sure enough, we thought ourselves to be just like Louis and Clark. We was young and strong!" The old man chuckled then added, "And greener 'n aspen leaves in spring. One day we happened upon somethin' that just plumb overtook us with 'Gold Fever.' What a sight! It were a shining all to beat the band and layin' atop the ground. Easy as pluckin' a fat dewberry off a vine! 'Tweren't nothin' but fool's gold. 'Course we didn't know that at the time. So, Tar and me just grinned at each other and started in diggin'. We dug down thirty feet or more. One long shaft straight down 'til we hit granite. Then we used our dynamite! It's a pure wonder we didn't blast ourselves to the moon! What we did do was blast the roof off a mountain cavern. We cleared off the rubble but never did see hide-nor-hair of any more *gold!* We didn't care, we was as curious as a couple fox cubs. We wanted to see where that cavern went. There were three spurs that led from where our shaft dropped into the cavern. Two led to deep grottos that turned out to be death traps!" Jack chuckled, "'Course, we learned that the hard way. The third cavern had fresh air that got sweeter as ya went. But dang—it sure was a long walk! We got plum wore out, so we stopped to sleep—got up and walked—then slept again. After that second sleep, we woke up with the sun shining on our faces. Ya never seen two more surprised fellers than me and Tar! Been in the dark so long we near forgot the glory of sunlight. We was so happy we danced about like it were the fourth of July! 'Course that's when we realized that we weren't cut out to be no miners—we was mountain men—through 'n through! Didn't find gold—but we found treasure just the same. 'Twas a hidden meadow, prettiest place ya ever did see! Surrounded by flat sided granite walls with a river running straight through the middle. That water was as clear as the cry of an eagle. We looked down and saw deer and a band of wild horses grazing in grass that tickled the horse's bellies. We clapped our hands and shouted but they just looked up and snorted at us, as if we was being rude to disturb their breakfast. Them critters had never seen a man before—or they sure would a scattered. I've thought on it some and reckon the Indians in these parts probably know 'bout that place—but they don't hunt it. Most likely they stay away 'cause its kind o' sacred ya know—strong medicine in a place like that—sure 'nuff! Jack paused as he gazed into the fire and spoke of the hidden meadow then added softly. "Sure 'nuff—*strong medicine.* If Tar wanted to hide something real special, I reckon that'd be the place!"

Dirk recalled Jack's words: "Strong medicine…" he scoffed. The story smacked of an old man's memory of a young man's folly. It didn't matter; all he cared about was finding the gold that Tar O'Leary had hidden. Just then, a gust of wind blew across his face. It was fresh and cool, and he quickened his step, hoping he might soon be free of this mountain tomb. And then suddenly, there it was before him, the great opening from the cavern. He wasn't greeted with golden sunlight, as Jack and Tar had been, but found instead a shadowy moonlight. Perhaps he had walked faster or slept longer, he didn't know which, but he stepped to the mouth of the cave and looked out on the valley beyond.

"Well, I'll be!" He groaned, then let out a long slow whistle. "That old codger got this right, anyway." Dirk looked on in awe seeing at least in part what Jack had described. A winding river sparkled in the moonlight, and it shimmered like a silvery ribbon curling and rolling down the center of the valley. The twilight didn't allow Dirk to see nearly as much as he wanted. It didn't matter—morning would come soon enough and he was tired. He laid himself down at the cavern entrance to sleep but his eyes refused to close as he gazed up at the expanse of sky above and listened to a lone wolf singing to his mate. She answered with her own tune and soon they were joined by their pack, adding a sad, shrill melody to the chorus. When the pack grew silent, sleep once again crowded in, but then he sensed more than heard the faint whoosh of wings as a night owl swooped low and then came the hapless cry of his prey.

Dirk awoke to the sight of the whole valley covered in a heavy morning dew that sparkled in the sunlight. When he saw how truly beautiful and pristine it all was…somehow the sight shamed him and he wished he hadn't come. A strange feeling came over him; he had asked God to show him if he had any worth, but he didn't like the answer this unspoiled valley gave him. He didn't belong in a place like this—he was an unfit intruder. Suddenly, he wanted only to leave, and he began hurriedly packing his things. It was only then that he remembered the gold! It had been a tortuous trek and he'd probably walked miles from the mine shaft. He had finally made it to the cave entrance and was shocked when he realized that he hadn't given a thought to Tar O'Leary's *hidden treasure*. Gazing around the entrance, he saw nothing but sand and dirt. He kicked over a few piles of rock in frustration, and then his foot landed on something soft. Dirk dropped to his knees and cleared away the debris. There he found a brown carpetbag, covered in years of dust. At first glance it seemed to be filled with dirty laundry, and yet this laundry was as heavy as an anvil. Groaning, he carried it outside then lifted what looked like a canvas vest from the bag and laid it down. It was a strange garment, covered with tiny pockets. He opened one and withdrew a coin. It was a gold eagle and it shone in the sunlight. There were dozens of pockets and each one contained at least one or more coins. He looked into the carpetbag and withdrew a second vest and it was filled just the same as the first!

"Well, I won't be a millionaire…but this will do!" He laughed, "This will surely do!"

Dirk flipped a gold eagle into the air and pocketed it. Still, he was surprised that he wasn't more thrilled with his discovery. Perhaps if Mariah had been there, they might have laughed and danced about. Instead of celebrating, all Dirk could think of was that now he would have to face another long walk in complete darkness, carrying that heavy bag all the way. He was already dreading the return trip. Then he remembered Jack's advice. "It'll take ya at least two days to get to the valley and longer coming back if it's gold Tar hid. Best you stay and soak up some sunshine before ya come back. Days in that kind of darkness—it—well it takes a lot out of a man!"

Jack didn't need to explain that to Dirk. He already knew what darkness could do to a man or to a boy. He knew it all too well!

Chapter 28
Redemption

"In him we have redemption through his blood, the forgiveness of sins, in accordance with the riches of God's grace." Ephesians 1:7

Once Dirk found the gold he gave no more thought to it. He pushed the carpetbag to the side, slung his canteen over his shoulder and stepped into the sunlight. The mountain air was fresh and sweet. Suddenly he realized that he was hungry enough to eat a bull moose. As his eyes searched his surroundings for game, instinctively he checked his rifle—but somehow he didn't want to use it. Dirk was pleased when he spotted a Franklin grouse, also known as a Fool's Hen, for they sat in plain sight on the ground hoping not to be seen. He didn't need his gun, he simply picked up a sharp stone and threw it hard!

An hour later he was feasting on roasted grouse. Along with his hot coffee he gazed around him and drank in everything he saw. Earlier in the day he had felt too unworthy to even step into this valley, and though that might be true, just now he couldn't bear the thought of leaving it. Never in his life had he been in such a peaceful place. There were no enemies to run from or to chase after. No one making him feel odd. No one to fight. He was surrounded with freedom and peace, and a profound beauty!

He spent the day exploring this strange valley with its flat granite walls that kept it separate from the world beyond. The river that cut through the deep meadow grasses seemed to dance and sparkle in the sunshine. It was about two feet deep and a dozen feet wide and with its rock bottom, it was as clear as glass. He knelt down on the soft mossy bank and drank. It was pure, cold and sweet, and he drank from the river until he thought he might burst.

Although it was still spring, the day was hot! He stripped out of his clothes, undid his long braid, and jumped in; *gasping* as the frigid water took his breath away. After a very quick wash he rolled onto the bank and allowed the sun to dry his body.

As evening approached, the clouds were painted in shades of bronze and crimson, while a strange sadness settled over him. He did not want to bid farewell to such a place as this, or the way it made him feel. He pushed these thoughts away as his stomach rumbled, reminding him that he hadn't eaten since that morning. Returning to the river he was pleased to find mountain trout swimming lazily in the slow moving current.

"Nothing like fresh trout for dinner." He mused, tasting them even as he knelt on the bank and slowly lowered his hands into the current and waited. It wasn't long before a fat trout swam right into his hands and just as quickly out again. He had done this before and knew patience was its own reward. Keeping his hands perfectly still, he moved only his pale pinky finger, mimicking a juicy white worm. Just when the hungry fish sprang for the worm, Dirk instantly closed his hands around the trout and flung it over his head and onto the grass just behind him. Silvery scales sparkled in a shower of water, reflecting the last rays of sunlight. Soon a second and third fish joined their cousin. Dirk's hands were numb with cold and they shook as he made a small fire then cleaned the fish. By the time the sun and moon had traded places, he was completely warm again, had filled his belly and was more content than he had ever been!

That night he made his bed under the stars and awoke the following morning wanting only to relive the day before. He breakfasted on biscuits and jerky, then explored a little farther into the valley. When he spotted a high, level patch of ground beneath an overhang of solid granite on the north side, he was surprised to hear himself mutter, "Good shelter from winter storms, close but not too close to the river. Nice high ground in case the river flooded in the spring. Perfect place for a cabin!"

A scornful chuckle rumbled from his chest, taking his hat off he slapped it against this thigh. "Since when, Dirk Culley have you ever wanted to build a cabin?" The next thought shocked him, "Dirk Culley, never would have, but there was a time when Ladd O'Culla wanted a home and a ranch of his own! Could Sis be right? Could I have another chance at being a different kind of man—a better one? Make the right choices!"

This place was making him think and feel things he hadn't thought or felt for ages. He knew he needed to head back soon, knew that Mariah would be worried, but he hated the idea of leaving this place even more than he hated the idea of returning through the dark cavern. Once again, his eyes roamed over the granite walls that surrounded him, “Lord, is there another way out?” Dirk scowled at his own words, they sounded like a prayer. “Sure,” he hissed. “Ask God to show ya that yer worthy! Ask God to open up these mountains and make a way out!” Shaking his head scornfully, he groaned, “If I'm not the biggest fool there ever was.” Though he ridiculed himself and God, he was finding it difficult to hold onto his cynicism. He hadn't thought once of the bag of gold since he'd found it. And it shocked him to realize that finding it meant so little. Knowing that Mariah was no longer in need, it just didn't seem important any more.

He awoke on the third day with sunlight shimmering on the meadow grasses, bathed again in heavy dew drops. Once again he spent a languid day exploring the valley and searching desperately for a miracle passageway out. He called himself ten times a fool for even looking. “Give up,” he told himself. “Like me—this meadow is a freak of nature. It's good that there is no easy way in and out. That's how come it's so clean and pure.” Still, he couldn't seem to stop himself from searching just a little longer.

He walked all morning and had only eaten some greens. So far he hadn't needed his guns, hadn't wanted to use them in this special place. Whenever he got hungry it seemed another way always presented itself. Just then his stomach growled and sure enough when he checked his snares he found a fat rabbit. He'd found it just as the sun stood straight up in the dark blue sky, so he roasted it for his noon day meal, and then went to the river to drink.

The sound of the water soothed him. He laid down and listened to it as he watched silvery strands of water rolling over rocks and pooling in small quiet places along the bank. The sights and sounds all blended together, the sparkling water, the breeze blowing against the tall grasses, making them sway like rolling waves. He watched and listened until his eyes grew heavy and he fell asleep.

At first his dreams were melodious; Mariah was sitting beside him. Her hair was the exact shade of sunlight as she strummed the heart-shaped zither and began to sing. Then suddenly she was gone and once again he was surrounded by darkness. For once he wasn't in the cellar at the ranch, and his back wasn't throbbing from a beating. No, at least he wasn't there.

Instead he was back in that long dark cavern. He walked and walked until he rounded a corner and found himself surrounded by light. His stomach clenched when he realized, to his horror, that he had walked right into a brightly lit courtroom. A stout looking bailiff stepped forward and said, "They're all finally here my Lord." Dirk realized that he was in line behind other men awaiting their sentence. At the very front was a man with his back turned, he couldn't see his face but he would recognize his step-father—Ruxton Hunter from any angle. He knew the next man too, it was Jimmy Todd, then Ox Hennessey, after him stood Claw with his long black hair and next to him, Zeno.

Dirk tried to see the judge who sat behind the enormous desk, but when he looked up the sunlight in the room was so bright that he couldn't make out his features. He could hear the judge's voice though. It was like no voice he had ever heard before. It wasn't harsh or even demanding; instead it was the kindest voice Dirk had ever heard. It didn't make sense, but the judge sounded as if passing down these judgements broke his heart. And it was with great sadness, He said, "The justice I give you men today is of your own making. I sentence you to live out the eternity you have chosen." Again Dirk was touched by how tender the voice sounded and yet, it was as sharp and final as a surgeon's scalpel, "I loved you, enough to die for you, but you have chosen to reject my love, my salvation, and the redemption I have offered you so freely."

Dirk's step-father turned and stared at him, fear and regret marring his once handsome features. Then the pompous and hard man began to cry and weep as two horrible looking creatures slithered towards him and took him away. He cried out for mercy, but no one tried to help him. Dirk had always thought of himself as a better man than Ruxton Hunter, but now in the bright light of this courtroom he realized that his step-father had chosen his own fate—just as Dirk had chosen his. Though their paths had been different in many ways, they both were ending up in the same place.

Dirk watched as each man was taken away, Jimmy Todd, and then Ox and the two others. One by one they were ushered from the courtroom, screaming and begging for mercy but—none was given. The judge did not weigh their good deeds against their acts of crime and corruption. Instead the great judge told them that they were condemned for committing the unpardonable sin—they had rejected the Son of God!

Suddenly it was Dirk's turn to step to the desk for sentencing. He knew without question that he was not appearing before a mere judge but before Jesus Christ himself. "I am sorry," Dirk tried to explain. "It's just that I've never been a religious man."

"Ladd, I did not die on the cross to give mankind religion." The judge said tenderly, "I came to earth to rescue them. To have a bond, a relationship with them. Not the kind you had with your step-father, but the impenetrable bond between a cherished son and his loving Father. It is up to you to choose. You can be a child of God or God's enemy. If I give you another chance, Ladd—what will you choose?"

Dirk was lying on his stomach in the soft grass when he awoke to a warm breath against his cheek, and then he felt a gentle tugging on his long white braid. Normally he would have sprung to his feet, pistol in his hand, cocked and ready. However, for some reason, he slowly rolled over. Why he didn't react in his normal way—he would never know. However, he was glad he hadn't for he surely would have frightened the little bay filly. Probably no more than a few weeks old, she had discovered him sleeping in the grass and was of course filled with baby-like curiosity. A few yards away, her mother grazed hungrily on the lush meadow grass. The bay mare raised her graceful head, scented the air and then unperturbed, she returned to cropping grass. Dirk lifted his hand to the foal's muzzle allowing her to sniff and then nibble his fingers. Slowly Dirk sat up, and that's when he saw three other mares. Two already had their babies, playing and cavorting about them, but the little buckskin mare had bulging sides, and looked as if she might drop her foal at any minute. Turning his attention back on the little filly, Dirk was pleased and surprised when she allowed him to run his hand over her soft burgundy coat. Her black mane and tail were short, curly, and soft as down. He couldn't help but smile at the little thing.

Suddenly, he heard what had to be the call of the band stallion, trumpeting a greeting to his mares. Though he wasn't close enough to see, they lifted their graceful heads and nickered their welcome. The sound of hooves thundered across the meadow, and Dirk knew he needed to be cautious. Every stallion can be dangerous, they were born to fight, especially wild ones, and he stepped away from the colt. The sun was blocking his view of the beast at first, but then he realized that he was hard to see in the sunlight because the animal was as white as a winter snow. As the horse drew near,

Dirk realized with a start that the stallion—was an albino! And—he was magnificent! His conformation from nose to tail was flawless. Dirk stood mesmerized as the animal came to a stop and the two considered one another. The stallion called to the little bay filly who was still standing a bit too close to the stranger. She obeyed instantly, approaching her sire with her mouth opening and closing, a greeting of submission and repentance. The white stallion touched noses with the young filly, then with a slight nip and squeal he sent her off to find her mother.

Smiling at the gentle reprimand, Dirk slowly picked up the bag of salt he'd use while roasting the rabbit. Dumping a handful onto the ground, he stepped back about a dozen feet and then looked away, inviting the big stallion to accept this small token of friendship.

The stallion turned his gaze on his mares then looked around the meadow. Finally, he returned his attention to the two legged creature standing in the tall grass, and breathed in the tangy scent of salt and the less familiar scent of man. He licked and chewed, thinking about the salt; he took a step closer and snorted a warning. But Dirk didn't move. The cautious stallion debated this invitation for nearly an hour. Little by little, keeping his head low and his ears back in warning he finally got close enough to stretch his long neck, then lip a bit of salt into his mouth. Having succeeded in the small theft, he reared and danced away, licking and chewing—enjoying the treat. But the few grains of salt weren't nearly enough and he wanted it all. When he returned to the pile of salt he found that the strange two legged creature had moved closer to the prize. This give and take continued for most of the afternoon until the great beast simply lowered his head and licked up not only all the salt but every blade of grass around it, even with Dirk standing quietly beside him.

"Good man." Dirk said softly, "Want some more?" He sprinkled another small pile onto the ground, only to have it devoured in a second. Next, Dirk poured some granules onto the palm of his hand. He wasn't a stranger to horses and he knew he could lose his hand doing this. But he was in the place of strong medicine. Everything was different here, he was different here! He held out his hand, it was a clear invitation for this horse to extend his trust and though it seemed that the stallion had no real fear of men, he was still by nature a very cautious creature and it took some patience on Dirk's part to stand perfectly still while the powerful horse made up his mind. Finally, the stallion stretched his neck and his lips as far as they could possibly go…and managed to get a few grains of salt from the man's hand into his mouth. Nodding his great head, he grew bolder, stepped a little closer and took a bit more. The sun was about to set when the stallion came close enough to lick the salt from Dirk's hand. He licked that hand until it felt raw and Dirk just wanted to laugh! The mares weren't nearly as cautious and he divided the rest of his salt among them.

It wasn't until all the stars had spread across the night sky, that Dirk was finally able to rub the stallion's wide forehead. When he turned and walked away—the stallion followed. They walked together all along the river bank. Just then the big stud stopped, looked back and called to his mares. They raised their heads but the grass was sweet and they didn't respond. Apparently, they were happy where they were. But the stallion nickered again more insistently, then he galloped back to the little buckskin mare, who was farthest away, put his head down and ears back and snaked after her and the rest of his band of mares and colts. The mares lifted their tails as they trotted passed Dirk. He found himself grinning at their antics, he had always loved working with the horses on the ranch, but this beat any experience he had ever had.

He stared for a long time at the totally white stallion with glass-like eyes, and it was as if in he were looking at himself. Of all the wild stallions in the Rocky Mountains, it was an albino that led the herd in this sacred valley—this place of purity and—yes indeed—strong medicine!

"Dear God!" he whispered reverently as he stared into the night sky. "Could it be that You are speaking to me through all this? You are—aren't You? I've never seen another man or beast that was an albino like me. I asked You to show me if I had any worth in Your sight, and—You let me come to this special place and You allowed me to see this amazing creature. He stared up at the sparkling black canopy overhead, his eyes misting. "God—I believe You are who the Bible says You are! You are listening to me right now. More than that—You're speaking to me—a worthless outlaw. Being an albino wasn't Your punishment! All my outlaw partners are dead. But You allowed me to find my sister, and You allowed *me—me of all people*—to live—and—to come here to see this special place!"

Suddenly, he remembered the dream he had earlier that day. "Was that dream from you too? You said, 'If I give you another chance,

Ladd—what will you chose?'" Dropping to his knees he groaned, "I choose You God! I want to ask You to forgive me—but I'm so ashamed. I'm guilty of so many wicked things—but now I humbly ask that You allow me to be your child. Please God, I know I don't deserve Your mercy, but I beg You for it anyway! Please forgive me and please make me into the kind of man You want me to be."

He stayed on his knees in the grass for a long while. Cleansing tears of brokenness, pain and shame were shed. Finally, when he lifted his eyes, he realized that the bay mare and her filly and the rest of the small band of wild horses had simply bedded down all around him. He didn't even bother with his bedroll; he just laid down and fell asleep. When he awoke the following morning, he realized that it was Dirk Culley who was dead—and that albino—Ladd O'Culla—had been born all over again!

When he looked up he was surprised that the pale stallion was standing over him, and that the rest of this little band were peacefully grazing all around him as if he were an old friend. When Ladd got to his feet, the stallion walked in a circle around him, as if he sensed something new. Then with a snort and a shake of his head the snow white stallion raised his muzzle into the air, scented the wind then nickered loudly. As if following orders, the bay, who was apparently the lead mare, headed towards the far end of the valley with her little filly at her side. The other mares instantly followed behind. When the little buckskin with the bulging sides seemed to doddle, the stallion pinned his ears back and ran after her, forcing her to catch up with the others, while he trailed after them. Soon the small band was trotting down a pathway through the tall grass. This was a horse trail that Ladd, as he was now trying to think of himself, had missed seeing.

As if he were part of the herd, he trotted behind these horses and laughed as he went! True, heart felt laughter bubbled all the way through him. He felt so different—he felt light—he felt clean! He looked down at himself, his hands were the same as ever. He even pulled his white braid around and stared at it. He was just as white all over as he'd ever been! God hadn't changed him on the outside but he felt brand-new! After his experience with God the night before he knew he was just in the beginning stages of becoming someone different—Lord willing someone better! He wanted so much to tell Mariah and he knew he should even now be heading back towards the cave.

"Well, Lord." he said out loud as he followed the stallion. "I don't know what to do with myself. I've never felt like this before. I feel—good! I know I need Your direction. So—what am I supposed to do with this day—with—this life?"

Just then he stopped and listened, just as Mariah had told him. He didn't hear a thing, but after a while he did feel something. It was kind of like an inner, silent whisper. It seemed to be saying. . *follow.* Looking around he realized that the only thing to follow was the band of wild horses. He smiled, and then hurried after them, even though the direction they were heading—was a dead-end. In fact, it began to worry him as the herd went from a trot to a brisk cantor. It looked like they were about to run themselves into the granite wall. Confused, Ladd stopped and watched as the bay mare with her filly at her side, made a sharp turn. Then, it seemed as if she disappeared right into a wall of solid granite! He believed the valley was boxed in by that impenetrable wall. But now, he stood in amazement as the pretty dappled gray mare with her matching colt disappeared next, and then the others. Before the stallion followed after them, he stopped and looked back at Ladd. Then he let out a long, loud nicker, as if to say, "Well, are you coming or not?"

Ladd had searched diligently for a pathway leading out of this valley. But this band of horses had known all along what he had not been able to discover. It was nature's hoax, a simple trick of the eye. Somehow the granite slab forming the side of the mountain was grained and patterned in such a way that it made the stone before him seem like one solid rock! When in fact, there were two granite slabs set apart at just the right angle to make the pathway that went between them nearly invisible! Smiling at this wonderful discovery, he quickly followed the herd. Of course it was possible that he might become hopelessly lost in these mountains but he knew the horses would return to the hidden valley at some point. More than that, he felt God's peace! He'd been told to follow and so for whatever reason—this was the right thing to do! They walked for a long while through what felt like a complex mountain labyrinth of narrow pathways twists and turns.

The herd's destination had simply been a large box canyon where they immediately dropped their heads and began cropping grass.

It was disappointing. He had hoped that since the band seemed to be going in what he thought was the general direction of The Two Fools Mine that this might very well be another way back to its entrance!

Then he heard someone singing. His throat seemed to close and his eyes began to cloud as he recognized his own sister's familiar alto floating on the breeze. Sound travels well in the mountains but still he felt that she had to be close. After climbing a fairly steep hill, he caught his breath and looked down on the campsite he had left nearly a week ago. He shot his pistol twice into the air and when they all saw him, they shouted and called to him.

He would not have to travel through the dark cavern after all! Then a thought brought a brand new kind of smile to Ladd O'Culla's face. For in a very real sense, he knew that he would never have to travel in darkness—ever again!

EPILOGUE

18 months later

"Therefore if any man be in Christ, he is a new creature: old things are passed away; behold, all things are become new." 2 Corinthians 5:17

Mister and Missus Quincy Long rode in amiable silence as they enjoyed the beautiful day in the mountains. Since Mariah's horse, Steel, followed Flints every move, she really didn't have to pay attention. Instead she rested her hands on the saddle horn and allowed herself to be captivated by the scenery of rolling hills, jagged mountains and forests of pine and aspen. Quin had given her a journal to write in, and tonight she would describe the ride to the McKenna's as outrageously beautiful and supremely joyful! She had so much to be thankful for that she was always trying new words to describe a happiness she never could have imagined!

Indeed, the scenery along the winding mountain path was magnificent and in many places it was quite terrifying which added to the excitement! The sky overhead was as blue as her husband's eyes, and the clouds were as delicate as a lacy wedding veil. Mariah smiled at her romantic thoughts; everything seemed to remind her of the special day she had become Missus Quincy Long. Everything these days made Mariah happy—made her smile! The mountains only added to her joy for they were truly in their glory! She breathed deeply of the sweet pine scented breeze as it whispered its age old melody while sliding through the evergreens and turning the aspen leaves into wind-chimes. Being here again reminded her of just how good God had been! He had taken a broken woman and miraculously filled her with a peace beyond understanding and an overwhelming sense of gratitude! The leather of the saddle creaked as she leaned forward, asking Quin, "Shouldn't be much farther now. Is it my love?"

Quin chuckled, "I sure do like the way you phrase your questions—Missus Long—but I see you've been day-dreaming again—look around you—we've arrived!" He cupped his hand around his mouth and called, "Hello in the cabin!" The man's greeting was followed by Flint's loud whiny, for he too had old friends to greet.

When there was no sign of anyone in the cabin or barn, Mariah impatiently nudged her horse down the path leading to the hot spring. Her beautiful mare was a wedding present from Quin. He'd been intent on purchasing her horse from the Bar 61, and was especially pleased when the old man, Joseph was still there to personally choose the sweet-tempered gray mare for Mariah. Just as he had chosen Flint for Quin years earlier. As it happened, Quin and Mariah received a warm welcome from the also newly married Tytus and Augusta Grainger. Their story was bittersweet. Augusta was the widow of Ty's twin brother and one of Quin's dearest friends, Timothy Grainger. She had arrived at the ranch pregnant and alone. After a year of mourning, Tytus asked Augusta to marry him. The Grainger's had only been married a short while when the Long's arrived. Mariah and Augusta became instant friends and there was a lot of laughter and shared story-telling throughout their visit. Looking forward to starting their own family, Quin and Mariah were especially taken with the adorable little toddler, Tessie May. Mariah thought she was the most beautiful child she had ever seen. However, when Quin looked at the child, he couldn't help but see his old friend, Timothy. The child was the image of her late father. Curly wheat colored hair, bright blue eyes and a dimpled smile. The two couples grew close during that visit and the Grainger's were also quite interested in Quin and Mariah's idea for a ministry for women of the west.

"Come on Steel," Mariah urged as she passed her husband, heading down the path behind the cabin, "Let's go see if we can find our friends!" As they came near the hot spring they heard the sound of laughter.

"Hello McKenna's." She called, "You have company. An old married couple have come for a visit!"

Copper could have recognized her friend from a mile away for Mariah's hat had fallen behind her back and with her pale blonde hair coiled about her head, she looked as if she wore a crown of sunlight!

The two women started laughing and crying the moment they saw each other. Shad walked just behind Copper with a smiling toddler in his arms.

The little boy had raven black hair, and as they drew near his large green eyes shown with excitement and curiosity.

"Welcome!" Shad's voice boomed across the valley. With a grin that matched his son's, he held the boy high for them to see, "Come and see how much Tanner Josiah has grown!"

Mariah quickly slipped from Steel's back and threw her arms around Copper. Then she hugged Shad and little Tanner at the same time. When Mariah lifted her hands, the little rascal giggled and instantly dove into her arms, which made them all laugh!

Not wanting to be left out of the party, Remy's loud braying could be heard for miles as she trotted up the path from the river. The trees were so thick that she could be heard, but not seen. Copper and Shad exchanged amused glances, then Copper announced, "And we'd like you to meet another addition to the family. A *surprise* addition—to say the least!"

Quin and Mariah stared curiously at the McKenna's only to have them point back to the pathway where Remy was still braying her loud greeting. While they waited for the mule to make her way into the clearing, Shad asked, "Have y'all ever heard of a mule having a colt? Always heard it was next to impossible!"

Just then Remy burst into sight and Copper added, "But then, if you'll remember, Remy has always liked doing things she wasn't supposed to do. And with Boone's help she—well—you can see for yourselves!"

Just then both Quin and Mariah began to laugh, for coming down the path just behind Remy was a surprisingly pretty mule filly. She was a deep buckskin appaloosa, complete with white blanket and dark brown spots.

"A fine looking mule if ever I saw one, Quin remarked with a chuckle, "No offense to Remy, but thankfully that filly looks more like Boone! Other than her ears of course; she doesn't seem to take after Remy at all!"

Shad started laughing, leaving Copper to explain, "Yes, she does look like Boone but she's clever like her mama. Little Bonny is outrageously curious. We woke up this morning with her standing in our bedroom. And just wait till the sun comes up!"

Later that night over wild plum tarts and hot coffee, Copper was the first to bring up the gold. "So were you able to find the rightful owners?"

Quin smiled, "Yes, and it's an amazing tale of God's perfect timing. When Mariah and I got back from our honeymoon, we were going over the letters written to The Long Foundation asking for support for various charities. As we read one of the letters, it struck us both that it was obviously written by the wife of one of the men who had died in that mudslide. It told of how her husband and her friend's husband had run out on their families, taking all their savings to open gambling houses and brothels throughout the Rocky Mountains, but had never been heard of since. The letter went on to say that both she and the other man's wife were fortunate enough to have godly families to help them. When I contacted these women, they even told me about the special vests both men wore to conceal their money whenever they traveled. That's when we knew we had the right people. The interesting part of this story is that these two women, early on, realized that they were just two of many women and children who had been abandoned by men searching for easy money. Therefore, they opened a home for forgotten and destitute families. Over the years they've done a fine job and helped a large number of people, even with limited resources. Of course now with the funds we brought them, which was their late husbands' own money, they will surely be able to continue their success! Naturally, The Long Foundation will support them as well!"

Mariah took Copper's hand, "I wish you could have met those women. They introduced us to so many others who had stories, just like yours and mine. Women who had no resources, no family and nowhere to go! Thankfully God had a plan for us and He has a plan and a future for them as well." Mariah suddenly grew thoughtful, and then she looked to Shad, "I've been afraid to ask. Have you—have you seen or heard from Ladd?"

Copper couldn't contain her smile. "Oh, Mariah, he truly was sincere when he told us of his decision to trust in Christ! I know you were concerned when he returned to that mysterious valley, but Shad and I think it was the right decision for him—for now anyway."

"Have you seen him since that day he brought us that carpet bag full of gold eagles?"

It was Shad who answered, "Yep, he came and spent a few days with us last spring. He told us he'd built himself a small cabin right into the side of the mountain. Said it was the most beautiful place in the world and that he was mighty content! He also said that he wasn't gonna shoot his gun, since the deer and horses in that valley aren't afraid of men; he wants to keep their trust. But there are plenty of other critters up there to keep him fed. We loaded him up with supplies and we also gave him some tools and seed so he could grow a vegetable garden this summer. He looked happy and healthy. He's been reading the Bible Preacher gave him and you wouldn't believe the change that's come over him. You can see it in his face, hear it in his voice! He knows there are wanted posters out for him and so he kind of feels like his staying away from the world is both a penance and a privilege—he sure ain't complaining—he seems like a happy man!"

"Now that you know your brother is doing well, we want to know what about, Mister and Missus Long," Copper asked with a smile, "What are your plans now?"

The newlyweds exchanged a meaningful look then Quin answered, "Well, we had a good idea what The Boss wanted us to do. Even more so after we took the gold back to those women. We prayed about it all through our honeymoon trip, and God just seemed to be confirming his plan for us all along the way! There are so many women who could use the kind of help we could give. We plan to go into saloons and offer any woman who is wants it…a way out! We can give them a chance at a whole new life. We'll buy them out of bondage if necessary! As you know, The Boss has been leading me towards this for a while but the time was never right—" he smiled at Mariah and took her hand, "until now! Workers will be arriving soon, to start building a large Mission House. Once we have quarters for them, John and Willy Haze will be coming up to help!"

"Where ya plan to build?" Shad asked.

Quin's grin was infectious, "There's a beautiful waterfall just a few hours ride up Ute Pass. It has for many years, been one of my favorite places and it quickly became special to Mariah as well! We've decided to build our mission house there. It will be a place for women and for children who have no resources, no family or nowhere else to go!"

"Just like me," Mariah added. "It will be a healing place for those who have been abandoned or abused." She smiled warmly at Copper and Shad. "A place like you two provided for me not so long ago. We'll welcome those who feel broken and useless and introduce them to God—the Master Craftsman. The one who can indeed, make all things new. In these mountains they'll find a safe haven—a shelter and refuge for those who are sick in mind, body or spirit. We'll teach them useful skills, but mostly our desire is to share with them that when you think you have no hope…that's when God tells us to take shelter under His wing. Quin and I have been praying about what to call our mission. Psalm fifty-seven, verse one, kept coming back to us. *"In the shadow of your wings I will make my refuge, until these calamities have passed by."* This mission is for **W**omen **I**n **N**eed of **G**od's **S**helter so we have decided to call it WINGS...

Wings on the Mountain!"

THE END
(Please see Discussion Points next!)

Yes friends, please don't stop turning pages just yet!
Discussion Points are next.
Then see the Prologue for
Book One on the Colorado Trilogy –

GIANT in the VALLEY

DISCUSSION POINTS

1. The realities of abuse.

All forms of abuse are sin, be they verbal, physical, or sexual. How and why were women and children abused centuries ago? With increased rights and advocacy centers, why is abuse still such a widespread problem? How has the breakdown of the family been a factor? Discuss the impact abuse had on Copper, Mariah and Ladd. Discuss the dangers of running and why victims often blame themselves instead of their attackers?

2. The servant's heart.

Although Christ encourages us to have a "servant's heart", how do you feel when people treat you as their servant? We may no longer have indentured servants, but we do have spouses, parents, landlords or employers that might treat you like a servant. How are Christians supposed to handle relationships like this?

3. Are Christian's always good?

Discuss the relationship between Copper and Ma Riley. How were Ma's actions descriptive or non-descriptive of being like Christ? Have you known people like her? Or been like her? Discuss how Ma used Copper to help her son, even at Copper's expense. List Ma's strengths and weaknesses. Can you understand her?

4. Between a rock and hard place?

What was going on with Mariah's mother? Discuss the situation with her husband and children. How could she have been a better mother? Discuss the dilemmas that face victims of abuse (i.e. family, financial, social, etc....).

5. **The shame of Otter Run.**

It's easy to be angry with the townsfolk of Otter Run—and rightly so! Discuss the difficulties of providing for a stranger—indefinitely—knowing that to do so would take food from your own family. Discuss how and why you might help a stranger even if it meant potential danger to your family? What might the ramifications be? What could the townsfolk have done to assist Mariah without hurting themselves?

6. **God desires mercy and not sacrifice.**

God gave Quin a message through John and Willy Haze. Discuss the ways in which Quin's heart was being pulled in two different directions. How was this manifest in Quin's struggle to know what to do about his strong attraction to Mariah and his fear of losing his ministry? Discuss how this verse might have meaning in your own lives. What does God desire from you?

7. **Can a broken vessel be made whole?** 2 Corinthians 5:17

Discuss the transformation of Dirk to Ladd. How is it possible for someone who is truly evil to become a person of honor? Discuss the symbolism of Mariah and her zither—broken—then restored by the touch of the Master's hand. Discuss how their experiences with Christ changed all the main characters in this novel.

Remember with Christ—All things are possible.

PROLOGUE PREVIEW

GIANT IN THE VALLEY
COLORADO TRILOGY – BOOK ONE

"God helps the righteous and delivers them from the plots of evil men." Psalm 37:40

Summer, 1865 - Denver, Colorado

Her golden eyes reflected in the window glass as she watched and waited in the dark. Finally, she saw it: the quick strike of a match, a bare wink of flame, and then it was gone. Quietly, she slipped from the house like a shadow, and made her way to the secluded arbor in her back garden.

The man waiting for her was dirty and saddle weary. Dressed in dark buckskins, he wore a double brace of pistols and his boots bore heavy Mexican spurs with long, sharp rowels. His grizzled face looked even more fierce in the moonlight. Brazenly, she met his cold gray eyes as he glared at her from under the wide brim of his hat.

Taking the thick envelope, she placed in his outstretched hand, he cursed her and grumbled, "I'm callin' it quits—ain't doin' no more jobs fer ya. Done workin' fer a woman!"

His disdain meant nothing to her. Instead, a sly smile played about her rosy lips and her eyes flashed with a look of evil anticipation. Moving closer, her velvety voice became animated as she whispered, "If that's what you want. But remember? You still owe me! You promised you would help me—and then—you would bring her to me—when the timing was right. Well—my sources tell me that he won't be able to protect her much longer. And—if things continue as planned, that worthless little *mistake*...will be delivered right into our hands!"

Then her dark-rimmed, golden eyes sparkled as her countenance turned from malicious to venomous, as she hissed:

"It's going to be…almost…too easy. It's only fitting—after all, she ruined my life, my dreams. And now—I'm going to turn her life—into a nightmare!"

Please visit author website at: http://lfaulknercorzine.com